The Willow

MARK KRAVER

The Willow

Edited by Shari Shallard
Cover and book design by Cathy Gibbons Reedy

DEDICATION

For Nita,
Who has always been the wind at my back,
and the harbor I return to.
My steadfast willow,
bending with every storm yet never breaking.

As if touched by a demon,
Her gaze turned wild,
She glanced o'er her shoulder,
No longer mild.
The wide-eyed students froze in place,
As a spark lit up her pirating face.
Her emerald eyes flashed, sharp and steady,
And with a wicked grin, she whispered,
"Ready?"

FOREWORD

The Willow knows the dreams they chase

EARLY 1700S AMERICA was not only a period of growth for the colonies, separated by vast wilderness, but also a time of imminent change in the era's societal norms.

Among these norms was the limited educational opportunity available to young women. Education was primarily reserved for males, and most women were expected to remain in the home, learning only what was necessary to fulfill their roles as wives and mothers.

Especially in communities with strong religious convictions, education for boys was seen as a moral imperative. They were primarily taught to read so they could study spiritual texts. Still, even this limited scope of education represented a significant step toward acknowledging the importance of basic literacy for all.

However, some challenged these gendered restrictions. In progressive circles, both affluent and less privileged, there was a determined effort to educate all children. Some families went to great lengths to ensure their daughters received an education. They hired tutors, shared books, and sometimes sent their daughters to schools in disguise or under the pretext of traveling to an adjacent town to assist a relative with their health. These families believed in the power of education to enrich lives and minds.

This is how the struggle for women's education in early 18th-century America began: a quiet revolution taking place in homes, out of the public eye. It was driven by the love and wwdetermination of those who believed in the equal worth and potential of every mind. This era laid the groundwork for the gradual progress towards educational equality, a journey that would reshape the landscape of learning and opportunity for women across America.

CHAPTER 1

On the Hudson River, October, 1712

THROUGH THE SHIFTING CURRENTS OF TIME, Manhattan pulsed with hidden dealings and whispered bargains, where a murmured promise in the dead of night carried as much worth as a hefty sack of gold or sparkling cascade of cut diamonds. Along the uneven, rock-strewn banks of the Hudson's eastern shore, just beyond the Fort and Windmill, stood a stately two-story home. Before the Dutch ceded New Netherland to the English without bloodshed, this estate had already claimed its place—its walls raised with the spoils of plundered fortune.

The interior of this grand estate stood as a silent homage to bygone eras, its walls adorned with the watchful eyes of ancestors and enigmatic associates immortalized in portraits, while its spaces overflowed with age-old curiosities gathered from across the globe. Surrounding this venerable house was a garden steeped in mystery, where a vigorous wisteria wove itself into the landscape, its sinewy arms embracing an architecturally distinct backyard bump-out room—an intriguing extension of the main edifice. Within this singular feature lay a fortified stronghold, housing a cannon whose unyielding gaze remained fixed upon the sweeping tides of the Hudson. This steadfast guardian protected the very core of the estate's enterprise—a venture shrouded in secrecy. To the rest of the world, it was little more than a whispered legend, drifting along the fringes of the clandestine and the infamous, but its reach extended across the seven seas.

The room holding the cannon was more than just a storage space for bygone weaponry, but it concealed a heavy, locked door—the secret entrance to a labyrinth of cellars beneath the house. Strangely, the stairs to the basement began with a sharp descent into what appeared to be a narrow, flooded corridor. Only at the lowest tide could one descend these stairs to reach the bottom and uncover a heavy, dropped gate. Lifting this barrier revealed the path upward into a series of hidden spaces. Within this covert cellar lay chests brimming with gold, silver, and precious gems—treasures deposited by some of the most notorious pirates in the world.

Contrary to the myth of pirates burying their treasure on deserted islands, corsairs of the sea often sought trustworthy individuals or families to store their ill-gotten gains safely. This practice allowed them easy access to their booty for future use and ensured their loved ones could obtain the plunder in the event of the pirate's untimely death. These secret deposits served as a financial safety net, blending their daring exploits with practical foresight in what became known as the Pirate Bank.

Abigail Spragg, the current guardian of her family's secrets, was a figure woven from the same cloth as her great-grandfather, the legendary and fabulously wealthy Dutch Barbary pirate Jan Janszoon van Salee. Her lineage was steeped in piracy and adventure, a family tree that branched over oceans of dark deeds and buried truths. From her mother, Annica, she had inherited not just her fiery emerald-green eyes and a spine of iron but the world's most valuable trove: a treasury whose fortunes were amassed through gunpowder, sharp swords, and death.

While navigating the intricate webs of the family business, Abigail understood that piracy's wealth was not always counted in silver and gold. The actual currency of the trade extended beyond gleaming coins to commodities like cotton, molasses, and rum—goods that, in the right markets, could rival or even exceed the value of traditional treasures. The vault was more than a place for plunder; it served as a beacon in the shifting tides of fortune, offering sea marauders a rare and elusive promise—security. It was a safeguard for their future, a means to orchestrate their final wishes. Whether securing a quiet retirement on some nameless shore or ensuring a bequest reached kin across the seas, the repository stood as an anchor in an otherwise precarious existence, often fulfilling its purpose only after the pirate had met his inevitable fate.

Her family's operation thrived in the shadows, fueled by a network of ambiguous figures and coded messages. It was an underworld built upon a foundation of trust forged in the unbreakable code of the sea. This code was not written but understood; it was a bond as strong as any chain, a commitment to secrecy and loyalty that bound the pirating world to the Spraggs.

On this particular autumn day, with the wind murmuring hush-hush through her window, Abigail sat at her desk, gently bouncing her fussy son in her arms while trying to read the letter clutched in her hand. The seal upon the letter bore the mark of a ghost—a pirate king who had vanished into legend. To Abigail, he was Long Ben; to the world, he was Captain

Henry Avery. He was the man who had dared to defy empires, seizing the opulent ship, Ganj-i-Sawai, the Mughal of India's floating mountain of treasure. And then, as if taunting the world, he had vanished into history, leaving behind only whispers, speculation, and the lingering specter of his death in legendary shades of gray.

Henry Avery had not only entrusted the Spraggs with a fragment of his ghostly existence, ensuring his disappearance from the world, but he had also left behind a fortune in diamonds, silver, and gold—treasures that even now lay concealed beneath the house, their opulence known only to the walls that guarded them. But this letter was different. Unlike whispered instructions and secret exchanges of the past, this was a tangible summons, a deliberate and irregular reach from the shadows. A pause settled over Abigail as she studied the seal, knowing that whatever message lay within carried a weight beyond mere wealth.

The letter was addressed to Abigail's late mother, Annica, the founder of the Pirate Bank. Though the sight of her mother's name still stirred something deep in her chest, it wasn't unusual for correspondence to be directed to Annica. Even ten years after her death, news of her passing had been carefully kept secret, and her clandestine banking network continued to operate across the seas, passed discreetly from one pirate captain to another. The letter was penned in a script that quivered with urgency and peculiar desperation, detailing an unusual request: he wanted her to give a significant portion of his wealth to a lady acquaintance he had met in New Haven, Connecticut. He wished to fulfill that woman's dream of establishing a school for girls. Abigail paused to look out her studies' florid window to muse softly, "Girls' school?" The purpose of the bequest was noble indeed, especially from a pirate.

"Meow," announced the sleek, well-fed cat with a ruby earring, his amber eyes glistening like polished marbles. Mr. McDermot was no ordinary house cat; his life began aboard Captain Kidd's ship amidst the undulating vastness of the Indian Ocean, born to the ship's cat named Molly. As Kidd's favored feline companion, he had weathered storms and calms, seeing parts of the world most men would only dream of. Now comfortably ensconced in Abigail's eclectic household, Mr. McDermot served as a living reminder of adventure, weaving together the threads of history and legend with every purr and pounce.

"Mr. McDermot," Abigail cooed, her tone affectionate as she regarded the orange tabby pacing near her feet, its tail flicking with impatience. The cat meowed plaintively, hopping up onto the chair's armrest to sit closer; his amber eyes locked on hers with an almost human expression. "I'm terribly sorry, but you see, there's no room at the moment," she said with a soft laugh, nodding down to the bundle in her lap.

Nestled in a cocoon of fine linen and Abigail's steady arms, her newborn son was rooting against her bodice with relentless determination. His tiny hands batted at the air as though grasping for something just out of reach. Abigail set the letter down at a safe distance and moved closer to him, her expression equal parts amused and exasperated.

"You'll have to wait, Mr. McDermot," Abigail murmured, addressing the cat as though he understood. "This little one never gets enough." She adjusted the baby, letting him latch again, and sighed. "The doctor says I don't have enough milk for him," she added, her voice softening in confession.

The tabby tilted his head, ears twitching as if deep in thought.

"Oh, don't look at me like that!" Abigail laughed, brushing a damp strand of hair from her forehead. "I had enough for my other six—why is this one different? Am I… too old?" Her smile faltered, worry flickering across her face. As if sensing it, the cat let out a soft, sympathetic meow, curling his tail around his paws.

"Well," she said, her lips quirking, "too bad I can't just feed him some of your fish. That'd be convenient—at least for me." She chuckled as the cat blinked in mild offense. "The way he's eating, Mr. McDermot, you might be out of luck."

The baby suckled noisily, his tiny fingers clutching at the folds of her gown.

The cat meowed again, sharper this time, almost accusatory. Abigail arched an eyebrow. "Oh, don't you start complaining. I'm doing my best," she teased. "It's all hands on deck for this little sailor."

With an exaggerated yawn, Mr. McDermot stood, whiskers twitching, casting one last pleading look before stretching into a resigned loaf.

She turned her attention back to the little boy in her arms, his soft breathing mingling with the faint creaks of the old house. "Well, little one," she murmured, her voice tender, "you've got quite the appetite, don't you? But you're worth every moment of it…" Her words trailed off as her eyes fell back on the letter, only an arm's reach away.

Abigail's mind drifted back to thoughts of academia. A 'place where girls can receive an education on par with Harvard' is how Avery had described it. Was such a place possible? Could a future exist in which young women learn and thrive? Could the female gender's destiny be as boundless as the ocean her cat once sailed? At that moment, her own daughters came to mind. Contemplating the possibilities for their education, the quiet room seemed to flicker with the shadows of the past and the glow of tomorrow's promise. Suddenly, her reflective thoughts were interrupted by a pounding on the front door.

In the grand foyer of the stately home, Lawton, the ever-dutiful Butler, answered the resounding knock by pushing open the stout door. On the threshold stood the young Dr. Jones, the esteemed physician who had aided in the delivery of Abigail's latest child, accompanied by a timid young woman whose eyes were pools of apprehension and hope.

"Who is it? I'm busy," Abigail voiced from her office.

Bypassing the Butler's apologetic frown, Dr. Jones said with a raised voice, "Tis I, Dr. Evan Jones, with a matter of importance."

"Please, come in," Abigail beckoned, her voice cascading from her office across the parlor.

"Oh, thank you," Jones said with a slight bow to Lawton's outstretched hand and then led the woman toward her voice. They both stood silently at her office doorway, reluctant to take another step.

"Enter, please! Dr. Jones, are you here for my and William's check-up?" Abigail called out, rocking back in her chair.

"I am not," the doctor replied, a man of gentle demeanor and kind eyes. "I pray all is indeed well with you and the little one—he was a most difficult delivery. And Jacob's boy, Andreas, is recovering well, I presume? Chickenpox involving the eye is nothing to sniff at. I am surprised it hasn't spread to all your children by now."

"Yes, of course. And no, he's recovered quite well. Upstairs with his cousins, if you'd like to see them?"

"No need. How is the boy taking to his new life here? Being adopted by another family can be traumatic—even if that family is blood."

"My son has not seen him yet, if that is what you are asking. Lord only knows how many other children he's spawned about the Hudson and beyond. I'd say we were lucky to have found this one. An—ah—old acquaintance alerted me. For a fee, of course," she added with a wry smile.

"No, I'm here on a different matter." He gestured toward the young woman beside him. "This is Clara. She's one of the forgotten German Palatine souls, forsaken by her family due to an unwed pregnancy. Tragically, she lost her child two days ago. She's in need, and I thought of you... for her to serve as a wet nurse."

Abigail halted, rocking, her initial reaction a blend of surprise and dismissal. But when she thought of the poor girl losing her child, she looked down at the babe in her arms and could not imagine. "I am sorry for your loss," she said with heartfelt sympathy before protesting, "but I do not feel the need for a wet nurse at present." Her voice was firm yet not unkind. "Dr. Jones, I have seven children; I hardly see the need for assistance now."

The doctor met her gaze steadily. "But you're not just any mother, Abigail. You're a pillar of the community, a woman with ambitions that extend beyond the hearth. You mustn't overextend yourself, or you will overtax your constitution and invite ill-fortune. Your years have bestowed upon you a wealth of wisdom and grace that only time can provide," he said with a gentle, respectful emphasis, "and there's no harm in helping yourself while offering this young woman a new start."

Abigail's eyes drifted to the note lying before her. Long Ben's greed and lust for power and treasure had astonishingly transformed into a quest for women's education. She was, of course, skeptical of his intentions, but his commitment seemed to outshine her own efforts to empower women through kindness. A sigh escaped her, and her resolve softened. Here was a young woman, much like the ones the pirate Henry Avery aimed to uplift with a school, needing shelter and work — both would offer a chance to broaden this woman's horizons. How could the pirate be so compassionate, and she not? She chastised herself, thinking, "No wonder women are uneducated; not even their peers see the need."

Adjusting the baby in her arms and rising to her feet decisively behind her massive desk, Abigail nodded to the young woman. "Come, child," she beckoned, her voice sincere, inviting the girl to take her baby and demonstrate her nursing abilities.

Clara, overwhelmed and inexperienced, fumbled when she first held the infant against her breast, uncertainty painting her features. But the young babe already knew how to feed and took to her right off, causing the young girl to cringe, squirm, and grit her teeth before getting used to it enough to deliver a forced smile of acceptance as the swollen pressure inside her breast began to lessen.

"Ah, he seems to have taken a liking to you already," Abigail said. She glanced at her desk, where the letter that had captured her attention lay among a small pile of other correspondence—unpaid receipts and records from her various business interests, including the alehouse, shipyard, real estate holdings, farming ventures, and the slaughterhouse and tannery. A sigh of unexpected relief washed over her as she took it all in.

"I had thought, with this last one at least, I might nurse him myself 'til weaning, but alas, 'tis simpler thus. Dr. Jones, do guide her and be at hand for her queries," Abigail instructed before turning to Lawton. "And Lawton, see that Miss Clara is shown to the nursery, where she'll bide. The other servants shall show her how to swaddle, change, and bathe the babe with little trouble. He can be a fretful child when denied his will," she laughed lightly.

As Dr. Jones reached the doorway, he remarked with a touch of humor, "I think you are correct. The house servants know better how to teach breastfeeding than I ever could." He glanced at the clock above Abigail's desk. "Besides, I have three other pregnant patients to call on today."

Abigail called out, her voice carrying a mixture of resignation and resolve, "Dr. Jones, I — I thank you for your devoted consideration. I do have much to attend to."

The doctor paused and turned back slightly, an understanding smile touching his lips.

"And thank you for filing the birth certificate with the Hempstead magistrate. This baby—the last one," she didn't hesitate to add, "was too obstinate to make an appearance before we had to leave. I wanted all my children to be born in my home township, but…"

He nodded once more, acknowledging the depth of trust and regard their relationship held, before stepping out onto the front steps, charting his next course.

Once the heavy front door shut, the room's silence was broken only by the soft meow of Mr. McDermot jumping into Abigail's now-available lap. Stroking the wise middle-aged cat, Abigail murmured, "It seems, Mr. McDermot, this arrangement benefits all, you and me included." The ensuing purring suggested agreement, echoing the quiet satisfaction in Abigail's heart.

The house seemed to breathe around Abigail, the air thick with the weight of impending change. As always, she felt the presence of what lay beneath her—silent, waiting—the vast treasure below the foundations, its secrets intertwined with her family, sworn to guard it. Then, with unusual clarity, an epiphany struck: What was the point of hoarding such immense wealth if not to wield it for something grand?

Her mother's once-perplexing words fluttered through her mind, finally making sense after all these years: Fortune favors the bold, but it enslaves the timid.

For much of her life, the hidden riches had felt more like a curse, their cold fingers threatening to twist the future she so fiercely sought to shape. But now, she understood—this was a moment for action. The gold could be more than a relic of conquest; it could be the key to seizing control of destiny itself.

Abigail entered her eldest daughter's bedroom to find Hannah studying the large thunderbird tattoo on her forearm, her journal open in her lap. At her mother's unexpected arrival, Hannah moved hastily, sending her pen flying and splattering ink across the papers on her writing desk. In one swift motion, she snapped her journal shut and buried it beneath a stack of other documents on the cluttered surface.

Despite the hurried attempt at concealment, Abigail immediately recognized that her daughter had been deeply engrossed in writing something she didn't want her to see. What stood out even more was that Hannah had chosen to hide her words—but not the two small musket pistols resting openly beside her bed.

Hannah raised her eyebrow in curiosity, asking, "I saw Dr. Jones earlier from the stairs. I didn't want to interfere with your appointment. Is everything as it should be with you and little Willie?"

"No appointment. Who are you writing to?" Abigail asked, knowing her daughter was intrigued by the poor doctor who'd lost his wife and two young daughters to diphtheria the year before. When her questioning was ignored, Abigail's face turned stormy with worry. "You're not writing to that pauper, Andreas, again, are you? Well, at least a doctor is preferable to a penniless German immigrant fresh off the boat. How could you even consider involving yourself with that... that grown man taking on such a silly pirate name—Andreas Andreas?" She scoffed as she said his doubled name, her words cutting like the edge of a sword.

Hannah's secretive actions with the journal only ignited her mother's aggravation, deepening the mistrust in her already troubled disposition. "Your father and I have gone to great lengths to find someone of our standards for you to court. Men of good standing and birth with means to support you in comfort, wanting for not."

Hannah, every inch her mother's daughter, met Abigail's fiery gaze without flinching. "Mother, are you still in a tiff? Andreas was here, what, two, no, three years ago? Put it behind you, please. And as for those other leeches, honestly, Mother, I don't know how you and Father ever got together. The men you picked for me didn't know the first thing about loving someone other than themselves and were only on the prowl for your money. So know this: I am the master of my own fate," she declared, the defiance in her voice an instrument of the pirate blood that indeed ran strong in her veins. "My heart is my own, and I shall give it to whom I choose, be he prince or pauper."

For a moment, their looks cracked with the intensity of unspoken challenges and silent battles of wills. Then, as if adopting a new strategy, Abigail's demeanor softened, but her eyes remained as calculating as ever.

"If you are so determined to chart your own course, Hannah, you must first understand the waters you navigate. You will accompany me to New Haven. Consider it part of your education," Abigail proposed, her words carrying the weight of an ultimatum rather than an invitation.

"What? New Haven? But that is in Connecticut," Hannah blurted, her brows knitting together in confusion.

Abigail hardly seemed to notice, her gaze distant, focused inward. She pressed a hand to her writing desk, fingers drumming lightly against the wood as the pieces began to align in her mind. "Yes... New Haven," she said, peering out the window across her gardens off into the Hudson. "A town still young, still malleable. A place where fortunes could be made, where influence was not yet cemented, where the right investments could turn whispers into legacies."

She exhaled, eyes sharpening as she continued thinking aloud. "Land, business, alliances... if carefully placed, they wouldn't just support a future; they could define it." A slow, knowing smile touched the matriarch's lips. "And what better way to ensure control than to build the foundation yourself?"

Hannah's expression was a mixture of incredulity and something else—wary intrigue. "I don't understand what you're talking about, mother."

"A place where girls can receive an education on par with Harvard," Abigail said, reciting Henry Avery's words and nodding to herself. "We can make it happen."

You can't be serious," Hannah said, but the uncertainty in her voice betrayed the fact that part of her knew her mother was.

Abigail finally looked at her oldest daughter, eyes bright with conviction. "Why shouldn't I be?" she countered. "We've spent our lives protecting the past, guarding what was. Maybe it's time to use it for what could be."

The room settled into silence, save for the steady rhythm of Abigail's fingers against the desk, like the measured ticking of a clock counting down to something inevitable.

Hannah harbored the suspicion that her journey to New Haven was merely a pretense to transform her into the de facto nanny for her new infant brother, William. Her instincts bristled at the thought, yet she could not help but feel a flicker of intrigue at the prospect of leaving behind the familiar for the uncharted terrains of a bustling colonial town in Connecticut. When her mother casually mentioned hiring a wet nurse, Hannah felt genuinely surprised and pleased. But her pleasure came laced with an acerbic twist. "So, you're already weary of the maternal embrace? This feels like a familiar tune," she remarked dryly, recalling past siblings and the patterns of upbringing that came with them.

Her mother stood with stoic resolve, a visage of fortitude chiseled into her features. The stiff upper lip she maintained was a bastion against the swell of emotions that threatened to betray her composure. Every fiber of her yearned to offer a word of caution to her headstrong daughter, to urge patience until the day Hannah herself would navigate the turbulent waters of motherhood. But such words remained unspoken, caught in the silence between them. She harbored no desire to cast the shadow of such weighty expectations upon any of her children's shoulders, especially not while the ink of youth still glistened on the pages of their lives. In her silence was a quiet benediction, a hope that Hannah would be allowed the luxury of time to explore the breadth of her own existence before the mantle of motherhood beckoned.

As the echoes of her unspoken advice faded into the quietude of her own heart, a plurality of thoughts perched at the edge of her consciousness, whispering with the gentle insistence of autumn leaves stirred by a nascent wind. 'Take your time, my child; drink deeply from the cup of youth and savor its heady brew,' she thought. Yet, in the exact reflection, a counterpoint rose, a subtle reminder of the inexorable march of time and the perennial cycle of life that their family, like the sturdy oak, must endure through the sprouting of new branches. 'But, Hannah,' her heart silently implored with a quiet fervor, a soft maternal plea to the wheel of time, 'do not tarry too long in the throes of youth, for grandchildren are not merely the joyous continuance of our lineage, but the essential threads that will one day complete the image of your birthright.'

But she said none of this. Instead, she flashed a playful smile. "And naturally, don't forget the twins. We leave in the morning," she said, gesturing to her daughter's brazenly displayed musket pistols.

"Without a doubt," Hannah responded, her expression tinged with sobriety. "Oh, but mother? We leave tomorrow? I was going to shop for a new hat. Sarah took my favorite and dropped it in the mud." She cast her eyes to her muskets. "She's lucky she is my sister," she added.

"Then you must be off to do it today, my child. The tide waits for no one, be they princess or pauper."

Hannah jumped up, brushed her hand across the muskets, grabbed her shawl and purse, and left, dancing down the hallway toward the stairs.

"Oh, and don't forget your new pattens this time," Abigail called out after her.

"Mother, iron ring soles on my feet just slow me down—like an anchor! You don't want me to trip and fall?" she complained as she descended the stairs.

"You need to wear them! The last time you came home, you trampled horse pucky all over the house," Abigail shouted, unsure if her daughter could still hear her. She listened for a moment, then smiled with contentment as she heard her headstrong daughter heed her call, slipping on the platform overshoes at the front door before leaving.

Abigail stood in the bedroom doorway, delighted by her daughter's energy. Something caught her eye as she reached for the handle to close the door, and she froze. A piece of red ribbon stuck conspicuously out from her writing desk, peeking from under a stack of parchment. She knew it was a bookmark holding a place in Hannah's clandestine journal.

Abigail began to close the door, but at the very last moment, she bit her lip, hesitated, and stepped back into the room. Carefully noting how everything on her desk was arranged, she slid the leather-bound diary out from beneath the pile. She paused, listening intently for any footsteps in the hallway before she dared to crack it open and scan her daughter's handwriting.

As she flipped through the pages, her heart sank. She wasn't disappointed in what Hannah wrote but in her struggles to put her thoughts down clearly — the creative spelling, fragmented sentences, and endless run-ons. Her daughter was passionate about writing, and though Abigail treasured that spark, it tugged at her heart to see the words still wander across the page with the sweetness of childhood, not yet settled into the quieter strength of a young woman finding her voice. A wave of disappointment and sorrow washed over her, mingling with a sense of failure she hadn't expected. If she had noticed sooner how much Hannah's writing skills had fallen behind, she could have spent more time helping her.

After Abigail left the bedroom, she sat alone in her quiet office, surrounded by the invisible presence of her ancestors and the whispered conversations of ghosts. In that solitude, she better understood the perilous game she had long played with her children — especially her oldest daughter, who now teetered on the edge of adulthood. Balancing business and motherhood was a pursuit of shadows and intrigue, where pirates' secrets were currency and her daughters' futures the prize she sought to secure. But now, she couldn't shake the sinking feeling that she was failing.

After a brief, hypnotic trance staring out the window, she picked up the ex-pirate's message and showed it to the cat. When the pet was clearly uninterested, she mused, "Am I mad to consider this? Education for young women? Have you ever heard of such a thing?"

Mr. McDermot meowed, sensing the attention.

"Well, it seems there is a need, after all. One, I suspect, may find a start in New Haven." She sat, and the cat jumped into her lap, purring and brushing its whiskered chin on Abigail's obliging hand. "Now it seems I have impediments removed from my traveling," she said, adjusting her tightly fitted blouse. Captain Avery's request tugged at something deep within her pirated spirit, a longing she had harbored for her daughters to get a proper education.

Then a thought crossed her mind—Sarah?

Her fingers paused briefly against the cat's fur as she contemplated her next-older daughter. Hannah was one thing: older, sharp-minded, already learning the weight of secrets and the careful architecture of the world Abigail had built. Hannah understood risk. Hannah listened.

But Sarah—

No.

The answer came almost as quickly as the thought itself. Sarah was still too soft, too untested. New Haven was no place for indulgence—especially for a lass, where privileges were so easily dulled by danger. Abigail would not have her youth shaped too soon by a world that smiled sweetly while sharpening its knives.

She exhaled and resumed stroking Mr. McDermot, careful of the ruby earring. The notion dissolved as easily as it had formed.

The cat leapt from her lap, the decision sealed.

"Only one daughter," Abigail murmured. "Sarah is not yet ready to know the world as it is."

Dreams of a future where women's ideas wouldn't just be whispers behind closed doors but voices that roared in the grand halls of learning and commerce resonated in Abigail's thoughts. However, she knew the world women inhabited today demanded a more practical approach than just intellect; it demanded alliances and marriages that ensured their children's place among the elite. Love was a luxury, often sacrificed for family duty and survival—not to mention children and grandchildren.

The flirtation of her headstrong older daughter, Hannah, with a penniless Palatine German immigrant had been a dangerous brush with disaster. Abigail wouldn't allow it; the blood of pirates and warriors coursed through her veins, and the two forceful entities yearned for unions that would fortify their empire, not crumble it to sentiment and folly.

With a resolve carved from the same iron as her forebears, Abigail summoned her Butler, Lawton, a former slave whose loyalty had been forged through years of silent complicity in the Spragg family's darker pirate dealings, to run a message.

After asking him if Clara was comfortably settled in the nursery, Abigail turned to employ the tall Butler with a decisive tone that brooked no argument. "There's been a change in plans," she began, her eyes reflecting the strategic mind behind her composed demeanor. "Inform Captain Holloway that Ms Hannah and I will require his services navigating The Atlas to New Haven along the Long Island Sound in Connecticut." Her words were precise, leaving no room for misinterpretation. "Make haste, my sloop must be ready by sunrise. Time is of the essence. The tides wait for no one, queen or concubine, and we cannot afford delays."

"As you wish, Mistress Spragg," Lawton nodded, his face betraying no emotion.

She could see his mind swirling with unspoken questions, his eyes shifting purposefully, and his steps silent but swift, aware that time was a luxury he seldom could afford. Lawton was accustomed to Abigail's brisk efficiency, and he immediately set off to convey the instructions with the urgency she demanded.

The Spragg sloop sat moored, rig-ready, waiting for the outgoing tide before Abigail's dockside Albany Investment Firm. Lawton relayed the message to the captain, who growled out orders to his crew, "This boat better be ship-shape by morning tide, or you'll be kissing my cat-o'-nine tails arse over a cannon."

Captain Henry Holloway, a figure shrouded in as much mystery as the treasure he allegedly buried on Maine's Jewell Island, had long been part of the Spraggs' clandestine circle. Abigail and her mother, Annica, had played a crucial role in orchestrating his supposed death by hanging for piracy, a necessary deception to shield him from the relentless pursuit of those he had crossed. In return, Holloway had become her trusted ally in laundering their notorious booty and an adept pilot of her private sloop, his life now intertwined with the Spraggs' secrets.

Holloway growled to the dutiful Butler after glaring up at the sun and then down at the tide, "Tell Mistress Abigail she'll be ready at dawn."

CHAPTER 2

THE FOLLOWING DAY, as the Manhattan skyline dwindled into a fine line on the horizon, the sloop, guided by the Captain's deft hands, sliced through the waters of the East River. The gentle slap of waves against the hull played a rhythmic counterpoint to the creaking of timbers and the snap of the sails overhead. Her gaze fixed on the water's ever-changing canvas, Abigail took a moment to address the Captain.

"Captain Holloway," Abigail began, her voice carrying the warmth of genuine concern over the sea's breath. "How fares your wife and little ones? I trust the provisions you've received have served your family well?"

The Captain, a man weathered by brine and gales, glanced over his shoulder, a rare smile breaching his ordinarily reserved demeanor. "Aye, Mistress Abigail," he replied, the gratitude in his tone being more telling than the content of his words. "Thanks to your generosity, they're weathering life's storms far better. My Anne's cough has cleared, and the little ones are plump as partridges. We're in your debt."

The softness in Abigail's eyes belied her reputation for stern leadership. "No debt between us, Captain. That was the deal struck years ago," she said firmly yet kindly. "The sea takes enough; it's only right to give back where possible."

A knowing nod was exchanged, a silent acknowledgment of the bond forged through business and a kinship of shared piracy—a connection as vast and profound as the waters they navigated together.

The journey was pleasant, the world around them a blur of changing colors and distant horizons. Yet, despite the beauty of the open water, an invisible weight hung between Abigail and Hannah, thick with unspoken resentment. Abigail resisted commenting on Hannah's sour mood. She knew it was about more than just the forced journey to New Haven—it was the ongoing tension over Abigail and her husband's quiet efforts to arrange a suitable match for Hannah. Hannah longed for the freedom to choose love on her own terms, and being brought on this journey was a reminder of how elusive that freedom remained.

"Would you like some water, my child?" Abigail asked as they stood on the main deck, her voice measured, careful.

"Mother, I am not a child anymore," Hannah snapped, her tone clipped and distant.

Abigail held out the water-filled skin anyway, but Hannah turned her back, rejecting both the offer and the gesture behind it.

The silence between them stretched, taut and uneasy. But between them simmered something more profound—the raw, quiet defiance of a child evolving into an adult, pushing against the force that had shaped her, testing the limits of a mother's control. Abigail understood this unspoken battle of wills was as old as time itself, a storm brewing beneath the surface, waiting for the moment when restraint would shatter, and the true reckoning would begin.

Hannah's grip tightened on the railing as she stared out over the waves, her jaw set while old conversations replayed themselves, unbidden. She had never forgiven her mother for forcing her to forgo her one true love, Andreas, years earlier—nor for the carefully laid designs meant to bind her future to a man chosen *for* her, not *by* her.

And now she understood it went deeper still. Even her brother's son had been spared the name. Andreas quietly set aside, softened into Jan, as if a syllable alone might reopen wounds Abigail preferred sealed. Not for her sake, she suspected, but for her mother's own peace. The past was dangerous when named aloud, and love— spoken aloud—had a way of refusing to stay buried.

Abigail, watching her daughter's rigid posture, sighed but said nothing. Some battles were not won with words—but that did not mean they were not fought.

Their quiet standoff continued unbroken until they reached the notorious passage known as Hell's Gate. Here, the Harlem River crashed with a surging current into the East River, birthing a maelstrom of treachery over lurking boulders, a test for even the most seasoned sailors. The sloop pitched and yawed as the waters churned around and over the decking, the passengers and crew holding tight to whatever fixtures they could find.

Without notice, the ship jolted violently, nearly capsizing to its side. What was once the flat deck now appeared as a wall, with the turbulent waters below reaching out in a chaotic embrace. The mast and sails slapped violently against the water, adding to the blurring scene.

"Hannah!" Abigail screamed, lunging forward, grabbing for her daughter's arm just as Hannah slipped toward the water below.

The deck was slick with seawater, making stable footing nearly impossible. Abigail's heart pounded in her chest as she rolled across the wet planks, her grip on Hannah's sleeve tenuous at best. The violent motion of the ship threatened to tear her grip apart, but Abigail held on with every ounce of her strength.

"Hannah, hold onto something!" Abigail shouted, her voice pleading with anguish.

With a final surge of effort, Abigail pulled Hannah back from the brink, the two collapsing in a heap on the uprighting, swaying deck. They lay there momentarily, gasping for breath, the reality of their narrow escape sinking in. The ship's tiller regained complete control as they stopped pitching and swaying, and for now, they were safe.

"Are you okay?" Abigail asked, her voice trembling with concern.

Hannah nodded, tears streaming down her face. "I'm okay, Mother. I thought I was going over, for sure."

Abigail hugged her daughter tightly, relief washing over her. Amidst this turmoil, the ice between mother and daughter began to crack.

Holloway, indeed, proved his reputation as an able seaman. His familiarity with these capricious waters was evident in his unwavering confidence as he steered their vessel. Despite several heart-stopping moments when their ship seemed to brush the jagged teeth of hidden rocks, they emerged unscathed into the calmer embrace of the Long Island Sound. Scrambling across the main deck, counting his crew and passengers, the Captain saw the two women no worse for the wear and called out, "Ah, Ms. Abigail. Sorry for the mishap. It seems we struck the masthead of a downed ship. Poor bastards kissed the bottom, raking open their hull."

"What of our ship?" Abigail asked with concern.

"So far, it seems sound. We'll know better after I inspect the bilge, ah, and the cargo hold," Holloway said, looking around to check the stern's rudder.

Finally, Abigail kissed her daughter's forehead, the salty sea breeze teasing loose strands of her hair, realizing she had almost lost her beloved daughter—the daughter to whom she one day wished to tell stories of her past and the one she'd picked to take over the family's pirate bank. She had long felt Hannah was too young to hear about her mother's mistakes, but now, after almost losing her, she sensed this was the time to share one of her deepest secrets.

In the ensuing calm, Abigail's expression was contemplative. Her eyes were lost in the horizon as if they held specters of her past. The silence was a living thing, an entity that had wrapped itself around both mother and daughter. Then, without turning her head, her voice barely more than a whisper, Abigail spoke aloud a secret carried on the wind, "I was married before I met your father."

Hannah, taken aback, turned sharply to look at her mother. A tide of surprise and curiosity quickly drowned her previous emotions. Every fiber of her being was now attuned to her mother, the world around them fading away.

Abigail continued, her gaze still fixed on the distant point, her voice steady but laced with the soft pain of old scars. "I was about your age. He was older, and I believed I loved him."

"Who was he? What happened?" Hannah asked, her voice a mixture of concern and the innate thirst for knowledge that youth cannot help but possess.

It seemed as if Abigail wouldn't answer for a moment, the past locked behind her lips. But then she took a slow breath, resigning herself to complete honesty. "His name was Jan Aertsen van der Bilt," she said, the name foreign yet familiar, a ghost from her past. "He owned the Van der Bilt Brewery on Wall Street."

Hannah's eyes widened slightly, and she recognized the name of the prominent establishment now owned by her mother. The revelation drew Hannah closer to Abigail's side, not because of the man's significance but because of Abigail's vulnerability and trust in sharing her hidden past.

Abigail finally turned, meeting her daughter's eyes. In them, Hannah could see the reflections of memories long buried. "My mother eventually found out," she said, a bitter edge sharpening her words. "She told me never to see him again and moved me to Long Island to live with relatives. The marriage was annulled before I could even grasp what was happening."

"But why?" Hannah implored. "She broke up your true love because he was older? Is that why you took Andreas away from me?"

Abigail shook her head. "You were too young to know what you wanted."

"I'll never do that to my children."

"Don't be so sure. When the time comes, you'll understand."

"You mean because I learned it from you?"

The world around them felt thick with memory; the weight of past pains pressed between them. Abigail instinctively took her daughter's hand, searching for a bridge between their experiences, a thread of shared history to show that, in many ways, they were navigating the same uncertain waters.

"Then, after about a year, my mother arranged my marriage to your father," Abigail continued, moving the conversation forward.

Hannah gasped, pulling back her hand. "So you are saying you didn't fall in love with Father before you married? How unromantic," she said. "What did Grandfather do about you running off and getting married the first time?"

"Nothing," Abigail said with a quick shake of her head. "I think he knew it was women's work. Ha, I think my mother forbade him to act on the matter for fear he would do something dire, like kill my beloved Jan. Grandpapa was so passionate."

"I can't believe they just assigned you a husband after that."

"Your father was somewhat attractive. A Spaniard with a dark Moorish complexion and green eyes like your grandmother." Abigail tried to explain the reasons for her consent. "It was a marriage born of strategy rather than passion. With Edward often away in Albany, his attention was divided between political machinations, rumored secret affairs, and another family in Albany; he served his purpose."

"Mother!" she exclaimed.

"What? I've got seven children."

"What are you saying? Does father have another family? In Albany?" Hannah asked.

Abigail shrugged as if she didn't care anymore what he did. "I remember your Grandmother Annica found out about his escapades. She had dealings with Captain Kidd, a client whose name was often cloaked in danger and intrigue."

"You mean Uncle Willie?"

"The very same. Ha, I'm surprised you remember him. You were only what, nine or ten at the time?"

"Seven," Hannah inserted as if the correction was significant.

"Seven?" she asked, tilting her head, trying to remember. "But of course you were."

"He taught Jacob, Sarah, and me how to wield a sword and shoot a musket. I suppose Sarah might have been too young to remember." Hannah folded her hands in front of her chest, saying, "You know, he was the one who gave me my twin pistols before he left. Sarah and I have wagered that you named William after him. And now I realize you call Jacob's son Andreas Jan after your, uh, first love?"

"Ha, I believe I did just that." Her mother sighed with nostalgia and discomfort. She shrugged, tugging on her blouse under her coat to rearrange her cotton pads over her achingly full breasts. "I just wish the babe were here now to lighten my load."

"How long does it take to stop, ah, hurting — after?" Hannah asked, frowning with curiosity.

Abigail waved a hand dismissively, uninterested in discussing her discomfort. "Wield a sword and shoot muskets," she said instead."I remember having our butler, Caesar, dull the blades so you wouldn't hurt anyone with your sneaking jabs. Perhaps you can pass those skills on to little Willie in Captain Kidd's honor." She half laughed, then nodded solemnly, reflecting as she fixed her eyes on the distant banks. "I do remember. I also remember Kidd threatened your father with retribution should he continue breaking his marital vows in a protective rage over my honor."

Hannah stood as rigid as a ship's mast braving a tempest, her face registering shades of shock and disbelief at her mother's candid revelation about her father. Wide-eyed and momentarily voiceless, she grappled with the weight of the words that had fallen upon her ears.

When her voice finally found its way through the thicket of her astonishment, it carried a tremor of curiosity and trepidation. "What kind of retributions?" she asked.

"I believe it had something to do with his stones?"

"Stones?" Hannah naively asked.

"Nuts. Cods. Privy members, whatever you call them, it worked on your father."

Hannah's expression initially contorted in shock but swiftly transformed into a broad smile regarding the precious masculine jewels. "He must not have been caught because you kept having children," she laughed.

"Well, we did, but it wasn't exactly as it seemed—" Abigail abruptly paused, causing a frown from her daughter. Abigail softened her expression and sighed. "You have to understand this was a complicated time. My father eventually died, and Edward and I moved back to Manhattan to run the family farm. We lived there until we eventually retired to our current abode, grandmother's house on the Hudson, where she ran her business. My first husband, Jan, was now engaged to be married, and all was forgotten—or so it had seemed."

"Wait! So it had seemed? No, what did you do?" Hannah hissed, sensing a scandal.

"I didn't start it."

"Mother?"

"Our farm was very productive. As you may already know from childhood, it was north of the Wall Street wall where the land was fertile and the roads well-worn. Jan was a brewer and had a reputation for making the finest ale on the island. After establishing a line of credit to sell grains to Jan, one day Edward invited Jan's fiancée, Juliet, to the farm to discuss donations to her church. He lied to her that others would be at the meeting, and when a sudden rainstorm delayed her departure, well. I wasn't at home when it happened."

Hannah held her breath, afraid to breathe.

"When Juliet became pregnant, Jan knew it wasn't his. He ended their engagement."

"What happened to her?"

"Juliet? Things only turned worse. Her family kicked her out, and she lived on the streets."

"Oh, mother, that sounds awful."

"Finally, someone stepped forward and set her up in a place to stay and gave her food and clothing."

"Someone?" her daughter asked. "Who would be so kind?"

Abigail's reply did not come at once. The air between them tightened as she considered what could be said—and what must remain unspoken.

"It was you?" her daughter pressed. "How did you know she was in trouble?"

"I still followed Jan's actions—and, consequently, her," Abigail said at last. "Not long after he'd so abruptly rejected the poor girl, I came upon her one day in the street, filthy and starving. I passed her by at first, telling myself she would find her way to an almshouse eventually, but then—" She frowned, the memory closing in. "I turned around and led her to a nearby wayfarer's rest until I could find a lodging house to take care of her. One day, when I was delivering supplies, she mentioned that she thought it was Edward who was sending the food." Abigail's voice was unwavering. "This surprised me, of course, and, with my insistence, she eventually told me what he did to her—but I didn't believe it could be Edward's child until it was born. You see, Jan and Juliet shared blonde hair and blue eyes, and when the baby was dark-skinned, like your father, I knew she was telling the truth. I went to Jan to let him know what had happened. That it wasn't her fault and, in the process, we—well, had an affair."

"Oh no. The sin of adultery?" Hannah asked, her voice trembling with shock. Her mother nodded before lowering her head. Hannah's eyes shifted back and forth, her mind racing. Finally, she exclaimed, "Mother, did he leave you with a child? Oh, mother... how? I mean, oh my, it was my brother Jacob? That is why he looks… different."

Abigail reacted as if the confession had gone too far and wanted to recount her words, but it was too late.

"That's why my older brother Jacob looks nothing like anyone in our family. Blonde hair and blue eyes—and taller than father by a head."

"At the time, I felt it was Biblical justice: Eye for an eye and a tooth for a tooth. And now, come to think of it, it may have been why your father has strayed from me ever since. Oh, my child, I want to protect you from something just as heartbreaking."

"Mother," Hannah said with a look of incredulity. "But wait. How did you inherit the Van der Bilt brewery?"

"I said my father died, not my mother," she said with a pause, as if that was explanation enough. Then she added, "She got a whiff of all this and gave Jan an offer he could not refuse for his brewery and for him to disappear forever. I think she may have mentioned something about his stones as well."

"What is it with men and their privy members?"

"Child. With a question like that, I no longer need to worry about you running off with a man." Abigail waved a hand over the edge of the boat. "As turbulent as these waters we cross," she said thoughtfully, "I tell you these stories to paint a more vivid picture of the world you are poised to traverse as an adult. The truth is, love, danger, and duty collide at every turn."

Hannah leaned over the side of the ship's bulwarks to ask, "Are you telling me this about Father because of what you told me about Andreas all those years ago?"

Abigail looked at her maturing daughter and frowned as if she could not remember what she had said.

"You told me men are not to be trusted to be loyal to one woman. They always have an agenda that doesn't include me."

"Oh, daughter, see your life through my eyes just once. Where would you be today if you had run off with that penniless German mercenary?"

"I'm not sure, but I feel we'd both be happy."

"Would you now? You and Andreas Andreas?" She laughed sardonically at the man's pirate name.

"We could purchase a plot of land and farm—I have the money. Grandfather had a farm north of the wall."

Her mother laughed wholeheartedly, "Yes, he did, and never got a single finger dirty. That farm was within an hour's ride of anything you'd wish to buy. You'd be lucky to find a sack of flour out in the wilderness. No, I am sad to say, my dearest daughter, I have raised you and your sister, Sarah, to be obligate city girls. You like pretty dresses, styled hair, and elegant foods like chocolate."

Hannah smiled cavalierly, trying to insinuate she didn't like chocolate when everyone knew she loved that confectionery delight. She stood thinking about her mother's wisdom. Did her mother's mother, Grandmother Annica, have the same sentiment for her mother as the young girl who wanted to run off and marry the older ale brewer at her age? Then the thought came to her mind: would she do the same for her daughters when the time came?

"But Sarah?" Hannah asked. "Why didn't you ask her to come along?"

"Oh, I wanted some alone time with you. Besides, she hasn't yet shown any interest in—"

"Boys? Mother, Sarah is taken with the young gentleman as well."

"No? I was going to say our family business, but—oh my." Abigail laughed, shaking her head. "Now that you tell me this, maybe you can fill me in on boys and Sarah?" She gave her daughter a knowing look, amused by her own naivety.

"Well, perhaps boys play a small part," Hannah admitted.

"She's shown no interest in the family business. And this is, in many ways, why you are with me on this business education trip, and not Sarah." Abigail's brow furrowed with concern, second-guessing her decision. "You think I should have added her to the mix? There's nothing like a sister's comfort and counsel to keep your course steady and strong." She turned her gaze toward the horizon, eyes scanning the landmarks off the starboard side. "My sister Eunice has always been my compass," she murmured, lost in thought.

"What are we to do in New Haven, Mother?" Hannah finally inquired, turning the subject in mid-stream, her curiosity alight with the day's revelations and adventures.

Abigail, her gaze steady on the horizon swelling before them, replied with a simplicity that belied the complexity of their mission, "Paying dividends, my dear. What dividends we will pay and to whom, I am still working out. But remember, in our world, debts are not only settled with gold and silver, but they are often from promises, shrouded in secrets, and sometimes, they're the whispered wishes of ghosts long past—and—" she hesitated before saying, "I now realize we will be needing more help."

"Captain!" Abigail called out as he climbed down from the command deck ladder, her voice and gait steady as she left her daughter to speak with him.

The Captain turned to her, his eyes squinting against the sunlight that reflected low off the water. "Miss Abigail, the ship is sound. I think the mast of the downed ship only careened barnacles off our port side," he nodded. "Is there something you be needing?"

Abigail clasped her hands behind her back, her posture straight, exuding the confidence and grace she was known for. "I've settled on a slight alteration to our planned course," she began. Her tone was diplomatic but low, so her daughter wouldn't hear the exchange.

The Captain raised an eyebrow, a silent prompt for her to continue.

"We'll need to stop in Flushing before we proceed to New Haven," she explained. "It's imperative that we pick up an additional passenger there, my widowed sister, Mrs. Eunice Fowler — though she doesn't know we are coming for her."

The Captain considered this momentarily, his gaze drifting toward the horizon. "That'll add a fair bit of time to our journey—at least the night, if not a full day—if we cannot contact her right away, ma'am," he mused, his voice gruff, like gravel tumbling in the surf.

"I believe we have time for this," Abigail replied with calm reassurance, "and for another diversion I've planned for you."

"Another diversion, ma'am?"

"Yes. After dropping us off in New Haven, I wish for you to sail on to Old Saybrook."

"Old Saybrook, ma'am. I'm familiar with those waters."

"And I need you to become even more familiar with the terrain." She held up a hand to forestall his reply. "There is a school there—the Connecticut Collegiate School. They may have tutors who are interested in relocating to a better educational system. Your job is to assess how steadfast the school's administrators are and whether there are any weaknesses we might exploit—if need be, you understand. Only if need be. If you catch my drift, but odds are your investigation will yield nothing."

The Captain's forehead furrowed with surprise at the mention of a school and tutors, but he had worked with Abigail Spragg for years enough to know not to ask questions when she had that driven look on her face. He gave a curt nod. "Very well, Miss Abigail. We'll set course for Flushing. But I must warn ye—these waters can be treacherous. Aye, we've a stout crew, but we mustn't tarry long."

"Agreed, Captain," Abigail replied, her expression one of genuine gratitude.

The sloop carved through the gentle waves of the long waterway separating the mainland from Long Island, its main sail billowing with the serene, steady eastern wind, changing course to the starboard, guiding them along the coastline. The vessel was modest, its wooden sides worn from the many voyages it had weathered, but it was sturdy and reliable, much like its current passengers.

As Abigail returned to Hannah, she felt a sense of relief. The Captain's cooperation was crucial, and the idea of having Eunice at her side while she embarked on what was still a somewhat nebulous mission was too appealing to bypass. She hadn't yet revealed the full scope of their journey to Hannah, and as she made her way back to her daughter's side, she prepared herself for the barrage of questions that would undoubtedly follow her announcement of their unscheduled stop.

True enough, as the shoreline in the distance began to shift, Hannah's curiosity bloomed like a sail in the wind, and Abigail readied herself to provide reassurance and kindle excitement for the unexpected detour that lay ahead.

Hannah stood at the prow, her hand shielding her eyes from the evening sun that glistened off the water. The excitement of the journey was evident in her stance, the slight bounce in her posture. She turned to her mother, who was consulting a much-folded hand-sketched chart, and the unanswered question she'd been pondering finally spilled forth.

"New Haven sounds so thrilling, Mother," she said, her voice carrying the melody of adventure.

Abigail, her expression contemplative as she traced a route on the map with her finger, glanced up, her eyes meeting Hannah's. "Yes, my dear. Every new place is thrilling. Especially when it is shrouded in mystery, but I am beginning to get an idea of what we will find," she said. "But first, we have an important way-point."

Hannah's curiosity was piqued. "A stop? Where?"

"In Flushing," Abigail replied, folding the map precisely.

Hannah's eyes widened in surprise. "Flushing? Aunt Eunice lives there, does she not?"

Abigail's gaze drifted toward the horizon, a determined set to her jaw.

"We're to pick her up."

Hannah gasped at the mention of her aunt.

"Yes," Abigail continued, surprised at her daughter's reverie. "Eunice possesses a unique skill set that I realized I needed before it was too late. She is crucial for our plans in New Haven. Her insight is sharp, her judgment unparalleled, and I don't dare pursue these endeavors without her guiding hand. She's been residing in Flushing for some time now, and her knowledge of the terrain and local dynamics is invaluable."

The excitement of the reunion dawned on Hannah, and she nodded, her initial confusion giving way to an excited anticipation. "You know," Hannah said, a bright smile playing on her wide-set lips, "this reminds me of the summers I spent at Aunt Eunice's old estate in Hempstead before Uncle George died. The way the light hits the water, it's almost magical."

Abigail turned to her, intrigued. "You've always mentioned her fondly, but never really taken the time to talk about her. What was it like with her?"

Hannah's smile grew at the memories. "She was—is—wonderful. The kind of person who lights up the room when she walks in. Everyone adores her, not because she tries to please but because she's genuinely herself. And her wit! She's the sharpest person I know."

Abigail chuckled. "Please, enlighten me."

"Of course," Hannah laughed. "There was this one time, a gentleman who fancied himself a poet, who read her some verses. Aunt Eunice listened with the utmost attention, and when he finished, expecting praise, she said, 'Well, sir, I do believe you're the only poet who has successfully made rhyme an enemy of reason!'"

Both burst into laughter, the sound carrying over the water.

"And her sense of humor is so dry, sometimes people don't know she's jesting. She once told a woman, straight-faced, that her dress was 'a marvelous effort to make roses endangered single-handedly.' The woman took it as a compliment!"

Abigail wiped tears of mirth from her eyes. "Oh, I would love to have been there! But alas, I was either with child or neck deep in our family business." A ghost of a smile flickered across Abigail's lips. "I know my sister and I are different. That's why I require her company on this particular quest. Her mind works in mysterious ways, always crafting, always planning. I'm sure she will love coming with us, too."

"Mother, you shouldn't work so hard," Hannah said, her expression turning tender. "Aunt Eunice taught me the importance of being true to oneself. She's strong, independent, and unapologetically herself. I love her so much, not just for her humor but for her heart. She's been like a second mother to me when I visit."

"Should I be jealous?"

The laughter faded as a comfortable silence settled between them, the sky now a vivid orange surrounding the sun's last twilight gleaming.

"What do you think about Harvard?" Abigail said, changing the subject and postulating on the highest form of education she could conjure.

"Isn't that a school for rich boys?"

"So it seems; for now, at least, it is."

Abigail offered nothing else, and they stood there, lost in their thoughts; the only sounds were the gentle lapping of water against the hull and the distant dying cries of seagulls. The unforeseen challenges ahead seemed a little less daunting, their spirits buoyed by the love and lessons of those who had shaped their lives. After a few more moments, Abigail gave her daughter a kind, parting nod and turned to her cabin.

Abigail sat at her private desk, affixing her seal to the letter she had penned to her sister. The wax, still warm and malleable, was imprinted in the middle with an upright, rose-shaped flower whose stems were entangled in a criss-crossing, a tangible mark of her identity and heritage. While it was whimsical and pretty, it also served as a visible mark for a pirate, the skull and crossbones of their trade.

Letter in hand, Abigail then moved swiftly to consort with the Captain as the sloop's sails yielded to the embrace of the approaching shore, billowing gently as the vessel decelerated, the rhythm of the waves playing a softer melody. The sun fell from the vast sky's eternal canvas, kissing the horizon one last goodbye before disappearing, casting hues of orange, crimson, and gold across the clear heavens, a masterpiece only nature could render.

Against this spectacular backdrop, the Captain informed Abigail he had changed his mind about docking and would instead anchor some distance away. There was not enough room for their sloop amongst a line of nefarious-looking vessels.

As the crew moved about, pulling on lines, securing sails, and calling instructions to one another, Abigail approached Hannah. "We'll be bedding down here tonight, I'm afraid. Not enough room at the docks," Abigail said, her voice steady but carrying an undercurrent of excitement — an emotion mirrored in the heightened color on her cheeks and the sparkle in her eyes when she said to her sleepy daughter. "This won't be the last time you brave a night on board. It's in our blood, a legacy that binds all the sons and daughters of our Barbary pirate grandfather."

Hannah stood beside her mother, taking in the day's closing scenes: the bustling crew securing the ship's sails, the last rays of light shimmering on the water, and the beleaguered lights of Flushing drawing them into its nocturnal embrace. She watched as her mother dispatched a message to the shore, a note swiftly transported by a nimble dinghy destined for her Aunt Eunice: a request for her company at dawn to go with them on the remainder of their journey to New Haven. A sense of profound anticipation swelled within her, a wave of exhilaration mixed with a dash of trepidation. This journey, Hannah thought, was more than just a change of scenery or a simple errand. Being here with her mother and aunt was more like an education into the inner workings of the family business, the Pirate Bank Business: a rite of passage, a bridge to an inheritance she had only glimpsed in a blending of pirates' stories and the legacy that hummed in her veins.

The adventure, Hannah realized with a heart thrumming like the sails in the wind, was only unfurling its life. Ahead lay mystery, challenge, and the undeniable pull of destiny.

CHAPTER 3

Hannah's Twins

THE VEIL OF SLEEP was abruptly torn from Abigail as the jarring sound of musket fire shattered the stillness of the night. Her heart pounded against her ribcage, a frantic rhythm that mirrored the chaos erupting outside her cabin.

Sitting straight up in her corner bed and showing the whites of her eyes, Hannah watched her mother move cautiously to secure a musket from under her mattress.

With foresight threading her every move, Abigail placed her finger to her lips and then lowered her hands in a motion that signaled her daughter should stay put and quiet before cocking the musket and inching towards the door. The wood was cool against her bare feet, every sense straining into the darkness. She listened to the cracked-open door with her ear.

As she dared a peek through the narrow opening, the world tilted on its axis. A forceful hand latched onto her sleeping gown, yanking her with such ferocity that her feet lost their purchase. She tumbled out, sprawling unceremoniously onto the deck, discharging her musket ball into the wooden planks, a harsh welcome to a nightmare.

Disoriented, Abigail's eyes darted around, struggling to make sense of the commotion she'd been thrust into. The moon, a scant witness from above, cast an eerie glow on what was unmistakably a robbery. Her breath caught in her throat as she took in the sight of their captain, a man she'd entrusted with their safety, now compromised and held at knife-point by one of the three menacing figures who'd boarded and seized the ship.

"What is happening?" she cried out, her voice a mix of fear and burgeoning anger, seeking answers from the aged captain, who looked as helpless as a lamb before wolves.

"These gentlemen are in search of treasure, ma'am," the captain replied, his voice strained but eerily calm given the blade kissing his throat, his eyes apologizing for the tumult he couldn't control.

Gathering the hem of her sleeping gown to stand, Abigail's fear rapidly coalesced into fierce indignation towards the marauders, her every word slicing through the hostility like a whip. "Well, you're sorely misguided. Your concerns should lie elsewhere — with your own well-being. Do you have any idea who I am?"

Her words hung heavy in the salt-tinged air, a challenge wrapped in steel. The audacity of these looters, thinking they could ambush her ship and crew and, most of all, disrupt her mission, was more than a mere inconvenience. It was an insult she could not, would not, tolerate. In that moment, the deck of the sloop transformed from a scene of disarray into a stage where Abigail stood, formidable even in her sleeping gown, every inch the descendant of pirates and privateers. Her heritage, a silent strength coursing through her veins, rose to meet the danger head-on as the night echoed with uncertainty, courage, and power.

One of the other robbers approached Abigail and slapped her face with such brutality that she almost fell again. The one with the knife to the captain sneered, his face a map of scorn illuminated by the moon's pale light. "I don't give a damn if you're the Queen of England herself. Where's the Crown Jewels, eh?" he jeered, pulling the blade and nicking the captain's flesh, his laughter a sinister melody that lingered with the ocean's whispers.

Abigail, her resolve hardening like steel in a forge, stood defiantly amidst the chaos. Her sharp and calculating eyes darted between the intruders, assessing them with the cold precision of a strategist on the battlefield.

"There are only three of you," she stated, her voice steady. Her words were not a question but an assertion, like a lioness marking her territory in the face of hyenas. "How far do you expect to get once you leave this ship?"

Imbued with undisguised contempt, her challenge lingered ominously as she rubbed her swelling face. This was more than just a question about their escape plan; it was a stark reminder of their grave miscalculation. To their disadvantage, they didn't know they weren't up against just any woman; they were up against a legacy, a lineage of seasoned seafarers and staunch defenders who yielded to no intimidation. But how could they? The pirate bank was a well-placed secret known only to those captains who'd met on the seven oceans. And now, they had unwittingly trapped themselves in a web of their creation, and at its heart stood Abigail, a formidable foe disguised as a victim.

The deck was still for a heartbeat. The only sound was the ship's creaking and the distant crash of waves, as if the ocean held its breath, awaiting the intruders' next move. In that sliver of silence, the balance of power teetered precariously, the outcome of this nocturnal confrontation as mysterious as the waters that cradled them.

Undeterred by Abigail's fortitude, the knife-wielding robber grinned, his rotten teeth a grotesque display in the ghostly moonlight. "You should not care where we are going next. I reckon you'll be in no state to give chase when I'm through with you." He laughed haughtily, then spat at the captain's boot tips, his spit carrying a peril that slithered through the night like a foul fog. "Why should we be the ones to leave? The size of this ship and crew already feels quite cozy to me," he said, drawing his blade tight enough to cause blood to drip down the captain's neck onto his white-collared nightshirt. "This appears to me to be the beginning of a splendid career. And there can be only one captain of a ship—"

"You? Ha!" Abigail shouted. Her taunt drew his attention away from his dirty deeds. "Pirate? Don't dilute the name. We're the only pirates here!" She laughed out to the brazen face of the moon, nodding her head with crazed excitement.

Before the echo of her laughter could fade, the night's darkness ruptured with a flash of burning smoke and a deafening concussive blast. The explosion consumed the knife-wielding raider's head in a hellish burst, leaving behind the acrid stench of smoke and the weight of imminent uncertainty. As the musket recoiled from the back of the raider's neck, his knife clattered across the deck. Every marauder and crewman jolted, seized by raw terror, as the ship descended into chaos and noise.

When the smoke cleared, the figure that had once been a menacingly confident knife-wielding bandit dramatically transformed. Grotesque lines carved through his facial features. His sneer had become a grimace while blood blossomed from his mouth like a crimson confession under the moon's unflinching gaze. His body swayed, and then he crumpled. For a moment, his chin rested on the captain's shoulder before he slowly slid down his back, revealing behind him the slender, determined figure of Hannah. She stood resolute, a musket in each hand, extending her smoking gun at arm's length over the captain's shoulder. Her thunderbird tattoo on her forearm thrust its majestic head from beneath her nightshirt sleeve, and the barrel of her discharged weapon still whispered the promise of more retribution. Her steely green eyes shifted like a cat to the other two predators.

Tendrils of smoke dissipated through the pristine glow of moonlight, signifying the end of the standoff. Hannah, her eyes alight with the fierce impact of triumph and the lingering adrenaline of action, met her mother's gaze across the deck. In them, Abigail saw the reflection of her own indomitable spirit, the legacy of their lineage burning bright. The air, now tinged with gunpowder and resolve, thrummed with newfound respect and an unspoken understanding — they were not victims of this night but the powerful orchestrators of their survival.

In the aftermath of the gunshot's echo, action resumed fervently on the deck. The captain and crew, their resolve reignited by Hannah's bravery with musket in hand, moved swiftly to secure the remaining intruders. Like prey ensnaring their predators, they bound the would-be robbers to the mast, their faces etched with the stark realization of their foiled plan.

"Check every corner! And find out how they boarded us," the captain bellowed, his voice slicing through the lingering smoke and confusion. "There could be more rats hiding in the shadows!" The crew scoured the ship, their footsteps a drumbeat of urgency against the wooden planks. Though they sighted a lone canoe adrift off the starboard, the vessel yielded no more threats; the trio had been ambitious but ultimately unwise.

With the immediate danger quelled, the captain, ringing his finger in his deafened ear, turned to Abigail, a heavy question furrowing his brow. "What shall we do with these two scallywags?" he asked, nodding toward the defeated picaroons. Their fates were now as uncertain as the sea that cradled the ship.

Abigail's eyes, usually so decisive, flickered with hesitation. This moment, she understood, was pivotal—not just in terms of justice but as a lesson inked in real time for her daughter. Her gaze shifted to Hannah, who stood with the residue of smoke and valor clinging to her. The muskets, now silent sentinels in her crossed hands across her nightgown, had transformed her from a spectator to an active scribe in their family's storied history.

"Hannah, you will decide their fate. What will be done to these intruders?" Abigail asked the question as an invitation for her daughter to step into the legacy that was her birthright.

Hannah, the echo of the musket's blast still ringing in her ears, felt the weight of her mother's inquiry. The impact of what she'd done — the life she'd taken in defense of their own — anchored her to the moment. Gathering the fragments of her composure, she met her mother's gaze squarely.

"Call the constable," she said, her voice a surprising bastion of calm in the storm's wake. "Let the law handle their fate." A pause, a breath, and she added, "But before they're taken away, have them swab the deck. I don't want the sun to rise on the remainder of this night's darkness."

Her words, firm yet tinged with the vulnerability of her youth, resonated with a wisdom that belied her years. Abigail heard not just her daughter's orders but the echoes of the leaders who'd come before, the strength and resolve that twined through their family tree like the tendrils of a blooming vine ready to strangle any opposition in its path. They would survive, the dawn would come, and they would continue — not just for themselves but for the legacy they carried forward.

CHAPTER 4

Thaddeus Pudding

THE FOLLOWING DAY, Aunt Eunice stepped into the dinghy and told the watermen, "Nothing like an early start to remind you that old bones and chilly mornings don't mix well."

"Yes, ma'am."

"Well, if I am to meet my sister on her sloop, The Atlas, at least the sunrise will put on a good show for us early risers."

An elderly gentleman caught what she had said and addressed it: "Am I to believe that this ferry is heading out to The Atlas? A certain Abigail Spragg?"

"My sister's private sloop is indeed named The Atlas. State your name and business, kind sir."

"Constable Pudding, it is. Thaddeus Pudding at your service, ma'am?" the soft-spoken gentleman said, removing his hat with a bow and rocking the small craft as he embarked. He inquired her name with his raised bushy eyebrows, but she evaded his unspoken question.

"You have been summoned by my sister as well?"

"Yes, ma'am. As I said, a Mrs. Spragg, to be exact."

"Whatever for, pray-tell?" she asked as the watermen made haste towards the moored sloop.

"She didn't say specifically, but it was emphasized that it was of grave importance. The seaman who delivered the message was quite insistent. Ha, I thought he would kidnap me from my bed if I didn't comply. Unnerving at best, I grant you."

"Why do we always meet at the crack of dawn? I think my sister enjoys seeing me grumpy."

"I'd say not grumpy," he countered with a roguish grin. "If you ever tire of these sunrise escapades, I know a charming fellow who prefers moonlit strolls and leisurely breakfasts."

"Yes, that sounds more agreeable. Is it too much to ask for a mid-morning start?" Eunice said, recognizing the clean-cut man of the law as a newcomer to the Flushing area. "I've heard good things about you, sir."

"Me, ma'am?"

"It was mentioned that your ability to stay calm under pressure is legendary; you treat every crisis as if it's a minor inconvenience, much like your presence. Ah, here we are. Give me a boost?" Her words confused his concentration as their ferry boat bounced off the hull of The Atlas, and he stood to assist.

They both boarded the sloop in a manner lacking any semblance of grace, with Eunice sitting her bottom on the top of the constable's head. Clambering awkwardly up the ship's shroud until she reached the deck, she promptly enveloped her sister and niece in a hug that, though unexpected, brimmed with reassurance. "I expected your needy mother, but not you, Hannah, my darling! Whatever are you doing here?"

"I was ordered to accompany her, just as you were."

Eunice pulled back, a wry smile playing on her lips as she quipped to her sister, "Truly, with you, it's never a dull moment. These impromptu reunions of ours — you'd think I have nothing better to do than sit around, twiddling my thumbs, awaiting your sudden appearances to add a dash of excitement to the vicissitudes of my dreadfully mundane existence!" Her light and jesting tone took the edge off the recent events, her words serving as a buoyant counterpoint to the night's earlier distress.

Eunice's gaze then drifted to the two sinister figures bound to the mast, and her eyes widened slightly as she observed the captain showing the constable what seemed to be a lifeless body under a tarp. She turned back to her sister, her expression theatrically shocked, and teased, "Oh, sister, you didn't have to go to such lengths to pique my interest with an actual murder. It's not one of my ex-husbands, is it?"

Abigail pursed her lips and indicated with a thrust of her head that the man's death was Hannah's doing.

Eunice was halfway through a sharp retort when her eyes caught Hannah's, and the punchline died on her lips. Her niece's mood glistened—just a shimmer at first—stopping Eunice, as if she'd spotted a crack in a fine piece of porcelain before it cut her tongue. She blinked, tilted her head, and softened her voice to a teasing lilt. "Well, blast it, darling, if you're going to look at me like that, I'll have to cancel the levity portion of tonight's exchange." She leaned closer, her expression folding into a sly, maternal smile. "Now, tell your old auntie—did someone insult your baking again, or are we mourning something dire, like the loss of good wine?" Her hand found Hannah's, warm and firm, her thumb brushing the back in quiet rhythm. "Come on now, love. No tears without tea. Or whiskey. Preferably the latter."

They all watched in solemn silence as the crew dragged the body to the bulwarks and unceremoniously heaved it over the side into the waiting dinghy below. The thud of the body was followed by the subdued parade of the other two captured filibusters, their heads bowed in defeat and shame.

Now piecing together the night's dramatic events, Eunice couldn't help but comment as she saw the last of the marauders escorted past. With a sardonic smile, she mused, "Well, what grand fools these rogues were, daring to cross swords not with one but two lady pirates on their own turf. It's almost pitiable how sorely they underestimated the notorious blood of our lineage." Her words, though light, carried a swell of pride for the resilient women of her family.

Having observed the exchange between the women from a respectful distance, Constable Pudding chose this moment to approach. The morning sun cast long shadows on the deck, and the ship swayed gently, a calm contrast to the previous night's chaos.

"Madams," he began, addressing both Eunice and Abigail but pausing to offer a reassuring nod to the younger woman. "What transpired here last night... it was an act of remarkable bravery." His voice was steady, the timbre resonant with the authority of his office, yet softened by genuine admiration.

"These three river rats," he continued, gesturing in the direction of the tied dinghy where the dead one lay, "have been like eels, slipping through the law's grasp time and again. But your actions," he paused, his gaze sweeping across the deck where the signs of struggle were still visible as stains in the morning light, "will put an end to their reign of thievery."

He straightened up, and there was a certain formality to his stance as he prepared to take his leave. "The community owes you a debt of gratitude. Your courage likely saved many from future torment at the hands of these scoundrels."

Constable Pudding bowed slightly, then tipped his tricorn hat — a practiced, fashionable gesture that seemed entirely natural coming from him.

He said to Eunice, "You know where to find me."

Eunice gasped as if she didn't know what he meant, holding her hand to her neck before giving him a shaded smile.

Without another word, he turned on his heels and walked with measured steps to the ship's side. He descended into the dinghy that had remained tethered with the dead and bound criminals, his departure as understated as his arrival, leaving behind the promise of justice finally within reach.

Eunice whirled toward her sister, the constable's departing figure now barely registering in her mind. Her face was a portrait of sudden consternation, her voice pitching to a note of maternal urgency. "Good heavens—the baby?" she exclaimed.

Abigail's response was swift, calming to her sister's flaring anxieties. "The baby's fine. William is not on board."

As Eunice absorbed this, the storm of concern that had gathered in her eyes was replaced by a fog of confusion. "But where—?" she started to ask, her voice trailing off as she searched Abigail's face for answers.

Hannah stepped in, her tone gentle. "The little one is safe at home with the wet nurse," she said, nodding with a frown to her mother struggling to adjust her tight blouse.

Eunice's shoulders dropped with understanding, and a sigh of satisfaction escaped her lips. She drew her sister and niece into an embrace that seemed to gather up all the scattered worries of the moment, holding them tight in a wave of familial relief.

CHAPTER 5

New Haven

AS THE HARBOR ALONG THE CONNECTICUT shoreline approached, the outlines of New Haven emerged through the afternoon mist. The Captain deftly steered the ship past a large low tide sandbar off their port, with Abigail standing at the helm, her gaze fixed on the view ahead. With sails slacking but still proud against the backdrop of the vast Sound, the sloop cut through the waters with a grace that belied its sturdy build. The structures hugging the waterfront were rudimentary at best, their forms hinting at practicality over aesthetics. They were more reminiscent of warehouses than homes where lives would be woven together in domesticity.

When Hannah emerged from the cabin onto the deck, she saw her mother and aunt huddled together. She approached, hoping to catch the thread of their conversation. Eunice's voice carried a note of disbelief. "And here I thought he was dead. But why on earth would he want you to start a girls' school here, of all places—for heaven's sake?"

"A girl's school?" Hannah chirped. "Is that why I'm going to New Haven, to be put in a girl's school?"

Taken aback, Abigail inquired, "Hannah, my dear. Do you feel the need to better your education?"

"Well," she said, hesitating to say, looking back and forth between her mother and Aunt Eunice's wry smile.

Eunice quipped, "Well, bless your boots; you've stumbled into the middle of the pudding before the bowl was set on the table."

With her sharp eyes, Eunice turned back to her sister, wanting more. "New Haven hardly seems the place for fineries, let alone building a school for young ladies," she remarked, a tone of skepticism threading her voice.

Hannah, young and hungry for the unfolding world, looked on with a blend of wonder and curiosity as if pondering the distant shores of a country like India. "You're going to build a school for girls here?"

Abigail turned to her sister and daughter, the light rain matting the hair that escaped her veil to her face. "We're not just here to idle in the tide, my dear," she began, her voice carrying the undaunted spirit of the sea. "Our quest is to find a woman, the acquaintance of a man whose favor we enjoy and whose purse strings are as open as the sea is wide. We are to settle her debts and assist her in anchoring a place to nurture the minds of young girls, no less. A school, right here in this growing colony." Abigail's hand swept across the view of the coast as if painting the future with her words.

The idea moved in the moist draft between them, a concept so alien yet now entrusted to their care. Eunice's brows furrowed in thought, and Hannah's eyes were alight with the possibility of change, the potential of education for her own gender stirring a silent excitement within her.

"But, Abigail, formal schools are for boys. What will the townsfolk say?" Eunice finally said. "Girls are taught at home, if at all, as our mother did."

Abigail's lips curled into a knowing smile, the kind that had seen storms and stars and the endless horizon. "Aye, that may be the tradition," she declared, her voice carrying the weight of a roaring ocean. "But the winds are shifting, and with them, the tides of time. We're not just here to deliver cargo or trade goods. We're here to chart new courses, to open doors long closed to the righteous of hearts and the meekest of gender."

Hannah's heart swelled with fierce pride for her mother, and Eunice's skepticism gave way to a reluctant admiration. The idea of educating girls was no less revolutionary than their pirating lifestyle, defying the norm with the same bravado that had defined their lives.

As the sloop approached the jetting rough-hewn dock and the buildings of New Haven grew clearer, so too did the vision of what they were about to embark upon—a venture that would defy convention and perhaps, in its own small but significant way, turn the tide of history.

The sloop's wooden hull made a gentle thud against the dock, and the eager trio—Abigail, Eunice, and Hannah—prepared to disembark. As soon as the gangplank was set in place, Abigail stepped onto the sturdy planks of New Haven's pier and turned back toward the steadfast Captain Holloway, inspecting him with the air of a superior officer assessing her crew.

"Captain, don't forget to look your finest," she reminded him with a raised brow and a tone that was playful yet commanding.

Holloway straightened to attention with a grunt, brushing off his coat and adjusting his collar, clearly feeling the weight of her request.

"Mother?" Hannah chided, watching the poor Captain squirm. "Why do you taunt our noble captain so?"

"Not a taunt, I assure you, daughter. The Captain has a mission."

"Mission? Here?"

"No. Old Saybrook, some thirty miles to our east," Abigail said airily, as though the matter were hardly worth concern.

"Whatever for?"

Abigail sighed at her daughter's insatiable curiosity and rolled her eyes toward Eunice for support. "A mission? Or maybe a reconnaissance, I should have said?"

"Definitely a pirating mission. Not the pelagic ship-to-ship barbarous rendezvous, of course, but ship-to-land—much more leisurely—and safer, with letters of marque for only the scholarly of heart," Eunice interjected with a knowing glower.

"Pirate? But I thought he wasn't a pirate anymore," Hannah said, watching the sweet Captain pull up his stockings.

"Once a pirate, always a pirate," Abigail scowled. "He'll be sneaking into the Connecticut Collegiate College to tabulate a list of instructors, to see what there is to know about them. Identify the more adventurous among them."

"Oh, Mother. Why do you need to pirate away tutors? Aren't there learned people here in New Haven?"

"Perhaps. But with the Captain widening the enthusiasm with a smattering of coin—"

"Pirate coin," Eunice added, smirking.

"—We will know the lay of the land better and be able to recruit the best instructors money can buy when the time comes," Abigail finished, nodding with satisfaction toward the Captain, who was now overseeing the offloading of their luggage.

"If the time comes," Eunice was quick to add.

Behind them, the crew moved with practiced ease, hauling the ladies' heavy sea chests down from the sloop's deck. Each chest was packed to the brim with the essentials and treasures of genteel women—silks, petticoats, ribbons, and other wardrobe necessities that spoke of refinement and grace.

With a wink, Eunice caught Abigail's gaze and added, "And mind your manners, Captain. We don't want any tales reaching us of rough sailor language at the college."

The Captain rolled his eyes with a chuckle and tipped his hat to the sisters. "Aye, ma'am, I'll be the very picture of civility," he replied with mock solemnity, giving his vest another brush as if it would somehow polish his scruffy demeanor.

Watching the exchange with a grin, Hannah leaned over to her mother. "Do you think he'll really be able to charm those scholars?"

"Oh, I have no doubt," Abigail whispered back, her smile mischievous. "Even a pirate can be persuasive when he has to be—"

"Especially with a large sack of silver greasing his welcoming palms," Eunice teased.

As they made their way down the pier, Abigail cast one last glance over her shoulder, watching Captain Holloway smooth back his unruly hair, pick an unseemly louse from his coat sleeve, and stride purposefully along the dock. The women exchanged amused looks as Abigail called back, her tone stern yet laced with playful authority. "Keep those chests under a watchful eye! I am sure it would be well-nigh impossible to replace our wardrobes in this weather-beaten town."

"Aye, aye, ma'am," the Captain barked at his men, scratching his whiskered chin. "You've got your orders. Look sharp!" The crewmen, as if jolted by his command, gripped their belted muskets and stood watch like loyal sentinels.

With a shared laugh, the women turned and headed toward the town, leaving the Captain to his task of impressing the learned men of Old Saybrook—whether they liked it or not.

The harbor was tranquil, swaying as if waiting for an event of note. Eunice breathed a sigh of relief at the lack of crowds. "Fortune smiles upon us," she observed. "With the town so empty, we'll easily find a roof to sleep under tonight."

Yet, as they moved away from the waterfront, the sisters fell into a familiar debate, each convinced her direction was best for securing accommodations. Their words crisscrossed like the rigging of their ship, each argument a knot tighter than the last.

Unfazed, Hannah, with the fearlessness of youth, approached a local—a young man holding a stringer of fish, his gaze following the ship's crew with quiet curiosity.

"Sir," she inquired with the confidence she had inherited. "Might I ask your name?"

"'Tis John Prout, ma'am," the soft-spoken young man said, wearing the unaccustomed look of one who a young lady at the docks did not often address.

"Where might we find the finest lodgings in town, John Prout?" she asked with a warm smile of appreciation.

The young man, taken aback by her directness, pointed without hesitation toward the end of the waterfront, stammering, "Pa-Peck's Inn, Long Wharf off of Fleet Street, before old East Creek."

Looking in that direction, she saw a modest but well-maintained two-story inn, its windows gleaming with the promise of comfort.

"Much obliged, John Prout," she said, repeating his name while looking him up and down, making his ears glow red. Then, as an afterthought, she added, "You a fisherman?"

"Nah. Like to fish. Work for my father in the fur trade."

"Ah, then you're a businessman?"

"Try to be," he said, smiling at the ground. "When I'm failing as a fisherman, that is."

She nodded in appreciation, turned, and ran to catch up.

By the time she reached her mother and aunt, their heated exchange had reached its natural, inconclusive end. Once at their side, Hannah interjected, "This way." With her voice steady, she gestured with an outstretched hand. "The best inn is just along the waterfront."

Her assertiveness drew a momentary frown from both women, their pride pricked by the young girl's decisive action. Yet, in the absence of a better plan, they followed Hannah, albeit with murmurs of other unexplored directions.

As they walked, the inn grew closer, its presence robust yet inviting against the backdrop of the utilitarian buildings dominating the harbor. By the time they reached its doors, the indignant murmurs had given way to nods of approval. Hannah had led them right to the threshold of the finest inn in town, standing as a witness to the changing times.

The robust wooden door of the inn creaked open, surrendering to the firm push from Abigail, who entered with the air of a sea captain docking her ship. Eunice trailed just a step behind, her eyes sweeping over the quaint establishment, while Hannah lingered on the threshold, taking in the warmth and chatter spilling from within. A fire crackled in the hearth, casting dancing shadows over walls adorned with nautical charts and a mounted figurehead of a unicorn, presumably salvaged from a shipwreck, seeming to leap from an invisible watery grave.

Abigail approached the innkeeper, a stout man with a ruddy complexion and a smile that reached his eyes.

"Good evening, sir. We require a room to stay, perhaps for the month," she declared, laying a heavy purse on the counter with a thud that suggested ample recompense for their lodgings.

Hannah's eyes widened slightly, the length of stay catching her unawares, but she held her tongue, trusting her mother's foresight. Her gaze was inexorably drawn to the majestic unicorn figurehead that crowned the fireplace, its spiraled horn pointing toward realms of legend and myth. She turned to Eunice, her curiosity piqued.

"That figurehead above the fire—why a unicorn?"

Eunice leaned in, her voice carrying the tone of an imparted secret. "You see, in ancient times, seafarers would carry with them the head of a beast, sacrificed to appease the gods for safe passage across treacherous seas."

Hannah nodded, her mind conjuring images of solemn rituals on creaking decks.

"The unicorn, though," Eunice continued, her eyes twinkling with a mix of whimsy and wisdom, "is a creature of purity and grace, often elusive and shrouded in mystery—much like the character of this town. It stands as a symbol, a beacon, if you will, reminding us that even the most fantastical tales hold a kernel of truth."

"So, this town…" Hannah began, seeking clarity.

"Ah, this town," Eunice interrupted, gesturing broadly. "It's like every other township I've been to. It may seem straightforward at a glance, but beneath its surface, it's as magical and unpredictable as any unicorn tale. This figurehead is an apt reminder that there's more to this place than meets the eye—a nod to the unknown adventures that await us here."

Hannah's eyes returned to the unicorn, now seeing it not just as a decorative artifact but as a silent guardian of the inn's hearth and the mysteries of New Haven.

Adjusting the feather in her hat, Eunice said with a playful lilt, "I daresay, at first glance, this town wants for the grandeur of elsewhere but must persevere." The innkeeper's grin broadened, misreading her jest for flattery.

"I am James Peck, and who might you be, fine ladies, if I may ask?" the innkeeper inquired, twirling his feathered quill as he spied their coin with a knowing wink.

"We're the Harringtons," Abigail replied, offering names that were not their own but served their purpose well enough.

With the pleasantries swiftly dispatched, Abigail leaned closer, her voice lowering to a conspiratorial whisper while moving her plump purse closer to the innkeeper's hand. "We're seeking a Miss Hope Terwilliger. Perhaps you've heard the name?"

The innkeeper stroked his nubby chin, a furrow of concentration creasing his brow. "Terwilliger, you say? Can't say that I have. We recollect most visitors around these parts, and that's a name I'd remember. Sounds like a name that would belong to someone from beyond the town's borders. Or perhaps someone who doesn't get out and about?"

Disappointment flickered across Abigail's face but vanished just as quickly, replaced by a steely resolve. Observing this silent exchange, Hannah sensed that their quest had become more challenging.

Eunice, ever quick with a word, laughed softly. "Well, it seems we'll have more of an adventure finding our Miss Terwilliger than we would sailing through this tempestuous little town!"

The innkeeper chuckled. "If she's around, you'll find her, or she'll find you," he said, his eyes focusing on the tempting purse. "New Haven may be small, but it has ways of revealing its secrets to those with a keen eye."

With keys in hand, the women ascended the narrow, creaking staircase of the New Haven inn, their boots tapping out a tired rhythm on the worn wooden steps. Candle sconces flickered on the walls, casting warm light on plaster cracked from salt air and time. A modest but well-kept corridor awaited them above, and one by one, they approached their quarters.

Eunice disappeared over her threshold first, emitting a faint sigh of satisfaction. Before the sturdy oak door could close behind her, Hannah peeked inside, saying, "I hope my boarding room will be this cozy." The room was sparse but tidy, with a single bed, a fireplace already laid, and a writing desk pushed beneath the window.

A few paces down, Abigail opened the next door, revealing a slightly larger room with two narrow beds, heavy woolen coverlets folded neatly at the foot. A simple washbasin stood by the hearth, and a small wavy glass-paned window overlooked the bright harbor.

Hannah followed her mother inside, silent, eyes sweeping their next-door room with equal curiosity and approval.

They each passed the time in quiet industry, checking each dresser drawer, testing the mattresses' comfort, and inspecting for pesky insects. Abigail was hanging Hannah's discarded shawl on a peg by the door when, from the hallway, came the Sound of boots clomping up the stairs—heavy, deliberate. The muted thuds of trunks being set down in Eunice's room echoed through the inn, followed by muffled conversation and the familiar clink of buckles and clasps. The sloop's crew had arrived with their luggage. Abigail paused, her fingers lingering on the bed's fabric, her thoughts already shifting from unpacking to strategy.

Scanning the delivered luggage at the foot of her bed with a satisfied nod, Abigail heard a muffled voice calling out, and she looked at her daughter in amusement.

"Abby," Eunice said loud enough to be heard through the thin walls. "This woman we're to find... are you certain of her name? Perhaps it's a mistake or another town. Show us from whence you know this name."

Abigail shifted uncomfortably, hearing her sister's voice clearly through the walls. Before she could speak, Hannah interjected, "Oh, Mother, if you cannot trust your own kin, then whom can you trust?"

"I tell you, I don't trust the walls of this inn," she remarked. "Eunice, if you want to speak to me, address your questions to my face."

Eunice sauntered into the room with a nonplussed expression, exclaiming, "I was just trying to test the place's acoustics. What do you think?"

Abigail felt the weight of truth pressing at the edges of her resolve. She longed to tell her daughter everything—no more cryptic answers, no more evasions. But this truth, this particular truth, needed to be shared in full, and only with the right ears present. She waited until Eunice entered the room, meeting her sister's steady gaze. No surprise flickered there—only quiet understanding.

With the door now closed and the room sealed in silence, Abigail turned to Hannah.

"The one whose treasure we've been safeguarding in our—" she paused, clearing her throat as if the truth itself carried the dust of too many years. Then she leaned forward, her voice barely above a whisper. "Is none other than Long Ben... Henry Avery."

Eunice gave a single, knowing nod, her expression unreadable but firm—as if to say, 'It's high time the child knew.'

Hannah's eyes widened, saying too loudly, "The King of Pirates?"

"Shush! The very same," Abigail confirmed, reaching into her coat to reveal a well-hidden letter, creased and tattered. "You were too young to remember when he visited our home with his… chests," she emphasized. "His gold, silver, and jewels were most impressive."

"I do remember him—from my," Hannah stopped short of revealing that she wrote about him in her journal. It wasn't written as well as she'd liked, but, as her mother had alluded, she was still a young lass when he visited.

Abigail carefully unfolded the letter, its words penned in the flowing script. "Annica," she read, then paused to clarify, "It was your grandmother he dealt with, not I." She looked back at the letter, her voice taking on the cadence of the past, "I hope this finds you well. I continue to enjoy the free lifestyle thou hast so cleverly arranged for me. As I wane in years, the reflections of my past deeds weigh upon my soul, and I find myself desiring to reconcile with said past."

Abigail's eyes glanced between Eunice and Hannah, ensuring they hung on every word. "One constant reminder is of a woman, peculiar in her ways, yet brimming with grace and vitality. Aye, she was lively and not without her share of mischief. Her ambition to educate lasses in literacy and numeracy inspired me greatly. Given that my bounteous treasures have lain idle under thy care, I now beseech thee to seek this woman and fulfill her noble aspiration for a school."

She paused for a moment, allowing Avery's words to sink in before reading on. "Her name, as memory serves, is Hope Terwilliger. A Dutch moniker for 'willow,' she led me to believe." Then she lowered the letter from her eyes, adding, "Truly grateful, Long Ben."

Hannah exchanged a look of astonishment with her knowing aunt Eunice. The task at hand was formidable, yet exciting. Behind the challenge lay the legacy of one of the most infamous pirates to ever sail the seas—fodder for her journal—and a legacy that might pave the way for a future where girls like her could aspire to an education and a life beyond the domestic sphere.

Abigail folded the letter and tucked it back into its secret pocket. "So, we set forth not only on a mission for this estranged woman but for the enlightenment of all," she concluded, a determined gleam in her eye that mirrored the adventurous spirit of their storied ancestors.

Hannah furrowed her brow, a thread of skepticism woven into her voice. "What do you suppose he meant by 'not without her share of mischief'? Perhaps she was no lady in the strictest sense?"

Eunice, leaning against the heavy oak dresser, picked up on the other peculiar detail. "And what of this 'willow'? Why include such a thing? Is it a clue or merely the ramblings of a man too long at sea?"

Abigail, whose experience had taught her to look for meaning in even the smallest of details, nodded thoughtfully. "It may well be the only shred of her identity he clung to over the years—a distinctive trait, perhaps, or a nickname that stuck. It could be the very thread we need to unravel this mystery."

As twilight gave way to the deep blue of a New England evening, the room was filled with an almost tangible worry born from the collision of anticipation and the uncertainty of the quest before them.

Eunice paced, her mind racing with strategy. "The constable should be our first visit," she declared with conviction. "Lawmen have a way of knowing the goings-on of their townsfolk."

Abigail shook her head, her fingers tracing the elaborate stitching of her bodice. "No, the church. Parish records, baptismal scrolls, and marriage banns are meticulous in their documentation. If Mistress Terwilliger made a life here, the church will know of it."

The room fell into a momentary silence, each woman ensconced in her own thoughts. Hannah, the youngest but by no means the least astute, mulled over her mother and aunt's suggestions. Her intuition nudged her toward a different path—one more aligned with the undercurrents of a town's daily life. Yet, she chose to keep her own counsel, preferring to watch and learn from the seasoned tacticians before her.

The flicker of candles and the aroma of roasting meat greeted Abigail, Eunice, and Hannah as they descended the narrow staircase to the inn's standard room for their evening meal. It was a modest chamber, alive with travelers' chatter and the clink of earthenware. The atmosphere mingled with wood smoke and the earthy scent of stewed vegetables.

The innkeeper, Mr. Miles, a rotund man with an ever-watchful eye, bustled between the tables, his wife at his heels. While pausing to observe the dining area, both older women warned the younger. An innkeeper and his wife were well-known for their insatiable appetite for gossip; any word spoken too loudly could become the morrow's common knowledge.

With a practiced ease, the trio found a small, unassuming table near the hearth, its fire crackling merrily, and sat with their backs to the wall. They exchanged pleasantries with a nod and a smile but kept their words sparse and their voices low.

A maid, cheeks flushed from the kitchen's heat, soon arrived at their table, laying out the fare for the evening: thick slices of salted pork, brown bread still warm from the oven, and a hearty pottage teeming with fish, root vegetables, and barley. A pitcher of hard cider accompanied the meal, its tartness a welcome counter to the meat's richness.

They each took a moment to savor the simple, robust flavors of the New England autumn—flavors that spoke of the land and sea, of harvests gathered and fishing nets hauled. It was food that nourished both body and soul after the day's long journey and the heavy burden of their quest.

As they ate, their conversation was little more than whispers over the meal, mostly passing remarks about the quality of the cider or the tenderness of the pork, nothing to betray the true nature of their visit to New Haven.

Upon finishing their meal, Abigail caught the innkeeper's wife's attention and offered her a genuine and strategically terse compliment. "Goodwife, your skill in the kitchen has made our long journey's end a comfort. We thank you for this meal."

The woman, plump and rosy, likely from leftovers and the steam of her pots and pans, beamed at the praise. "'Tis nothing, good madam," she replied, her eyes darting between the guests, hungry for more than the returning pleasantries. "I'm pleased to hear it's to your liking. Rest assured, we aim to keep a welcoming house."

As the night grew older and the inn's patrons dwindled to a sleepy few, Abigail, Eunice, and Hannah withdrew once more to the privacy of their rooms, acutely aware that the walls listened—and that it was best to keep one's cards close to one's chest until the game was well and truly won.

As dawn unfurled, casting the first assertive rays of light that wove through the sheer curtains, a silent competition stirred among them. Eunice, with her steadfast practicality, set her bonnet firmly, ready to prove her methodical approach superior. Abigail, ever the strategist, plotted her route with meticulous care, determined to be the one to decipher the riddle of Hope Terwilliger's whereabouts. And Hannah, her quiet determination now a smoldering fire, clasped her cloak, eager to outshine the seasoned acumen of her elders. This was not merely a quest; it had become an unspoken challenge—a race against time and each other to uncover a piece of the past that would leave an indelible mark on the legend of a pirate king.

CHAPTER 6

Docks

WITH THE DAY ALREADY AWAKENED by the cock's crow, the air felt crisp and sweet, tinged with the scent of autumn's advance. Abigail left first, leaving Hannah in the care of her Aunt Eunice's steady resolve as she stepped out through the inn's entrance—each sister a different arrow loosed from the same quiver, each aimed at her own target.

With a seasoned pirate's intuition, Abigail made her way with an unassuming grace toward the town's venerable church. Her presence was commanding yet subtle, a balance befitting a woman who navigated the realms of privilege. She understood the power of faith and the church's role in the townsfolk's daily lives well. Her mission was clear: to coax the priest for hints of Hope Terwilliger's family or friends' whereabouts.

Eunice's practical nature underscored her pursuit of the constable's office. With composure as her shield, she left with haste to unearth any official records or recollections of the woman whose existence seemed as elusive as the evaporated morning fog over the harbor.

Hannah, the youngest yet no less determined, turned to find herself abandoned with neither of her older escorts in sight. So, instead of wandering around the town aimlessly, she turned her sights to the nearby bustling harbor. Beneath the flow of her cloak, discreet bulges hinted at the presence of twin muskets—her assurance against the unpredictable tides of human nature. She traversed the waterfront, a seemingly casual onlooker, yet her gaze missed nothing. The loose cobbles, the sway of the mooring ropes, the faces of those she passed—all were noted with an innate understanding. While her mother and aunt sought answers in the light, Hannah's path veered towards the shadowed doorways and raucous taverns, where truth and rumor often joined in a clandestine waltz.

The sun hung low over the bustling docks, shadows giving way to a piercing glare as Hannah made her way along the waterfront, the timbre of the harbor alive with the cries of gulls and the creak of docked ships. Amid the tangle of sailors and merchants, her eyes found the young fisherman who had earlier guided them to the inn—a stroke of fortune in her search, she hoped.

"Good morrow, John Prout!" she called out with a bright smile. Her voice sliced through the din of the docks, halting the man in his tracks.

He turned, his expression one of mild surprise at being addressed so openly by a lady of her standing. "Mistress," he replied, nodding with a deference that the gap between their stations demanded.

Hannah closed the distance with confident strides. "I wanted to thank you for your guidance yesterday."

His cheeks took on a touch of color, unaccustomed to such direct thanks. "I've done naught but my duty, mistress."

Curious, she ventured further, "Tell me, have you lived in this town for long?"

"All my years," he affirmed with a trace of pride.

"And the sailors," she continued, "do many come here to find respite from the sea?"

His brows arched, betraying his surprise at her line of questioning. "Aye, they do. The sea grants little peace, so they seek it where they can."

Emboldened by the conversation, she took a daring step forward. "And where might a... girl go to enjoy such company?"

The question hung like a challenging breeze. John shifted uncomfortably, the weight of her question evident in his awkward stance. "There's a tavern," he began, voice trailing off, the implication of her question dawning upon him.

Her eyes followed his gaze towards the far end of the docks, a flicker of understanding passing between them. "The one over there?"

He nodded, not speaking the establishment's name as if it were a summoning charm for trouble.

She thanked him with a nod and turned to walk away, but his concern overrode his reluctance. "But, mistress," he stammered, a note of caution in his tone. "That place is not fit for... You should not venture there. No telling what or who you may encounter."

She paused, her back to him, and glanced over her shoulder with an assuring smile. "My interest is guided by curiosity alone, not mischief," she said, though the mischievous twinkle in her eye might have suggested otherwise.

He looked at her, his expression a mix of skepticism and worry, then nodded slowly. "As you wish, mistress," he said quietly before turning away, his pace quickening as if to distance himself from the potential repercussions of their exchange.

The waterfront boardwalk creaked under Hannah's measured steps, the waters mingling with the musk of tar and the faint stench of spilled piss and ale. She watched the seafarers, some hauling ropes and sails, others singing and bellowing sea shanties that had no doubt been passed down through generations. Each ship was a hive of activity, a world unto itself, and she admired their synchronous chaos.

Her gaze settled on the tavern at the end of the line—a building that seemed to sag with stories of vice and revelry. Men stumbled out from its darkened doorway, laughter and curses spilling into the air, a stark contrast to the disciplined bustle of the ships.

Hannah's attention was captured by a lone figure emerging from the tavern—a woman, her graying hair askew, clothes hinting at a profession as old as the sea itself. Quickening her pace, Hannah intercepted the woman before she could disappear into the anonymity of the crowd.

A steely resolve halted the woman's initial retreat as she faced Hannah, fists clenched.

"What d'ye want?" she spat, the edges of her words blurred by a working-class accent of the period.

Hannah's advance was not aggressive, but the woman was defensive, mistaking her for a scorned lover. "If 'tis 'bout yer man," she said sharply, "I ain't to blame. Men come to me o' their own accord."

"No, you misunderstand," Hannah interjected, her voice soft but firm. She hadn't expected this kind of confrontation and wasn't sure how to steer toward her true intent.

The woman's posture relaxed marginally, though suspicion still narrowed her eyes. "Then what is it? Ye here to scorn me for my trade? Or is it charity ye game offerin'?"

Hannah couldn't help but let a small laugh escape at the mistaken identity. "I assure you, I'm not here to judge nor to offer alms. And most certainly not wanting to supplant your profession. I seek knowledge of the past, not a score to settle."

This disarmed the woman somewhat, her fists uncurling. But her demeanor remained wary. "Ye think I'm old as the hills, then? Some ancient mariner?" she scoffed, a smile playing at the edges of her lips, mocking the absurdity.

"No, nothing of the sort," Hannah said, and then, with a sincerity that reached her eyes, she posed her question. "Have you, perchance, heard tell of a woman named Hope Terwilliger?"

At the mention of the name, the woman's brashness faltered. "Hope?" she repeated as though the name echoed from some distant memory. Her face closed off momentarily as she searched the recesses of her mind.

"Yes, Hope," Hannah pressed gently, sensing a lead.

The woman eyed Hannah skeptically. "And what's she to ye?"

Without missing a beat, Hannah presented a few silver coins from her glove, her gesture discreet yet unmistakable. "For your troubles," she said smoothly. "The why need not concern you. The question is, can you assist me?"

The promise of coin glinted in the woman's eyes, mirroring the metallic sheen in Hannah's palm. The allure of easy money wrestled with the remnants of her caution.

"Hope Terwilliger, ye say?" the woman mused, her voice lowering. "Aye, a tale or two is wrapped up in that name." She let her voice trail and eyed Hannah's coins pointedly, making sure Hannah took note of her hesitation.

Hannah's reply was a smile tempered with the patience of one who knew the value of information. "I have enough to make it worth your while. Shall we talk?"

The salty tang of the sea mixed with the tangy stench of fish and tar as Hannah and the woman stood by the harbor, the sounds of the water and gulls their only companions. The woman, still eyeing Hannah's stance with suspicion and curiosity, leaned against the weathered pylon, her eyes squinting against the glare of the sun reflecting off the water.

"Listen, Miss," she began, her voice carrying the rough timbre of one accustomed to shouting above the roar of singing sailors. "Hope Terwilliger ain't a name that's been whispered 'round these parts in a long spell. Folk here don't take kindly to dredging up old tales, especially ones with shadows as long as hers."

Hannah's eyes didn't waver from the horizon, but she tilted her head, indicating she was listening. "Shadows? What kind of shadows?"

The woman glanced over her shoulder, her expression hardening. "The kind that darkens a reputation. She was a rare one; Hope was. Had her hands in all sorts of jars, some filled with honey, others with vinegar, if you catch my drift."

Hannah turned, her gaze settling on the woman. "And these shadows—

could they be why no one remembers or is willing to speak of her?"

"Could be," the woman conceded, pulling her shawl tighter around her shoulders as a gust of wind whipped past them, carrying the scent of adventure and the whispers of the past. "Or maybe it's 'cause those that do remember ain't in these parts no more. Time has a way of clearing out the old to make way for the new."

She took the coins from Hannah's outstretched hand with a swift, practiced move, and her eyes softened just a touch. "If it's Hope Terwilliger you're after, you might try looking where the willows meet the water. That's all I can give you. Now, best you move on, and me as well, before suspicions rise like the tide."

"Willow?" Hannah echoed, the word laced with frustration and intrigue.

"Don't prick me with your witch-pricking needle," the woman snapped, her patience wearing thin like a sail long battered by the storm. "I'm no soothsayer nor witch to be conjuring tales from the aether. No one can prove it, nor can you."

Sensing the conversation had reached its end, Hannah nodded, her mind racing with possibilities. "I understand. Thank you," she said, though the woman had already turned to leave, melting back into the crowd like the shadow of the shack she worked.

Left alone with her thoughts, Hannah pondered the woman's cryptic words of advice. Willows by the water — witch-pricking needle — both clues as elusive as the woman Hope herself. With a deep breath, she turned her gaze toward the end of the town, where the verdant arms of trees joined at the river's edge. There, she suspected, her next step would begin.

After spending the morning fruitlessly snooping around the docks and wandering along the waterway homes in search of willow trees, Hannah's exhaustion led her back to the comfort of their rented abode. The tavern's warmth enveloped her in solitude, a sharp contrast to the cool debate constantly brewing between her mother and aunt.

When her two chaperones stepped inside, their argument faded into the background hum of low conversations and the clinking of pewter mugs from the other guests. They found Hannah thoughtfully fixating on the unicorn figurehead, her gaze circling it with an ember of curiosity flickering in her eyes.

"Child, have you been here this whole time?" Abigail questioned.

Diverting the question like an adept sailor changing tack, Hannah inquired, "What have you uncovered?"

Abigail huffed her exasperation with the Reverend while it was still fresh on her mind. "Nothing but a man more concerned with lining his pockets than aiding his flock. His need for a donation was as pressing as a hole in a ship's hull. I nearly told him where he might hoist his appeal, but alas, he might be of use yet. So, I held my tongue."

Eunice was eager to cast her findings into the fray, her voice a mix of triumph and irritation. "The constable had crumbs of knowledge, at least. He's heard the name, tied to tales old as the cobblestones. He pointed me to his aged mentor, living on the town's fringe."

"And where might he dwell?" Hannah asked, a flicker of insight dawning. "Where the willow hangs over the water?"

The two matriarchs paused, looking at Hannah with a blend of surprise and disregard, questioning her relevance in this endeavor.

Ignoring their glances, Hannah held her ground, remembering that if Hope Terwilliger is as connected to the willows as whispers claim, then that's where their search must lie. Then, for a brief moment, she wondered whether there was any real significance to the willows. If that prostitute took her as an easy mark and bamboozled her way into earning a few ill-gotten coins.

"Shall we go find this constable's mentor now?" Hannah asked, trying to sound astute.

"Now?" Eunice questioned. "We know not how far we will be traveling, and I, for one, do not wish to be caught out in unfamiliar territory in the dark."

Without further discourse, the sisters retired to their chambers, leaving Hannah amidst the tales told by the crackling fire and the silent sentinel of the unicorn.

The following day, on the outskirts of the bustling town, the change was detectable; the scent of the sea gave way to earthier notes of the countryside. Here, the roads were less trodden, the houses more spread out, each nestled in its pocket of solitude. The trio's steps kicked up little swirls of dust as they made their way, stopping occasionally to inquire of passersby about the whereabouts of the constable.

Each person they asked provided a piece of the puzzle, pointing them further along the road, through a copse of trees, or down a winding path. Their journey was punctuated by brief encounters: a farmer leaning on his fence offering directions with a cautious squint; a group of children playing by the road, their directions delivered with giggles and wild gesticulations; and an older woman with a basket of herbs, her finger directing them with the presumption of known wisdom.

At last, they arrived at a modest homestead that sat in the gentle embrace of a wide bend in a small creek. The structure was old but kept, with smoke lazily curling from the chimney and chickens clucking from the back. A garden rich with the last squash of autumn added a splash of color to the thinning willow trees.

This had to be the abode of the retired constable, Barnabas Jenkins, the man Eunice hoped still possessed enough of his wits to guide them to Hope Terwilliger. They approached the door, the wood worn smooth by years of weather and use, and raised their hand to knock, each of their hearts a mix of apprehension and Hope. When no one came to answer, Eunice began to snoop around the side to see if anyone was near.

Then, with caution, the intrepid trio approached the slumped figure carefully, the sharp scent of spirits dangling heavy around him. They observed the fallen man, his breath shallow and uneven, creating a somber vignette against the autumn leaves.

Hannah clutched her chest, her voice quivering slightly, "Is he dead?"

Eunice, ever the pragmatic one, leaned closer, her nose wrinkling in anticipation of a far worse scent. "If he is, it hasn't been very long. He doesn't yet reek of death."

Abigail stepped forward, her hands deftly pulling the bottle from the man's limp grip and setting it aside. She nudged him with a firmness born of necessity, her voice stern, "Mister Jenkins, awake!"

The man grumbled a low, gurgling noise that clawed its way up from his throat, confirming his tenuous grip on life. His body shuddered with the effort to face the intruders of his inebriated peace.

With a shared glance, the sisters realized that their quest for answers would not end at the lips of a drunken slumber. They exchanged a silent agreement to wait for the haze of alcohol to clear from the old constable's mind, hopeful that when he awakened, he would be a fount of information regarding Hope Terwilliger.

They settled at a respectful distance, the riverside willow trees providing a tranquil backdrop to their grim wait—Barnabas Jenkins's somnolent form a reminder that even the best leads can sometimes end in a snarl of unexpected complications.

Hannah watched the leaves fall, each one a reminder of the passing time they could afford to waste. Eunice paced with a slow, deliberate gait, her mind no doubt turning over every other stone by their inquiries. Abigail looked lost in her own thoughts, piecing together what she would do if and when they locate the elusive woman.

After an hour of snoring and mumbling in his sleep, the man, who lay amid the autumnal detritus, stirred, looking like a remnant of another time—his eyes, when they met theirs, held turbulence that spoke of long-gone storms.

"Who the hell are you?" he grumbled, his voice gravelly with the scars of time and drink.

"We seek an audience with Constable Barnabas Jenkins," Abigail stated firmly.

The man pushed himself up on his elbows, squinting against the light that dappled through the leaves. "Tis I," he declared, though his tone carried the instability of a question.

"We are looking for information on Hope Terwilliger," Abigail continued, ignoring the rank smell of spirits that emanated from the man.

At the mention of the name, his face remained impassive as though he wasn't listening, but a visible shudder ran through his body, and their hopes turned expectant. Then, as though his visceral reaction had finally reached his mind, Jenkins' bleary eyes suddenly sharpened, and a discernible tautness knitted his brow. He scanned the trees and underbrush, his movements quick and fearful—a hunted animal checking for predators. "Is she here?" he hissed, his voice suddenly laced with jitters that belied his previous stupor.

The women exchanged glances, noting the shift in his demeanor. It was clear that the name Hope Terwilliger was more than a mere whisper from the past; it was a shadow that still seemed to loom in the man's nightmares.

Eunice stepped forward with a tact borne of years of navigating her late husband's moods. "No, good sir, she is not," she assured him with a gentle firmness. "We merely seek her whereabouts for a matter most pressing."

Jenkins' shoulders, which had bunched up to his ears, dropped slightly, but the wild look in his eyes did not abate. He pulled himself to a sitting position, the comfort of his drained bottle out of his grasp. The silence that followed was filled with the sounds of nature, a stark contrast to the man's heavy breaths before them.

"Then why?" he demanded, his voice a mix of curiosity and residual dread. "Why summon old ghosts?"

Abigail stepped forward now, her gaze steady. "Because, Constable

Jenkins, those ghosts have unfinished business, and it seems they haunt us now as well. We mean to lay them to rest."

The old constable studied their faces, searching for sincerity or perhaps the shadow of the same phantoms that seemed to clutch at his soul. Slowly, painstakingly, he climbed to his feet, steadying himself with the trunk of a nearby tree.

"Unfinished business," he echoed as if tasting the words, trying them for truth. "Then we have that in common. Come inside," he gestured with a gruff nod toward the cottage. "The tales involving Hope Terwilliger are not ones for the open air—they're best shared with walls to hold them, lest they slip away into the wind once more, to repeat their sorrowful song."

With that, he turned and began to shuffle toward his home, leaving the women to follow in the wake of a story that seemed to stretch its tendrils out from the depths of time.

In the dim confines of the cluttered cottage, they stood awkwardly as Jenkins tossed an empty bottle toward the fireplace, which shattered against the stone with a crack. The remnants of the day's light fought through the grime-smeared window, throwing long shadows across his weathered face as he sank into a creaking chair with resignation.

"Have a seat," he rasped, though it was clear there were none to be had. The women stood, watching him, each wrapped in their thoughts, until Abigail's voice cut through the heavy air.

"Hope Terwilliger?" she prompted, commanding the space.

Jenkins' gaze swung to her, a spark of clarity in his bloodshot eyes. "Ah, you're the ringleader of this quest," he said, a bitter edge to his tone. "Why dig up old graves?"

Before Abigail could retort, Hannah stepped forward, her presence like a gentle wave smoothing the sands of contention. "What do you know about the witch?" she asked, her voice clear and curious, causing her elder relatives to turn to her with furrowed brows.

The old man's eyes darted to Hannah, wide and startled. "Witch?" he echoed, and then a heavy sigh escaped him, laden with memories. "No, she wasn't the witch. She was the pricker—a necessary evil, some believed. She held the truth, but was drowned out by the lies. That truth haunts me."

Eunice tried to make sense of his ramblings, asking, "What truths haunt you?" but he feared answering.

Hannah persisted, softening her approach. "Why was she known at the dock taverns?"

Jenkins' gaze fell, and he nodded, the action weighing him further. "Aye," he murmured, almost lost in thought. "She thought she'd find a real malevolence amidst the bawdy songs and spilled ale. It was... for professional purposes."

His hands twitched, perhaps seeking the comfort of a bottle that wasn't there. "She finally knew it was wrong, and I was so very wrong not to listen."

Hannah cut in, "*What* was wrong?"

Jenkins ignored her. "The zeal, the fervor of the townsfolk—they pushed, and I... I obliged. It was easier to believe the loud majority than the quiet truth."

"Who pushed? Why were you wrong, and she was right?" Abigail asserted, but instead of freeing his words, it smothered them like a blanket over a fire.

The women sat still, waiting for him to speak, but the silence enveloped them as much as the dust motes that wandered in the slanting light. Here was a man, broken by his past, offering them a thread of the story they had been seeking—a thread that wove through taverns and town squares, through righteousness misplaced and penance never given. They were no closer to finding this woman than when they started.

Hannah leaned in slightly, her voice a beacon in the dim room. "What happened to Hope Terwilliger?" she pressed gently, hoping to unravel more of the past from the tattered old man's memories.

Jenkins lifted his head, eyes meeting hers with a flicker of something akin to fear—or perhaps it was regret. "That," he said, "is a tale soaked in mystery. Sit on the floor if ye must take the weight off your feet. I'll tell you what little I know of Hopestill Merriweather Terwilliger, the one who knew too much and was heard too little."

Abigail, Eunice, and Hannah exchanged wary glances. Each could tell the other was thinking the same thing: Jenkins' revelation that Hope was a witch-hunter—a figure feared and reviled during times of hysteria—raised fundamental doubts about whether this woman should be the head of a school for girls.

"Hopestill Merriweather Terwilliger — is that her christened name?" Hannah asked. "And she was a witch-hunter?"

"Pricker," he corrected.

Their heads slowly nodded as the breaths in the small room grew still, as time itself paused to bear witness to the revelations being unearthed. Hannah's question lingered, a key poised to unlock further secrets of the past.

Jenkins' recollection materialized like a fog lifting, revealing previously hidden landscapes. "Hopestill Merriweather Terwilliger... David Yale of Boston was her unmarried father," he mumbled, his voice barely above a whisper. His gaze drifted to the window, half-expecting his ghost to peer through the dirty pieces of drooping glass.

Eunice's voice cut through the solemn atmosphere, her tone sharp with the era's judgment. "So she's a bastard?" she concluded, a harsh term that stung the ears.

Jenkins' nod was almost imperceptible, a slight dip of his head, as though acknowledging the word aloud would somehow summon ill fortune or worse.

"Yale?" Abigail prompted, steering the conversation back with a determination that seemed to anchor Jenkins to the present.

"Yes," he affirmed. "Quiet man. Loved his plants."

"Was he eating them?" Eunice interjected.

"No, no..." Jenkins waved off the confusion. "He collected them, studied them. Wrote about their healing properties in a book." His eyes grew distant, as if he were viewing a scene only he could see. "A scientist of sorts, he was—trying to document the Indian's herbal knowledge. But his quest... it ended tragically; shipwrecked at sea on his way to publishing his works in Wales."

Hannah reached for the thunderbird talisman on her forearm for protection, a subconscious gesture born of her past. The talisman, an emblem of strength and a guardian against evil, felt cool against her palm, offering a silent reassurance amid the grim tale.

Silence followed his words, a respectful pause for the fate of Yale, whose scholarly pursuit led him to an untimely and violent end. The mention of his death was a grim reminder of the perils that shadowed the edge of colonial settlements and the dangers that raged beyond them.

The three women absorbed the tale, each processing the fragments of the past that slowly pieced together the mosaic of Hope's heritage—woven with threads of intellect and inquiry, now stained with the blood of her father's demise. The knowledge of her illegitimate birth and her father's unfortunate fate cast Hope in a new light, not just as a crazed accomplice running around accusing fellow citizens of being witches but as the daughter of a man who sought understanding in a world quick to fear and slow to comprehend.

Hannah put a gentle hand to Jenkins' arm and began, "What about—" but before she could fully attempt to steer the man back to the story of Hope and the townspeople, he spoke again."Hope pricked me once." The old constable nodded with a glint of satisfaction as he looked to see if the mark was still visible, but it was not.

"Pricked you? Why would she do that?" Hannah asked.

Abigail, Hannah, and Eunice sat opposite him, arranged like a tribunal—though none of them had truly come to judge.

"I was a different man in those days," Jenkins slurred, his eyes glassy but his voice steady as he stared into the empty fireplace. "Twenty years ago. Hope... She was employed back then. Employed to be a witch-pricker."

Abigail narrowed her eyes. "Employed? By whom? And why?"

Jenkins gave a crooked smile, baring too many yellowed teeth. "Do you know your history, ma'am?" he said, lifting his hand like a mug to wipe his crusty lips.

"History of what?" Abigail asked coolly.

"Of New Haven," he said, voice dipping into something rehearsed but deeply etched in memory. "Five hundred Puritans left Massachusetts Bay Colony, under Reverend John Davenport and merchant Theophilus Eaton. They aimed to build a theocracy. A community where church and government were the same."

He cleared his throat and leaned forward, his eyes catching some reflected sunlight. "But after the land was divided, it became clear not everyone was a loyal Puritan. Some stirred trouble. Other colonies were no better."

"So what did they do?" Hannah asked.

He paused, letting the question hang. "They found ways to rid themselves of the undesirables," he said darkly. "And what better way than to call them witches?"

Hannah blinked. "You mean to say they hired Hope to accuse people of witchcraft? To get rid of them?"

Jenkins nodded slowly. "That's right. Hope would seek out the designated troublemaker—tag them as witches—and then I'd arrest them. Gave them a choice: trial, which I suggested could mean death... or exile." He put his hand to his chin and recalled, "Never got anyone to ask for a trial."

Abigail's voice grew sharper. "But who? Who gave the order?"

He leaned back, expression grim. "Do you really need to ask? Who had the most to gain? Who wanted to purify their perfect little church-run government?"

Eunice's voice was low, saying, "The colony's founders?"

Jenkins didn't dispute it. He just nodded.

"Once I was ordered to evict a witch and their whole family. A man, his wife, a baby, and a child," Jenkins said, the words falling from his lips like the last embers of a dying fire. "I help put all their worldly possessions into a wagon. It was sad to see how little one's lifetime accumulated."

He stared into the hearth before him, where only cold ash remained, the faint scent of old smoke lingering in the stone. "That's how they looked," he continued, voice low and distant. "Like a hearth without flame—just the shape of what once was warm. Their wagon held barely more than a few threadbare blankets and a tin kettle. The mother cradled the baby beneath her shawl, trying to lend her body's heat to a child that never cried. The father... he didn't say much. Just kept one hand on the reins, the other holding the older girl to his side. And their eyes—God help me—their eyes looked like this hearth. Empty. Cold. Waiting for a fire that never came."

He bowed his head, hands clasped tightly in front of him, as if in silent prayer or penance. "I walked them past the town line. Watched them disappear into the snow. And it stays with me... the memory of them—like the cold hearth that never burned again. I found out later they'd all frozen to death. Who knew a blizzard was coming? That was when I knew. I wasn't just an officer. I was a monster. A demon of the Devil himself in a constable's coat."

"And that's when Hope saved me," he said, his voice cracking slightly.

Abigail leaned forward. "Saved you? How?"

"I went to the council. Ready to confess, to accuse the whole bloody conclave. Said I was as evil as the Prince of Darkness." He held up a trembling hand and pointed to a faint scar at the base of his palm. "And Hope, hearing this… she stood up. Didn't say a word. She just pulled out her pricker and stabbed me through the hand. Right there, in front of the whole council."

Hannah gasped. "She stabbed you?"

"Aye, right in this spot on my hand," he said with a dry laugh, looking down at his birthmark. "And it hurt like hell. Bled like a stuck pig. But it proved something. Proved I wasn't a witch. I wasn't a demon. Not a slave to Satan. Just a puppet. A fool doing the town's dirty work."

"And Hope?" Abigail asked softly.

"She was at the same meeting for her own reasons," he said. "She was quitting and ending her reign of terror as the pricker. After Salem went mad, every colony saw the writing on the wall. The trials were ending. And it was Hope who put an end to it in our quaint little New Haven."

The fireplace ashes swirled in the silence that followed. For a moment, no one spoke.

Then Eunice broke it with a quiet certainty. "So she was a weapon…Then, chose to become a shield."

"Aye. That's a good way to put it," Jenkins said slowly.

Abigail sat back, her expression unreadable. Hannah looked shaken, her eyes fixed on the cold, dark hearth.

Outside, the wind howled softly past the windowpanes, like a whisper from the past, begging not to be forgotten.

"She's alive and well. Nearby," he added, smiling with a brighter face. "She's tending to the needs of orphans."

The idea of Hope, a kind caretaker of orphaned children, was a complete antithesis to such a feared figure.

Abigail's reaction indeed bordered on the preposterous. "I spoke with the Reverend. A man I thought would be informed of his flock, yet he provided no clues."

Jenkins' knowing smile suggested a web of secrets that the newcomers to New Haven had yet to be initiated into.

"Terwilliger? Orphanage?" Abigail muttered, filing away the information. "Hope must have adopted a new identity, perhaps as a shield from her past or as a penance for her actions during those contentious times."

Jenkins' recounting of being pricked by Hope seemed almost intimate, a shared moment between the accuser and the accused, a memory that brought a smile to his worn features. He appeared momentarily lost in the past, his actions unconsciously echoing the memory of the prick he had experienced.

"And this mark," Hannah probed further, shaking him from his pensive somber. "How is it identified among so many?"

Jenkins' smile faded, replaced by a somberness that had likely settled in after years of reflection. "It's a dark art, finding these marks. You look for a spot that does not bleed, that feels no pain. But many a time, the marks were naught but blemishes, birthmarks, harmless and innocent. You see, mine was nothing more than this," he said, holding up his hand. "The pricking was a cruel test, wielded with deception to those who knew naught but fear and suffering."

The weight of his admission was apparent. It was the acknowledgment of an era marked by darkness, of innocence lost to the frantic hunt for witches. In this new light, the pricker was not just a figure of fear but also one of tragedy—entwined with the fate of those they tested.

Hannah and her companions absorbed this grim history, each no doubt contemplating the physical and emotional scars that such a witch hunt had left on the town and on Hope, who had lived through it all. They now knew they must tread lightly upon this history as they continued their search for the truth.

"It's strange," Hannah murmured, more to herself than to the others. "That someone who once sought to find witches is now a caretaker of the innocent."

Jenkins gave a nod, his eyes clouding over. "People change. In the times of witch trials, people were twisted. Hope, she's done with all that pricking business, been so for years. She's seeking redemption, I suppose, through her work with the children."

The revelation softened Hannah's stance, and her previous apprehension eased. "And you're certain she's there?" she asked again, perhaps needing the reassurance for her peace of mind.

"As certain as the dawn," Jenkins replied, "Hopestill Merriweather Terwilliger is no shadow of the past. She's very much alive, a woman who's traded her needle for nurturing."

Hannah nodded, digesting this new shard of truth. Hope was not a specter to be chased but a living, breathing piece of the puzzle they were trying to solve. Their journey for answers was far from over, but they had been granted a direction leading to the community's very heart.

With a new determination, the trio prepared to leave Jenkins to his memories and demons. Their next course of action was straightforward: They would go to the orphanage, to the heart of the mystery that embodied a woman who had walked through the flames of accusation and emerged as a guardian of the forsaken.

As they turned down the lane back into New Haven, Eunice threw an affectionate arm around Hannah's shoulder. "Child, I've seen your mother barter better than the shrewdest of merchants and negotiate like a siren of the sea. Your mother has power, not the kind that requires a witch's mark, but power nonetheless." The quip drew a begrudging smile from Abigail despite her lingering frustration. "But I have never seen such investigative prowess as you showed with that drunkard."

"Yes, well played," Abigail said to her daughter, a tone of pride evident for the second time on the journey.

The inn was a welcome sight, its familiar structure a bastion of normalcy in the whirlwind of their day. The innkeeper nodded, welcoming them back.

As they entered, they shook off the cold, respectfully stomping off any dust accumulated on their well-traveled shoes.

Once in the privacy of their room, the trio settled into a brief silence; each lost in their thoughts about the upcoming encounter with Hope. Abigail sat at the small table, methodically tapping her fingers on the wooden surface as she pondered their next move.

"We approach this delicately," Abigail finally said, lifting her gaze to meet those of her sister and daughter. "Hope has evaded attention for years. She might retreat further into the shadows if we're too direct."

Hannah nodded, her previous bravado giving way to contemplation. "The docks gave me insight," she admitted. "But I understand we're playing a subtler game now. This is about coaxing out a story long buried, not just finding a name."

Eunice leaned back against the headboard of her sister's bed. "We must be both the hawk and the dove," she mused. "Eyes sharp for the truth, yet gentle in our approach, lest we scare away the very one we seek."

"Tomorrow, then," Abigail decided. "We'll go to the orphanage with open minds and guarded hearts. Tonight, we rest and gather our strength."

As night fell over the inn and the town of New Haven, three women lay awake after their filling meal, their minds racing with possibilities, plans, and the potential for revelations that could change everything they thought they knew about the elusive Hope Merryweather Terwilliger.

CHAPTER 7

Searching for Hope

THE MORNING LIGHT filtered into the inn's dining room, casting a soft glow over the three women seated at a late breakfast table. The atmosphere was heavy with unspoken thoughts between the elderly sisters, a certain apprehension that had settled over them like a shroud. Each was lost in her own contemplations, mulling over the previous day's revelations and the encounter that lay ahead—the night had been long and sleepless, leaving each feeling irritable.

The clinking of utensils and the occasional scrape of a chair were the only sounds punctuating the silence. Hannah, ever the spirited one, had to fight against the quiet that stifled the room. She was bursting with questions, theories, and the impetuous desire to act. Yet, Abigail's disapproving grunts and Eunice's stern looks indicated to her that this was a time for caution and strategy, not impulsive curiosity.

They ate their meal efficiently, not a morsel wasted, yet each bite was regarded as if devoid of taste, a mere ritual to fuel the body for the day's endeavors. They stood almost in unison when they finished, a silent agreement that it was time to leave. There was no return to the rooms; the urgency of their quest had stripped away the need for further preparation.

Abigail led them out. Her mind was made up about their first move. "I'll speak with the preacher," she stated, finally breaking the silence. It was a declaration, not an invitation for discussion.

They made their way to the church, their steps synchronized—a formidable trio bound by blood and the shared purpose that now drove them.

However, when they neared the church's annex, they unconsciously steered past the church doors; the weight of their collective narrative seemed to merge into the solid heft of the orphanage's brass knocker in Abigail's hand. With a resounding echo, the sound of metal against wood cut through the morning air, a clarion call that heralded their arrival. The door swung open, revealing not the wizened visage they had braced themselves to encounter but the fresh, unlined face of a younger woman whose eyes held the spark of youthful energy and curiosity. In the background, a child shouted, "Ursula, we are hungry. When are we to eat?" followed by the wail of yet another child. Abigail adjusted her blouse as the sounds unwittingly brought her own children to mind.

"Soon. Mind your manners; we have guests," she shouted back, and then her gaze flitted over them, a hint of surprise at the sight of the three visitors. "Good morning," she greeted cheerily.

Abigail, the de facto leader of their trio, stepped forward. Her posture was one of controlled poise, though her heart hammered with the anticipation of the confrontation. "Good day," she replied, her voice firm yet laced with an undercurrent of urgency. "We seek a certain Hope Terwilliger. Might she be present today?"

The young woman before them paused, a flicker of recognition—or was it caution?—passing over her features before she offered them a polite smile.

"She is not here at present. May I inquire as to the nature of your business with my mother?" The young woman's tone was professional yet warm, an ambassador of the sanctuary beyond the threshold.

The three women exchanged surprised glances, silent counsel that spoke volumes, yet this twist united them further. Abigail cleared her throat. "When will she be back? We are seeking her counsel."

"I see. Is there something I can help you with? Our cow stopped milking this morning, and she has gone to secure another. The children are always hungry," she said with affection.

"We should have come here yesterday," Eunice said, causing her sister to bristle with frustration.

"No matter," Abigail said. "When do you expect her back?"

"Huh, I'm not sure. Depends on where she has to go to find another milk cow for sale. She's a very determined woman. I would not be surprised if she brought back two for the price of one."

Hannah leaned in to say, "She sounds like someone I know."

The church's tall spire cut a sharp silhouette against the crisp October sky, a sentinel amid the changing leaves. A cool breeze whispered through the open door as Abigail, Eunice, and Hannah stepped inside, starkly contrasting the church's interior, which held onto the warmth like a deep cellar.

"Are you still having discomfort?" Eunice asked, noticing her sister's restlessness.

"Oh, it's almost over. The sound of those hungry children just gave me a twinge, that's all."

Shadows played across the walls as the women walked down the aisle, the colored light from the stained-glass windows dappling their path with muted tones. A hush filled the expansive space, the quiet seeming to amplify the smallest of sounds—the creak of a pew, the rustle of fabric, the soft tap of their footsteps.

"Hello, Miss Huntington, is it?" The Reverend's voice seemed to float toward them, imbued with the serenity of the place. He and a determined woman, seemingly the same age as Abigail, were busy arranging the seating behind the altar.

"Yes, Reverend Morton," Abigail responded. "When I inquired about Hope Terwilliger yesterday, you gave me no indication that you knew of her, yet we understand she is employed at the orphanage next door."

The woman halted her furniture rearranging and faced them squarely. "That's because I told him to say nothing," she declared, her voice resounding with a clarity that belied her years.

Hannah moved forward, her breath cutting like a knife as she spoke. "And who might you be?"

A heavy and expectant silence settled among them as the woman met Hannah's gaze. "I am Hope Terwilliger," she pronounced, and the words seemed to mingle with the musty scent of old hymnals and the many shades of stained glass raining down on their heads.

The revelation struck them deeply, like the church bell's toll echoing in their chests. Here was Hope Terwilliger—no grand figure cloaked in the mystery of enlightenment, as they'd imagined, but a simple woman standing before them in plain light. This was the very person they'd journeyed to find, the one whose name had been wrapped in hushed tales and shadowy rumors. And now, on this cool October day, she was here, no different from anyone else, within the quiet walls of this modest church.

Abigail's heart sank as she took in the woman before her, weighed down by unmet expectations. Eunice's eyes held a wary disappointment, and Hannah's face revealed quiet contemplation, as if she were trying to reconcile the stories she'd conjured with the reality standing before them. Here they stood, four women bound by threads of shared and separate histories, yet the aura of mystery they'd anticipated was absent. The solemnity of the church walls and the crisp promise of autumn only deepened the sense of letdown, casting a somber shadow over the meeting.

Abigail maintained a steely gaze as she addressed the woman identified as Hope. "We are interested in donating to the orphanage," she stated, her voice measured and precise.

The Reverend, eyes alight with the mention of a donation, eagerly stepped forward, but Abigail raised her hand, halting his advance. "You will be dealt with later," she declared firmly. "My business concerns the orphanage directly."

Despite Abigail's insistence, the Reverend pressed on. "But the orphanage is an integral part of the church. Donating to one is the same as donating to the other," he countered, his smile stiffening as he sensed his control of the situation strengthening.

Abigail's response was curt. "I see. Yet I still wish to speak only with Hope, not with you now. Is there a place where we can converse privately?"

Hope Terwilliger's gaze shifted from Abigail to the Reverend, her expression vulnerable. "Whatever you have to say to me, you can tell in front of him," she said firmly. "After all, he is God's representative, whom I trust implicitly."

With a reluctant nod of acknowledgment, Abigail exhaled a weary sigh. She fixed her eyes on the Reverend, her following words laced with disappointment. "That's too bad. Then we have no other choice but to retract our donation."

"What? No," the Reverend interjected, the glaze of appreciation in his eyes now replaced with panic. "How could you consider such a thing?"

"It's simple," Abigail retorted, her voice growing colder with each syllable. "Our considerable donation stipulates that we discuss the terms only with Hope Merryweather Terwilliger. If you insist on intruding on this private matter, the donation will become null and void. We will take our offer to the next orphanage on our list. It's unfortunate, but we cannot deviate from our conditions. Sorry for the trouble, good day."

The situation grew heavy, laden with the unsaid and the undone. Abigail turned to leave, her relatives in tow, each step punctuating the silence that enveloped the church's interior. They left the Reverend and Hope in the wake of a decision that lay heavy on their shoulders—a decision that could alter the future of the orphanage and the children it sheltered.

Abigail listened as the Reverend's resistance crumbled, her deliberately slow march towards the door, and the weight of her words left no room for his interjection.

"Okay, okay," the Reverend said, his voice heavy with resignation, the volume afforded by his pulpit. "You could speak to Miss Terwilliger in private. I trust her decision in these matters."

Abigail stopped and turned with elegant ease to face the back of the church. "Are you sure?" she asked.

The Reverend squeaked, 'Yes,' then, with more control, said in a lower octave, "Yes, of course. Besides, I need to go and see about a cow." When the man of the cloth finally departed, she turned her attention back to the woman before her, her eyes unwavering, her presence demanding the space with unspoken authority.

"Please, Miss Yale," Abigail said softly, hoping to jar Hope from her guise. "Have a seat," she said with an outstretched hand to the wooden pew. Although her eyes seemed to flicker a frown at the word 'Yale,' Hope stayed anchored, standing. The anticipation filled the room, and the cross affixed to the altar bore witness to a reckoning of past and future.

"Hope, have a seat," Abigail said, pacing back and forth as if preparing to deliver a sermon. It was more of a command than an invitation, and Hope complied with little hesitancy. After a moment, Abigail sat down beside the woman and leaned in slightly. Her voice blending compassion and strength, she uttered, "Maybe it would be better if I told you a little tale—a tale from the past."

Hope, her expression a mix of confusion and apprehension, gave a hesitant nod, preempting her by adding, "The stories of yore often carry weightier truths than the present dares to acknowledge."

All in Abigail's circle nodded at the poignant meaning of her words, then Abigail began to speak, weaving the narrative that was all too familiar to Hope. As Abigail described a young, intelligent woman who held a strong moral compass and a suspicion of the supernatural, the threads of her tale intertwined with Hope's memories.

The room stilled as Abigail spoke of love found and feared lost to the capricious heart of a pirate, a man with a name like a chameleon, changing to suit his environment. Hope's eyes welled up with tears as she listened, a silent confirmation of the love she had once held.

"And tell me," Abigail continued, the timbre of her voice gentle yet insistent, "did you happen to tell him one of your lifelong aspirations was to start a school for girls on par with Harvard?"

Hope's confusion gave way to realization as the memory surfaced, a wish she had once confided in a moment of vulnerability. "A girls' school," she echoed, her voice barely above a whisper.

"Yes," Abigail confirmed, a knowing smile gracing her lips. "Are you still interested in building a school where young women can become as well educated, if not better than, men?"

"Well, yes, I suppose," she responded, wistfulness lacing her words. "But it is a silly dream. How could I ever do that? It would take a king's ransom to fund such an endeavor."

"Or," Abigail prompted with a knowing look, "a pirate's treasure?"

The statement stung her ears, and a proposition veiled in the guise of a question confused her. She pulled a handkerchief from the folds of her dress and dabbed at the edges of her eyes. As silence enveloped the group, the notion sparked a deep flame within Hope, a flame that had long been smothered by years and circumstances. Was this an offer of some sort? Hope dared to wonder. Was this redemption, a second chance born from the whispered legends of hidden plunder and a pirate's love?

Hope's gaze, still misty from the tears that veiled her sorrow, lifted slowly to meet Hannah's as she slid closer to her on the extended bench. The idea of a girls' school—once a delicate dream woven in the fabric of her younger self's aspirations—now resurfaced with the weight of a tangible possibility.

"What?" she whispered with confusion as if she'd heard the girl say something, but the words she heard were the fragments of some distant memory, too sweet to belong to the harsh reality she had come to know. "I dreamt of a school once," she said, voice distant. "A school for girls—not just needlework and scripture, but astronomy, mathematics, languages, the sciences. A place where they could ask questions and not be scolded for curiosity. A place where a girl could grow into the fullness of her mind."

She paused, her fingers tracing the curve of the wooden pew.

"A place," she added quietly, "where my own daughter might have attended."

Hannah, seated next to her, looked up. "We met your daughter. She's still young, is she not?"

"Ursula?" Hope's voice was a mixture of pride and pain. Her hand subconsciously moved to rest over her heart.

"Ursula? She's older now. I've schooled her at home—what I could manage. This school, were it built tomorrow, would offer her little benefit. The time for that dream has passed—for her, at least."

The silence stretched for a breath before Hannah spoke, her voice firm but kind.

"But what of all the other girls? The ones with no mother like you? No books, no letters, no second chances?"

Hope turned slowly, eyes settling on the empty pew beside her—the one her daughter had once curled in, years ago, with a book too large for her lap. Perhaps the dream wasn't dead; it had only grown beyond her own household.

"Ursula is a beautiful name," Hannah offered when Hope didn't respond.

"It was my grandmother's," Hope said softly.

"Grandmother Yale?" Hannah asked, prompting the connection and drawing the invisible lines between her past and present.

"Yes, how do you know?" Hope's inquiry was cautious, almost wary.

"Constable Jenkins," Hannah revealed, a soft sigh escaping her as she mentioned the man marked by the trials of his duty.

"Oh, that poor man," Hope lamented, the memories of the constable's torments briefly clouding her eyes. "He could not escape the witch's spell that cast him into the devil's brew of iniquity. So sad. I had to rescue him from his own transgressions."

"Yes, but you have," Abigail interjected firmly, her eyes locking with Hope's, instilling a conviction that seemed to say the past need not dictate the future. "And you can distance yourself and your daughter further from the sins of others in your past."

The word 'school' slipped from Hope's lips once more, her mind grappling with the enormity of the concept.

Hannah nodded, her eagerness to be part of this vision shining through. "Yes, a school for girls on par with Harvard. And I would like to be one of your first students."

The offer was a lifeline thrown across the expanse of time and circumstance. It was an invitation to rebuild, to create a legacy that could outshine the dark chapters of her storied past.

Hope's eyes finally brightened with a resolve buried beneath years of survival and disguise. The dream of a girls' school was no longer just a whisper from her past—it was a clarion call to the future. The presence of these women and the directness of their proposition all conspired to reignite the spark of Hope's long-dormant ambitions.

CHAPTER 8

Widow Clark

THE AUTUMNAL NEW ENGLAND BREEZE was brisk as it wove through the town streets, rustling the edges of the ladies' cloaks as they walked. The cobblestones beneath their feet echoed with the promise of a new era. Abigail, the stern matriarch with her indomitable spirit, led the way, flanked by Eunice, whose wit was as sharp as her tongue, and Hannah, whose youthful optimism was as contagious as her enthusiasm.

"Do you think a dozen students are too many?" Hannah queried, her eyes surveying the buildings they passed, imagining each as a potential cradle of learning.

Eunice cast a sidelong glance at Hannah, her lips curving into a knowing smile. "And how do we know she even has the intellect to teach a dozen or even one?"

Abigail turned to face them both, her expression resolute. "It doesn't matter if she were a borderline imbecile," she declared. "We have a duty to perform and all the money in the world to do it."

"Well, I don't think she's an imbecile," said Hannah. "Look at the way she's running the orphanage. I suspect Hope Terwilliger is quite accomplished," causing the others to nod in agreement.

They continued their survey, the town stretching before them like a canvas waiting for their brush.

"I think we should assign Hope the task of forming a curriculum, a challenge that would test her mettle and dedication to this nascent dream," Eunice declared.

Hannah, always one to envision the livelier aspects of life, chimed in. "What about dancing? That's an essential skill for a lady."

"Most definitely cooking," Eunice added. "One cannot subsist on books alone, and everyone knows, or should know, that the route to a man's heart traverses his stomach via his palate."

Abigail patted her still-deflating stomach and added, "Child rearing should be foremost on the curriculum."

"Oh, Mother. Not the birds and the bees all over again. I barely made it through the subject the first time without laughing," Hannah exclaimed.

"God only knows I needed that course before I started having children," Abigail mused. "I don't think I even knew how babies were made back then and hadn't the foggiest what he was trying to do to me until it happened."

Hannah laughed quickly, and her mother challenged, "So you are telling me you do? The one who asks, 'What is it about a man and his stones?'"

"Mother, you are twisting my words." Hannah pretended to be insulted. Then she added more tenderly, "Will she be teaching that too?"

"She'd better, or there will be a population explosion after the school's first dance," Eunice said, holding up one arm and feigning being twirled by a man as she smiled and batted her doe eyes.

"Yes! Our school must have a dance," Hannah said with excitement. "Ooh, Auntie Eunice, you must teach me a few of your moves."

"I will, my dear," she said, finishing with a curtsy. "My dance moves are so innovative that onlookers worry for my general well-being."

"But do you think there will be enough young men in this town to go around? I'd hate to have to share an escort with someone else."

"Good point, my dear. You have uncovered a crucial flaw in our school's location. The town is not nearly large enough or affluent enough to attract enough eligible young bachelors for our of-age young women's year-in and year-out enrollment at our school."

"Mother, you haven't been able to find a suitable suitor for me in a place as large as Manhattan after years of trying. Why do you feel you can do it here in New Haven for an entire class?"

Eunice added, "You can point a mare towards a puddle, but she'll only sip if it pleases her."

"Exactly," Hannah said.

Their laughter mingled with the sounds of the town. They were a trio of visionaries in a time when women were often seen but seldom heard. They paused before the first old building, its windows dusty but intact, its frame solid and promising. Each tilted their heads at the sloping front porch for several moments before Eunice said, "A straight line never dared pass through that house. If it were any more twisted, it would have to confess to witchcraft," and they moved on.

As the trio meandered through the town, they took in the grand manors, each inherently too small for its purpose. These homes stood like proud patriarchs of the community, silent witnesses to the town's prosperity and esteem. Among the more imposing of these architectural titans were neglected structures—dilapidated shells whose former glory was hinted at only by their skeletal grandeur. Poised on the brink of ruin, these houses seemed to whisper tales of decay and forgotten splendor.

"This one would need renovations so constantly that the house would develop an identity crisis," Eunice quipped.

Each loop around the town brought them past that particular two-story house; they paused to inspect it. It was neither grand nor visually decrepit, but it sat with quiet dignity on an extensive lot that seemed to catch their eyes each time they passed by. Though it needs a wash, its windows let sunlight filter through in a warm, inviting glow. The peeling paint covering the intricate, delicate woodwork spoke of skilled artisans who once took pride in their labor.

They would glance toward it with every pass, an unspoken acknowledgment growing between them. It was as though the house was calling out to be more than just a mere edifice; it was beckoning them to breathe new life into its walls.

Yet, no words were shared, and no explicit comments were made. It was as if admitting their mutual attraction to the structure would jinx their burgeoning dream. The house seemed to be a metaphor for their endeavor — not aspiring to the opulence of the grandest manors or surrendering to the desolation of the crumbling facades, but instead seeking a rebirth, a new purpose.

Finally, as the sun began to dip lower in the sky, casting elongated shadows on the cobblestones, they stopped in front of the house again. This time, it was Hannah who broke their shared silence.

"This one," she said, her voice laden with trepidation and conviction. "It's... right. Close to the harbor but far enough to escape a gale's tide."

Eunice nodded, her eyes appraising the structure as if seeing it for the first time. "It has character," she admitted. "And potential."

Abigail stepped forward, her gaze fixed on the house as if she could already see the future they might create there. "It's not too grand to be intimidating nor too shabby to be dismissed," she observed.

They stood before the house that had silently won their hearts, knowing it was the vessel they needed to embark on their noble journey. In this unassuming abode, they would lay the foundation for a legacy of learning and empowerment.

"But how do we know who owns it, and if they would even consider selling it?" Hannah exclaimed.

Abigail glanced back, her eyes gleaming with amusement and reassurance. "Trust me, dear, we'll strike a deal. And should they be reluctant, we've got resources they can't even fathom."

Eunice, always the pragmatic one, peered up at the structure. "Well, it never hurts to start a conversation. We'll know soon enough if they're amenable to reason or if we need to employ a bit of charm—ah." She stopped speaking, seeing the Constable walking in their direction with a fixed nonplussed smile. She put a hand to her sister's lower back and nudged her forward a step. "You can do the talking, Abby. My negotiation skills are so potent, I've often talked myself into an extra slice of cake."

Eunice raised an arm and began flagging down the man she'd spoken to yesterday, already making his way over. As he approached, he was wiping his hands on his coat, a look of curiosity quickly replacing his initial attitude, crumbs still clinging to the corners of his mouth.

"Ladies," he greeted them, tucking the remainder of his bread into a pocket. "What brings you 'round this part of town?"

Eunice, with her characteristic directness, pointed to her company. "Constable, may I introduce my sister Abigail—Huntington—" she said slowly, unsure if that was still the name she was going by. "And her daughter Hannah."

"Charmed," he said with a deep bow, hat in hand.

"We find ourselves intrigued by this property," she said, whirling around and pointing to the house behind them. "Would you happen to know who owns it?"

The Constable nodded, now with a look of understanding dawning upon him. "Aye, that I do. Belongs to the Widow Clark. It's been in her family for years, but I reckon she's been looking to sell at the right price. Her children have grown or gone—nine in all— and it's a sizeable home for one."

Abigail stepped forward, her mind already turning to the prospects. "Would you be able to introduce us, Constable?"

"Ya yes, Ma'am. Zachariah Hullabee, at your service," he said with another bow while clicking his heels together, showing he'd been in military service once.

Abigail nodded slightly, saying, "We're interested in discussing the future of this property."

Constable Hullabee, sensing the extent of their intent, tipped his hat up slightly to look at the tall building. "Certainly, Miss Huntington. I believe she would appreciate a conversation with such... distinguished potential buyers. But pray-tell, why this house? Surely you will not want to live here in its current state of disrepair?"

Eunice chuckled, echoing like light through the dense canopy of their earnest discussion. "Oh, Constable," she said with a wry smile. "This town's charm lies in its quirks. Living here is like dancing with a partner who steps on your toes—unpredictable but never dull!"

The Constable's face cracked a reluctant grin, appreciating Eunice's wit. But it was Abigail who stepped forward, her gaze locking with the Constables in a moment of earnest communication. "This house," she began, her voice imbued with a passion that belied the calm exterior, "is not destined to be a mere residence. We envision it as a school—a place of learning and enlightenment."

Constable Hullabee's eyes widened slightly, the corners of his whiskered mustache twitching in surprise. "A school, here?" he echoed, his mind visibly turning over the implications.

Abigail nodded, her posture straightening to embody the institution she proposed. "Indeed, a school. But not just any school—a place where young minds can be nurtured and encouraged to flourish."

The Constable looked between the women, their faces alight with the fervor of their cause. It was an excellent idea, especially in a town that held tradition as tightly as it did the railing of the church steps. He was about to speak when Abigail continued, her tone now of strategic discretion. "However, we're not keen on stirring the pot before we've had the chance to simmer the stew, if you catch my drift," she said with a knowing look. "We'd rather not court controversy until we have the foundation laid, literally and metaphorically."

Constable Hullabee nodded, a slow smile dawning upon his face as he began to grasp the magnitude of their ambition. "I see. You plan to educate the next generation and give them a fighting chance in the world?"

"That's precisely it," Eunice interjected, her voice firm. "And we'll need the support of understanding and progressive minds like yours, Constable."

The Constable tipped his hat, a newfound respect in his eyes. "Well then, Miss Huntington, Miss Eunice, Miss Hannah," he said with a bow that held more than a hint of gallantry, "you've got my attention—and my curiosity. A school, you say? Now, that'll be something nice to see."

As they followed the Constable's purposeful march toward Widow Clark's residence, Eunice leaned in close to Hannah and whispered, "I do hope he'll still think it's 'something nice to see' when he sees young women attending."

Hannah covered her mouth to suppress a conspiratorial giggle.

Abigail, Eunice, Hannah, and Constable Hullabee traversed the short cobbled street leading to the property they were interested in. The grandeur of the old estate was hidden beneath a veil of neglect; the front gate dangled precariously off one hinge, squealing in protest with every gust of wind.

The front yard, a tangle of overgrown dormant grass and wildflowers, whispered the stories of yesteryears—of laughter and play, now silenced and abandoned. As the four approached the porch, their steps cautious, they noticed the hole of broken boards gaping in the center, a maw that seemed to mock their aspirations.

Constable Hullabee, a portly figure with a cheery face, stepped forward with an air of authority. He avoided the pitfall in the porch, cleared his throat, and then rapped sharply on the door. The sound was a staccato in the stillness, a demand to be answered.

The women clustered behind him, the image of eagerness and anticipation— a chorus of Christmas carolers ready to sing praises to a new beginning.

The door groaned open, a slow creaking like the opening of a long-sealed tomb, revealing Mrs. Clark's slight figure. She stood clutching a large wooden spoon in her hand as if it were a scepter of defiance.

"What is it this time, Constable Hullabaloo?" she demanded, her voice sharp as the edge of winter frost, eyes piercing through the visitors like needles.

Constable Hullabee offered a conciliatory smile, turning slightly to present the women. "No taxes, tithes, or assessments due today, ma'am. These fine ladies were admiring your house and are quite interested in discussing the possibility of purchasing it."

The lines on Mrs. Clark's face deepened, and she examined them, her gaze lingering on each in turn—Abigail's composed certainty, Eunice's practical scrutiny, and Hannah's youthful optimism. Then, without a word of invitation, she let the door swing back with a force that resounded the finality of her feelings.

"It's not for sale," came the growl from behind the closing door, as if those words could sever the thread of hope they held.

The shut door left the women and the Constable in a silence punctuated only by the creaking gate. Yet the spark in Abigail's eyes had not dimmed, and the set of her shoulders spoke of battles yet to be fought and won. They turned away from the door, the dream undimmed, ready to strategize their next move in the quest to transform the Clark estate into a beacon of enlightenment and progress for the women of their time.

Constable Hullabee's smile had faltered, but didn't disappear. He turned to Abigail and her companions, his expression apologetic yet conspiratorial, as if to suggest a temporary setback rather than a defeat.

"Mrs. Clark is a bit... particular," he whispered. "Let me try again."

He knocked once more, a bit more gently this time. The door swung open promptly as if Mrs. Clark had been waiting just behind it.

"Mrs. Clark," began the Constable, his tone warm and conciliatory.

"Constable Hullabalooiah. I thought my intentions were made clear."

"Yes, ma'am. But these ladies are not ordinary buyers. They have a vision—one that could benefit the entire community. Please, just a moment of your time."

Mrs. Clark stood in the doorway, her frown slowly fading. "Fine," she said curtly. "But make it quick. I have bread in the oven."

Abigail stepped forward, her companions falling silent. "Mrs. Clark, we understand the value you place on your home. We have no desire to displace you without due respect and consideration. We're prepared to offer a fair price that reflects the market value and honors the care you've undoubtedly put into this property over the years."

The older woman's posture softened a little.

"I understand nine children grew up in this wonderful place. It must have been a happier time?"

She grunted proudly, "My oldest is a merchant in Boston. He is the only one who can afford to visit. He comes once a year, about this time, on his ship, to trade down at the docks. He brings me supplies to last the winter months."

"Oh my, you must be proud. But don't you miss your other children?"

"Of course I do. What mother doesn't?" she snapped.

"So why are you hiding here in this old house? It's too big for one person. You could use the money we are offering to move closer to your children; you would have more than enough to purchase a new place and offer financial assistance to your less fortunate children. Now, wouldn't that be nice?"

"I don't want to leave, and I don't want you to knock it down," she quickly said, casting her eyes down at the large hole in the front porch floor. "My husband, Thomas, built this house with his bare hands. If I leave it, I'll be leaving him behind," she added, wiping her nose with her sleeve.

Abigail touched the widow's arm and said softly, "I find departed loved ones don't inhabit buildings like ghosts but live in your hearts like angels."

Mrs. Clark dropped her hands in submission and held the door open, indicating they could come in. Eunice patted the Constable on his shoulder as they entered and said, "Good job. You are a good man." Then, just before he stepped over the threshold, she added, "Now run along and keep the town safe from grave robbers or the like," and shut the door behind her.

"And what do you plan to do with it?" Mrs. Clark asked as they stood looking at the ceiling beams. "Do you plan to live here or turn it into a fancy boarding house?"

"Not simply a boarding house," replied Abigail. "We aim to establish a boarding school to educate students in ways that go beyond what our current institutions offer. It would be a place of empowerment and learning."

Mrs. Clark eyed the trio shrewdly. "A school, you say? My children never had such chances. Worked their fingers to the bone they did, and I taught them everything they knew with nary a word of thanks."

"There's a change coming, Mrs. Clark," Eunice interjected passionately. "Learning to read, to write, to understand the world. The young need to know their worth."

A moment passed, heavy with the weight of her decision. Mrs. Clark leaned on a stout chair back, the wooden spoon now absentmindedly stirring her future as she thought.

"Education, hm?" she mused thoughtfully. "Perhaps..." she nodded. "My husband and I never had much schooling — we did alright. But it might be nice to leave behind something that truly matters. Boys always need a leg-up in life to get started before they become all high and mighty."

"Girls, too," Hannah blurted out, earning a sharp frown from her mother.

The older woman paused, her hand resting on the chair, then stepped back, raising her hand toward the kitchen. "A school for girls, you say? What kind of foolishness is that?" But when no one cared to say another word on the subject, Mrs. Clark shrugged. "Well, come into the kitchen and have a cup of tea. Let's hear this offer of yours. But I warn you," she added with a downturned smile, "I'm not easily swayed."

The sky was gray, and the rich scent of smoking fireplaces lingered in the air as they walked away from Mrs. Clark's home. The echo of the slammed door still faintly rang in their ears. Eunice let out a melodic laugh, instantly lifting the mood. "My negotiation skills are truly something, aren't they? I'm so persuasive, I often talk myself into paying more!"

Abigail smiled at her sister's humor and added, "That's why it's a good idea to let someone else do the talking sometimes." Then, with a wistful sigh, holding out the bill of sale in her hands and scanning over the wording, she said, "I do feel for the old woman, though. To have a house that echoes with the memories of children now grown and distant. It's a sad affair. We blindsided her with our offer, but I honestly think it will be better for her to move on. She truly wanted to die in that old house just as her husband did; she was doing little more than waiting for death to come for her."

Hannah moved closer to her mother, slipping her hand into hers. "I'm ever so grateful you're here, Mother," she said warmly. "After all, someone has to pay our fares on this grand adventure."

"Oh my God, child," her mother said, her mind drifting with other thoughts. "I truly thought you whad damaged our negotiations with your gaffe about it being a school for girls." She tilted her head and furrowed her brow the way the widow had. "A school for girls, you say?" Abigail quoted in a strained voice, attempting to mimic the widow's low, scratchy way of speaking. "'What kind of foolishness is that?'"

As Eunice laughed at her sister's re-enactment, Hannah shrugged with exaggerated modesty. "Well, I brought her around, didn't I? I think she might prove to be one of our most passionate advocates."

Abigail smiled proudly. "You certainly do have a way with words, my dear."

Hannah rolled her eyes over to see her Aunt grinning with the same fondness. Then the girl's thoughts returned to the business at hand, and she changed the subject. "I would have liked to have seen upstairs before you offered her such a generous offer. Do you think she is sleeping in the kitchen? It looked like a bed to me."

"Your compassion for your mother's purse, not mine, warms my heart," Eunice quipped, her eyes sparkling with humor. "And just as well, my budgeting skills are so proficient; my purse frequently enjoys the thrill of emptiness. It's practically an amusement for coins!"

They continued to walk, the weight of the encounter behind them transforming into a lighter, more hopeful stride as they contemplated the future. Abigail, ever the visionary, had already redirected her focus to the next important step. "Now, let's go visit our new Headmistress. We must ensure she is still committed to this cause before we invest in that purgatorial renovation," she said with determination, suggesting she would move heaven and earth to accomplish their mission.

The women's laughter and resolute footsteps infused the town with a purpose as they headed toward the orphanage.

CHAPTER 9

Hope

THE WHITE STEEPLE OF THE CHURCH pierced the clear sky, positioned as a beacon over the small community. Outside, Reverend Morton stood as if surveying God's realm, his arms crossed with the weight of many souls resting on his conscience.

"Good day, Reverend," Abigail greeted cordially, not breaking stride.

The Reverend's stern expression softened into a faint smile as he stepped off the porch to meet them, his long hair stirring slightly in the breeze. "Ladies," he acknowledged with a nod, though his tone carried a note of hesitation. "I understand you have not yet finalized your donation to the orphanage. You aren't putting all your funds into that cavalier girls' school, are you?"

Abigail's brows lifted as she stopped in her tracks to confront the indiscreet man of God. "Cavalier? Whatever do you mean?"

The Reverend cleared his throat, shifting his stance as if rethinking his words. "That is to say," he amended, "one must weigh the necessities of the orphanage against, well, such a new endeavor as your school for young ladies who are invariably destined to having and caring for their own children—one day in the future, of course."

"That is correct," Abigail confirmed, her voice even, her expression betraying nothing. "Good. I see Hope has confided in you. We are here to follow up on that very subject—privately, of course."

"Oh yes, of course," the Reverend quickly agreed, his gaze flickering with curiosity as he glanced toward the orphanage. "Hope and Ursula are with the children."

Hannah, her youthful face bright with concern, asked, "Did you find another milk cow for the children, Reverend?"

The Reverend pursed his lips and let out a slow sigh, shaking his head. "Not yet, I'm afraid. People may fear God's wrath, but they still hold their purses tight when it comes to His work."

Eunice, ever quick to find humor in a sobering truth, quipped, "Seems like the only thing tighter than a church drum is a sinner's wallet on collection day."

The Reverend let out a dry chuckle despite himself, rubbing his chin. "A regrettable reality, to be sure." He hesitated, then added more thoughtfully, "I will say, though, I acknowledge I am perhaps too quick to judge. The way you have been talking... well, I suppose education, even for young ladies, is an investment in the community."

Abigail's lips twitched with the barest hint of amusement. "Reverend, that almost sounds like an endorsement."

"Now, now," he said, holding up a hand. "Let's not get carried away. But I do admire a cause that stirs such conviction."

"You mean convictions regarding those who are seen but not heard?" Abigail countered with a stern look of conviction.

Eunice quipped, "And I do admire a man who departs a conversation before his opinions overstay their welcome."

"Yes, indeed." The Reverend gave an unexpected chuckle, the strain in his shoulders easing. "Quite so, Miss Eunice. Quite so. I'd best take my leave before my tongue sets sail without a map."

"You mean before your tongue knots a noose?" With that, he silently extended his hand forward toward the orphanage, leading them into a conversation that, perhaps, would prove more productive than anticipated.

They continued walking past him toward the annex, where children's laughter rose above the hum of the gusting trees. Out front, a group of children were playing tag, their joyful shrieks a stark contrast to the serious discussions of adults.

As they stepped into the cacophony of childish glee, the women's expressions softened, and it was clear that each child's laughter and smile fortified their resolve. This was the future they were fighting for.

The soft murmur of recited alphabets and the scratch of chalk on slate welcomed Abigail, Eunice, and Hannah as they entered the makeshift classroom within the orphanage annex. Hope, a woman whose gentle demeanor was etched with the subtle lines of persistent worry, oversaw a group of older children hunched over a single book. Beside her, her older daughter, Ursula, moved with patience well beyond her years, guiding tiny hands as they formed letters.

Abigail's eyes sparkled with unspoken dreams as she watched the scene. "Oh, I see you already have a school here," she said, her voice light but laden with implication.

Hope looked up from sweeping the floor, brushing a strand of hair from her forehead, and smiled resignedly. "Maybe this is all I wish for?" she mused. "Indeed, this is all I can afford. Most of my funding has been squandered on tangibles of the mind and not the intangibles of the heart."

Eunice chuckled, observing the children with a twinkle in her eye. "Children's minds are so inventive; they seem like an ongoing art project."

But Abigail was intent on her mission and asked, "Hope, have you considered a curriculum for the older children ready to take their place in society?"

A surprised silence fell over the group. Hope and her daughter exchanged a knowing glance, a silent understanding passing between them. Ursula's eyes, mirroring her mother's, held a mixture of faith and caution.

Ursula stood with her arms crossed, her sharp eyes scanning the room as her mother spoke excitedly to the three women from Manhattan about the prospect of building a school for girls. The sun-filled windows cast long shadows against the wooden walls of their modest orphanage, the warmth of the smoldering fire barely easing the tension in her rigid stance. She had lived in this town all her life, seen too much, endured too much, and she wasn't about to let her mother be trampled under the weight of the town's disapproval.

"Mother, this isn't wise," Ursula said, her voice low but firm. "You don't need to go stirring up the town with this—this impossible dream. You know as well as I do that people around here believe schools are for boys. They will not take kindly to you challenging that."

Hope sighed, setting down her broom against a table. "We cannot live in fear of what others think. Girls deserve to learn as much as boys do. You deserve to learn; do you not?"

"That is not the point," Ursula snapped, her frustration bubbling to the surface. "You taught me everything I need to know at home, just like all the other girls in this town. I need to make sure you don't get crushed by their scorn. Do you remember what they said when you first started taking in orphaned children and teaching them, including the young girls? The whispers? The looks? Do you think it will be any different now? They will call you foolish, arrogant—worse—pricker." She shook her head firmly. "And I won't stand by and let them prick your heart to death."

Hope reached and took Ursula's hand, squeezing it gently. "My sweet girl, you carry too much of my past on your shoulders." Her voice was calm, steady—the same voice that had soothed Ursula through childhood fears and sleepless nights. "I know you have spent your whole childhood protecting me, but this is something I must do. If we do nothing, nothing will ever change."

Ursula clenched her jaw, looking away, her heart warring between loyalty and frustration. She wanted to believe in her mother's dreams, but the risk was too significant. "People don't like change," she muttered. "And they certainly don't like women who think they can make a difference."

Hope smiled. "Then we'll have to teach them differently, otherwise."

Ursula exhaled sharply and looked back at her mother, reading the determination in her eyes. She had seen that look before—when fighting for the orphanage, when she had refused to let Ursula be treated as lesser by church parishioners, when she had built something out of nothing time and time again.

With a reluctant nod, Ursula relented. "Fine," she muttered. "But don't expect me to sit back and watch when they come knocking at our door with their righteous indignations." She squeezed her mother's hand in return. "I'll fight for you and be damned."

Hope chuckled, "I never doubted you would."

Outside, the wind howled through the trees, as if carrying the town's inevitable judgment on its breath. But inside, a quiet resolve settled between them. No matter what came next, they would face it together.

Hope nodded subtly to Abigail's expectant face, a faint smile appearing at the corners of her mouth. "I already have everything prepared at my home for just such a purpose," she admitted, catching them off guard with her quiet foresight.

She stood, the children's gaze following her with a mix of respect and affection. "Would you accompany me to my home, a short distance away?" Hope asked the trio. Her tone suggested more than a simple walk; it hinted at the possibility of something greater, an unvoiced truce projecting between them as Ursula turned to address a child's needs.

"But what of Ursula and the children?" Abigail asked, indicating she would be left alone with the children.

"Not to worry. If you haven't noticed, my daughter is the one who runs this place," she said, watching Ursula moving from child to child like a mother hummingbird watching over her garden of beautiful flowers.

"Then, of course, lead the way," Abigail replied, her gesture open and encouraging.

They left the hubbub of the orphanage behind, the echoes of learning dissipating as they stepped out into the tranquil afternoon. As they began walking, nobody spoke of the mother and daughter's heated conversation until Hope broke the silence. "I was like her, you know," Abigail said quietly. "It was my mother who pushed me outside of my comfort zone." The other women only nodded.

The road to Hope's house curved gently through the thinning trees, the kind that whispered when the wind caught them just right. The sun had slipped low behind the hills, casting the path in that soft gold that makes everything feel remembered.

"I never knew my mother," Hope said quietly, as they walked side by side. Her voice wasn't bitter, just distant—like she was pulling a thread from somewhere deep. "Not even a face in a locket or a scribbled note. Just absence."

She paused as her house came into view, shoes crunching over leaves that had wandered through the woods in search of eternity for the past year.

"My father raised me alone. Most of my memories of him are… well, they live in the house. The creak of the stair that he said he would fix, the smell of his pipes mounted over the hearth, the way he'd read aloud, looking out the window when he thought I was asleep." She smiled faintly. "He built the shelves crooked in the study. Claimed it gave the books 'character."

As the house came closer—weathered but standing proud, its chimney tall and cold—she added, "When he died, he left it to me. Not just the house, but the silence inside it. That's where he lives now. In every worn floorboard and sun-faded curtain."

She reached for the gate but didn't open it right away.

"Sometimes I think the house remembers him better than I do."

The history and affection Hope held for her father began to paint a picture of a man who was not just a scholar but also a visionary, someone who saw the world not only for what it was but for what it could be.

"My father showed me his gifts of knowledge at a young age," Hope said, her voice tinged with reverence. "He was a remarkable man."

With youthful admiration sparkling in her eyes, Hannah tilted her head slightly. "And he was a botanist, was he not?" she asked, recalling fragments of previous conversations she had heard.

Hope nodded solemnly. "That, and other things. He excelled in mathematics, physics, engineering, and..." Her voice trailed off as if her father's talents were too extensive to encapsulate in a single breath.

Abigail and Eunice glanced at each other, their expressions tinged with quiet skepticism, as if wondering whether she had gleaned such knowledge from her father before he died—rather than inherited it outright.

"My goodness," Eunice exclaimed, "He sounded like a regular Renaissance Man."

"That he was," Hope replied, a touch of pride warming her words. "Some had indeed called him a genius."

Abigail's doubt lingered, reluctance flickering in her gaze. She wondered if these stories of Hope's father were mere fabrications, tales inflated over time. Yet, as Hope spoke with conviction, the three women exchanged more glances, each acknowledging, however cautiously, the value of such knowledge if it proved true. There was a reluctant murmur of agreement, a shared understanding that, despite her misgivings, there might be more to Hope than first met the eye.

Hope's residence, nestled next to a picturesque willow-shrouded creek, was the manifestation of the genius she spoke of. The home wasn't just a structure; it was hidden within a paradise of greenery, curated by someone with a profound understanding of art and science.

"Oh my. You say your father built this?" Abigail breathed out as the beauty of the landscape unfolded before them.

"No, my grandfather. He moved to New Haven from Boston in the 1660s, after my father was born. Uncle Elihu lived here, too."

"What a beautiful menagerie of plant life," Abigail added wistfully.

"Yes," Eunice concurred, with a hint of jest in her voice, "and that's coming from someone who has an entire crew of slaves tending her garden."

"Ha, father had no use for slaves—after all, he had me," Hope laughed.

Abigail, slightly affronted by her sister's comment, quickly set the record straight. "They are not slaves, at least not anymore," she corrected firmly. "I've given them their freedom and a working wage. It would be dreadful to own someone who might one day become your friend. Let's enfranchise the whole lot as citizens. Then they would pay their own taxes and pick their own cotton, if you will."

There was a moment of silence as they each reflected on the moral complexities of the times, the weight of history, and the potential for change. The garden's beauty around them bore witness to what could be cultivated with care and respect—ideals that they hoped to plant and grow within the walls of their new endeavor.

As they followed Hope along the stone path that weaved through the verdant oasis she had referred to as a front garden, they couldn't help but marvel at the meticulous care with which each plant was placed and pruned. The vibrant colors and varied textures conversed, creating a symphony of nature that hummed with life.

Eunice said, "I wish I could see this in the spring after everything has sprung."

As they ventured into Hope's ancestral home, her father's legacy became increasingly apparent. The drawing room, not unlike the spotless reception, held the tangible remnants of a life dedicated to the pursuit of knowledge and the esoteric.

In the corner stood a tall, imposing athanor, its surface dulled with age but still imposing. The furnace, used for alchemical experiments, hinted at her father's endeavors to transmute base metals into gold, or perhaps the effort to achieve transmutation was also an act of piety and an exercise in self-purification.

Hope led them further into the study, her eyes tracing the spines of ancient books and lingering on the worn edges of maps that adorned the walls. "My father," she began, her voice taking on a note of pride mixed with a tinge of sadness, "was not just confined to his studies here. He went on several pilgrimages in his quest for knowledge."

Abigail listened intently, her interest piqued. "Pilgrimages?"

"Yes," Hope continued. "When I was too young to remember, we journeyed to Constantinople, with stops in Venice, Leghorn, Pisa, and Florence, on an alchemical pilgrimage." She gestured to a shelf lined with aged tomes and a collection of exotic-looking instruments. "This was the first of several journeys he made to expand his understanding. He built networks with fellow alchemists, collected books, and learned various experimental techniques."

Examining a curious-looking astrolabe, Eunice remarked, "A man of the world. I always thought alchemy was confined to hidden chambers and secret rituals around a large black cauldron."

Hope chuckled softly. "You mean a witch? Alchemists can find themselves in precarious situations. Often, to hide this, they sought knowledge far beyond their shores. And his last journey," she paused, her gaze distant, "was to meet with Native tribes. He was fascinated by their knowledge, connection with nature, and what they might know about alchemy."

Abigail's interest deepened. "And did he find what he was looking for?"

Hope shrugged. "I'm not sure. He went to Wales to publish his findings, but never returned from that journey. He did leave behind these." She waved a hand around the room. "His legacy. I believe he found some truth in his quest – something transcending the mere transmutation of metals."

Her gaze softened into resolve, and she said with a quiet heart, "I'd always hoped he had simply found what he was looking for and had transformed into something, an angel perhaps. To look over my life."

The room, filled with the echoes of Yale's quests, seemed to hold its breath, preserving the spirit of a man whose search for knowledge knew no bounds. For Hope, this legacy was not just an inheritance of physical objects but a lineage of insatiable curiosity and a passion for discovery.

Hannah's gaze wandered through the room, taking in the exotic furnishings and the personal touches that made it home. She turned to Hope with a question lingering in her mind. "What does a young girl do in a place like this after her father was lost in the wilderness? Did you have nearby relatives to assist you?"

Hope's expression shifted, a shadow of past grief crossing her features. "When my father ventured into the unknown, he always knew the risks," she began, her voice a whisper of reflection. "He told me if something were to happen to him, I was to sail to England and live with his brother Elihu, who had made quite the name for himself upon his return. He was celebrated as one of the wealthiest men in the Kingdom."

Intrigued by Elihu's mention, Abigail responded, "I've read about him. He was the President of Fort George, involved with the Eastern India trading company, wasn't he?"

Hope nodded, a faint smile appearing as she thought of her relative. "Yes, that's him. His life is worlds apart from mine, filled with commerce and grandeur. Yet, he was my father's chosen guardian for me, a link to a life never lived."

Hannah's brow furrowed. "So you never went? You stayed here alone?"

"Oddly enough," she lamented. "What tethered me to New Haven was not blood or property, but a man of the cloth with sharper eyes than most. Reverend Warham Mather."

"Mather? As in Cotton Mather?" Abigail asked.

"Reverend Warham Mather was Cotton Mather's untempered cousin, a man inflamed with zeal and rigid to the point of cruelty. In retrospect, he proved a rather unsuccessful preacher, yet a feared figure nonetheless—no less relentless than his cousin in pursuing the Devil's undoing. He married into the powerful Davenport family and thus enjoyed the respect of the colony's elders and the ear of its council, which he used to twist the laws to his cruel favor—advantages his character alone would never have earned. I believe he sensed in me grief, not fragility, mistaking it for an untapped well of conviction he might bend to his righteous purposes."

"Righteous purposes?" Eunice scoffed. "He recruited you."

"To be a witch pricker," Hannah added, and Hope's brief silence filled in the answer.

Hope began to pace as she continued, "At first, he made it sound like an assistant, a scribe, a witness. But it wasn't long before my own hand held the pricker. I did not always draw blood, but I always drew fear. And sometimes, a confession from the weakest of minds."

Hope fell silent. Her gaze dropped to the floor, as though the boards themselves might remember what she had tried so carefully to forget. When she spoke again, it was with the cadence of words long rehearsed—less explanation than echo, shaped by years of taught certainty.

"The Reverend taught me to look for signs: an herb garden grown too lush; a woman who healed without tincture; a child who dreamt too vividly. He said the Devil cloaks himself in kindness. To watch not for malice, but for benevolence. It is being one chief project of that old deluder, Satan, to keep men from the knowledge of the Scriptures."

"Benevolence? But that is a desire to do good," Hannah asked.

"Not all that the Reverend said made sense. So, I found myself looking in areas where I felt the Devil lurked: the docks."

Each of the women nodded in agreement with her assumption.

"The docks are where I began my search more intently. Seamen returning from Barbados, traders bearing unfamiliar spices, fishermen with salt-dulled eyes. The docks brimmed with stories and strangeness—and it was there that I met my pirate, Benjamin."

"And had Ursula," Hannah said with a hard swallow of hesitation.

The conversation lingered in the room, a mix of curiosity and unspoken emotions. Abigail could sense the depth of Hope's past, a fabric of family ties and what-ifs woven with the threads of loss and resilience.

Eunice, ever the skeptic, held up an old manuscript, asking, "And have you read all of these books in your father's impressive library, or are they just scattered about to oggle the eyes of visitors?"

Hope reached for the book in her hand and read the cover, which was written in Greek: "This one was written by Archimedes, titled 'On Floating Bodies.' It's not an original, of course."

"Archimedes?" Eunice asked. "I don't believe I've heard of him. Is he married?"

Taken aback, Hope opened her mouth, not knowing if she was serious, then answered, "He lived before Christ, and no one seems to know if he was married or not. You may borrow it if you want to read his works."

Eunice raised her eyebrows at the foreign lettering.

Hope laughed, "Not to worry. As soon as you familiarize yourself with the Greek alphabet, the words will flow off your tongue like poetry, and you too will be able to find your own eureka moment."

"Oh," Eunice said. "But don't get me wrong, child. I'm not picky. It's alright if we have to dig him up. But I'm afraid you and I have an entirely different definition of eureka when it comes to a man."

Hannah, seeing the familiar confused expression many have had at her Aunt's dry commentary, stepped closer to Hope. "Show me your pricker," she said out of the blue.

Hope drew in a sharp breath of surprise, and the room fell silent. The room's jovial ambiance shifted as if a haunting shadow had crept over the sun following Hannah's abrupt request. Abigail and Aunt Eunice, though surprised, watched the lady of the house with a blend of apprehension and curiosity.

Hope, her initial irritability giving way to resolve, turned slowly to face an old chest sitting in the corner of the room.

The room's silence was broken only by the creaking floorboards as Hope's tentative steps carried her toward the chest. Her fingers, betraying a hint of reluctance, brushed against the cool metal of the key that hung around her neck, tied to her skin by the thinnest strand of rawhide. The gentle scrape of the key turning in the lock echoed too loudly in the expectant quiet.

The lid of the chest opened as if emitting a soft groan, and for a moment, Hope paused, peering inside as though she might find something other than what she sought. Then, her hand emerged, cradling the small cylindrical pricker with a reverence that belied its sinister history.

The tool's simplicity did not match the complexity of its past, and as the three women beheld it, they felt they were peering into a time when fear reigned, and innocence was no shield.

"How does it work?" Hannah's voice broke the silent reverence, her intrigue evident.

Hope's smile was tinged with sadness, a reflection of wisdom from one who had witnessed too much. "People are creatures of belief and can believe just about anything if told from a point of authority, such as the church," she explained.

Hannah gasped, "The church invented this tool?"

"No, they didn't have to. They only needed to comply with their congregation's imagination. By allowing rumors to spread freely without guidance, witches began to sprout wings everywhere," Hope replied.

"So, how did the pricker come about?" Hannah pressed.

"That's an excellent question that I've asked myself every day to no avail. I suppose the answer lies as far back as our pagan roots. You see, witches are believed to be servants of the Devil, marked on their bodies by Lucifer himself," Hope explained, her eyes glancing down at Hannah's tattoo peeking beneath her sleeve. "This mark is said to feel no pain and bleed not when pricked."

"Really? What kind of mark?" Hannah asked, skeptically pulling her sleeve down to cover the thunderbird.

Hope's hand shot out like a striking snake and grasped Hannah's arm, revealing the tattoo. She then jabbed the pricker into the bird's head. As she let go to observe the mark, they all waited for a reaction, but none came. Hope suddenly backed up, feigning shock, and screamed, "She's a witch!"

Hannah's mouth fell open as Hope continued her reaction, "Look, she does not bleed!"

Hannah's face paled as the weight of persecution bore down on her. She saw her own mother and Aunt step back as if she were plagued.

Hope's face softened, making it clear her dramatics were entirely for show. Abigail and Eunice exchanged embarrassed looks and stepped in closer to inspect Hannah's arm.

"Did it hurt?" Abigail asked.

Hannah shook her head in disbelief. "It wasn't even sharp," she confessed.

Hope nodded calmly, as if expecting Hannah's response, then suddenly pursed her lips and leaned forward to prick Hannah again on the other arm. This time, she drew blood.

Confused and disoriented, they all looked to Hope for guidance. Her accusatory stance softened as she wiped the blood from the pricker. "Belief can turn the simplest object into a weapon of great power," she said, showing them the device's dual nature — one side blunt, the other sharp. "Before you burn your daughter at the stake, consider the power of suggestion."

Hope's audience was captivated as she went through the motion of twisting the wrist to present the sharp or dull point with a slide of the hand. Still recovering from the shock, Hannah rubbed the thin streak of blood on her arm and asked, "Why would a woman of your intellect ever become a charlatan?"

"Indeed?" Hope replied while cautiously locking the object away. "As I had alluded to before, intelligence does not always equate to common sense. Insatiable curiosity is a better description. I was put to the task and wanted to find a sorcerer—a real demon."

Hannah's abrupt questions seemed to roll through like a fog bank, with Abigail and Eunice's expressions painting a perfect picture of understanding. Hope, once statuesque in her calmness, now betrayed a hint of agitation, a swift change that did not go unnoticed. The atmosphere in the room had taken a credible turn as Hope's revelations settled like fresh dust on the furniture.

Hope's composure wavered momentarily, the memories washing over her like an untamed river. She took a slow breath before turning to face Abigail, her eyes holding depths of untold stories.

"It has not been without struggle," Hope began, her voice a soft echo of resilience. "After my father's... disappearance, I was left with this property and a modest sum from his investments. I've had to be rather... inventive with finances, especially since...Ursula." A flicker of shame touched her lips. "I'm grateful the community has been more tolerant of me than I likely deserve. They may believe the blame for a murder doesn't lie with the musket ball itself. And those truly responsible for my mission... they hide in plain sight, each in their own way."

Hannah added, "Since your prickering days are now over?"

Hope gestured vaguely towards the verdant expanse outside, where every plant and tree seemed to be positioned with intention as a diversion to her question. "The orchard yields fruit we use at the orphanage, and the herbs have been more than just decorative. They've provided for us, as well."

Abigail nodded, understanding the unspoken fortitude it took to manage such a feat, especially for a woman in her position. Yet, the second question hung in the air, a specter from the past that seemed to darken the sunlit room. "Ursula's father..."

Hope paused, the weight of history momentarily bowing her shoulders. "He was a seafarer traveler, unlike my father."

"He was a pirate," Hannah prompted.

She answered unapologetically, "By his own accord. When," she wiped her eyes, "he did not return, he became a part of my pricking story that ended abruptly when Ursula arrived."

The atmosphere in the room shifted as Hope's revelation lingered among the trinkets of her heritage.

"Benjamin," she said. "Or this Henry Avery, as you know him." Her voice was barely above a whisper, as if speaking the name might conjure the real man from the shrouds of her memory. "He was unlike anyone I had ever met, a man of the sea with tales as tall as the mast of his ship. He brought a sack of strange gold coins and jewels as colorful as the stories he wove."

With a slight hesitation in her hands, Hope reached under a nearby well-worn table stand and unlatched a secret compartment, revealing a small, weathered sack. She loosened its strings and poured its contents into her hand, her trust evident as the contents glittered and sparked even in the room's muted light.

"He said they were treasures from his travels, gifts from a life he was ready to leave behind." Her smile was touched by sadness and the knowing look of someone who had dared to dream of love only to awaken alone. "He spoke of a new life here with me. But one day, he vanished as swiftly as he had appeared, swallowed by the horizon from which he came."

The women leaned in, their eyes reflecting the myriad of colors that spilled out from her hand onto the table. Abigail reached out to touch one of the coins, her finger tracing the familiar foreign symbols embossed into its surface.

"I dare say these must be worth a fortune," she murmured, her business acumen assessing the potential value of such rarities.

Hope nodded a resigned acknowledgment in her gaze. "Perhaps, but they are foreign, and their value here is... suspect. Once, when I tried to sell one of the stones, the constable quickly came to me, demanding that I tell him where I had stolen it from."

"Constable Jenkins?" Abigail asked, and Hope nodded.

"Since I've held onto them more for their sentimental worth than any hope of fortune they might bring, perhaps Ursula will find them more valuable one day."

"And have you tried to find out more about them? About him?" Eunice inquired, her curiosity piqued by the mystery of Hope's enigmatic lover.

Hope sighed, the weight of a story half-told resting on her shoulders. "I have made inquiries discreetly, but it seems Benjamin was as much a mystery to the world as he is to us. A pirate, he was, but one with a conscience and a desire for redemption, it seemed."

Abigail also nodded, saying, "Yes. Truly, it seems."

Hannah, moved by the romantic and tragic tale, whispered, "It's like something out of a novel..."

Eunice smirked. "Well, at least he had good taste in parting gifts."

The room filled with gentle laughter, acknowledging the bittersweet truth that life often writes stories more compelling and complex than any fiction. And in the center of it all was Hope, a brilliant woman who had learned to weave her tale from the threads of the unknown and the remnants of a pirate's promise.

As Hope's gaze drifted, they saw the shadow of a young woman who had weathered storms of sorrow and had grown middle-aged, now standing before them, an instrument of quiet strength.

Sensing Hope's delicate heart, Abigail said, "You've done remarkably well to honor your father's legacy, Hope. This house—your home—it's clear it's been tended with love and remembrance."

Hannah stepped closer, her voice a soothing balm. "You've built something beautiful here, not just in the garden, but in your spirit. That's a rare thing to find these days."

An agreeable silence fell until Eunice chimed in with a light-hearted tease, "And here I was, thinking my knack for growing a single potted plant was an achievement."

After leaving the unusual home, the trio made their way down the cobbled streets that wound through the heart of the township. The ambitious task ahead of them sparked an exhilarating and daunting fervor.

Eunice shook her head in mock dismay, "From coins to bricks in the blink of an eye. Who would've thought we'd become patrons of construction?"

Abigail, whose resolve seemed to harden with each step, replied, "It's not just about construction, Eunice. It's about foundation—the foundation for a future that burgeoning young ladies deserve."

Hannah's eyes widened at the scale of their undertaking, yet a smile still spread across her lips. "We'll need more than just a good builder. We'll need supplies, labor, and someone keen on planning, or this building will not be complete until I am an old maid."

Eunice halted mid-stride, a sudden thought dawning upon her. She turned to her companions, her expression a blend of earnestness and a twinkle of mischief. "Ladies, should we circle back and inquire if that kind-hearted Constable knows who might be a good builder around these parts?"

Abigail paused, casting a sidelong glance at Hannah, whose attempt to stifle her amusement was betrayed by the mirth dancing in her eyes. "You mean Constable Hullabaloo?" Abigail corrected with an arched brow. The corner of her mouth twitched upwards, threatening to evolve into a full smile.

Hannah, unable to hold back any longer, let out a snicker. The name 'Hullabaloo' conjured images of the constable's flustered attempts to maintain order in the face of the disagreeable widow Clark.

"He might just direct us to the town's handyman, who's more adept at mending fences than constructing buildings," Eunice's lips quirked into a playful smirk. "Well, between Constable Hullabee and mending fences, I'm sure we'll find a fine patchwork of expertise."

"That's where the innkeeper comes in," said Abigail confidently. "He's well-connected and well-informed. If anyone knows the lay of the land, it's him."

"The inn sounds comforting. My feet are not used to walking for so long," Eunice said, her face looking uncharacteristically somber.

"You two can go back to the inn to freshen up. As for me," Abigail said, slapping the handwritten bill of sale against her sleeve, "I need to file this with the town clerk before the ink dries."

As they approached the inn, a stout building with a wood-shingled roof that whispered stories of many a traveler's respite, the innkeeper himself was stepping outside. Eunice whispered to Hannah, "Your mother perhaps should have purchased this establishment for her schoolhouse. At least here, you can find a comfortable bed and a delicious meal without too much trouble."

"Good day, ladies," he greeted, wiping his hands on his apron. "How was your day?"

Eunice was quick with her wit. "We're in the market for a builder, and not the kind that puts up walls only for them to fall with the first gust of wind."

The innkeeper laughed, a deep, hearty sound that filled the inn with its richness. "Ah, a sturdy hand you're looking for. Well, I might know a fellow. John MacCreedy's his name. He built my stables last spring, and they're still standing strong despite our storms."

Hannah nodded, taking mental note of the name. "We'll need someone who can do more than stand a pole barn. We want to transform Widow

Clark's property into a boarding schoolhouse."

The innkeeper raised his brows, visibly impressed. "A schoolhouse? That's noble work. I'll tell you what—MacCreedy is as reliable as they come, and he's fair with his pricing, too. Want me to send word to him?"

"Please do," Eunice replied with Hannah in agreement. "And let him know we're serious and ready to begin as soon as possible."

The innkeeper tipped his hat. "I'll send my boy to fetch him immediately. Anything to support a good cause—and the education of our young'uns."

The women thanked the innkeeper and returned to their rooms, their hearts a little lighter, one step closer to making their vision a reality.

As they climbed the narrow wooden staircase, Hannah remarked, "It seems the entire town might rally behind our school."

Eunice smirked, "Indeed? I'd be willing to bet a king's ransom the innkeep meant those 'young'uns' are boys."

Hannah frowned, glancing back over her shoulder as if the innkeeper might be listening. "You think if we had mentioned it was for girls, he would have changed his mind about helping us?"

Eunice let out a knowing sigh, pulling her shawl. "I think it best we keep that detail to ourselves—unless, of course, we want an organized opposition at the most inconvenient moment."

CHAPTER 10

John MacCreedy

THE MIDDAY SUN poured generously through the inn's leaded windows, casting dappled shadows across the wooden floorboards. Abigail, Eunice, and Hannah sat finishing a hearty, refreshing lunch perfect for the afternoon's endeavors. As they sipped the last stout ale, the door swung open to admit a figure as robust as the meal they had just consumed.

The innkeeper indicated to them with his stance and glaring eyes that the local builder was indeed a sight — broad-shouldered, with arms that bespoke years of labor and a complexion kissed by the sun. He greeted the innkeeper with a nod and a smile that seemed to light up the room, and they began walking about the inn, pointing out various nooks and crannies in need of attention.

Abigail watched them for a moment, her gaze analytical, appraising the man's movements, confidence, and the assured way he took stock of the repairs needed. She was pondering the potential quality of his artistry when the innkeeper gestured towards their table, drawing their meeting to a head.

"Mrs. Huntington, may I present John MacCreedy, the general contractor I spoke of?" the innkeeper introduced.

"How do you do, Miss Huntington? I am John MacCreedy. How may I be of service?" Mr. MacCreedy said as he approached, extending a hand that swallowed Abigail's in a firm but not overbearing grip. His voice was welcoming, his accent hinting at distant shores.

Abigail's response was a nod of recognition, "We are quite well, thank you. I understand you're the man to see about building works?"

"That's right," he replied with a grin, turning his eyes towards Hannah and Eunice. "I hear you have a sizable project on your hands?"

"Indeed," Abigail confirmed, "We want to transform the Clark house into a high-end boarding school."

"High-end, you say? How high?" His eyebrows raised in genuine interest.

"Exceedingly," Abigail asserted with a tone that left no room for doubt.

At the same time, Hannah offered a flirtatious smile, her eyelashes fluttering in a manner that could turn the heads of saints and sinners alike. MacCreedy's answering smile was one of open appreciation.

"And when can you begin to assess our needs?" Abigail pressed on, rising from her chair with determination.

"I am at your disposal now if you are ready," he answered, stepping forward to pull Hannah's chair. Her touch was light on his arm, a silent thank you that seemed to warm him.

Eunice's throat clearing was audible and deliberate, and MacCreedy hastened to afford her the same courtesy. "Thank you, young man," she said as she rose. "You're both a gentleman and a roustabout, it seems."

His laughter was easy, unaffected. "Yes, ma'am, both titles have been bestowed upon me in my time."

"And which do you prefer?" Hannah's voice was soft, teasing.

MacCreedy met her eyes, his twinkling with good humor. "I reckon a wise man knows when to be a roustabout and when to be a gentleman. But I'd hope to be considered the latter in your company."

After exchanging introductions and pleasantries, the group stood ready to embark on the journey towards their shared vision of turning the dilapidated Clark house into a bastion of learning and hope.

The firm scent of potential accompanied their steps as they stood before the Clark house. John MacCreedy, with the keen eye of a man well-versed in assessing a building's structure, carefully surveyed its exterior. He spoke only after thoroughly considering his words.

"A few dimples in the roof, but she looks sturdy," he finally declared, a note of respect in his voice for the enduring craftsmanship before him. "They don't make them like this anymore."

Abigail, ever the pragmatist, pressed for clarity. "So you believe it has life in it yet? It's not destined to be kindling for the hearth?"

He chuckled, a sound that seemed to vibrate through the very foundation of the old house. "I'm not sure, ma'am. It's begging for a second chance, not a mercy killing by fire. However, closer inspection is needed to see if a deeper rot inhabits from within."

His request to inspect the inside was the moment Hannah had been waiting for — her opportunity to interject with etiquette and concern. Yet, as her mother nodded assent, her words lingered on her lips until they could no longer be caged. "Mother? You just bought the house this morning. What will the poor woman think when we barge in and begin discussing tearing out walls and fixtures true to her heart?"

MacCreedy laughed at her concerns and said, "Don't worry your pretty little head, missy. I've got it handled."

MacCreedy's stride was confident as he approached the house, his hand firm against the front porch posts. Hannah's indignation at being referred to as 'missy' bloomed silently within her — a mixture of affront and secret amusement.

The door creaked open, and there stood Mrs. Clark, the matriarch of the home they sought to transform. MacCreedy's response of recognition of her warmed the air, nostalgia mingling with the scent of baking bread.

"Do you remember me? I used to play with your children right here in the front yard and on the street. You baked the most delicious bread," MacCreedy reminisced, his voice laced with the shared memories of youth.

Mrs. Clark's features softened, her past recollections coloring her present smile. "I'm just baking some now," she confirmed, a trace of pride in her voice.

"I hear you are moving. Gosh, my parents loved moving closer to their grandchildren. It was a real blessing."

And then, with a gentleness that belied his large frame, MacCreedy followed her into the sanctum of the past, his eyes now critiquing the space through the lens of the future. Hannah trailed behind; her disappointment at his mention of his parents' delight over the grandchildren cast a shadow over her thoughts.

The interior walk-through was ablaze with potential and pragmatism, with MacCreedy pointing out what was salvageable and what required reimagining. He touched a main beam and felt the residue between his fingers, asking, "How long has the roof leaked?"

Mrs. Clark fell silent until all eyes looked upon her. "I'm not sure. The years have flown by. I don't go upstairs on account of my rheumatism." Hannah looked at Eunice, who puckered her lips and lowered her chin.

"Ever see any bugs?" he asked. When Mrs. Clark raised her eyebrows, he added, "Vermin? Beetles? Ants? Goblins?"

"Just the usual," she answered with a plain face.

When he pointed to the stairs, he asked, "You don't mind?" Mrs. Clark only shrugged.

While climbing the stairs slowly, each step creaked and gave as if it were on its last leg. "Be careful, ma'am. I'm not sure they can take the weight."

"I beg your pardon?" Abigail asked indignantly at first, and when she saw his dismay, she laughed. "I'll be alright if you are alright, I am for certain."

He made a genial sound of agreement as he approached the top step. "Here we are," he said, stepping onto the landing of the second floor. He looked straight up at the ghoulish network of water stains in the ceiling, and he tapped the nearest wall with his knuckles to provoke a swarm of giant ants to spring out. "Carpenter ants." Then he rubbed his thumb on a beam and pointed out all the tiny holes, saying, "Powderpost beetles."

As they concluded, MacCreedy's confident tone returned to Abigail's attention. "You said you already purchased the property?"

Abigail nodded.

"Maybe an assessment would have been a better first step?" he muttered, more to himself than to Abigail. "I'll write down some thoughts and meet you at the inn later tonight," he proposed, his words punctuated by the smell of burning bread as Mrs. Clark sputtered curses downstairs in the kitchen.

As the group disbanded, each with their thoughts and tasks, Hannah lingered a moment longer, gazing after the builder. For all his talk of structure and solidity, she found herself intrigued by the foundations of the man himself. Was there room in his well-ordered life for the dreams she harbored? Or was she just another part of a day's work to him, a 'little missy' while planning a school? The evening at the inn would tell her more, not just about the fate of the Clark house but of the potential narratives that might unfold within its resurrected walls.

The rest of Hannah's day was a whirlwind of anticipation. She was consumed by meticulous grooming, from fixing her hair into elegant curls to ensuring her teeth gleamed like pearls in the filtered sunlight. Her preparations were interrupted only by stolen glances out the window, her thoughts dancing on the possibilities the evening might hold.

As evening drew its curtains, the women gathered for a hearty dinner. Their conversation was light, tinged with the excited undertones of their shared venture. The clinking of cutlery against the plates provided a comforting rhythm to their plans and laughter.

After noticing the moonlit sky, Eunice teased her sister about the potential need for a nightcap, suggesting the evening's excitement might not yet be over. Abigail, too, was poised in expectation when the door swung open, and John MacCreedy entered with the promised parchments tucked under his arm.

"We were about to give up on you for the night," Abigail greeted, her tone a blend of reproof and relief.

The innkeeper's wife, quick to sense the shifting focus, cleared the remnants of their meal to make way for MacCreedy's plans. With a deliberate grace, Hannah leaned in to observe the plans, her earlier preparations now playing their part as she drew MacCreedy's attention from the parchment to herself.

They discussed the potential to transform the plans. Each new idea Abigail introduced was met with an eager nod or a thoughtful tilt of the head from MacCreedy. Hannah took this opportunity to weave a personal thread into their conversation and inquired about his accent, which was laced with exotic European notes.

Caught in Hannah's charm, MacCreedy didn't immediately notice the shift in her demeanor when she posed the question.

"Ah, yes, you noticed," he said with a smile. "I was indeed born in Hungary."

With a frown, she asked, sliding back in her chair, "Well then, you couldn't have played with the widow Clark's children. Weren't you in another country?"

Her questioning caught the attention of the others, who slowly turned their heads to look at him suspiciously.

"Well, yes, I knew a few of the Clark children," he said as if it was nothing. "We moved here when I was five. Being raised by Hungarian parents leaves its mark on one's speaking. Of course, as an adult, I rarely see them — once a year perhaps — so now I mostly sound like a born and bred New Havener."

He grinned cheerily as he spoke, not noticing the way Hannah's face hardened at his words.

"Wait a minute. You told the widow Clark that your parents moved closer to be with their grandchildren. Was this a lie?"

He looked confused. "A lie? I wanted to put the old lady at ease, that's all. Why would—"

"You just said you haven't seen them in a year. How do they live close to your children?" Her cheeks flared with the accusation.

Abigail and Eunice leaned back in their chair to assess the man with more scrutiny, making him nervous.

MacCreedy's mouth pursed as if he were unsure whether he was the butt of a joke. "What? I don't have children. I'm not even married."

"Mr. MacCreedy, I do believe you are not as honest as you seemed to be," Abigail said, her tone firm. "If you think you can bamboozle through this project, you are mistaken."

"No, no, you're getting the wrong idea. I didn't lie. My parents moved closer to my brother's children. And they are pleased about it. I'm not a pirate," he insisted. He looked at the women defensively as they considered his words.

Finally, Abigail spoke. "Alright, alright. I believe you were deliberately vague with the widow Clark and not trying to be dishonest with us. We can put this matter behind us."

Eunice added, "But if you cross us," then nodded her head to Hannah. "Especially her—because the last person who crossed her received a real headache."

MacCreedy nodded, eyes wide open. His flustered explanations under the ladies' scrutinizing gaze only heightened the edginess, leaving him to navigate the delicate line between being personable and maintaining professional integrity.

Once the dust settled and they were back to the business at hand, the plans grew more complex, and so did the discussions around them.

Abigail asked for additions, and he began to write them down. "What if we hung a large chandelier in the main hall?" she asked, watching his reaction closely.

MacCreedy, his eyebrows raised ever so slightly, nodded and made a note. But before he could fully commit pen to paper, Abigail continued, her voice rich with inspiration. "And crown molding, not just in the common areas, but throughout every bedroom."

With each new proposal, the builder's hand moved furiously, scratching his pen a counterpoint to Abigail's melodic voice. It wasn't long before he reached for a second sheet of paper, then a third, and finally a fourth, his previous organized scrawlings now a sprawling attestation to their grand design.

When Abigail finally paused, MacCreedy looked like he had been through the physical labor of building rather than merely planning it. He pressed a large hand to his forehead, sweeping it back over his head as if to clear away the fog of work lingering in his mind.

"Mr. MacCreedy? You are not overwhelmed so soon?" Hannah asked.

"Well, there is a lot to consider," he said, stacking his notes. "Is that all?" he asked, a faint note of hope threading through his voice.

"I think we are finished for now," Abigail replied with a smile that hinted she was far from finished. "But rest assured, if anything else comes to mind, you'll be the first to know."

He shook his head, a slight smile tugging at the corners of his mouth despite evident exhaustion. "This sounds more akin to a royal palace for princesses than a boarding school for a bunch of foul-smelling young men," he half-joked.

Abigail's eyes sparkled with pride and anticipation. "Maybe not a palace, but you're half right. This will be a girl's finishing school," she clarified as if unveiling a well-kept secret.

Understanding dawned on MacCreedy's rugged face, transforming his weary expression into one of realization. "A girls' finishing school," he repeated. "Here? Are you sure that makes sense in New Haven Colony? This isn't Manhattan or Boston."

"Why? Do you think there will be a problem?" Abigail asked, her tone even.

MacCreedy scratched his chin, considering. "Well, I'm not sure. It's definitely bold." He was quiet for another moment before nodding with satisfaction. "Bold indeed," he said. " So, hey—why not?"

Abigail allowed a small, knowing smile. "I believe it is customary to leave a down payment for your upfront expenses."

"Ah, yeah—about that," but before he could tell her more, Abigail tossed a sack full of gold coins onto the table. His eyes widened in disbelief.

Before MacCreedy could speak, Abigail added, "No need to count it now; I know how much it is." As she turned to leave, she stopped to say, "Don't get foolish with your estimates, or the next contractor will laugh in your face each time he sees you."

The exchange concluded with Abigail's casual yet authoritative stance, signaling the end of their business. This left the room, unspoken, with excitement and trepidation as MacCreedy stood, stunned, gathering his faculties.

"Oh, just one more thing," MacCreedy said with a sobering look at the sack of coins weighing heavily in his hand. "Where did you say you wanted this building built?"

The women sat perfectly still, looking at each other with a perplexed expression.

"Because now that I realize this is not a school for smelly boys, if you wish to attract respectable families to place their daughters in your care, you will need a different site than the one you've chosen."

Each woman tilted their head with a frown until he said, "The Clark building is rotten from within, and all the money in the world cannot fix that."

Shocked, Abigail gasped, "What are you suggesting?"

"Moving to a different location?" Eunice asked, shifting her eyes around to assess everyone's reaction.

"Or we knock it down where it stands and build what we want from scratch?" Hannah asked with jolted shock.

Mr. MacCreedy rolled up his papers and braced against the back in his seat, only offering a shrug as a solution.

CHAPTER 11

Thomas Clark

THE MORNING DEW held the crisp edge of autumn, carrying the sharp echoes of hammering and sawing from down the lane. With the steadfast Eunice and the ever-eager Hannah, Abigail had set out to visit Hope, but first made it their business to pass by the Widow Clark's house. The sounds were those of dismantling, not of repair, as men pried and pulled every scrap of metal worth salvaging from the old abode. Iron hinges, brass handles, nails, and other fixtures were gathered with practiced efficiency and placed in carts lining the street, ready to be hauled away. It was a purposeful day, one in which plans and prospects were to be measured by more than mere intentions.

As the trio neared the house, the distinct sounds of industry gradually gave way to an escalating crescendo of raised, combative voices. The rhythmic clinking of metal tools around the old house gave way to a discordant symphony of anger and accusation.

"'Tis not my doing that the wood's rotten! Once stripped of value, weather allowing, it will be torched to the ground to make way for a new structure," protested Mr. MacCreedy, thick with frustration, slicing through the morning's peace.

"The devil, take your men and your workmanship!" came the biting retort from a man, his voice laced with a venom that could wilt the hardiest of flowers.

Eunice's eyebrows arched towards the heavens, and Hannah felt a buzz of curiosity tinged with a shard of concern. The voices grew louder and more vehement, and as the women approached, they became puzzled by the commotion.

Mr. MacCreedy, whose reputation as a carpenter was as solid as the oaken beams he shaped, stood nose to nose with another dressed in mercantile apparel. The air around them was filled with insult and accusation, the strain winding tighter like a fiddle string, ready to snap.

They were poised on the brink of violence, a push away from turning their fists into weapons.

A shrill whistle cleaved the moment before the spark of their hostility could set their tempers alight. It was a sound that commanded attention, piercing and assertive, leaving no room for doubt or disobedience.

Every head turned, eyes wide, seeking the source. The two men halted their quarrel, momentarily stunned into silence. The whistle had emanated from Abigail, who stood a short distance away, her posture the very embodiment of authority. Her fingers pressed to her lips, and as she lowered her hand, the expectant gaze of the men fell upon her, the altercation jutting unfinished between them.

"Gentlemen," Abigail's voice was a force, her tone measured but brooking no argument. "If you intend to entertain the street with this... performance, then pray, proceed. But please move it out into the street to make room for your replacements. That building's interests are my own, and I'll not suffer its advancements hindered by the likes of this."

Her words carried the weight of civic respectability and personal investment. Eunice and Hannah stood firmly behind her, a united front of feminine resolve.

Mr. MacCreedy, recognizing the woman's stance was not to be trifled with, swallowed his pride and stepped back, his expression morphing from anger to embarrassment. The other man, sun glinting off the silver braid of his beaver-felt tricorn that had gone askew during the heated exchange, dropped his fists and shuffled his feet, the heat of the quarrel dissipating like fog before the rising sun.

The street fell silent once more, save for the distant caw of a crow and the subdued mutter of hired workers now keen to resume their work without further ado.

"Whatever do you mean, this building is yours?" the man with the hat said to Abigail. His voice was lower and more controlled, though his cheeks still flared with heat. "My father built it with his own two hands. My mother still lives here, for God's sake." He nodded toward his weathered mother, now standing at the front door in a tattered dress and stained bonnet with a piece of parchment in her hands.

Abigail's expression softened slightly as she realized the man in the fine coat was the widow Clark's son. But the moment of recognition did little to ease the tension crackling between him and Mr. MacCreedy. The civility of the front yard stood in sharp contrast to the heated standoff unfolding before her.

The man stood with unreserved restraint, watching the laborers with narrowed eyes, his hands clasped tightly behind his back. Mr. MacCreedy, eyes never leaving him, sneered openly. His eyes dropped to the gentleman's polished black leather shoes—fanciful things, gleaming like obsidian, each silver buckle engraved with curling ivy. With a snort of disdain, MacCreedy turned on his heels and marched through the front yard, barking clipped orders to his men with exaggerated authority.

Seeing the stripping away of old doorknobs and hinges from the house he had grown up in gave the man an expression of mingled indignation and confusion. His dark, intent eyes flicked over each piece of metal, struggling to reconcile the dismantling of a home he believed was still under his mother's care—and would one day be his.

"Mother?" he shouted to the old lady hunched over in the front door, appearing afraid to come out. When she didn't respond, he muttered, "You must be sparing no expense with this renovation. I will not be bearing the bill."

Abigail turned her attention to the man. She approached him with the poise of one who knows her standing and her business.

"Sir, might I inquire about your business here? This property is now under my care," she restated, her voice carrying the gentle but firm tone of ownership.

The man's smile faltered, his brows knitting together. "Under your care?" he echoed, confusion tainting his words. "But this is the Clark residence. My mother—"

"I'm afraid you are under a misapprehension," Abigail interrupted softly yet firmly. "This property was sold to me not a day past. Widow Clark will be relocating." She frowned and glanced toward the doorway, seeing that the woman wasn't ready to leave the premises.

For a moment, silence fell, then the realization hit him visibly, a blow that robbed the breath from his lungs and the color from his cheeks.

"But the house... it was to be mine by inheritance. By rights, it should still be mine," he stammered, his voice a hoarse whisper of disbelief.

Abigail looked sharply at the woman and then at her son, saying, "We weren't informed you were an encumbrance."

The man stood tall and proud to have conquered the moment until his mother roared, "He is not."

The gathered workers and onlookers watched the drama, the yard filled with dread and unspoken sympathies.

"What do you mean?" her son impugned, scoffing.

The elderly woman spewed with spittle from her trembling lips, "This house is mine. Mine to do with as I please. And I am pleased to sell it, as is, before it falls around me whilst I sleep, waiting for you to visit me."

"Ha, you do not know what you are talking about. I am the eldest. I only let you stay according to your dower rights, allowing you to use the estate during your lifetime."

Mrs. Clark stood defiantly, clutching a piece of parchment in her fisted hand. Her mouth hung open, laboring to breathe as she scanned everyone in the streets who had stopped to look and listen. She looked like she would have preferred to be behind closed doors in this embarrassing situation with her own blood, but he chose the place and time of the argument. Then, as with an afterthought, she straightened up her posture and placed her hands on her hips to say, "You didn't even bother to come to his funeral."

"What? I was away on business," he said, nodding to the crowd of people standing about.

"Business? Blah—you are trying to dilute your neglect. You couldn't bother yourself with the whole affair. You were always too busy with your cotton, molasses, rum, and other black market pirated goods."

"Ah, mother! Listen to yourself," he said, turning to the townsfolk who had gathered around to watch the demolition for parts and pieces they could use at their homes. "She is old and senile. She knows not what she speaks of."

"That is why your father left the house to me, and me only. So you would not come and evict me before my time had come."

"You know I would never do that."

"Your father thought it so. So he made sure of my care and safety in his will." After a long pause of disbelief from her son, she added. "It's a shame you didn't even bother to read the will. You just assumed, in time, you would inherit the house and land, only to sell it, lock, stock, and barrel, to the highest bidder. Well, I beat you to it."

Abigail's expression softened ever so slightly. She understood the intensity of this moment for the man, the loss, the confusion, the sense of a world upturned.

"I am truly sorry for your surprise, sir," she said, "but the sale was lawful and stands solid. The records are clearly recorded and held in the presence of notable witnesses. I assure you, no duplicity has colored this transaction."

The man's speechlessness gave way to a crest of anger, his hands clenched at his sides. "But I..." He struggled to find words, his sense of injustice an evident force. "I was not informed! I should have been allowed to claim what is rightfully mine."

The crowd sensed a new confrontation brewing, but this one carried a personal sting, a sense of intimate betrayal. Abigail stepped forward, her presence a calming influence.

"Come," she urged gently. "Let us discuss this like civilized folk. We shall review the documents together, and I will hear your claims about any furniture or keepsake you wish to acquire for your family's antiquity. But I will not tolerate an unruly scene outside what is now my property."

The man, caught between the rising tide of his emotions and the firm, compassionate offer before him, was at a crossroads of choice. The anger simmering in his eyes was at war with the despair and the sudden, crippling doubt of his position.

Eunice and Hannah watched as silent witnesses to the unfolding drama, ready to stand in and support Abigail if needed. But at the same time, they felt a little sorry for the man. They knew the weight of inheritance, the legacy of land and home, and the sorrow of its loss.

Finally, the man's shoulders slumped, the fight seeping out of him as if through unseen wounds. He nodded, wordlessly acquiescing to Abigail's proposal. She whispered so few could hear, "There would be no more scenes in the street today, only the pursuit of truth and perhaps, in time, the understanding and acceptance of a difficult reality."

The house's interior, still smelling of baked bread and mold, seemed to hold its breath as the man followed Abigail inside. His steps were uncertain, each one heavier than the last, carrying the weight of years and memories that clung to the walls and floors of the once-familiar home.

The Widow Clark stood by the fireplace, the flames casting dancing shadows upon her fading features, etched with the lines of time and softened by new tranquility. She looked up as her son entered, her eyes betraying a flicker of old affection buried under layers of practical resolve.

He stood there, a boy lost in a man's frame, his voice barely a murmur as he asked, "Mother, why did you sell the house?" The hesitation that greeted his question was apparent, a pause that spoke of the sacrifices and unspoken agreements that had led to this point in their estranged relationship.

It was Abigail's subtle yet persuasive nudge that broke her silence. The

Widow Clark exhaled a breath that seemed to carry the weight of her decision. "Because I am lonely," she began, her voice tinged with a melancholy resolve, "and I do not want to die alone in this emaciated carcass of a house."

Her words hung between them, poignant and irrefutable.

Once taut with confusion and anger, the man's face softened as the reality of his mother's vulnerability became apparent. "Then, where are you going to stay? Where are you going to go?" he asked, the depth of his concern replacing the ire in his voice.

Widow Clark reached out, her hand trembling slightly, seeking the warmth of her son's. "I am going to stay with you, I'd hoped. Maybe find a smaller space nearby?"

Abigail watched the exchange, a silent sentinel to this tender family moment. She knew that houses, like the lives they contained, had chapters; some written in the bold script of birth and growth, others in the faded ink of parting and change.

"You are her son, the merchant she was so proud to tell us about?" Abigail asked.

The man seemed to wrestle with his emotions, the yearning to protest warring with the understanding that his mother's happiness was not something he could deny. "I... I wish I had known," he finally said, his voice cracking with a mixture of regret and relief.

"And I wish I could have told you," Widow Clark replied softly, her eyes glistening. "But life moves swiftly, and sometimes, we must make choices that are best for us, even if they surprise others."

Abigail watched the son's face as he digested the information and noted the flicker in his eyes shift from soft concern to the hard glint of avarice.

"How fortuitous, you may now transport your mother's household goods and furniture back to Boston," Abigail stated firmly, her voice leaving no room for interpretation. "They are not part of the sale; instead, part of the continuing life your mother is choosing."

With a resigned sigh, his mother extended the parchment to her son—the bill of sale. "Look here," she said, her voice steady. "See what they have given me. It is more than fair."

The son's eyes darted over the document, tracing the figures with a growing sense of disbelief and indignation. The amount was substantial enough to ensure his mother's comfort and care, but to him it suddenly seemed like a starting point rather than a settlement.

He scoffed, a harsh sound that seemed to scrape against the soft murmurs of the flame in the hearth. "This? They give you this for a lifetime's worth?" He waved the bill dismissively, his expression contorted with derision. "If they're willing to pay an old woman this much, they'll surely pay more to me."

Widow Clark recoiled as if his words were a physical blow, her face etched with disappointment.

Abigail stepped forward, her eyes alight with an unspoken warning. "Your mother has made her decision. This transaction is concluded with satisfaction on both sides. Your attempt to leverage more out of this situation is not only unseemly, but it is also unnecessary and unwelcome."

The son's ire rose, flushing his cheeks. "Unseemly? I am her son! I have rights! This—"

"Rights do not grant you license to greed," Abigail interrupted, her tone as sharp as the edge of a blade. "The sum paid was agreed upon by your mother, who is of sound mind and clear intent. It is not for you to question or covet."

"Sound mind?" he scoffed, causing his mother to lower her head in shame. He stood there, the bill of sale crumpling in his tightening grip, his mind racing with the figures and the possibility of what he believed he could wring from the situation. But in the face of Abigail's unyielding stance and his mother's obvious distress, his resolve began to crumble.

Widow Clark, mustering the dignity that had always been her cloak, finally spoke, her voice slicing through the suspense. "I am content with the agreement. I will not have you tarnish these final days in my home with your greed."

The son looked between the two women, and the realization dawned upon him that the figures on the paper did not truly reflect the value of what was being transacted here. It was not merely about property and money—it was about respect, dignity, and the quiet acceptance of life's ebb and flow.

His mother had made her peace with the sale, and now, reluctantly, he had to do the same. With a curt nod, barely acknowledging the defeat of his avarice, he folded the bill of sale and handed it back to his mother.

"I... I will acknowledge the sale but not your wishes," he muttered, his voice barely audible.

"Mrs. Clark," Abigail said, addressing the elderly woman who was still processing her son's words. "You failed to mention your son was of such... low character."

The man's eyes sparked with offense. "How dare you!" he blustered.

Eunice, no longer able to bite her tongue, retorted, "I would suggest you restrain yourself lest your words only heighten your disgrace. Indeed, if folly were to be harvested, you would surely be a magnate in this New World, with riches unending."

Abigail nodded toward the front door. "Now, should you require assistance transporting your mother's possessions to your vessel, I am confident Mr. MacCreedy can direct you to some robust helpers."

The man's stature wilted under the weight of collective censure, his schemes and bluster reduced to ash in the face of Abigail's steadfast resolve and Eunice's piercing wit. His sneer grew with each step he took, a silent exemplification of his disgruntlement. His concerned mother met him at the threshold. She opened her mouth to say something reassuring but paused as he cast a venomous glance around the room, a clear promise that, in his mind, this unsavory business was far from concluded.

"You may think this is the end," he hissed, his voice a serpentine whisper that slithered through the air. "Beware, for shadows turn and fortunes spin. This isn't the last you've heard of me. Come on, Mother," he growled, tugging on her arm. "You won't need any of this rubbish. Burn it, for all I care."

With that ominous parting shot, he stormed off with his mother, a reluctant but willing prisoner, his exit more a strategic withdrawal than a retreat. The heavy door closed with a resounding thud behind him, its echo a harbinger of troubles yet to come.

CHAPTER 12

Manhattan, 11/1714

THE STREETS OF MANHATTAN buzzed with commerce and noise. Yet in Abigail's quiet study, only the rustle of letters and the scratch of a quill could be heard. Back in the city to settle business, Abigail faced a tall stack of post.

It had been almost two years since the New Haven property was razed, and months since Abigail had been in her own home. She traced the edges of Mr. MacCreedy's latest letter, its ink barely dry. His words brimmed with excitement and offered a vivid, heartfelt account of the schoolhouse—a vision fast becoming reality. He wrote of toiling, orchestrating a large crew of carpenters from across the region. Each contributed unique craftsmanship to the grand project. The school's stately architecture neared completion; ample bedrooms were ready, beds made and adorned with frilly quilts and coverlets that, in his poetic description, seemed to whisper goodnight. Abigail smiled—a rare, unguarded moment—as she pictured the twin harpsichords, recently arrived from the Ruckers family of Antwerp via Boston, poised to fill the halls with the harmony of music and learning. The letter was more than an update; it was a promise unfolding before her: hope inked by the labor of many hands.

Abigail knew elsewhere that Hope Merryweather Terwilliger—a name that always brought a brief chuckle—had taken up the mantle of tutor recruitment with commendable zeal. She traveled with a sizable budget, speaking with the passionate conviction that could move mountains—or at least persuade potential educators to join their cause.

But it wasn't just the construction and staffing that demanded Abigail's attention. Word of the school had already spread across the colonies, thanks to the Albany Venture Investment Group. The group—the money-laundering arm of the Pirate Bank—had included the school as a loan-backed enterprise now admitting female students in its memorandum to the Proprietors. Her desk was awash with letters from prospective students' parents and guardians. Each sought assurances about the living arrangements and the caliber of education offered. Abigail replied with eloquence and precision, leaving no question unanswered and no concern unaddressed—most especially when it came to tuition.

As she sealed another letter with wax, Abigail realized they had more than enough interest. The seed of an idea that had sprouted amid adversity was flourishing, promising to grow into a haven of learning and opportunity for young women. And that, she knew, was worth every pirated shilling's effort they poured into this dream.

Abigail smiled at the memory of Eunice's laughter, a sound as comforting as the warmth of a hearth on a winter's day. Eunice had a way of finding humor in the simplest of invitations, and her response to Hannah's earnest suggestion that she come home with them to live was no different.

"Oh, Hannah," Eunice had said with a twinkle in her eye, "Manhattan may well swallow me whole! I'm content among my potted plant and my quiet contemplations." She laughed when remembering she said, "Why, my knitting is so avant-garde; each scarf is a labyrinth of yarn. But I thank you for the offer."

Hannah entered the room, cradling her aging cat, Mr. McDermot, in her arms. With all the theatrics of a royal procession, the old tom flicked his tail, surveyed the space like a conquering general, and then—in a single, spectacular bound—launched himself out of her arms, straight into Abigail's lap.

Abigail let out a soft "oof," her hands instinctively rising to steady the creature.

Before she could comment on his dramatic arrival, Hannah announced, "Mr. McDermot clawed little Andreas. Made him bleed."

Abigail's head snapped up, eyes sharp with maternal alarm.

Hannah quickly lifted a palm. "Well—Andreas, ah, Jan, was pulling his tail."

Abigail exhaled through her nose in a low grunt, the kind that carried both judgment and understanding. It was clear she thought the cat had shown remarkable restraint, but wasn't so sure about her daughter's restraint in the use of the name Andreas.

Hannah rolled her eyes with a faint smirk. "Honestly, I can't blame either poor creature. And I'm grateful the boy's been rescued from Jasper's clutches. Heaven knows what would've become of him if he'd stayed there longer."

Abigail's brows rose.

"I remember Jasper," Hannah continued, settling into a nearby chair.

"Former pirate, pretends reform because he lost his sword. His wench of a wife, Maggie, fusses but can't stop her husband from drinking or getting into trouble. And to think—she raised Jacob's son after he left for Albany to escape tavern maid entanglements."

Abigail made a soft hum of agreement, stroking the contented cat purring in her lap. Mr. McDermot kneaded at her skirts as though he disapproved of little Andreas's living arrangements.

"Well," Abigail murmured, half to herself, half to the cat, "at least someone in this family still knows when to defend himself."

Hannah laughed. "Him or the cat?"

Abigail didn't answer—she just continued to stroke the purring beast, her silence saying everything.

Entering the room with a determined purpose etched across her young face, Sarah, the younger sister, whose fiery spirit was the perfect foil to Hannah's nurturing nature.

"Mother," Sarah demanded, her tone brooking no arguments. "The next time you venture to New Haven, I insist upon accompanying you. Hannah will not cease her tales of it, and it's all become far too compelling to hear about secondhand."

Hannah's eyes sparkled with reliving their adventures. Abigail knew Sarah, always eager for new experiences, would not be content to stay behind next time.

Abigail leaned back, watching her daughters with affection and amusement. "Sarah, my dear," she replied, her voice laced with mirth, "If you wish to see New Haven, we shall do so. For now, let's focus on the present. Mr. MacCreedy, our superintendent, is finishing the school. We can visit soon—unless you'd rather go now and learn how to decorate a house?"

Later that evening, Hannah and Sarah perched side by side on the ornate settee in their family's parlor, holding cups of tea delicately between their fingers—the warmth of the porcelain a welcome contrast to the cool evening air wafting through the open windows. Their conversation, as had become customary during these twilight hours, drifted from the day's mundane events to the far more thrilling topic of potential suitors.

Hannah's mind, ever so often, drifted back to New Haven, to the rugged framework of the new schoolhouse rising from the decayed splinters, and more so, to the man whose hands shaped its destiny. "Mr. MacCreedy," she began, a blush tinting her cheeks. "He's not like the young men here in Manhattan. He has calluses on his hands and a seriousness in his eyes that speaks of purpose and passion."

Sarah giggled behind her teacup, her eyes gleaming with the excitement of shared secrets and sisterly confidences. "And did those serious eyes ever find their way to you?" she teased, nudging Hannah playfully with her elbow.

"Oh, stop it," Hannah retorted, but the corners of her lips betrayed her with a smile. "But there's something about a man who can build and create with his hands. It's... It's captivating."

The room filled with the warm glow of candles and the scent of lavender, rosemary, dill, sage, cumin, and thyme stalks drying from the kitchen rafters over a white sheet, yielding the seedy spices. Each sister took turns describing the young men they had encountered, the fleeting glances exchanged on the cobblestone streets, the polite nods at church, and the more daring smiles at social gatherings.

Sarah leaned in closer, her voice dropping to a conspiratorial whisper. "What about young Mr. Marshal at the general store? He has the most fascinating stories of the ships coming into the harbor. And his eyes, Hannah, they're as deep and mysterious as the Atlantic." She then gave out a carefree laugh, fingering her necklace. "He told me he liked my necklace."

"Oh, he did!" Hannah gasped. "You think he was looking at your—your—cleavage?"

Sarah's mouth went agape with surprise before blurting out, "Of course. Why wear a shiny trinket around your neck in the first place if you don't want someone to notice it?"

Hannah squealed, "I know!"

They held hands with excitement as their minds painted images of each young man they named, their virtues, and their quirks. Yet, despite the allure of these Manhattan beaus, Hannah's heart remained anchored to the vivid memory of New Haven's resilient spirit, embodied in Mr. MacCreedy's unyielding form.

The sisters' conversation meandered through dreams and desires. The heavens around them filled with the heady perfume of possibilities. They were at that tender age where the line between girlish fancy and the burgeoning desires of womanhood was as delicate as the china in their hands. With each passing day, they were more aware of lingering eyes, the implications of a well-timed smile, and the power of an innocent blush.

As the night drew in and the candle flames flickered and danced, shadows fell upon their faces. Hannah and Sarah continued to weave their tales—each a figment of hope and fancy—spinning from the golden threads of youth and the bittersweet tang of growing up.

Every evening, Hannah returned to her upstairs room to the small writing desk facing the expansive Hudson. Here, quill in hand, she recounted the tales told by the pirates who had, over the years, frequented their home. The house, with its secluded backyard leading to the river, had been a covert haven for those weary of the high seas and the authorities, namely, the Admiralty and pirate hunters. Her mother, a woman of formidable acumen, was known across the seven oceans as a provider of sorts, sheltering and discretionary, while ensuring their visits were profitable for all parties involved.

Hannah's fascination with the roguish mariners of the sea had evolved from innocent childhood curiosity into a more vibrant and passionate endeavor. As a young girl, she began writing in her journal, which she boldly labeled "A General History of the Pyrates." Back then, it was a simple collection of stories and rumors she'd overheard, tales of the fearless men who frequented their family's Pirate Bank, bringing with them whispers of danger and adventure. She fancied that one day, her journal would become a grand compendium of exploits and treachery, an intimate chronicle of those who lived by the sword and the compass.

But now, as a blossoming young woman, her feelings toward her writings had deepened. Her words took on a more intimate tone, no longer merely a child's fascination, laced with admiration and longing. Each tale she penned was about adventure and freedom—the freedom these men embraced and the lives they carved out for themselves beyond the strict confines of society. She found herself drawn to their defiance, to the spirit that would not be bound.

The sea held secrets and stories wrapped in salt and starlight, and Hannah was determined to be their scribe, regardless of her mother's disapproval.

Her mother had always viewed such tales as childish fancies, urging Hannah to focus on more "practical" matters—like ledger keeping and the management of trade inventories. But Hannah felt a fire within her that longed for more than the mundane.

In every stolen moment, she poured her thoughts into her journal, its leather cover worn soft with use. Each line became a testament to her dream of capturing the spirit of the pirates—their courage, their ambition, and, perhaps, their loneliness.

In pirates, Hannah saw the distilled essence of freedom and danger, a world far removed from the structured confines of society. From Caesar, the steadfast family servant who found his liberation and departed to mingle with legends such as Bartholomew Roberts, Black Sam Bellamy, Blackbeard Edward Teach, and Calico Jack Rackham, to the stories she overheard whispered by other such shadowy figures in the dim light of their secretive gatherings, Hannah collected each tale like a precious gem.

Lawton, their butler—who had taken Caesar's place at her mother's side after he left with Blackbeard, Edward Teach—was a wellspring of sea lore and sharp opinion. He spoke of pirates with a blend of reverence and disdain, like a man who had once felt the sea's freedom in his bones but had lived long enough to mourn those it dragged to Davy Jones's locker.

From him, Hannah learned the rogue's cant—the gruff tongue of sea dogs and cutthroats. She now wrote "cutwater" instead of prow, and knew better than to say a man had died—he'd been marooned, scuttled, or swung from the yardarm. She described storms that blew the deadlights out of a man's skull, and coins earned under the creed of "no prey, no pay."

Her journal wasn't just stories—it was a chart of pirate life, drawn in salt and blood, with every slang-laced line proof that she understood the cost of freedom on the open sea.

In her book, she emphasized the characters who visited their household's pirate bank, though not necessarily to deposit treasures. Monitoring these pirates closely, she depicted Calico Jack with flamboyant flair, his sartorial taste as distinct as his predilection for swift, sudden raids. Blackbeard was the nightmarish legend who waded into battle with his beard alight with fuses. She remembered each had sat in this house, their stories unfolding as she listened from the hole cut through the kitchen pantry, adjacent to her mother's study, or, in some cases, from the secretive entrance to the Pirate Bank's cellars, before and after they turned to their pirating ways.

The tales poured from Hannah's quill, a mix of secondhand accounts, embellished rumors, and her own imaginative flair. She spoke of their governance, the Pirate Code that bound them, and the democracy that ran as deep as the waters they traversed. Her prose spewed with the romance of piracy yet never shied from its brutality.

As her manuscript grew, so did her secrecy. Whispers throughout the colonies of a young authoress from Manhattan crafting the pirates' tome would have violated her mother's strict family code and potentially jeopardized their most profitable business. Yet, Hannah's literary journey was not merely an act of historical record. In the lives of these pirates, she found a reflection of her own yearnings—a desire to break from the fetters of expectation, to sail on the winds of ambition, and perhaps, to find her own story among the echoes of their legendary escapades.

CHAPTER 13

Books

THE NEXT MORNING, Abigail once again sat at her desk in her Hudson River home, with the familiar hum of winter's wind circling through her sleeping garden outside her window. She knew that Hannah, ever the dreamer, had envisioned the schoolhouse in its nascent stages and had dreamt of the eager minds, new friends, and companions that would soon populate its rooms. Now, Abigail, the ever-practical matriarch, shared in the culmination of those dreams, though not without the familiar tug of maternal concern. The joy of the school's completion was tempered by the bittersweet recognition of its demands on their time, resources, and, most poignantly, on their family—namely, the departure of her two older daughters for school and possibly a new life.

Scrutinizing another letter, Abigail sifted through Hope's list of prospective tutors. Her eye caught on one name in particular—the Reverend Cotton Mather. The possibility of securing such a renowned, controversial figure as a visiting tutor for her school was both a coup and a potential quagmire. His reputation preceded him, as did his writings, which Abigail had perused with a critical eye—not to mention his role in the Witch Trials that Hope was so determined to leave behind.

She set the letter down and glanced at the stack beside her—letters from less polarizing scholars, lesser-known ministers, and even a handful of recent Harvard graduates who claimed to teach scripture and science with equal conviction. Alternatives existed, though none carried the same thunder as Cotton Mather's name.

Just then, she thought of James Holloway—the Captain of her yacht, The Atlas—a man as dutiful as he was discreet. Just as she, Eunice, and Hannah first set foot in New Haven, Abigail had dispatched Holloway on reconnaissance to the Collegiate School in Old Saybrook. She pulled open the lower desk drawer and rifled through a folder of documents until she found the list he had compiled and mailed to her last year. He had been tasked with finding tutors whose minds were as sharp as their morals and who bore loyalty—but not enough to ignore a new posting at The Willow for the proper incentive. She looked over his list once again, now with fresh eyes given the imminence of the school's opening. Were any of these worthy of consideration, she wondered—or was Mather, hailstorm cloud and all, the only one who might lend their school a lasting name?

Hope Merryweather Terwilliger had proven an invaluable ally, her correspondence sprinkled with the names and credentials of potential tutors as well. She had journeyed with indefatigable zeal, courting the best minds and persuading them with the promise of a new frontier in education—though careful not to let anyone know beforehand that it was a school for young women who were not just future mothers but learners and thinkers, contributors to the more excellent dialogue of knowledge wherever knowledge was needed.

Coming to the bottom of her pile of correspondence, Abigail examined a package from William Bradford, the printer and manager of her publishing company, Metropolis. Bradford had sent her a reem of parchment detailing an unusual but significant acquisition. The acquisition of which he wrote was a pirates' deposit, but not of gold or jewels; instead, it was a collection of almost two thousand bound books seized en route to Virginia from England. In an age when knowledge was as coveted as wealth, these books represented a treasure of a different kind.

Bradford's letter outlined a proposal to capitalize on this unexpected windfall. He suggested opening a bookstore, a novel idea for efficiently distributing this cumbersome bulk of literary riches. The concept was innovative yet clashed with Abigail's appreciation of the intrinsic value of education, literature, and silver.

Running through the list of books, one title stood out—circled in pen, almost certainly by Bradford himself. Next to it, a note mentioned he might already have a buyer.

Curious, she traced her finger along the ink and read the title aloud: Philosophiæ Naturalis Principia Mathematica by Sir Isaac Newton.

She paused, startled. Of all the volumes, she hadn't expected this one. Newton was known as the greatest natural philosopher of the age, a man whose ideas about gravity, motion, and the very structure of the cosmos had changed how scholars across Europe understood the world. His name was whispered with awe in scientific circles—and with suspicion in religious ones.

She considered the title and author more carefully. It was not merely a book, but a cornerstone of knowledge, the kind of work kings and universities vied to possess.

At the right price, it could bring her considerable gain.

But part of her wondered if it belonged, instead, on the shelf of her own library—a quiet rebellion against the limits placed upon a woman's mind.

Commodities other than precious metals and gems were channeled through trusted brokers on the docks, where they were processed like other covert cargo, such as cotton, sugar, rum, and molasses. All expenses, including bribes and taxes, were paid. This unconventional acquisition of books exemplified the broader operation of Abigail's secretive enterprise.

Abigail penned a letter to Bradford that said, "Keep under lock and key. Books are not for sale—yet." In that moment, an idea took root—an epiphany. These books, she realized, were more than curiosities or investments; they were the foundation of something greater. A library. A proper library at The Willow. Not just novels and needlework guides, but works of mathematics, philosophy, natural science, and history. Knowledge that could educate and elevate, that could sharpen a girl's mind as surely as manners might smooth her edges.

She began drafting a list, methodically at first, then with growing urgency. The Principia Mathematica by Sir Isaac Newton would crown the collection. Though complex, its very presence would be a symbol of inquiry, of ambition, of intellect unbound by gender. She added other essential volumes to the list, each representing a stone in the academic foundation she envisioned for her school.

She enclosed the list with a second note to Bradford, asking that the specified titles be set aside and sent directly to her sloop for discreet transport to New Haven. The Willow, she resolved, would house more than refined girls—it would foster thinking women.

As Abigail contemplated her next steps, Hannah floated into the room, her thoughts clearly adrift in some romantic daydream, perhaps of Mr. MacCreedy, whose name she always uttered with a sigh that spoke volumes of her young, fluttering heart. Abigail smiled, knowing well the tug of young love, yet remained anchored by the weight of responsibility that now lay upon her shoulders and Henry Avery's hefty purse strings.

The school's opening had the potential to be a heralded event, not just in

New Haven but across the colonies. It could be a beacon of enlightenment in a world ensnared by the trappings of ignorance and superstition.

With a determined breath, Abigail began penning her approval for the tutors, namely the locals who possessed practical skills, sealing the letter with a sense of purpose. This school would be her legacy, a fortress of learning where the daughters of the colonies would be armed with the most powerful weapon known to humanity: education. And as the schoolhouse readied itself to welcome its first intake of bright, eager minds, Abigail knew Hope stood at the vanguard of a quiet revolution, one that would echo through the annals of time, proof to the power of dreams fortified by the unyielding strength of the human spirit. Or so she hoped.

As she dripped wax to seal the letter approving Hope's appointments as tutors, Abigail whispered a quiet prayer—not for ceremony, but for clarity. She hoped, with all the weight of her name and influence behind the decision, that entrusting Hope with such authority would not prove to be a gross misjudgment.

She admired the woman's conviction, yes—but conviction could be blinding, especially in matters of education, doctrine, and reputation. The school was more than a dream now; it was becoming real. And real things had a way of bearing consequences.

Abigail pressed the seal into the wax with a final sigh, murmuring, "Let this not be my folly."

CHAPTER 14

Arriving at the Willow, July, 1715

IT HAD TAKEN DAYS BY RIVER AND SOUND, while stopping off to pick up her Aunt—but now, as the boat edged toward the town under a bruised afternoon sky, Sarah leaned forward with a mix of excitement and nerves, her eyes scanning the clustered rooftops of New Haven rising beyond the shoreline.

"I've never been this far from home," she whispered, clutching the rail. "It feels... lighter than I imagined. Certainly not Manhattan."

Later, when they stepped off the carriage and onto the cobblestone streets, Abigail, Hannah, Eunice, and Sarah were met not with the usual bustle and warm familiarity of New Haven, but with a strange and unsettling quiet.

The town, typically alive with lighthearted greetings and neighborly exchanges, felt drawn in on itself—as though holding its breath. People who might have nodded or tipped their hats now turned their faces, their eyes shadowed with something between skepticism and reproach. It was clear that word had traveled faster than they had.

The group made their way through the town, feeling the weight of the locals' unspoken judgment. Whispers fluttered from doorways and windows like leaves disturbed by a chilling wind. It was evident that word had spread about the school's purpose, and it had not been received favorably.

As they approached the new building, a small group of residents had gathered outside, their judgmental murmurs deliberately loud enough to garner attention.

"A finishing school for girls, here?" one woman holding a basket of bread clucked disapprovingly.

"What's next, women in politics?" scoffed a man leaning against a post, his arms folded defiantly.

Eunice, ever the one to cut through hostility with her sharp wit, leaned in to whisper to Abigail, "Seems we're about as popular as a cat at a mouse convention."

Abigail offered a tight smile but remained undeterred. She addressed the small crowd with a calm, steady voice. "Good people of New Haven, this school is an institution of learning and growth. We aim to give young people the knowledge and skills they need to thrive in society."

A murmur ran through the crowd, a mix of curiosity and continued skepticism. Hannah and Sarah stood close, their excitement about the school now tempered by the reality of the town's reaction.

Despite the chilly reception, the four women continued past the sneering group, their heads held high. They passed through the school's gate and, though the murmurs and stares did not abate, they felt as though they were stepping into a world of their own making, where the future promised endless possibilities.

The facade of the schoolhouse exuded charm and elegance, with its neat brickwork and genteel proportions—a structure that suggested order, refinement, and purpose.

Just to the right of the door, a large wooden placard was neatly nailed to the brick, its surface darkly stained and smoothed to a fine finish. The name—The Willow Finishing School—was carefully engraved into the wood. Visible even from the street, each letter was filled with gold paint that caught the daylight in quiet, dignified brilliance.

The school was the culmination of ambition and vision. Yet as Abigail stood before it, flanked by her family, a noticeable sense of trepidation wove through the crisp New Haven air—a hush of uncertainty gilded just beneath the surface.

It had seemed a noble endeavor, a necessary stride toward enlightenment—a place where young women could be educated to the standards of their brothers. But as they observed the bustling street, an unspoken question hung between them: Would the community ever embrace such a revolutionary concept?

"It's unnatural, this," voiced a stern-faced matron, her words carrying weight as she passed the school's gate. "A woman's place is at the hearth, not the head of the table."

From the road behind them, voices rose—not loudly, but with the sharpness of stones flicked into still water.

"Mark my words, they'll have the girls reading Latin next—then what?"

"Next thing, she'll be calling their husbands to do her chores."

"A finishing school? More like a place to let Satan dilute a woman's place, making her unfit to raise a proper family."

Each biting comment seemed to cast a shadow longer than the sun could account for, and Abigail and her kin stood beneath it—a cloud stitched from tradition and fear.

With a spirit not easily doused by the torrents of narrow-mindedness, Sarah stared defiantly at the words on the placard. "I like it—kinda," she declared, her voice attempting a resolve beyond her years. But her eyes betrayed her pride. She caught sight of a young girl standing just beyond the gate, looking with a sort of longing at the gold lettering. The girl's mother began tugging her daughter away, whispering behind a gloved hand. There was urgency in the woman's posture—warning, almost panic—as though the words themselves carried contagion.

A flicker of doubt passed through Sarah like a chill. "Maybe it should just say The Willow," she murmured, eyes falling to the ground. "Let people figure out the rest for themselves?" It was a concession—a subtle retreat, a cautious nod to the noise swelling behind them.

Abigail's eyes met Sarah's, steady and searching. She saw the fear behind the suggestion, the instinct to protect rather than provoke. Her gaze drifted back to the sign, its engraved gold letters catching the light like a quiet bell ringing truth. "And what would that teach our students?" she asked softly. "That we must hide our purpose? That we should bend to ignorance rather than educate it?"

Sarah hesitated, torn between boldness and the urge to keep the peace. "Yes," she said at last, voice small but honest. "For now, at least. In the beginning. Until things... quiet down."

The wind tugged lightly at their coats. Somewhere behind them, another voice sneered: "Mark it—before long, they'll be giving sermons from the lectern."

But Abigail stood unmoved, her eyes fixed on the placard. "Let them whisper," she said. "We'll teach our girls to speak aloud."

Hannah stood beside them, her heart pulled between the romance of the idea and the hard reality pressing in. She thought of the old tales—of the sea, of pirates and adventurers who sailed into the unknown despite every warning. "Pirates did change their flags," she said thoughtfully. "When they wanted to lure unsuspecting prey into believing they were someone else."

Aunt Eunice, the most detached of them all, laid her hand upon the sign. "The Willow is strong because it bends with the wind but never breaks. Let this school—let this sign—be our Willow. We will bend beneath their words, but we will not break." She paused, then added, conceding Sarah's point, "They will learn soon enough that willow bark soothes pain only when given slowly and in the proper dose. But yes—ditch the 'Finishing School.' Let them discover the rest on their own. Their children are not compelled to attend at all."

Their bruised unity restored, the women turned toward the open doors of the schoolhouse as the murmurs outside swirled like fallen leaves. Within The Willow, there would be a different kind of whispering—pages turning, pens scratching, minds opening to a world hungry for knowledge that only a place like this could offer.

At Abigail's nod, they stepped inside, leaving the crowd's judgment where it belonged. In time, those voices would fade—not through force, but because they would be outnumbered by the confident voices of educated women, their wills as unyielding as the tree for which the school was named.

Hannah's earlier excitement—the handsome builder, the promise of something new—had dimmed as reality settled in, replaced by quiet contemplation of how the school would be received.

Aunt Eunice placed a steadying hand on Abigail's shoulder. "Change is like the ocean," she murmured. "Both balm and tempest. You never know which it will be until you set sail."

Abigail's gaze lingered on the carved sign—The Willow, its graceful boughs meant to suggest resilience. Now it seemed almost to taunt her. "Did we misjudge the winds of change?" she asked softly.

Sarah shook her head. "It's not education that chafes—it's who receives it. We knew it would be a battle, yet..." Her words faded as she glanced through the window at the disapproving faces beyond the glass.

Hannah watched, her romantic vision colliding with the weight of custom she had not fully reckoned with.

"It isn't just about reading and writing," Abigail said at last, resolve returning to her voice. "It's about giving women a voice—space to be heard, and the means to contribute. Perhaps this silence is only the stillness before the leap."

Aunt Eunice nodded. "This kind of change comes not with fanfare, but with whispers that grow louder over time. If women wait another three hundred years for permission, it will be because we chose silence over resolve."

A door creaked open, and a young housemaid peeked out with wide, curious eyes—a small flicker of the future they all hoped to protect.

"Good day," Hannah said gently. "Do you serve in this house?"

The girl shifted her weight and gave a wary glance before answering, her voice quick and clipped. "Aye, mistress—I sweep the floors an' lay the linens for Mr. MacCreedy, 'til he sees the work done."

"I see," Hannah replied, catching the builder's name with quiet satisfaction. "And do you find the work fair?"

The girl gave a half-shrug. "Far as I can tell, ma'am. Ain't for me to say what's fair, only to keep the dust down." She dipped a brief curtsy and ducked back toward the kitchen, saying, "Beg pardon—I've a broom to fetch."

Abigail stepped forward and sniffed, the weight of the moment upon her. "Let's not judge the day by the sunrise," she spoke with newfound determination, using her sister's euphemism. "The Willow may indeed bend, and does not break. We shall stand, and we shall see this through. For every girl who dreams of more, for every woman who is told she cannot, this is where we plant our feet and say, 'We can do it too.'"

The group's uncertainty began to dissolve, replaced by the familiar warmth of shared conviction. They knew the journey ahead would be fraught with challenges, but their vision for The Willow was clear and unwavering. It would be a sanctuary of learning, a cradle for the minds and spirits of women who would one day turn the tide of history—not with swords or conquests, but with words, wisdom, and an unrelenting thirst for knowledge.

As the day passed, the sun's final rays draped golden over the facade of the newly christened school. Hannah turned to her mother, inspecting the front porch after she and her sister had snooped out every nook and cranny the building had to offer. With a quirked eyebrow, a question danced in her eyes: "Who named the school The Willow?"

Abigail couldn't suppress the chuckle that bubbled forth, a fond note in her laughter as she remembered. "That was Hope's doing," she said, her smile deepening with the memory. "When she had her daughter, Ursula, out of wedlock, it was no small matter of gossip. To protect her child from cruel whispers and the stain of scandal, she couldn't use her maiden name, Yale. So, she took up the name Terwilliger—it's Dutch for Willow. It was her alias, her shield. And now, it's become our standard, our moniker—a symbol of resilience and protection."

"There you are?" shouted a stern man from the street, a look of concern splashed across his handsome face. Mr. MacCreedy stepped down from his carriage with the care and confidence of a man who knew his work would endure the test of time. But his usually bright eyes were downcast until they swept over the building's facade, noting the symmetry of the windows, the sturdy doors, and the neat lines of the brickwork and side boards that climbed toward the clear sky.

Approaching the group, his stride was sure but reverent, and the slight dusting of dirt on his coat testified to his hands-on approach. His presence commanded the space, a blend of ruggedness and refinement mirrored in the school's construction, yet something in his stance suggested a somber tone.

"Mrs. Huntington," he said, doffing his hat in respect as he reached her. "It is with great pride that I present The Willow to you. She's as sturdy as she is graceful. May she stand long and nurture many a bright mind."

"If they let us," she nodded to the passerbyers, who were leaving, shaking their heads.

"Oh, you get used to them. The ways of God can be unsettling to the best of us. They are afraid to admit to their vices."

Abigail's eyes reflected the school's windows, full of light and promise. "Mr. MacCreedy, your craftsmanship has exceeded our highest hopes. This school is not just a building but proof of what we value. Thanks to you, education, strength, beauty—it's all here, including ample space for my captain and crew to populate the shelves with our library of books."

Eunice nodded in agreement, her eyes tracing the lines of the building, "Yes, I'm honestly surprised at how well this turned out; I didn't expect someone with your experience to do such a good job."

MacCreedy stepped back, taking the outspoken woman in stride with a tip of his hat. "T'wasn't all my doing," he said with a modest grin. "Credit the generous budget—'tis what let me hire the finest craftsmen from every corner of the colony."

Eunice laughed, commanding the last words. "You know, for someone who often seems so simple, you certainly have a knack for complex work. It's quite a talent to hide that skill level under such an impressive exterior."

MacCreedy chuckled good-naturedly, tugging at the brim of his hat. "Well, ma'am, I'll take that as a compliment—of sorts. I'll be away for a spell, up in Wallingford, overseeing another sizable construction project. Fine folks there, but not half so generous as you." He glanced toward Abigail and then back to Eunice with a respectful nod. "If there's need of me, send word through the blacksmith in town. He'll see it gets to me quick enough."

At his words, Hannah's expression faltered. Her fingers worried the folds of her dress as she looked between the three adults. "Oh," she said softly, a faint note of disappointment threading her voice. "I'd hoped you might still be around when—well, never mind."

Sarah leaned towards Hannah, her voice a conspiratorial whisper that carried with it the thrill of shared secrets. "I see what you mean about his exterior," she murmured, her eyes following Mr. MacCreedy's every movement. "He's handsome indeed. And his work..." Her gaze returned to the school, appreciative. "It's as if he's crafted it with the same care he'd give to a cherished ship."

MacCreedy's kindly smile lingered a moment longer before he tipped his hat again. Yet as he turned to go, a flicker of worry crossed his face—something quiet, pressing, and seemingly unrelated to their conversation. His gaze drifted down the rutted road leading into town, brow furrowing as though weighing a thought he chose not to share.

Sarah grasped her sister's hand, seeing his visible strife, and asked, "Is he alright?"

Hannah only frowned, her cheeks flushed with a bloom that matched the climbing roses adorning the school's entrance. Worried that her flushed cheeks would give away her nerves, Hannah quickly changed the subject. "Have you seen Hope? Is she at the Orphanage now?"

MacCreedy's eyes conveyed the sobriety of the situation. "Haven't you heard?"

"No, we've just arrived," Hannah said with apprehension, sensing something was wrong.

"Yes, she's there. She wouldn't leave the children's side, especially not now. The sickness came on fast, spreading quicker than wildfire throughout the Orphanage and in some homes throughout the town."

MacCreedy's gaze dropped momentarily before meeting theirs again, his expression taut with concern. "It's not the pox, I heard."

"Oh dear," Eunice exclaimed.

"The children are sick—fever and swollen neck. Hope's been up night and day with them. Doctors are scarce, and she's doing all she can. I might have heard mention of the barking bull neck or the purple death?" His voice trailed off, and he shook his head. "She could use some help?"

Hannah's hand went to her mouth, a silent prayer escaping her lips. "Children have died?"

He nodded.

"We must go to her," Hannah said firmly, her voice laced with determination. "She needs us, and those children need all the help they can get."

Sarah nodded, her youthful face set with an adult resolve. "Let's not waste a moment," she said, already pulling up her dress and moving towards the road.

As they hurried to the carriage, Abigail's voice, usually calm and assured, was laced with an edge of fear. "Sarah, Hannah," she began, turning to her daughters with a fierce protectiveness in her eyes. "You must stay here at the school. I cannot—will not—allow you to go. If it is as bad as it seems, this sickness could be deadly. I will not have it take you from me."

"But Mother—" Sarah started to protest, her face a mask of indignation.

"No," Abigail cut her off, stopping mid-stride to face her daughters. "I have lost enough in my life; I will not gamble with you," she continued, her tone brooking no argument. "You are my most precious treasures, and I will keep you safe. I'd just as soon burn this building down with my own hands and leave this place never to return than to let you die from some horrid disease."

Hannah's expression softened, seeing the poorly concealed panic behind both her mother's and aunt's stern demeanor. She reached out, taking her mother's hands in her own. "We understand, Mother. We will stay safe," she said, her voice a soothing balm to Abigail's frayed nerves.

Abigail squeezed Hannah's hand before dropping it and continuing to the door of MacCreedy's carriage with her sister.

Sarah bit her lip and grasped Hannah's arm, drawing her sister in as though for comfort—but instead of a hug, she leaned close to whisper sharply, "What do you think?" Her eyes darted past the carriage and down the road in the direction of the Orphanage. The rebellious spark that had lit her expression moments before now faltered. The weight of their mother's voice—never turn from those in need—seemed to echo in both their minds.

Hannah's expression flickered, torn between caution and conviction. "She would tell us to help," she said softly, the words half confession, half challenge.

Sarah's grip tightened. "I know," she admitted, her voice trembling. "But what if this is different—more than we can see?"

The sisters stood still in the school's yard, their silhouettes framed against a gray, gathering sky, watching their mother—and then Eunice—climb into the carriage. Mr. MacCreedy stood a short distance off as they commondiered his ride, silent and rigid, helplessness written plainly across his face as if he wished to intervene but could not find the right to do so. Beyond the quiet neighborhood, the Orphanage lay somewhere out of sight—but not out of mind.

Though no sound carried that far, the thought of the sick children drifted between them like a chill in the autumn air, unsettling in its silence.

Around The Willow, the world remained deceptively calm: the soft rattle of dry leaves along the walk, the faint jingle of passing carriages. Fear pressed close, yet conscience refused to retreat, whispering of duties they could not ignore, no matter how far removed they stood from the suffering.

Finally, Sarah drew a breath and straightened, her tone bolder now. "Maybe we'll help… from a distance," she called out to her mother. "At least until we know what's needed. It's the least we can do."

The sisters exchanged a look—one of uneasy resolve—then turned their eyes back toward the town and Orphanage, hearts heavy with both love and hesitation.

The carriage creaked forward, its wheels biting into the road. The girls held their breath, the moment stretching thin as a thread.

Then—without warning—the carriage jolted to a halt.

The sudden stillness was louder than motion. The door swung open.

The girls hesitated, uncertain, the pause heavy with questions no one dared speak, until Mr. MacCreedy nodded toward the carriage. It was Sarah who moved first. She reached for her sister's hand, her grip firm despite the tremor in her fingers, and tugged her toward the open door.

The Willow rose behind them, silent and watchful—a sanctuary meant for the future, now standing guard over an uncertain present, waiting to learn whether any future at all would be claimed.

CHAPTER 15

Purple Death

THE CARRIAGE TRUNDLED ALONG the cobblestone path leading up to the orphanage, its wheels clattering with an urgency that matched the heavy thumping of Abigail's heart. The sight that met their eyes was far from the sanctuary of care and laughter one might expect of such an establishment. Instead, the Reverend emanated quiet desperation, his face a canvas of restrained panic as he paced before the large oak doors, the hem of his cassock catching the winter breeze.

A small knot of townsfolk had gathered outside the chapel gate, their breath fogging the morning air; their voices were hushed but urgent.

"They say it's a cough," whispered one woman, clutching her shawl close. "Sort throats, or worse."

The Reverend turned to them, drawing his hands together in gentle appeal. "Good folk, please—let us not stoke fear with speculation. The children are under watchful care, and their suffering is not without purpose in the Lord's design."

A murmur of doubt rose, but the Reverend held firm. "Yes, there is a terrible, deadly sickness inside. But not pestilence, not plague—only the cruel visitation of a winter ague. We have caretakers tending them, and Dr Snodgrass has prescribed tinctures and clean linens."

"But what of little Matthew?" asked an elderly woman, her voice thick with concern as she gazed upon the small frame wrapped in a stained white sheet outside the front door. Her hands trembled as she took a tentative step forward, her instinct to comfort and tend overcoming all hesitation.

The Reverend turned toward her, his expression solemn. "If your heart compels you, Mrs. Thorne, you may do the tending. The Lord knows he deserves a gentle hand to guide him home."

For a fleeting moment, compassion overpowered her fear. She clutched the folds of her shawl and began to move toward the child—until a firm hand landed on her shoulder. Her husband, jaw tight and eyes fixed on the small bundle, shook his head slowly.

"No," he said, his voice low and trembling with restrained dread. "You'll not go near that sickness."

The woman froze, torn between duty and obedience, her eyes lingering on the still form. The faint wind stirred the sheet, whispering like a last breath, while the townsfolk behind her turned away, unwilling to meet her gaze—or the boy's ashen semblance of innocence.

The Reverend's expression softened with sorrow. "He is in God's hands now. We pray, we tend, we wait. And you—" he gestured gently to the crowd—"you must pray as well and not spread unrest. These children need our strength, not our fear."

The orphanage door creaked open, and the young maid, Ursula, stepped out carrying a basin of linens stained with grim proof of what raged within. Abigail descended from the carriage, her heart sinking even as her resolve hardened.

"Reverend!" she called, recognizing him as they hurried forward. "Is there anything we can do to help?"

He turned, his face drawn tight with exhaustion. "Yes—thank God," he said, relief edged with sorrow. "Hope and Ursula are beyond their strength. They've been tending the sick without rest. If they don't step away, they'll fall to this hellish purple death as well."

Purple death. The words settled like a chill fog. From inside came the moans of children, raw and relentless, each sound a reminder of how thin the line between life and loss had become.

Then a voice cut through the din—Hope's, stripped of composure. "Mary, breathe… that's it, just one more breath," she urged, clinging to hope like a fraying rope.

Silence followed—brief, terrible—then a scream that hollowed the air.

"Mary!"

Abigail froze, the cry echoing in her chest. The risk no longer mattered. This was not a choice—it was a summons.

Before she could speak, Hannah and Sarah vanished through the doorway, propelled by instinct and courage. Abigail's breath caught, fear and pride tightening together in her chest.

She turned to Eunice, her voice steady despite the storm within. "Go. Ask the townsfolk for food, water—anything. We'll need it all. This night will test us."

Eunice nodded once and moved without hesitation.

Abigail faced the gathered crowd. "Will anyone help the children?" she asked, her voice sharp with urgency. "Will any of you join us?"

No one met her eyes; fear ruled them, nailing them in place as they hid behind bowed heads, mistaking prayer for courage and using it as their excuse for doing nothing.

With a tired shake of her head—part disappointment, part resolve—Abigail turned away from the murmuring mass and crossed the threshold. Behind her, the townsfolk lingered in sorrowful knots, eyes fixed on the orphanage doors yet bodies rooted by self-preservation. Compassion tugged at them, but fear prevailed, leaving them silent witnesses to a battle they dared not enter.

Hannah and Sarah had rushed inside without hesitation, their skirts brushing against the weathered doorframe, into the scent of sweat, sickness, and desperation clinging to the stale air. Their hearts pounded, and faces flushed—not from fear of disease, but from the urgency of those who had no one else to fight for them.

Moments later, when Abigail looked through the front door, she found her girls not standing still, scanning the space and assessing the situation, but in full action, caring for the nearest child's needs. The air within the orphanage was stifling—warm not with comfort, but with fever, with the cloying scent of sickness, of stale broth, soiled linens, and despair. The coughs of the ailing echoed down the halls, a heartbreaking chorus that would have sent many retreating. But not her daughters. They had rushed in before her, without protest or fear, sleeves already rolled, now baskets of fresh cloths already in hand. It had shaken her, at first—that they had moved so quickly, so decisively, while she had lingered, weighing risk against duty, fear against compassion.

Now, standing just within the doorway, Abigail's heart shifted. Dread melted slowly into pride, warm and unwelcome as tears. These girls, her girls, had become something more than she'd dared hope: brave, principled, and willing to act.

She straightened her back. Let the townsfolk murmur and wring their hands—her daughters were doing the Lord's work. And she would do no less.

Abigail allowed herself one final glance at the gathered onlookers, their faces shifting between shame and reluctant admiration. The Reverend stood casting a long shadow over the hesitant townsfolk, their boots rooted to the ground as though bound by invisible chains of self-preservation.

At the last moment, Abigail saw mothers clutching their children to their skirts—just as she longed to do with her own—and fathers gripping the brims of their hats with white-knuckled hands, unwilling to risk themselves for the forsaken, offering only their prayers instead.

The orphanage doors groaned shut, severing the unspoken barrier between those who acted and those who merely watched. Inside, fragile cries pierced the stillness, the frail voices of the abandoned echoing in the dimly lit hall. Abigail tightened her jaw. Hannah and Sarah turned to look at their mother, and the three silently agreed: There was no room for hesitation, no patience for cowardice.

Rolling up their sleeves, the three women moved with determined purpose, their presence a beacon of hope amidst the sea of suffering. But before they could begin, a familiar figure came rushing down the corridor—Hope, her apron streaked with sweat and stains, her brow damp and her voice tight with urgency.

"Thank God," she breathed, clutching Abigail's arm. "We need help—badly." Her eyes darted involuntarily to those children already lost, not yet wrapped in shrouds. "The air's thick in here. We've opened every window, but it's not enough."

"What can we do?" Abigail asked, scanning the grim hallway lined with makeshift bedding and purple faces, huffing, restless children.

Hope pointed to a half-toppled laundry basket near the corner hearth. "Those clothes need rinsing—Ursula has been trying to manage that along with everything else. If we can freshen the rooms, maybe it'll lift the miasma. Hannah, fetch lavender, rosemary, or whatever from the kitchen—we need to burn something pleasant to sweeten the air. And we need more broth heated—anything to keep them warm and sweating."

Abigail turned to her daughters. "Ursula is overworked. Heat the broth and water to steep the tea."

Hope gave a grateful nod, already moving toward the next room. "Good. Anything that clears their throats and drives the foul air out. God bless you, all of you."

Then, one by one, each caregiver knelt beside the fevered children at every free moment, pressing cool cloths to burning brows, whispering reassurances into ears too small to understand their sacrifice.

Abigail wrung out the linen cloth over a chipped basin of tepid water, the slow rivulets dripping from her fingers echoing the quiet desperation in the room. The feverish child before her stirred with a faint whimper, and she pressed the damp cloth gently to the girl's brow, her movements practiced but tender.

Her gaze lifted—not to the child, but to the opened windowpanes across the room, where light filtered through like the faint memory of a better day. She couldn't see the crowd from where she knelt, but in her mind's eye, they lingered—villagers and parishioners, shifting from foot to foot on the gravel path, their faces turned away in shame or held firm in stubborn judgment. Mothers clutching their children, shopkeepers pretending to pass by by chance. All of them, outside the threshold, untouched by the sickness but not by the fear.

They watched, Abigail imagined, as she and her daughters moved from cot to cot—outsiders by name, yet the only ones who had stepped inside.

A fresh cloth landed beside her—but she didn't look up at first. Instead, she soaked the new linen in the lukewarm water, twisted it tightly, and thought, 'It's not just these children who are ill.'

She exhaled sharply, her breath ragged with exhaustion and resolve. 'It's the town itself. It festers in fear and pride. Afraid of what it doesn't understand. Proud enough to turn its back on mercy.'

As she moved to the next cot, pressing her hand to another clammy cheek, she thought, 'Perhaps healing must begin with love before it can ever end in health.'

The scene inside the orphanage was weighed down by illness and despair. The children's cries and coughs created a cacophony that filled the room; each sound was a dagger to Abigail's heart. However, it was the sight of her daughters, with their sleeves rolled up, revealing Hannah's magical Iroquoian Thunderbird totem—meant to protect her from harm—and their expressions, grave yet determined as they assisted wherever they could, that cemented her resolve.

She moved through the room with purpose, her skirts sweeping the floor as she passed beds of stricken children. Her hands, though gentle, worked with the efficiency of one accustomed to crisis. The comfort she offered, the water she helped them sip, and the brows she soothed were all done with a mother's love—a love fierce enough to brave the storm of sickness.

The night stretched, hours blurring into an endless cycle of care and worry. Eunice returned, arms laden with supplies, her arrival a beacon of hope in the dim light of the orphanage. They worked tirelessly, united against the relentless tide of the purple death.

As dawn crept upon the weary world outside, inside the orphanage, a battle was being fought—not just for the children's lives but for the very soul of a community. Abigail, standing amidst the quieting sobs and the softening coughs, knew that this night would be etched in her memory forever, a night when the truest test of humanity was not just surviving but ensuring that others did as well.

The adults, steadfast in their vigil, became phantoms moving through the dim, candlelit room, their faces etched with fatigue, their bodies moving on nothing more than sheer will. In the rare moments of reprieve, they collapsed into uneasy rest, their dreams haunted by the echoes of the sick. Meals became afterthoughts, consumed mechanically to sustain their strength. The sickness that had befallen the children now crept insidiously among the caretakers, manifesting as ghostly shadows under their eyes and weariness in their bones. They frequently coughed discreetly into handkerchiefs, a grim chorus accompanying the recovery of their young charges.

As the children's fevered cheeks began to cool and their spirits rekindled with the gentle touch of health, a collective breath of cautious hope was drawn. The caregivers tended to their ailments in whispered solidarity, each coughing a reminder of the ordeal they faced. Muscle aches and the iron vise of headaches became common grievances, shared with knowing looks and half-hearted smiles.

The frigid embrace of chills came without warning, sending shivers cascading through them even as they huddled close to the fireplace for warmth. In the wake of the illness, the orphanage became a crucible of shared suffering and resilience, a witness to the human spirit's endurance.

When, at last, the tide of the disease ebbed, leaving behind the delicate bloom of recovery on the children's pallid faces, the caregivers allowed themselves a moment of quiet triumph. The worst had indeed passed, but it had left in its wake a sobriety that bound them all, a sincerity born from struggle and the profound relief that came with survival.

They had faced it head-on, standing among the sick, wiping the brows of fevered children, comforting those too weak to cry, and, when the time came, closing the eyes of those who would suffer no longer.

CHAPTER 16

THE SUN HAD BEGUN ITS descent, casting a golden haze over the quiet town as Abigail, wearied to her very soul, stepped outside the orphanage. The past days had been an endless cycle of care and worry, and as she looked around, she noted the absence of the once vigilant crowds. They had dissipated, just as the disease had through the bodies of those it claimed.

The orphanage door groaned as Abigail and her daughters stepped out into the cold morning light, their skirts heavy with the weight of labor and their faces lined with exhaustion. The stench of sickness clung to them, woven into their clothes, their skin, their very breath.

The town was silent.

The townsfolk had gone home to their own families, locking their doors, tending to their own, as though distance could shield them from grief. But for Abigail and her family, there was no home untouched by sorrow, no safe place to retreat to. They met the Reverend Morton standing alone, his hat in his hands, his face pale and drawn, the lines of his brow etched deep with sorrow and contemplation.

For a long moment, he said nothing. He watched them, his gaze drifting over Abigail, Eunice, and Hannah, taking in the weariness in their limbs, the grief they carried like a cloak, the quiet resolve that had not yet shattered despite the weight of death surrounding them.

Finally, he spoke, his voice low, reverent.

"I have always believed men and women are not the same, and now I know it to be true—because I have never seen a man do anything so brave as what you just did; myself included."

Abigail stared at him, surprised by the words, by the undeniable sincerity in his tone.

Eunice exhaled softly, her fingers still stained from the work they had done inside.

Hannah, who had fought back tears for hours, felt them sting her eyes anew, not from grief this time, but from the simple acknowledgment of what they survived—what no one else had dared to do.

Reverend Morton shook his head slightly, as if struggling with his own thoughts. "If I had a daughter," he continued, his voice breaking just slightly. "I would only hope that she could learn from the likes of you."

A breeze stirred, carrying the first scent of rain, but still, the town remained silent, as though it, too, was mourning the loss of those taken too soon.

Abigail took a slow breath, the weight of his words settling deep within her.

"We did only what was right," she said at last.

The Reverend nodded. "And yet, you were the only ones who did."

The words hung between them, a truth both painful and undeniable.

Then, without another word, he placed his hat back on his head, gave them one last look, and turned away, stepping into the empty church, leaving Abigail and her daughters standing in the wake of loss, courage, and the knowledge that they had done what others would not.

Within hours, word spread that a heavy toll had been exacted around the township: twenty-five souls lost, the innocence of childhood making up the majority, with three of the town's elders counted among them. Abigail's heart ached with the news, but her body screamed for rest, the kind of deep sleep that was as much about healing the mind as it was about resting the body. Hope had extended an invitation to her home while she and Ursula would stay at the orphanage, her voice insistent despite the fatigue that clung to every word. But Abigail could not bear the thought of imposing their exhaustion and lingering sickness onto another household. No, she decided; they would retreat to the sanctuary of The Willow.

The new school, with its untouched bedrooms, seemed the most suitable place to rest without risking further spread of the illness. A sense of belonging enveloped their tired spirits as they walked through the doors—so different from their arrival not long ago, though it already felt like weeks had passed, and memory had begun to blur. Back then, they were met with judgmental eyes and whispers upon entering The Willow.

Now, the streets were devoid of life, save for the rustling leaves that whispered the day's sorrow. It seemed as though the town itself was in mourning—its energy spent, its people withdrawn into the sanctity of their homes, bracing for the dawn of a new day.

The bedrooms of The Willow were a welcome sight, their pristine condition a balm to their weary bodies. There was a credible sense of solace within these walls that had been absent in the outside world. As Abigail and her family settled into the unfamiliar beds, they were enveloped by the quiet comfort of the schoolhouse. It was a profound, albeit exhausted, realization that despite the day's losses, they had each other, and within the safe embrace of The Willow, they could find respite and, in time, the strength to face whatever lay ahead.

The schoolhouse's silence was broken only by the occasional creak of settling wood and the soft stirring in the kitchen. Time had lost all meaning for the weary; it might have been hours or days since they had surrendered to the deep embrace of sleep, their bodies sprawled atop the covers, too exhausted to undress.

Eunice, the stalwart pillar amidst the turmoil, awoke first and quickly found sanctuary in the kitchen's routine. The clatter of pots and the aroma of brewing tea were a soothing anodyne as Abigail drifted down the stairs guided by the promise of a warm cup. Her sister's speculative comment about turning the school into a hotel tavern drew a weary smile from her lips.

"It certainly has the bones for it," Abigail murmured, accepting a cup of tea with grateful hands.

As if summoned by the sound of domestic life, Hannah appeared, the remnants of sleep and the weight of the past days etched beneath her eyes.

"Is Sarah still okay?" The concern in Abigail's voice was plain.

Hannah's response came with the hint of a smile, the humor not quite reaching her still-clouded eyes. "She's fine. I think she'll outlast us all in sleep." Her laughter was fragile, like the first thawing ice in spring, and it was met with sighs of relief from Eunice and Abigail.

Eunice said, "The young at heart see a puddle and think of the splash; the elderly see it and think of the rheumatism."

"Aunt Eunice, why do elderly women mention rheumatism so much?"

"Oh my, am I already so old that I'm repeating myself?"

"Don't worry," Hannah said, sipping her tea. "Your jokes are so funny; they're private parties in your mind that we're all curious about."

"Oh, my child, you've inherited my plaguing wit."

With a mock sternness that fooled no one, Abigail chided Hannah. "That is absolutely the last time I will allow myself to stop you from helping children.

What was I thinking?" But the spark in her eye and the gentle curve of her lips betrayed her true feelings. She was proud—proud of the courage her daughters had shown, proud of their compassion.

As they sat around the kitchen table, sipping tea and sharing silent companionship, they knew that the true test of The Willow and all it stood for was beginning.

Several days passed, a necessary respite that allowed for the recovery and gathering of strength after the ordeal at the orphanage. The gentle period was a silent confirmation of the resilience of those within The Willow's walls; the women tested the school's every provision—from the comfort of the bathtub and beds to the acoustics of the harpsichords and the functionality of the spacious kitchen.

Hope's arrival was timely, bringing with her the winds of progress. In the quiet corner of The Willow's small library, where the morning light filtered through stained glass, casting a kaleidoscope of colors across the polished floors, she and Abigail convened for a crucial meeting. The rafters tinged with the scent of old books and the promise of new beginnings.

Hope, her expression a blend of excitement and trepidation, held a sheaf of paper tightly in her hands. These were the culmination of countless hours of research, correspondence, and careful consideration. They were her proposed list of tutors for The Willow; each name was a potential key to unlocking the vast potential of their unique student body.

"Abigail," Hope began, her voice tinged with pride and caution. "I have followed through with our final list of tutors for The Willow. But I must confess, even after discounting my contributions to reading, writing, and arithmetic, in my zeal, I may have... well, slightly, ahem," she said, nervously clearing her still scratchy throat, "exceeded our initial budget."

Abigail, her curiosity piqued, took the list from Hope's outstretched hand. Her eyes glanced across the page, taking in the names and accompanying qualifications. Each tutor was more impressive than the last, experts in their fields, from navigation and cartography to science, business, and political diplomacy. It was a list that promised an education as adventurous and unconventional as the lives of the students they would be teaching.

A soft chuckle escaped Abigail's lips, her eyes sparkling with amusement and admiration. "Hope, this is remarkable. But you know, that's the trouble with budgets," she said, her voice warm and reassuring. "You never truly know how big to make them until you get exactly what you want."

Hope's shoulders relaxed, a relieved smile blooming on her face. "I just wanted the best for our girls," she admitted, "to give them opportunities that perhaps we never had."

Abigail placed a comforting hand on Hope's shoulder, her gaze firm and encouraging. "And you have done just that. These tutors, this curriculum—it's more than education. It's a chance for these young women to redefine themselves, to be more than just the daughters of colonists. They will be scholars, adventurers, leaders."

The two women stood together in the library, surrounded by the wisdom of ages, yet focused on the future.

As they left the library, the list of tutors in hand, there was a sense of accomplishment and anticipation. The Willow was on the brink of something extraordinary, a beacon of hope and possibility. And at its heart were women, united in their determination to turn the tides of fate and forge a new path for those who had for too long been adrift in the shadows of their gender.

However, the conversation took a more serious turn as Abigail outlined the logistics of classroom placements and the designated areas for practical skills demonstrations, such as salting and curing meats. She described in detail the meticulous plans for the vegetable garden and the large, heavy table—intended to serve both as an altar and a serving table—highlighting how each element was thoughtfully designed to meet the diverse needs of their future students. Altogether, it pointed toward a comprehensive and well-rounded educational experience.

In this atmosphere of planning and potential, Abigail broached the subject of Cotton Mather's involvement. The question about Mather brought a somber note to the conversation, bridging the gap between days past and the present moment. It was a delicate topic, touching on history and personal trials—especially considering Hope's intimate understanding of the late troubles of witchcraft delusions in Salem.

Abigail, gently touching a fresh sheet near the window, said, "I know the fever has passed for now, but I can't help but worry what comes next. Especially if we must rely on the likes of Reverend Mather." She paused, then added, "He was most definitely involved. His hands are not clean."

Hope nodded slowly, setting down the empty basin she'd been carrying. "We've all been touched by sickness, one kind or another. The Reverend Mather has had his time to heal, just like the rest of us."

She stepped closer, voice calm but firm. "These past days, we've done more than mend bodies. We've sat in the town's silence. We've watched guilt try to dress itself as survival. And, in the doing, we've learned who each of us is."

Abigail looked at her, saying nothing, but Hope went on.

"Mather is… complicated. But even a man whose mind was once clouded by darkness and who looked away might now see more clearly. I don't trust his every word, but I believe in second chances. And I believe we can use whatever hands are willing—so long as they're now clean."

She offered a small, knowing smile. "We didn't come this far to let pride slow us down, did we?"

With the passing days acting as a buffer, they could address such issues with a clear head, considering the future of The Willow and its students with hope and careful, yet elusive, deliberation on Abigail's part.

Abigail failed to unveil a detailed list of The Willow's inaugural cohort of students, which she had nearly completed in Manhattan just days before leaving, for fear there would be a few no-shows. On the ledger she carried, the names of families and their daughters were neatly inscribed, each accompanied by a checkmark indicating that their reservation fee had been tendered.

"There will be no more than a dozen students in total. A few are still being considered, as their families are suggesting a confirmation tour before finalizing their commitments," Abigail said. "But I am confident this establishment will withstand even the most meticulous examinations."

The room hummed with a sense of achievement, a testament to hard work on the cusp of fruition. However, a practical concern hovered in the air, which Abigail voiced with hesitation and necessity. "Hope, I realize we have never spoken of one very important factor. Will you be staying here consistently while school is in session?" she inquired. "There are a myriad responsibilities that come with the title of Headmistress," she said, squinting, always assuming she would stay in the ample-sized first-floor master quarters.

Hope considered the inquiry deeply, the weight of the role settling upon her. "And what of Ursula?" she asked.

"I believe your daughter's fate to be equally crucial in your decision-making as mine is to me," Abigail asserted. "The master quarters are lavishly sized for her, too," she reassured, a softness to her voice suggesting the forethought of such arrangements. Hope's brow furrowed in concentration.

"When the school opens its doors to our first pupils…" Hope began, but

Abigail cut her off.

"You mean when the real work will begin? Are you already worried about the never-ending barrage of whining spoiled girls?" Before Hope could answer, Abigail continued lightheartedly, "The students will be arriving for the year in a fortnight. However, it seems the school is already operational. Sarah and Hannah are its inaugural students."

Hope's gaze lingered on Abigail, her questions like leaves caught in a gentle swirling breeze. "And how do you feel about me teaching your daughters?" she asked, her voice steady yet tinged with curiosity.

Abigail's response came with a knowing smile, the age-old adage falling from her lips with unwavering conviction. "What is good for the goose is good for the gander," she declared. "How can I expect others to entrust their daughters to us if I do not place the same trust in this institution for my own?"

Her words held the kind of sturdy truth that comes from a bedrock of faith—not only in the concept of their enterprise but in its execution and the security it promised. It was the ultimate gesture of confidence, a personal endorsement that would no doubt resonate with potential patrons. The future of The Willow, it seemed, was as promising as the resolve shining in Abigail's eyes.

CHAPTER 17

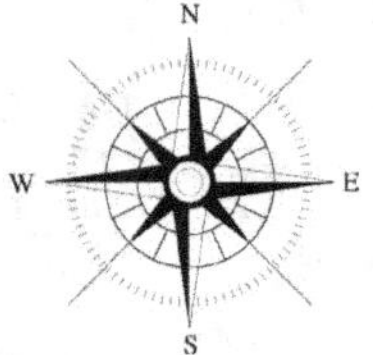

Meeting of Students, August, 1715

THE WILLOW WAS A HIVE OF ACTIVITY, tinged with the scent of excitement and the sounds of anticipation. Throughout the late morning, carriages and elegantly dressed couples arrived at the grand entrance of Willow Finishing School, where nervous glances and excited chatter filled the air as new beginnings awaited in this unfamiliar place.

Eleven young ladies of independent lineage from around the colonies, accompanied by their parents or guardians, gracefully glided across Willow's large central classroom that masqueraded as a reception hall and ballroom when need be. Their dresses rustled softly as they listened to the stately yet dignified duple meter tempo of the harpsichord, which usually accompanied the Pavane. Nervous laughter flitted between them like startled birds, rising in awkward bursts before settling into silence. Some girls clung to the sides of their mothers' skirts, others fidgeted with gloves or ribbons, casting furtive glances at their peers. A few attempted polite conversation, their voices tight and too formal, while others hummed softly to the music, eyes fixed on the polished floor as their feet shifted in uncertain rhythm.

In the corner of the grand room, set aside for preparations, stood Hannah and Sarah, along with bustling Eunice, who supervised the temporary staff hired from the church's congregation for the day's reception like a ship's quartermaster. All the students and parents were flushed with excitement, casting a mixture of downcast gazes and fleeting smiles as they moved to inspect the room architecture, library and especially the food and drink being laid out for everyone's consumption.

"I wonder who they will invite to that Ball?" Hannah said to her sister as she nervously rearranged the cookies and pastries around a flower display.

"Stop that. You're not going to distract my attention by mentioning the Ball," Sarah chided, brushing her sister's hand from the tray. "The kitchen staff has been arranging the hors d'oeuvres and pastries since noon, and the Ball is not until year's end—far too early to speculate about now."

"I know. I'm just covering up the empty spaces where I ate a few of these delicious cookies, that's all," Hannah laughed. "Anyhow, my dear sister, it is never too early to speculate. There will be male guests!"

"Me too," Sarah smiled cheerfully picking up a cookie, then looked at her sister with a mischievous glint in her eye while nibbling the edge. "Do you think the Headmistress might invite Mr. MacCreedy to the Ball?" She took her sister's hand and strolled across the spacious but crowded dance floor, her query an arrow aimed straight at her sister's bashful heart.

Hannah's cheeks bloomed a soft rose hue, betraying her emotions to the other girls standing apart with their parental escorts before she could muster a word. "I... I don't know," she stammered, her heart fluttering at the thought. "I wouldn't dare to ask her such a thing."

"But after all that has transpired, all that you and she have accomplished together, surely you could suggest it?" Sarah pressed, her brows arching in encouragement.

A sigh escaped Hannah, her gaze drifting toward the window as if she might find her courage there, but instead, her eyes fell upon a girl, the one she knew to be called Hirana, standing alone in the crowd. "The invitations will not be dispatched for months. What's the rush? Besides, who knows who I will fancy in that amount of time," she laughed softly, a hint of resignation in her voice. "If he were to be invited, there would inevitably be an odd man out. How would you feel if that happened to you?"

A playful spark lit in Sarah's eyes, refusing to allow her sister's spirits to wane. "Well, perhaps he might come of his own accord to ensure that his handiwork—the well-pump, perhaps—is working as expected?"

The idea brought a reluctant smile to Hannah's face, the notion not so far-fetched considering Mr. MacCreedy's dedication to his craft. "Perhaps," Hannah allowed herself to hope. The thought of Mr. MacCreedy's unexpected appearance at the Ball added a secret thrill to Hannah's steps, a silent wish in every beat of her dancing heart.

With a parting laugh, the sisters separated, Sarah rejoining Aunt Eunice in the kitchen. Hannah's attention, however, was drawn again to Hirana, who stood apart from the crowd. Her eyes reflected something deeper than the anxiousness Hannah had seen in all the other new students; this young woman's gaze conveyed a sense of being lost and lonely, like a minnow out of water amidst an opulent school of prized fish. She seemed vulnerable as if one misstep could throw her among their sharp teeth and voracious appetites, prowling the depths of the high society conversations around her.

At the head of the room on the grand staircase, Abigail, ever composed yet exuding warmth, stood beside the school's esteemed Headmistress, whose presence commanded respect and admiration. Hope, appearing as graceful authority, wore a deep emerald gown, her hair pinned meticulously in an intricate twist. Hannah spotted her mother and Hope on the stairs and moved swiftly to join them. Her mother gave her a pleasant smile but seemed intent on a quiet conversation with Hope, so Hannah turned to take in the scene before her. Her eyes widened with a hint of amusement as she observed the interactions, the subtle exchanges of glances, the polite laughter, and the careful choice of words each gave and received from strangers in high society. It was a promenade of social niceties that she was still learning the steps to. She'd fantasized, like she'd seen her mother do countless times before, that one day she too would navigate the room with an effortless elegance, her every gesture and word painting a picture of assurance and hospitality. She wanted to become the perfect hostess, with approachability but authoritative demeanor like her mother. She knew, in her element, her mother was the undisputed queen of her domain, and her confidence spoke of the promise of the exceptional education and learning opportunities that awaited the students of the Willow.

The classroom-turned-ballroom of *The Willow* school for girls shimmered in the golden glow of chandeliers, the candlelight flickering over polished oak tables adorned with silver platters of sugared fruits, fine cheeses, and delicate pastries. The scent of warm cider and fresh-baked bread wafted through the air as parents and daughters moved through the space, taking in the grandeur of the institution that promised to shape the next generation of well-bred young women.

Clusters of mothers in gowns of rich brocades and soft muslins conversed in hushed tones, some exchanging pleasantries, others peering keenly at their daughters' soon-to-be schoolmates.

Abigail surveyed the room, then subtly inclined her head toward a finely dressed woman and her bright-eyed daughter, whose long, curling locks were crowned with a striking blue ribbon.

Turning to Hope, she said, "Dorothy 'Goodyear' Whiting."

Hope's expression remained composed, though there was a flicker of recognition in her gaze. "We are lucky to have her," she murmured. "That is a name of high standards in these parts."

Abigail nodded in quiet agreement. "Indeed. Her lineage ties back to the governance of the New Haven Colony. Shall we make their acquaintance?"

Moving through the room with the elegance expected of women of their station, Abigail and Hope approached Mrs. Whiting, who straightened at their arrival, smoothing an invisible wrinkle from the bodice of her dove-gray gown. Dorothy, at her side, folded her hands neatly before her, though her eyes betrayed a barely contained curiosity.

"Mrs. Whiting," Abigail greeted warmly. "It is a pleasure to welcome you and your daughter to The Willow."

"The pleasure is ours, I assure you," Mrs. Whiting responded, inclining her head respectfully.

Hope studied the young girl before her, then focused on her mother. "Tell us, Mrs. Whiting—what do you hope this institution will provide for your daughter?"

Mrs. Whiting exhaled slowly as though choosing her words with great care before handing her daughter her teacup and saucer. She asked, "Dorothy, darling, would you be ever so kind as to fetch me one of those delicious-looking pastries and a mug of cider?" The girl forced a smile, curtsied to both women and shuffled her dress through the crowded room to the refreshment table where other girls had congregated to sample the sweets.

"Dorothy is a girl of fine breeding," Mrs. Whiting said. "She has a good temperament and a gentle spirit. But these things and her lineage have set her apart."

Hope arched a brow ever so slightly. "Set her apart?"

Mrs. Whiting nodded. "Her family name carries great weight in New Haven. Expectations follow her like a shadow, and it is a shadow she cannot seem to outrun. The young gentlemen—her peers—are hesitant in her presence, not out of disinterest but intimidation. Where she seeks companionship, she finds only distance."

Hope studied the girl standing behind the other girls, waiting for her turn at the pastries.

Mrs. Whiting continued, her voice softer now. "I do not wish for my daughter to feel burdened by her birthright. I wish for her to find confidence in herself, independent of her name. To be seen not as a legacy, but as a young woman with her own merit."

Hope was silent for a moment, then nodded. "The Willow is where young women cultivate grace, intellect, and self-possession. Here, she will learn what is expected of her and what she expects of herself."

Mrs. Whiting reached out and grasped Hope's hand, tears pooling in her pleading eyes. Her voice was quiet but unwavering. "That is what I want for her, Madam."

Hope's eyes softened at the sincerity. "Then I believe she will do well here, Miss Whiting."

Sensing a natural conclusion, Abigail smiled warmly and turned toward another mother standing nearby.

"Oh my," Hope said, her hand to her mouth and tipping her head to shield her words. "What, if ever, did you tell these families about this place?"

Her eyes then settled on the radiant beauty standing alone amongst the chatty girls. She couldn't help but notice that the girl's presence commanded attention, and her stand-offish nature towards the younger girls was apparent from the outset. "And who might that statuesque comeliness be there?"

With a knowing smile, she subtly inclined her head toward Margaret Van Hoorn, a woman of undeniable elegance dressed in a gown of deep sapphire blue embroidered with silver thread. She stood alone, watching her striking, beautiful daughter with an almost burdensome smile. Lena's golden hair fell in soft waves over her shoulders, her eyes downcast as though she wished to shrink into herself despite the vibrancy of her presence.

Abigail led Headmistress Hope Terwilliger toward the mother, her voice warm yet poised.

"Mrs. Van Hoorn," Abigail greeted. "Welcome to The Willow. It is an honor to have you among us."

Margaret Van Hoorn dipped her head in acknowledgment. "The honor is ours, Madam," she replied smoothly, though her voice carried the weight of unspoken concern.

Hope's keen eyes shifted between mother and daughter before settling upon Margaret. "Tell me, Mrs. Van Hoorn, what do you wish your daughter to gain from her time at The Willow?"

Margaret exhaled, her fingers tightening ever so slightly around the mug handle of her untouched cider. She glanced at Lena before speaking, her voice softer now.

"Lena has grown into womanhood far sooner than she wished to," she admitted. "Her beauty—though only one facet of who she is—has become both a blessing and a burden. It has drawn… attention, attention that she neither seeks nor welcomes."

Hope listened intently, nodding for her to continue.

"She hears the whispers," Margaret said, her expression tightening. "The warnings of women, the expectations of men. She is but fifteen, yet already she is made to feel as though the world demands something of her—something she does not yet understand, nor wishes to."

Hope noticed Lena's fingers curled around her long blonde hair comfortingly before turning her back to the chatty nearby girls.

Hope regarded the girl thoughtfully. "And how does this make you feel, Mrs. Van Hoorn?"

Margaret Van Hoorn hesitated, then lifted her eyes, strikingly blue and filled with quiet turmoil. "It makes me afraid," she admitted, her voice barely above a whisper. "Afraid of how they look at her. Afraid of what they expect of her. Afraid that no one will see her for who she is, only for what she appears to be."

A hush settled between them, the weight of her words tangible.

Margaret Van Hoorn's throat tightened as Lena returned to her mother's side.

"Lena, darling. I'd like to introduce you to your new Headmistress, Mrs. Terwilliger."

Lena smiled with bright eyes and deep dimples as she curtsied, saying , "How do you do, ma'am."

"You are such a lovely girl, but no. It is Miss. I am not married," Hope reluctantly offered while casting an eye between them to see if that fact caused any visual disturbances.

Margaret Van Hoorn reached toward her daughter's face and smoothed a stray curl behind her ear.

"Mother," the girl complained with dropped shoulders. "Why must you treat me like a child here, too?" the girl said with her lips pursed, before curtseying again, turning to leave towards the girls standing by the pastries.

"Lena was once a girl filled with curiosity and laughter," Margaret said wistfully. "Now, she withdraws. The joy of her youth dims beneath the weight of expectations she is not ready to shoulder."

Hope studied Lena from afar. The girl's expression was unreadable at first, but then something softened in her gaze.

"Mrs. Van Hoorn, let me assure you of one thing," Hope said firmly. "The Willow is not merely a place where young women learn refinement; it is a sanctuary where they learn to command their own narrative. Here, Lena will not be defined by others; she will be given the time and space to define herself."

Margaret swallowed a flicker of something—hope, perhaps—dancing behind her uncertainty.

"Your daughter is not alone in this struggle, Mrs. Van Hoorn," Hope continued. "Many young women will enter these halls burdened by the expectations of others. Our duty is to teach them to carry themselves with grace and strength and find their voice before the world decides to speak for them."

Margaret exhaled, her shoulders easing slightly. "That is all I could ever ask for," she murmured.

Hope inclined her head. "Then The Willow will be a fitting place for your daughter to find her footing."

Emboldened by the promise within Hope's words, she straightened just a little. "I do not wish my fear upon her any longer as well," she said quietly but with a growing determination. "And I was assured you are just the person we can trust to help."

Hope offered a small, approving smile. "Then I shall endeavor not to let you down."

"It's been a true pleasure, Mrs. Van Horne. Your daughter carries herself with such elegance," Abigail said warmly, offering a parting smile. With a graceful pivot, she turned back into the room, where small clusters of mothers and daughters lingered in cautious conversation, each pair subtly straightening or smiling in anticipation of the women's approach.

Hope stood, arms lightly folded, a trace of bewilderment in her expression. "I must say, you may have misrepresented me in your correspondence."

Abigail gave a soft laugh. "I did no such thing. I wrote that the headmistress of the Willow was intelligent, accomplished, and possessed of sound judgment—and you absolutely are." She said it with such confidence that Hope's cheeks brightened despite herself.

"Ha! Isn't it funny, then, that you implied I had suggested this whole undertaking?"

"Whatever do you mean?" Hope asked, her tone tight with a hint of animus. "I never suggested any such thing."

"But you did," Abigail replied with a knowing smile. "It was that remark you made about human nature. That was the seed. This may be the inaugural class at the Willow, and it is true you've never been headmistress before, but all I did was say aloud what people most wanted to hear—and they believed in you."

"But you twist words—"

"Into a circle of truths," Abigail said casually. "Or perceived truths—which, with your help, will circle back to the present truth of excellence."

Hope opened her mouth to protest, but the ambiguity left no clear point to challenge. Before she could compose a reply, Abigail had already turned, gliding toward who they should speak with next.

Abigail's sharp gaze drifted toward the edge of the room, where a young girl gripped her tea cup with two hands. Unlike the finely adorned daughters of the colony's elite, this girl had short-cropped hair and an air of restless energy about her. She shifted her weight impatiently, glancing toward the refreshment table as if longing for an excuse to escape the room's formalities.

Beside her stood a woman of quiet dignity, her dark silk gown modest yet fine. Abigail caught Hope's eye and discreetly gestured toward them.

"And there is the matter of someone near and dear to my heart—Sarah Bradley," she said, her voice holding an unusual softness.

Hope's scanning eyes flickered to the girl, then back to Abigail. "Sarah Bradley?" she repeated, noting the name.

Abigail nodded. "Yes. She didn't need any letter of application. I have been providing for her and her family's safekeeping all her life. I will continue to provide everything for her support."

Hope studied the young girl, sensing something unusual in Abigail's tone. "She has the same name as your daughter?"

Abigail's lips twitched with a wry smile. "Yes. Named after her mother, Sarah. My Sarah was born first, and it was an honor when their Sarah was born, but later, it became, well, confusing when discussing their child openly with my family." She half-laughed before adding, "We just call her 'Kidd' now, and I think she likes it."

Hope arched a brow. "Kidd? That seems detached."

The older woman standing beside Sarah—her mother—exchanged a glance with Abigail but said nothing.

Abigail sighed, lowering her voice. "Her needs, I fear, are based on anger. Her inability to express her feelings in a healthy manner leads her to destructive behavior and strained relationships. I fear, of late, she has been seeking the wrong company—somewhat reminiscent of you and our benefactor, Henry Avery."

Hope stiffened at the name. "Our benefactor? You say his name so casually!" Her face flushed for a moment. "Anyway," she said, regaining her composure, "what exactly is your relationship with Kidd's family?"

Abigail's expression darkened slightly. "Nothing. Just old friends of the family that are best kept secret."

Hope's voice lowered into a whisper. "Secret? Even from me? How do you expect me to know what to say or do without inadvertently eliciting more anger? I might end up pushing her away." She exhaled, then asked cautiously, "Or do I have to ask your daughters who this Sarah is to you?"

As if on cue, Abigail's own daughter, Sarah, crossed the room. Her presence was lighthearted and carefree, in stark contrast to the weighty conversations between the adults. She moved toward the refreshment table where Sarah Bradley stood and received a friendly punch in her arm in a welcoming gesture, eliciting childhood laughter, oblivious to their surroundings.

Abigail pursed her lips into a tight line before a feeling of resolution flickered in her eyes. "I must stress, with all importance, her identity shall remain anonymous."

Hope leaned in, nodding for Abigail to continue.

With a measured breath, Abigail whispered, "Her step-father is none other than Captain William—Kidd."

Hope's breath caught. Her fingers trembled slightly as she gripped the banister, and her eyes widened in shock. It took a moment for the weight of the revelation to settle in her mind. "Now her nickname 'The Kidd ' makes more sense. Does she know about his storied past?" she finally asked, her voice barely above a breath.

Abigail's expression darkened. "Only recently. When she found out about his colorful life, she changed. Her mother and I fear she will run off and do something unforgivable."

Hope's face grew pale, the confession striking a nerve she had long buried. When she finally spoke, her voice was hollow. "Like I did, laying with Benjamin… to have Ursula?"

The weight of her words lingered between them, unspoken truths passing in the silence.

For the first time in the evening, Hope Terwilliger was not merely the esteemed Headmistress of The Willow—she was a woman burdened by her past, standing before another woman who carried burdens of her own.

The candlelight flickered, casting long shadows upon the faces of the women who understood, perhaps better than anyone, the consequences of forbidden truths.

"Ah, here she is—the Kidd's mother Sarah." She nodded to Hope's new consideration for Sarah's nickname.

"Sarah!" Abigail said enthusiastically, reaching out to hold her hands and feigning a kiss on her cheek. "So happy you could make the trip. What have you been doing with yourself?"

With an unexpectedly gruff voice, Sarah replied, "Not getting married, if that's what you mean."

Hope's surprised expression framed the encounter in a somber mood, just as Sarah and Abigail burst into laughter at the Headmistress's reaction.

Abigail explained, "The aforementioned captain husband of hers was her third husband. Each of them wealthy."

Sarah nodded in agreement. "They were all wealthy men. But William, I think, was the only one I truly loved."

Hope's expression softened, and a small smile tugged at her lips as she said, "I completely understand. Men of the sea can be quite romantic."

"And other things," Sarah added with a big smile and raised eyebrows.

To change the subject, Hope cleared her throat and asked, "So, just to make it clear in my head, Sarah's surname, Bradley—"

"Is my maiden name," Sarah quickly responded. "Abigail and I wished to shield all my children from the ignorant scorn and ridicule cast upon them by the injustice placed upon my poor William's name."

With confusion still furrowing her brow, Hope pressed further. "But as only her stepfather, Captain William—"

"Let's not muddy the waters of the past," Abigail carefully cut off her train of thought, "and instead concentrate on the future—Kidd's future."

"Yes, about that. Don't you think her being called by that kindred nickname is problematic?"

"Ha!" Sarah laughed. "I think it is not only adorable but audacious, like a pirate. Besides, she likes it. I believe it gives her a connection to the only father she ever knew."

Hope nodded with acceptance as Abigail steered her away into the crowd.

Amidst the grandeur, Abigail and Hope stood together, focusing now on another delicate matter. Abigail glanced across the room before setting her gaze on a particular girl. She chose her next words carefully.

"There is something you should know about one of our new students,

Marie Allamby," she began, her tone serious but not unkind.

Hope, still absorbing the previous revelations of the evening, leaned forward. "Which one? Is there another problem? A pirate problem?"

Abigail shook her head. "Not a problem, per se, but a situation that requires our understanding and care." She subtly inclined her head toward a young woman sitting beside Hannah, the two girls sharing a moment of lighthearted laughter over a slice of pie.

Hope followed Abigail's gaze. The girl in question had a pleasant, delicate face, but there was a weight to her expression that didn't entirely fit, even in her laughter. Hope studied her carefully, noting she was the only student wearing sleeves that covered the full length of her arms despite the warmth of the hall. All the other girls and their mothers wore summery sleeves that ended in ruffles just below the elbow.

"She's different from the others, isn't she?" Hope observed.

Abigail nodded. "She is. Marie is not simply a young lady of good family sent here for refinement—she is already a wife and a mother."

Hope's eyes widened slightly. "Married? But she's so young. How...?"

Abigail exhaled. "Her parents arranged a match with Stede Bonnet, a wealthy planter from Barbados. He owns the Upton Plantation in St. Michael Parish."

Hope absorbed the information, but her expression was unreadable. "And where is he now?"

"Rarely at home," Abigail answered frankly. "Bonnet is often away, tending to business and his gallivanting ventures, leaving Marie alone for extended periods."

Hope's gaze returned to Marie, noting the fullness of her figure and the way she indulged in her pie with absentminded satisfaction.

"She's lonely," Hope murmured.

"More than that," Abigail replied gently. "She's miserable. She's showing signs of melancholy—perhaps worse. And those sleeves?" She gave Hope a meaningful look. "She has been harming herself, using it as a means to manipulate her parents."

Hope's face darkened with concern. "Poor child," she murmured. "That explains the sadness in her eyes."

Abigail sighed, nodding toward the dessert on Marie's plate. "And the need to fill her emptiness with pie."

Hope's brows furrowed. "She's not with child again?" she asked hesitantly.

Abigail tilted her head slightly. "That, I do not know. Her children—if they are still in Barbados—are being cared for in some capacity, but her parents are quite secretive. They came to Manhattan recently, handling some investments I arranged for them. That's when Hannah and Sarah met Marie."

Hope listened intently.

Abigail continued, "They saw how she was struggling—how isolated she felt—and invited her to come here with them. Her parents, eager for any diversion that might stabilize her, agreed. They have paid generously for her stay, though I suspect they see it more as a temporary respite than a true investment in her future."

Hope sighed, her fingers grazing the carved back of a chair as she considered the implications. "So, this may not be a permanent arrangement?"

"Possibly not," Abigail conceded. "But whether she stays a year or a few months, I believe she will benefit from the environment here. The Willow is not just a place of learning—it is a place to build strength. If she feels she belongs to something, even if only for a short time, this could even be a place of healing."

Hope nodded, her gaze settling once more on Marie, whose laughter had momentarily faded into quiet contemplation as she picked at the last crumbs of her pie.

"Then we shall do our utmost to provide her with the care and companionship she needs," Hope said firmly. "She must feel part of our community, not just a visitor passing through."

Abigail smiled, relief flickering in her expression. "That's precisely why I brought her here, Hope. If anyone can provide a nurturing environment for a young woman like Marie, it is you and The Willow."

Hope gave a solemn nod. "Then it is settled. We shall not let her fade into despair."

Their eyes met, a silent agreement passing between them—one of duty, care, and the quiet resolve to ensure that every girl under their roof found her footing in the world, no matter how uncertain her path.

Abigail and Hope stood at the periphery, taking in the room's energy as their discussion turned to another delicate case.

"Mary Dongan Nugent," Abigail said and exhaled deeply, scanning the room with a wry expression. Abigail's eyes fixed on the girl in question like a cat stalking its prey and began moving swiftly toward her.

"And Mary's mother? Which may she be?" Hope asked, being led through the pageantry, seeing there was no adult next to the young girl.

"It is Mary's aunt who brought her here today," Abigail replied with no further explanation. Several steps before reaching Mary, she surprised Hope by stopping abruptly next to a woman Hope hadn't noticed before.

"Hello, Bridget," Abigail said warmly as Hope looked on. The woman's posture was elegant but subtly defensive; Mary's Aunt carried herself with the poise of noble blood, yet something simmering beneath the surface—a tension, a quiet but unmistakable sense of grievance.

Hope tilted her head slightly, already sensing the complexity of what was to come.

Abigail clasped her hands before her and spoke evenly. "Hope, this is Bridget Nugent. Her niece, Mary, is the daughter of Colonel Thomas Dongan, the 2nd Earl of Limerick, and the former Governor of New York Colony."

Hope's brows lifted slightly in recognition of the name.

Abigail paused, watching Hope's reaction, before continuing.

"Bridget, it is so nice for you to escort your niece here today," Abigail said.

"Well, I couldn't very well have her travel alone, now could I?"

"Of course not. How are things in Albany? You haven't run into my wayward husband, have you?"

"Ah," she said with hesitation. "Yes, I have seen Edward occasionally," she acknowledged with a knowing nod. Then, turning her attention to Mary, she added, "Unfortunately, her father could not make it. His acknowledgment of her has never been made official. She has not been granted the rights or privileges her cousins enjoy, which has weighed heavily on her."

Hope's lips pressed into a thin line. "A child of noble lineage cast aside? That is a cruel fate indeed."

Bridget nodded. "And an infuriating one, from her perspective. She has spent her young life watching others live in the position she believes should rightfully be hers. It has fostered in her a deep sense of injustice and—dare I say—a measure of jealousy toward those cousins who bear the Dongan name with full honor."

Hope observed Mary as she spoke with another girl. Her chin tilted at an imperceptible angle, suggesting an unspoken expectation of deference.

"So, she struggles with resentment?" Hope asked, her keen eyes flickering with interest.

"She struggles with identity," Abigail corrected gently. "She was raised with the knowledge of her heritage but without its benefits. She is caught between two worlds—recognized just enough to be aware of what she lacks, but never enough to claim her place among them."

Hope folded her arms, mulling over the implications, and asked, "And what do you hope for her here?"

Bridget's voice softened. "As her Aunt, I hope The Willow will provide Mary with the support and guidance she needs to overcome her resentment. I fear if this jealousy festers, it will harden into something that could shape her future in ways that are... unbecoming."

Hope inhaled deeply, glancing toward Mary again, then back to Abigail. "You mean spiteful?"

Bridget hesitated before nodding. "Or worse, vindictive. A young woman of her intelligence, without access to wealth and social standing—however limited—could find ways to make her displeasure known in ways that would serve neither her nor her family's well being. I feel The Willow is her chance to learn that she is more than the shadow of her father's name. Here, she can become someone of worth in her own right."

"Ms. Nugent, are you married?" Hope asked, noting her name wasn't the same as her brother's.

"Never. He is my step-brother — different fathers. I adopted Mary and gave her a place to live," she said curtly. She turned her head, making it clear she would be offering no further explanation.

Hope bowed, saying upon their departure, "We will endeavor to meet all your expectations and look forward to teaching and nurturing your niece over the school year."

Hope and Abigail quietly stepped away from the gathering, their skirts brushing softly along the polished floor as they slipped toward the shadows of an alcove near the staircase.

With a glance to ensure they were momentarily out of earshot, Hope leaned in, her voice hushed but urgent. "I had no idea when I first agreed to your lofty scheme that I'd be swept into such an upbringing. From pirates to governors—what will be next, I fear to ask," she harkened, almost out of breath.

The soft glow of two large candelabra chandeliers illuminated the grand dining hall. Their warm light cast gentle shadows on their surroundings. The flickering flames created a serene ambiance, contrasting the weight of the conversation that was about to unfold.

Abigail, always the epitome of composed authority, turned to Hope with a thoughtful expression, approaching her once more with a way out of her commitment. "Hope, we are at a pivotal point in the future of this establishment," she began, her voice steady but hinting at something more profound. "Do you still wish to continue as the headmistress of this girls' finishing school, or are your fears surmounting into an unwillingness to go on? Should we reconsider our plans and perhaps repurpose the building as an inn for wayward travelers?"

The directness of the question took her aback, her eyes widening in surprise. She had always known Abigail to be a shrewd businesswoman, but this sudden turning point in their conversation left her momentarily speechless. Collecting herself, she realized the gravity of the decision being placed before her.

"Of course, Abigail," she replied, her voice firm but respectful. "I still want to be the Headmistress. This school is more than just a building to me; it's a place where young minds are shaped and futures are built."

Abigail's gaze remained steady, measuring Hope's resolve. "Very well," she said, nodding slightly.

"And who else do you have on your ominous list of needy students?" Hope prompted her to continue without reservation. She allowed herself a small, relieved smile, appreciating Abigail's unique blend of sharp wit and undeniable authority.

"There are a few more young ladies who could benefit from our guidance," Abigail said, returning to her ream of parchment for the next student. "Each has potential, though their circumstances are quite varied."

The banquet hall's candlelit glow flickered across the polished floors, casting dancing shadows on the walls as the evening progressed. The room hummed with the quiet elegance of conversation, the occasional clink of silver spoons against porcelain teacups, and the careful laughter of young ladies adjusting to the unfamiliar luxury of their new home.

Abigail turned slightly toward Hope, noting the earnestness in her expression.

"One of my many client relationships I feel obligated to help," Abigail admitted, her voice softer than before. "Sarah Marble must have heard about The Willow from someone—I don't know who, and I thought it best not to ask."

Hope's lips pressed into a thin line, waiting for further explanation.

Abigail sighed, shifting the parchment to the bottom of the stack before she continued. "Let it be said, they have the funds needed for her education and stay."

Hope nodded in acknowledgment but said nothing, sensing pirated charity as a source of creative accounting.

Abigail exhaled slowly. "However," she added cautiously, "she may become a flight risk. She's in love with a man of ill-repute—a pickpocket. Young love has a way of sprouting wings in the heaviest of showers, hoping for the day to turn fair once landing in the arms of another."

Hope's expression darkened, and she clasped her hands before her. "Let's hope not," she said firmly. "I do not want to set a precedent or find myself in the unenviable position of explaining a student's disappearance to the other parents."

Abigail tilted her head slightly, scanning the room, her eyes moving past clusters of young ladies and their mothers before settling on Eliza Marble.

The girl sat at the far end of the hall, her posture stiff, her gaze distant. Though constructed of fine quality, her gown was simpler than those of the other students, as if she sought neither attention nor approval. Even as other young women were beginning to engage one another in polite conversation, Eliza remained withdrawn, absently running her fingers along the rim of her untouched teacup.

Abigail subtly pointed her out. "There. At the table near the window."

Hope followed Abigail's gaze, studying the girl. "She carries herself as though she expects rejection."

"She does," Abigail confirmed. "Her birth was... complicated. She has lived under the weight of others' judgment, and I fear she sees herself as less than she is because of it."

Hope's sharp eyes remained fixed on Eliza. "And this young man she associates with—the pickpocket?"

Abigail gave a small, knowing sigh. "I think the less said about him, the better. She clings to him for the wrong reasons—seeking belonging in all the wrong places. He is not a man of promise. Just a boy who lives by his wits, feeding off the vulnerability of those who think they need him."

Hope pursed her lips. "We must tread carefully, then."

Abigail nodded. "Indeed. She will need encouragement but not pity. She will run if she feels this school is just another place where she is measured and found lacking."

Hope lifted her chin slightly, already forming a strategy. "Then we must make her believe that she belongs here—not because we allow her to, but because she is worthy of it."

Abigail smiled, a flicker of admiration in her eyes. "That is precisely why I trust The Willow in your hands, Hope."

Hope allowed herself the smallest of smiles before straightening her posture. "I will keep my eyes on her activities," she said, her voice laced with quiet determination.

Abigail's gaze returned to Eliza. She watched as the girl finally lifted her teacup, sipping hesitantly, as if unsure whether she had the right to take part in the comfort it offered.

"Let us hope," Abigail murmured, "that she learns she is deserving of far more than she believes."

And with that, the two women turned back toward the hall, ever watchful, ever mindful, as The Willow Finishing School hosted its lost and wandering souls.

Hope was silent for a long moment before she finally said, "Had I known what your grand idea would entail, I might have asked a few more questions. Now I can only wonder—who on earth is coming next?"

Abigail allowed herself a small smirk of sarcasm. "Perhaps we shall find the daughter of a king on our doorstep?"

Hope huffed, shaking her head. "The way things are going, I wouldn't be surprised."

The two women stood in quiet contemplation, watching the girls mingle in the warm candlelight. For all its elegance, the room was filled with broken, unspoken stories—each girl carrying her burdens, past, and uncertainties about what lay ahead.

Then, with a wry smile, Hope asked, "And who else do you have on your ominous list of needy students?"

Abigail chuckled, shaking her head. "Oh, you have no idea."

And with that, they turned back toward the room, ready to continue shaping the destinies of the young women entrusted to them.

Abigail smirked, guiding Hope toward a stately woman dressed in an elegant but subdued gown of Prussian blue. Her face bore the soft lines of a woman accustomed to privilege and burden, her composure betraying just the slightest undercurrent of concern. Beside her stood her daughter, a striking young girl whose auburn curls framed a delicate but uncertain face.

Abigail greeted her with the familiarity of old friends, placing a hand lightly on her arm. "Waite Carr, it's been far too long."

Waite gave a warm, if slightly strained, smile. "Indeed, it has, Abigail. But how wonderful it is to see you and The Willow flourishing. You've outdone yourself again."

"May I introduce you and Patience to the Headmistress?" Abigail asked with her hand outstretched.

Hope inclined her head politely. "Mrs. Carr, it is a pleasure to welcome you and your daughter, Patience, to our school. You are seeking a transition for your daughter or is it simply a scholarly venture?"

Waite's expression faltered just slightly before she regained her composure. She glanced at Patience, who stood with her hands clasped before her, but her gaze drifted elsewhere as if attempting to disappear into the bustling hall's background.

"Yes," Waite admitted, taking her arm to walk away from her daughter's ears, choosing her words carefully. "Patience has struggled since her last sibling was married and left home. The house has been too quiet, and with the passing of her Grandfather Caleb... well, it has only heightened her sense of loneliness."

Hope listened intently, nodding for her to continue.

Waite's eyes darkened slightly. "Caleb's name still lingers in conversations, even after all these years. Some speak of his business dealings with admiration, others with whispered caution. And Patience—" she hesitated, glancing at her daughter before continuing, "Patience has been caught in the shadow of that legacy. Having two Grandfathers being Governors of Rhode Island has made her question her place, worth, and goodness."

"Two?" Hope asked while studying Patience, who was now pretending to inspect the delicate china teacups near the serving table.

"Oh yes, my goodness. You would not know. Patience is a cousin-by-affinity to another former Governor of Rhode Island, Nicholas Easton—connected through my side of the family, the Stanton side."

"Does she believe herself tainted by her grandfather's reputations?" Hope asked, already recovering from the quiet shock of realizing her new student was kin to such infamous figures.

Waite exhaled slowly. "I don't think she knows what to believe. She has always been a kind and gentle girl, but I fear the young gentlemen's talk around her has made her question herself in ways no child should. And in that doubt, she has begun to withdraw, as if she must prove something to the world before daring to take up space within it."

Abigail glanced at Patience, then back to Waite. "And is she afraid? Or merely uncertain?"

Waite's lips pressed together, and for a moment, she seemed almost reluctant to answer. "She is lonely," she said at last. "Loneliness can be just as dangerous as fear if left unchecked. It makes one reach for anything that might fill the space."

Hope let out a soft hum of understanding. "Then she needs to be given space to fill on her terms. A place where she is not judged for a name but for her own merits."

Waite nodded, relief flickering in her eyes. "That is why I brought her here. The Willow is the only place I could think of where she might truly have the chance to become her own person—without the weight of our past defining her future."

Hope's gaze returned to Patience as they moved to rejoin the solemn girl. "Then we shall see to it that she finds her footing. No one should feel they are bound by the deeds of those who came before them."

Waite touched Patience's arm lightly as they strolled near, drawing her attention. "Patience, dear, why don't you introduce yourself to Headmistress Terwilliger?"

Patience hesitated for only a fraction of a second before turning to Hope and dipping into a graceful but reserved curtsy. "It is a pleasure to make your acquaintance, Madam," she said softly.

Hope gave her a small but approving smile. "Likewise, Miss Carr. I look forward to knowing you better."

Abigail, satisfied that the conversation had reached a natural close, turned to Waite once more. "You've made the right decision," she assured her old friend. "Patience will be in good hands."

Waite squeezed her hand gently. "Thank you, Abigail. For everything."

Hope and Abigail stepped away as the conversation ended, watching Patience tentatively approach a small group of girls, her expression unreadable.

"She will need guidance," Hope murmured.

Abigail nodded. "And patience. She is more than the sum of her family's past, but she must come to see that for herself."

Hope didn't miss the unintended pun; her expression softened into a knowing smile. "Then we shall see to it that she does."

With that, they moved on, ready to welcome the next girl into the folds of The Willow, where pasts were left at the door and futures would be shaped anew.

Around the room, clusters of young ladies stood in quiet conversation, some cautiously forming alliances, others asserting their presence more confidently. The atmosphere was filled with the hum of polite discourse, punctuated by occasional laughter and the rustling of fine silk skirts.

Abigail and Hope stood near the edge of the hall, scanning the gathered students as their discussion turned to their next pupil.

Abigail found the eyes of a woman who had finished her cider and placed the mug on a nearby table. As if wrapped in a warning, Abigail said, "I am afraid the next student will be a handful, Gulielma Maria Penn.

Hope gave a soft, disbelieving laugh, shaking her head. "A case of a spoiled child. Letting her do chores around the house would do her more good than sending her here."

Abigail smirked, "Indeed, but that is not the Penn way."

Hope arched a brow. "Penn? As in William Penn? Surely not."

Abigail sighed, turning her gaze toward where Gulielma Maria was standing near the fireplace with an accusatory finger pointed at one of the other girls. Gulielma Maria's posture was unmistakably poised, and her eyes keenly assessed those around her as though measuring them by an invisible standard.

"No, not the founder's daughter," Abigail clarified. "But his granddaughter, named after her grandmother."

Hope folded her arms, watching as Gulielma Maria adjusted the lace trim on her sleeve with an air of unconcerned confidence. Even from a distance, it was evident that she carried herself as someone accustomed to admiration—if not command. Having caught the edge of others' conversation, her sudden laughter rang out across the hall.

"You can wear one of my dresses the next time we have a social event," her voice was condescending.

Abigail's sharp gaze immediately followed who she was addressing—the plainly dressed Eliza Marble, whose attire, though clean, was simpler than the extravagant fabrics of some of the wealthier students.

Hope pursed her lips. "And that would be this girl's problem."

Abigail sighed, nodding toward the impertinent student. "That would be Gulielma Maria."

Hope exhaled slowly, observing the well-placed and downtrodden. The carefully reared daughters of society and the outcasted, now entrusted to her care. Their names were whispered in drawing rooms and courtly circles, their family ties woven into the fabric of colonial power and wealth and others condemned and scorned for not paying their taxes. Yet here they were, gathered beneath her roof, expecting refinement, education—and, in some cases, redemption.

She opened her mouth to speak, but nothing but a whisper came out. "What will I say to them? What do I dare say to them?"

Abigail placed a steadying hand on her shoulder. "Nurture them. Treat them as if they were your daughters."

Hope turned her head slightly, her lips pressing together in thought. "You mean get the switch after their hind legs if they cross me?"

Abigail laughed, shaking her head. "Maybe not that much nurturing."

She let out a sigh of satisfaction.

"Now, shall we?" Abigail asked, giving Hope a knowing look.

"Wait," Hope said, raising her hand to grasp Abigail's arm. "Haven't you forgotten someone? There," she pointed. "Or is this just one of the girl's sisters?"

Abigail nodded and turned with a sneaking look to say, "Hirana. She's another—ah—"

"Pirate's daughter?" Hope asked.

Abigail sighed. "Her mother has recently died, and her father is never around. It was my sloop's captain, Holloway, who suggested she come. It's on a probationary appointment. I wanted to wait until later to tell you so I could see how she blended in with the rest of the girls."

Then, with another sigh, Abigail suggested, "Time to address the students?"

Hope straightened her shoulders, inhaled deeply, and nodded. "Yes. It's time to meet our class."

And with that, the two women stepped forward and rose halfway up the grand staircase, ready to mold the future of the young women who would, in time, shape the world around them.

CHAPTER 18

The Welcome, August, 1715

HOPE AND ABIGAIL HAD ASCENDED halfway up the grand stairway, the imported mahogany bannister gleaming beneath their fingertips, when Abigail paused and turned with deliberate grace.

"I thought it best," she said quietly to Hope, "before we meet and greet the rest, that I make a proper introduction. An official one."

Hope narrowed her eyes slightly, suspicion tempered by curiosity. "Official, is it?" she murmured, her lips curling in a half-smile. She folded her arms as Abigail raised her hands and clapped twice, sharply. The sound echoed through the main hall, crisp and commanding, and drew the attention of every girl and parent milling about below.

The murmurs died down. Skirts were adjusted. Postures straightened. And Abigail, standing a step above them all, let her voice ring clear:

"Ladies," she began, her tone both warm and commanding, "it is with immense pleasure and pride that I stand before you today at The Willow."

A hush fell. Even the creak of the floorboards seemed to still.

"We gather here in the spirit of education and the pursuit of personal growth and mutual understanding. This place is not merely a school, but a sanctuary—where minds may open, voices may rise, and each of you may discover not just knowledge, but the strength to shape your future."

She paused, letting the words settle. Hope, feeling the eyes of every girl fixed on her, didn't lean for comfort—she gripped the carved banister so tightly her knuckles blanched. Her shoulders tensed, her jaw locked, and for a moment, it felt as though she might turn and flee back down the stairs. But she held firm, taking in the sea of youthful faces now looking to her for guidance—each one a fragile ambition, or perhaps each one searching for a chink in her armor, a fault line beneath the surface, a secret waiting to unravel, or a weakness poised to be tested. The sudden, silent understanding of what she had agreed to—a house full of lives to mold, protect, and discipline—settled into her bones like the first cold snap of winter.

"We come from different corners of the world, some of us scarred by hardship, others gifted with privilege—but here, those things do not divide us. At The Willow, we are sisters in learning, stewards of reason, and keepers of each other's stories."

There was a beat of silence before a single clap broke the stillness, followed by another, then a few more, until the stairwell trembled with applause.

Abigail smiled faintly and bowed her head before continuing, "I am honored to introduce the esteemed Headmistress of The Willow, Miss Hope Merryweather Terwilliger."

Everyone softly clapped.

"Under her guidance, this institution will blossom into a haven of learning, character building, and cultural enrichment. Ms. Terwilliger's dedication to your development is unwavering, and her approach to education is both innovative and deeply respectful of the traditions that shape us.

Please join me in welcoming Headmistress Terwilliger."

All the girls politely clapped again, making a soft, muffled sound with their gloved hands, as Hope smiled, hoping she had remembered her prepared speech. Then, when everyone stopped to listen, she said, "Thank you, Mrs. Huntington, for your kind introduction, and a warm welcome to each of you to The Willow."

Gulielma Maria, standing nearby, laughed out under her breath loud enough for the Headmistress to hear, "Mrs. Huntington? Is she daft? She is Abigail Spragg."

Hope continued, cheeks flushed, side-glancing at the woman standing next to her. "I am delighted to see such bright and eager faces ready to embark on this journey of learning and self-discovery.

"If you have any concerns or needs regarding your accommodations, please do not hesitate to let us know. We aim to ensure that your stay here is as comfortable and conducive to learning as possible."

Gulielma Maria shouted out, pointing to a list posted on the wall. "I've got one. Why do I have to share a room with someone from Boston?" This made her mother bristle with embarrassment, and the other girls gasped with shock at her impertinence.

"That's alright. I don't mind," Eliza said. "I'm sure she probably snores like my ma," causing everyone to laugh. Then she added, "Because she looks like my grandma."

Hope, not wanting to encourage this kind of discourse, continued speaking: "Tomorrow, we will begin our lessons with housekeeping—an essential skill that lays the foundation for discipline and attention to detail. This will be followed by lessons in table manners, a crucial aspect of social etiquette."

Gulielma Maria shouted out another protest, "We are not going to learn how to eat lobsters like Bostonians with our fingers?" causing Eliza to push her on the shoulder.

Hope continued, "Once we are all aligned in these fundamental areas of etiquette, our curriculum will delve into more challenging subjects. Rest assured, each lesson is designed to stretch your abilities and encourage you to think critically and creatively."

"You mean keeping your hands to yourself," Gulielma Maria said, sneering at her roommate. "I think she bruised my arm."

"Gulielma Maria? If you haven't noticed, we have a much larger corner room you might enjoy. I call it the Governor's suite," the Headmistress recommended.

"Yes, of course. My own larger room would be appropriate for someone of my station," causing the others to gasp, including the girl's own mother.

"My apologies," Hope said with a bow. "But you misunderstand. The larger corner room houses not just one student, but three. Like the three branches of government: The Monarch, Parliament, and Common Law Courts. Ah, we will be learning about all of those in our Elements of Civil Governance classes."

"We all know which one she'd like to be," snickered Eliza.

"Three girls in one room? I don't care how big it is, I shall not have it," Gulielma Maria responded. She looked imploringly at her mother, prompting the other girls to snicker. "Mother. Do something," she pleaded, but her mother shrugged with a smirking smile.

"I don't care who I room with," the radiant-looking Lena said, moving between the two to break up their quarreling.

Gulielma Maria's eyes widened as she looked at the beautifully developed girl in astonishment.

"Thank you, Lena. You are already showing leadership," Hope said with gratitude. "However, tonight, your task is simple yet equally important. As some have already noticed, room assignments are posted," she said with a wave of her hand, directing everyone's eyes. "I encourage each of you to engage with one another with civility. Learn each other's names, discover where you all come from, and share your hobbies and interests. This exercise is not just about making acquaintances; it's about building the bonds that will enrich your experience here at The Willow and, hopefully, the rest of your lives.

"Once again, welcome to The Willow. I am excited to witness your growth and accomplishments in the days, months, and years to come. Now enjoy the evening—plenty of refreshments remain," she said with a warm wave of her hand in the direction of Eunice, who was, at that very moment, stuffing an oversized pastry into her mouth.

The girls dispersed gradually, some curtsying awkwardly to one another before finding their way to the long refreshment table, where silver trays gleamed with sugar-dusted pastries and warm cider waited in abundance. A few wandered toward the tall windows, peering out into the candlelit courtyard as if it might offer answers to their unease. Others gathered around the Indian art set up in the corner, fingering the decorative feathers with casual interest, eager to appear interested. One pair had discovered a folio of music resting on a stand and began leafing through it, whispering their opinions on the pieces.

As they moved about the room, trying not to seem as lost as they felt, Hope leaned discreetly toward Abigail. With a sideways glance and a hushed tone, she murmured, "Spragg?"

Abigail's appearance remained composed, flexible, and informal as the name arose around them like smoke from a burning pirate's ship. Then she, seeing no resolve, commented, "My dear Miss Yale," the name itself reminding Hope that not everyone wishes their actual name to be known. "Are you enjoying the evening so far? Because I think it is moving along admirably." She paused to raise her eyebrows with solemn understanding. "I hear those splendid little cakes are absolutely malicious. As if baked by a singing chorus of angelic pirates." She emphasized the word 'pirates,' punctuating the sentence with finality.

As the evening unfolded with grace and gaiety, Abigail turned to Hope with a thoughtful gaze. "Let's mingle with the students and their chaperones," she suggested, her voice carrying the excitement of the night. "It's a perfect opportunity to foster connections and understand the families better, remembering they each put on their petticoats one leg at a time, albeit some, by a hand servant."

Agreeing, Hope nodded, and they began to weave through the crowd, the murmur of conversations and laughter serving as a backdrop. They soon encountered Mary Penn, standing with quiet dignity. With a gentle smile, Abigail introduced her to Hope, noting Mary's elegant poise.

Mary shared that her husband had intended to join the festivities but was unexpectedly detained by pressing matters.

"Yes, it has come to my attention that men of the families are conspicuously absent," Hope said, looking around the gathering.

"Men's only interests lie in their daughters marrying well," Mary said with a look of apprehension at her headstrong daughter.

The conversation naturally veered towards Mary's father-in-law, William Penn, the esteemed founder of Pennsylvania. Her tone softened with concern as she revealed, "He remains in London, his health in a delicate state." Then she confided, almost in a whisper, "And his financial strains are substantial. The grand vision of building a colony," she explained, "was proving to be more burdensome in both work and expenses than anyone could have anticipated—a venture teetering on the edge of being a losing proposition."

As they conversed, Mary's gaze drifted towards her daughter, Gulielma Maria, engaged in lively banter with a group of students. She sighed, a mix of affection and mild frustration in her voice. "I only wish Gulielma understood that money doesn't simply grow on trees and she is not a royal princess waiting to be crowned queen of the Pennsylvanian Kingdom," she said, her words laced with the concern of a parent grappling with the practicalities of life and a child's dreams.

Abigail and Hope exchanged a knowing look, each understanding the complexities and challenges of nurturing a family. The conversation with Mary Penn gave them a glimpse into the realities that shaped the lives of those carving out new paths in a new world, balancing ambition with the stark truths of their endeavors.

Abigail, with a gentle nod to Mary Penn, excused herself and Hope. Turning away, she subtly gestured for Hope to take note of the group as more people wandered in through the back door.

As they moved across the room, Abigail gently took Hope by the elbow and steered her near the edge of the hall, beneath a tall window veiled in lace. The sounds of polite conversation and harpsichord music softened around them, giving space for a more personal word as they both peered out in the direction of the backyard.

"Abigail," Waite said gently as she approached. "I hope you'll forgive me if this is too personal, but I feel compelled to share something that's lingered in my memory. Nicholas—my late husband—often spoke of your mother, Annica, with great respect. He recalled her assistance to his father during his time as Governor in Rhode Island. Naval assistance, I believe it was called then."

At this, Hope's brow lifted ever so slightly, her glance flicking toward Abigail, an unspoken thought passing between them like smoke from a shared candle—piracy, perhaps, beneath the varnish of duty.

Abigail's posture remained composed, though her eyes glinted with an old familiarity. "That would not surprise me," she replied with a polite smile. "My mother's sails caught many winds, not all of them conventional. I daresay our families' paths have crossed in more ways than one."

When the clock struck six, mothers and chaperones, filled with pride and anxiety, began to say their farewells and prepare to leave their daughters at the school for the first time. Hope clapped her hands to gather everyone in front of the impressive art situated next to the library. The piece consisted of twelve long arrows mounted vertically in a row on an ornately carved log featuring intricate depictions of local animals and trees. The feathers were arranged beautifully, with authentic arrowheads pointing skyward.

Holding her hands out for everyone to see, Hope began to speak. "This is a piece of great significance."

Mary Penn stepped forward and asked, "Yes, I noticed it. Which tribe does it come from?"

Hope examined the artwork more carefully and pointed to the log base. "This was given to my father by the local Quinnipiac tribe," she said, rubbing her hand over the wood as if trying to feel the memories. "The arrow shafts are dogwood from the Iroquois, namely the Mohawk. The arrowheads are from a much more northern tribe of Algonquin speakers, the Missisquoi, found at the top of Lake Champlain, nearer to New France."

She reached into a decorated bag under the display and pulled a giant clam shell with a purple neck near the hinge. "These are quahog clam shells from the coast of Maine. For all recorded time, the Wampanoag have made small purple and white beads called wampum out of them."

Sarah Bradley, one of the more serious students eager to share her knowledge, spoke up. "I know wampum. It's Indian money."

Hope nodded to acknowledge the student. "Excellent, Sarah."

But the girl corrected her, "I prefer to be called Kidd."

Hope nodded again, eyebrows raised, smiling at everyone's curious faces.

"Excellent, Kidd. But in their raw form," she continued, waving her fingers to indicate the shells each had a hole drilled through their middles, "these shells are not very valuable. But with a lot of hard work and skill, they can be transformed into something of beauty and value."

She pulled an intricately fashioned wampum belt from the chest drawer under the arrows, causing everyone to gasp in amazement. Eliza, one of the more outspoken students, asked, "Don't those belts tell a story?"

"Indeed, they do," Hope answered, looking at the multiple strings of carved and polished shell pieces woven into a pattern as long and wide as her arm.

"What does this one say?" asked Dorothy, one of the local girls whose family recognized the school's value early on.

"I'm not sure," Hope admitted. "It was given to my father on one of his many field trips to collect medicinal plants from the natives in the surrounding areas."

Mary Nugent piped up, "My father has lots of those hanging around. He was the Governor of New York Colony."

"Oh, can he read them?" Hope asked, intrigued.

Mary shrugged, touching the beads with only mild interest. "I don't know," she replied.

Hope looked to Mary's Aunt for an answer, but received only a downcast gaze.

Hope, sensing the unease, shifted her focus back to the students. "This belt, like each of you, has a story to tell. You are all here to learn, grow, and transform like the wampum beads. Your time at The Willow will shape you into a strong, capable woman."

Gulielma Maria snatched the clamshell from Hope's hand and examined it closely. "What is this hole in the middle of the shell for? Hanging it around your neck?" she said, laughing. She held the shell up to her neck with her tongue protruding, trying to elicit laughter from the other students. Some of them giggled nervously, but Hope merely smiled and gently took the shell back into her hands.

"So to speak," she said calmly. "These shells are used as indicators of your performance."

"Performance?" Gulielma Maria repeated, scrunching up her nose.

"Yes," Hope continued. "They are used to indicate how well you are doing at our school. If perhaps you cause a mishap that could have been avoided, I will place one of these shells over your arrow at the end of the day as a demerit."

"Demerit?" the quiet Maria Allamby gasped.

"Yes, and once you fill up your arrow completely with these shells, a letter to your home will be written. See, the arrowhead slips off with just a tug," Hope explained, popping one off to show how easy it will be to slip a clamshell over their arrow.

The girls exchanged uneasy glances as the reality of the school's disciplinary system sank in.

"Ha, this letter you speak of is like a report?" Gulielma Maria scoffed as if it meant nothing.

"No report," Hope said. "Just a notification."

"Oh, well, that doesn't sound so bad," she laughed, and her mother frowned at her embarrassing attitude.

Then, with a stern look at everyone in the room, students and parents alike, she announced, "A notification of expulsion."

"Expulsion?" gasped out several students.

"Your parents would be expected to pick you up within a fortnight and will find you lodging down by the docks in Peck's Inn. I know they have excellent amenities and a rather delicious ox cheek soup."

All eyes shot around the room with the fear of those consequences.

Hirana, having nothing to lose either way, curiously asked about the letters carved into a disk dangling at the bottom of each arrow.

"Yes, I am glad you noticed," Hope said, tasseling one with her fingers marked 'GM' and smoothing the feather base. These are your initials. Each one is assigned to a student. This particular one is Gulielma Maria's," she said, pursing her lips tightly together.

Hope held up the shell again, allowing the light to catch its purple hue. "This is not just about punishment, though," she said, her voice softening. "It's about learning accountability and understanding the consequences of your actions. But remember, it's also about recognizing your achievements. You can earn feathers to add to your arrows for outstanding performance, symbolizing your growth and success."

"What kind of feathers are they?" the beautiful Lena asked, feeling their softness with her fingers.

"The top feathers around the arrowhead are wild turkey."

"Oh, I love turkey," Gulielma Maria said haughtily.

"And these on the bottom," she said, pointing to the multi-colored plumage arranged in a spectacular pattern, "are chicken."

Gulielma Maria's defiance wavered as she considered Hope's words. "So, these aren't just for punishment?" she asked, a hint of arrogant curiosity in her voice.

"Not at all," Hope replied with a kind smile. "They are a way for you to see your progress and learn from your good and bad experiences."

The girls stood in thoughtful silence, absorbing the information. Hope's gentle yet firm approach was starting to straighten out their kinks. "Now," Hope said, placing the shell down, "let's move on to our activities. Tomorrow is the beginning of your journey here at The Willow, and I have no doubt you will all grow into remarkable young women."

Mary Penn expressed her gratitude to the Headmistress, standing closest with her hand extended to shake, and then nodded in approval to Abigail, who stood with her sister Eunice on the grand stairway. Eunice had just finished supervising the kitchen staff and was more interested in wiping her hands for the event than giving Hope more attention.

As Mary prepared to leave, she stopped abruptly before the arrows and picked up the lone clam shell sitting on the chest. She hesitated, fingering the rough edges with deep contemplation before reaching up and pulling off the arrowhead, then sliding the hefty quahog half-shell down over the one marked 'GM.'

"This one is for all the trouble you've given your father and me over the years," she said firmly.

"Mother!" Gulielma Maria cried out, her voice filled with indignation. "That's not fair."

She moved forcefully to remove the shell, but Hope caught her gently by the arm. "Once the clam is placed, only good deeds can remove it," she said softly but firmly.

Gulielma Maria's eyes filled with tears of frustration and hurt. "But I didn't do anything wrong HERE," she protested.

Hope gave her a kind but resolute look. "This is where you start, Gulielma Maria. Use this as motivation to prove to everyone, including yourself, that you can earn the right to remove that shell. Show us the remarkable young woman you are becoming."

Mary Penn stepped back, her own eyes softening with a blend of sternness and love. "I know you can do it, Gulielma. This is a place where you can truly shine if you put your mind to it."

The room fell silent as the other students watched the exchange, the weight of the moment sinking in.

Hope turned to address the group. "Remember, each shell placed on your arrow is a chance to reflect and improve. This is not just about discipline; it's about striving to be your best. And every good deed, every act of kindness and responsibility, will help you remove those shells and earn feathers instead."

The Kidd approached the stand of arrows and touched the one labeled 'SB,' which she assumed was hers, before commenting on the one with a GM: "GM? I like that better than the mouthful, Gulielma Maria."

"Ha," Gulielma Maria remarked with condescension. "That's funny coming from someone who goes by the name 'Kidd.'"

Abigail, watching from the stairway with her sister, felt a surge of pride and hope for the girls. She knew that the growth path was often challenging, but these very challenges would shape them into strong, capable women.

As the parents and chaperones began their farewells, the girls stood quietly, their belongings already placed in their rooms, leaving them with nothing to hold but the weight of parting. Some lingered near the doorway, reluctant to let go, tears brimming in their eyes. Others clung to final words, hoping they would stretch the moment just a little longer.

Hope moved through the crowd with practiced calm, offering gentle nods and quiet encouragement. Her confidence steadied the adults, reassuring them that their daughters would be well cared for. One by one, they took their leave, walking away with backward glances and forced smiles.

The silence that followed felt unfamiliar. The girls remained rooted in place, some wiping their cheeks, others blinking hard, determined not to cry. The threshold had been crossed—this strange place was now to be called home.

In the warmly lit foyer, Headmistress Hope stood tall, her figure casting a long shadow across the polished floor. Beside her, Abigail lingered with composed grace, a steadying presence beside the weight of new responsibility. Together, they looked upon the girls—not as strangers or wards, but as the seeds of something just beginning.

Gulielma Maria walked past the room that Hannah and Sarah were sharing as everyone was preparing for bed. She paused and asked, "So, what are you two?"

Hannah frowned and replied, "Students like you."

"No, that's not what I meant," Gulielma Maria added as others stopped in the hallway to listen in. "I mean, are you white or black?"

Startled by her audacity, the other nearby girls gasped with laughter, waving for others to join in and listen. Hannah frowned, asking, "Whatever do you mean?"

"I mean, your skin is darker than most whites. So, which are you? Black or white?"

Sarah pushed Hannah aside and said with veracity, "Our mother is Dutch-African if you must know."

Gulielma Maria's eyes widened. "African. I knew it. And your father is African as well?"

"Spanish," Hannah growled.

"Ha, where I come from—and point south," Gulielma Maria said, "you'd be working the tobacco fields and not attending a boarding school like this."

Hannah nodded, maintaining her composure. "Well, we'll just see who can finish school without being expelled first. I bet that you'll be the first to go. You're already in the hole, so to speak. So clam it up, or I'll clam you up myself."

"But that will earn you a demerit," Gulielma Maria said with an arrogant smile.

"It would be worth every shell," Hannah said with a growl, extending her arm to hold back her sister from earning a clam herself.

The tension in the hallway, high-pitched astonishment, and giggles filled the air as the other girls watched the exchange.

Hope, sensing the commotion, appeared at the top of the stairs. Her presence quickly restored order, and she addressed the group with a calm but firm voice. "Ladies, it's time for bed. We have a long day ahead of us, beginning at sunrise down at the dock to see your chaperones off."

"Sunrise?" Marie Allamby complained. "But my parents aren't even here."

"Mine either," Hirana added.

"Okay, breakfast will be served down at Peck's Inn," the Headmistress conceded. "Anyone who wishes to stay can prepare their own breakfast and pump water for the day from the well."

"Oh no," Marie complained. "I guess seeing the sunrise over the harbor would be more to my liking."

"And eating a hearty breakfast," Hirana said, rubbing the sleep in her tired eyes.

Gulielma Maria, still smirking at the sisters, backed away from the doorway. "Goodnight, then," she said with a haughty arched eyebrow that made it clear she would not quickly forget their earlier conversation.

Hannah and Sarah watched her retreat before closing their door. Sarah turned to her sister, her eyes filled with determination. "We can't let her get to us, Hannah. We belong here just as much as anyone else."

Hannah nodded, her resolve strengthening. "I know. And we'll prove it."

Back downstairs, Hope turned to see Abigail standing patiently with her sister, her eyes reflecting a depth of emotion that words could scarcely capture. "This evening..." Hope began, her voice a soft echo in the vastness of the hall, "It surpassed my every expectation. And yet, as the silence settles around us, I find myself wrestling with a restlessness that belies the calm." She paused, her gaze lost in the flickering shadows. "The weight of this responsibility, of guiding these young souls, is a burden far heavier than I anticipated. It presses upon me with a profound force, a piece of the lives and futures that now rest in our hands."

Understanding the fears hidden behind Hope's words, Abigail stepped closer. "Hope," she said gently, her voice a soothing balm in the quiet of the night, "you stand at the helm of a ship that is destined for uncharted waters. But your vision, your unwavering spirit, will guide these young women to the shores of greatness. The Willow is more than a school—a chart—a ship. It is a cradle of the future, a nurturing ground for minds that will one day change the world. And you, my dear friend, are the captain of this future."

The two women stood in a moment of shared silence, a silent pact between them that spoke of solidarity and unflinching support. As the clock ticked on, marking the passage of time, the night at The Willow grew long. But within its walls, under the watchful eyes of Headmistress Terwilliger, a new chapter was beginning – a chapter filled with promise, learning, and the endless pursuit of dreams yet to be dreamed.

CHAPTER 19

Lessons

BEFORE THE SUN ROSE the following day, Hope rang a large triangular bell, shouting, "Daylight's burning! Get up or clam up!" The mention of a clam sent everyone's heart racing as they rolled out of bed.

The soft glow of predawn barely seeped through the heavy dormitory drapes as a dull murmur spread through the rooms. A few girls were already stirring, some struggling to shake off the lingering grasp of sleep, others sitting upright in their beds, blinking at the dim candlelight illuminating the chamber from the hallway.

The chill of early autumn morning crept through the wooden floorboards, earning a collective shiver from those who had dared to leave the warmth of their quilts.

"It's freezing," exaggerated Eliza Marble, hugging herself as she sat on the edge of her bed, reluctant to stand.

"Do you think it will rain?" her roommate, Patience, asked, rubbing her swollen eyes and stifling a yawn.

In the adjacent room, Marie Allamby pulled on her stockings with slow, deliberate movements, her body still heavy with sleep. "Why must I go down to the waterfront at this hour?" she groaned.

"Because our dear parents wish to leave us on the outgoing tide before we've even had a proper breakfast," said her roommate, Sarah Bradley—the Kidd—throwing on a shawl over her nightgown before realizing that wouldn't be enough for the trip to the docks. She groggily ran a hand through her short-cropped hair, making it stand on end. When she finally walked out into the hallway to see what the other girls were wearing, she gazed into the next bedroom.

"Goodness, Kidd, you look like a barn cat dragged backward through a thicket!" giggled Gulielma Maria, still seated at her dressing table, dabbing at her face to wipe away the last traces of sleep.

The remark stirred more giggles and muffled snorts from around the rooms.

The Kidd scowled, though there was little heat behind it. "Well, at least I don't look like an overfed pigeon in a lace bonnet," she shot back.

The girls erupted in laughter, some clutching their sides, others covering their mouths to keep from attracting the Headmistress' wrath.

"Ladies," came a voice from the doorway, slicing through their morning sluggishness like a ship's prow through icy water.

Headmistress Terwilliger strode into the dormitory, surveying the chaos with an arched brow and the hint of a smirk.

"We are leaving. Now," she announced, her voice crisp but not unkind. "If anyone lags, there may not be any breakfast left for them."

A few girls groaned, but she patted her stomach and added, "I could eat for two... possibly three."

"And I can eat the rest," Abigail said, appearing next to her.

That was enough to send a wave of panic through the room.

Suddenly, the sluggish movements vanished. Girls grabbed at dresses, shawls, and cloaks, some barely managing to pull on stockings before yanking on their boots. Combs and ribbons were discarded in favor of speed, and within moments, the once-lazy rooms were a flurry of flying fabric and whispered curses as they hurried to dress.

A few minutes later, at the staircase, Marie Allamby, now fully bundled in a thick woolen cloak, glared at the open front door, where a gust of cold morning air swept through. "Boy, she doesn't wait for anyone," she muttered as the others scrambled past her.

From just outside, Hope's voice carried across the crowd. "That's because I have my eye on your breakfast, Miss Allamby. Keep up, or I'll eat your share!"

"Mother?" Hannah asked as her mother moved to her side to walk with her and her sister, Sarah. "You wouldn't really eat my breakfast, would you?"

"No, of course not, darling. But it did sound ominous, did it not?"

The other girls, still groggy but now moving at a determined pace, rushed out into the dim morning light, ready to bid their families farewell on the departing tide.

The cool morning air refreshed their faces as they shuffled along the uneven cobblestone path, the weight of sleep still clinging to their limbs. The girls of The Willow, their hair in various states of disarray, their gowns hastily thrown over nightclothes, plodded forward with sour expressions, eyes bleary and steps sluggish—as though each were being marched toward an unwelcome fate she hadn't quite agreed to

Ahead of them, Headmistress Hope Terwilliger and Abigail strode with purpose and poise, their shoulders squared, chins lifted, and bright, encouraging smiles on their faces, utterly disconnected from the miserable cluster of students trailing behind them. Every passerby who crossed their path—merchants setting up their stalls, sailors preparing for departure, women sweeping their doorsteps—was greeted by Hope's radiance, only to glance at the disgruntled gaggle of girls behind her and raise an eyebrow in amusement.

At the head of the bleary-eyed procession, Gulielma Maria still looked personally offended, huffing and clutching her cloak.

"I simply cannot believe there is no carriage," she said, for the third time that morning.

"Nor can I believe you still think there would be," Lena Van Hoorn muttered.

Gulielma Maria ignored the remark and continued, "It is entirely unreasonable to expect ladies of our standing to walk through the streets like common laborers." She cast an incredulous glance at Abigail, her voice rising slightly. "Surely there must have been a mistake? A carriage would have been the proper arrangement."

Abigail, who had been waiting for this moment, smiled and said, "No mistake, Miss Penn. At The Willow, we walk."

Gulielma Maria's eyes widened in sheer disbelief. "Walk?" she repeated, as though the word itself were foreign to her tongue.

Hope, without breaking stride, patted her own belly and called back over her shoulder, "Yes, Miss Penn. With our own two feet. You know, those things attached to the bottom of your legs?"

A choked laugh came from the Kidd, but she quickly disguised it as a cough when Gulielma Maria shot her a glacial glare.

"This is absolutely barbaric," she whispered under her breath.

"No, dear," Abigail replied with an amused smile. "This is how everyone in this town gets around. Or haven't you been paying attention?"

As they turned down Fleet Street, the girls dragged their feet as though being led to the gallows. The journey—a mere ten-minute walk—might as well have been to the ends of the Earth, given the way they trudged along, their blank stares fixed on the road ahead.

A group of dockworkers, already busy loading luggage onto a waiting ship, paused to watch the procession of weary young ladies with bemused smirks.

"Now there's a fine parade," one of them chuckled.

Gulielma Maria snapped her head toward them, glowering as though she might summon a storm on their heads.

The Kidd, still half-asleep, muttered, "If they say another word, I swear I'll throw myself into the harbor and let the tide carry me home."

At the front of the line, Hope remained unfazed, gracefully acknowledging every nod and smile sent her way as they neared the waterfront.

At last, Peck's Inn came into view, the warm glow of lanterns in its windows beckoning like a sanctuary. The girls perked up just slightly, knowing that soon, they could bid their farewells, eat breakfast, and, most importantly, return to the warmth of the school.

Gulielma Maria, still scandalized, shook her head. "This will not do. I shall write to my father about this disgrace."

Her roommate, Lena, rolled her eyes. "Do let us know when he sends a carriage for you. We'll be happy to wave as you ride away in style."

More stifled laughter followed as the girls came to a stop in front of Peck's Inn. The wooden door groaned as Headmistress Terwilliger pushed it open, leading her ragged procession of students inside. The warm aroma of roasted ham, fresh bread, and honeyed porridge filled the room, causing a few of the girls to cast a sidelong glance at the ominous Unicon head mounted prominently over the hearth.

Inside, their chaperones were already gathering their belongings, fastening coats, and brushing crumbs from their hands, their breakfast mostly finished. A few glanced up as their daughters straggled in, some with warm smiles, others with raised brows of surprise, as though seeing their offspring properly for the first time in their lives.

Gulielma Maria, still bristling from the indignity of walking unassisted to the Inn, scanned the room for her mother. Upon spotting her near the hearth, adjusting her sleeves, she stalked over with a dramatic sigh.

"Mother!" she declared, aghast. "You didn't have my breakfast prepared for me?"

Mary Penn turned, giving her daughter an even gaze, her expression betraying little sympathy. "It's high time you learn to fend for yourself," she replied briskly, tugging the buttons on her traveling cloak. "God only knows the sacrifices I've made for your well-being throughout the years."

"But Mother—" Gulielma Maria protested, as though she had said something scandalous.

"No 'buts' about it," her mother cut her off smoothly. "In your household, the servants won't always be waiting to lay your meals before you. Consider this an early warning lesson."

Nearby, Hirana and Marie Allamby, who stood next to one of the cluttered wooden tables, snickered into their hands.

"She should write to her father about this, too," Hirana muttered, smirking.

"Surely, he can send a carriage full of breakfast," Marie whispered back.

All around the room, farewells were underway.

Patience and Lena Van Hoorn embraced their mothers tightly, murmuring parting words that only those closest to them could hear. Dorothy, blinking back tears, let her aunt place a firm, reassuring hand on her shoulder before she turned away to compose herself.

Meanwhile, the hungriest of the girls, skillfully swiped leftovers from discarded plates as they hugged goodbye. Eliza Marble, stood beside a plate abandoned by a distracted mother, plucked a piece of bacon from its edge, slipping it into her mouth before anyone could notice.

The Kidd, unbothered by etiquette, casually grabbed a half-eaten biscuit from her mother's saucer, earning a look of amusement rather than scorn.

"You could at least pretend to miss me more than you miss breakfast," her mother quipped, adjusting her hat.

The Kidd merely winked before taking another bite.

Not all the girls had someone to bid them farewell. Hirana and Marie Allamby were conspicuously without chaperones and didn't seem to mind the solitude. At the far end of the hall stood Patience, Eliza, Dorothy, and Lena, their hands clasped before them, eyes flickering between the flurry of luggage handling and the grand Unicorn figurehead hanging above the blazing fireplace. Their expressions were solemn, tinged with unease, as though the moment carried more weight than they dared put into words.

As trunks were hoisted and final instructions exchanged, the young women gathered on the wide dock of the Inn, its rail damp with the morning mist that clung to everything like a whispered promise of autumn. Wrapped in shawls against the salt-tinged breeze, they stood shoulder to shoulder, their eyes fixed on the bustling harbor.

Still, none of them moved as their chaperones turned for one last wave before boarding their packet sloop. Hats dipped, gloved hands lifted. And then the girls waved back—silent, dignified, but with hearts slumping like the outgoing tide.

As the vessel pushed off into the gray-blue, its sails blooming in the breeze, the porch behind them creaked underfoot as the girls slowly filed back towards the Inn.

Headmistress Hope Terwilliger noticed everyone's grief, her perceptive gaze softening. Without hesitation, she strode toward them, her voice firm but kind.

"Come, girls," she said channeling everyone through the front door, motioning toward the tables now cleaned near the hearth. "Sit and wait for your food to arrive. There is no need to stand on the dock like statues saluting the horizon when you could be enjoying a meal."

Marie and Hirana moved with undeterred purpose, but the others, although grateful for the direction, hesitated before taking their seats.

Hope gave a slight, approving nod to the innkeeper to start serving before turning back to look out the windows toward the departing sloops.

After the brisk walk back to the school, the heavy wooden door of The Willow creaked as the girls entered, their steps slow and heavy from full bellies and lingering exhaustion. The early morning chill from the harbor had given way to the warmth of the school. As they stepped inside, a collective sigh of relief rippled through them, the first tell-tale sign the building was beginning to feel like home.

"Finally," murmured Eliza, already loosening the laces of her cloak as she shuffled toward the staircase.

"If I don't sleep for another three hours, I might die," Patience groaned, tugging off one of her gloves and stuffing them unceremoniously into her pocket.

Dorothy, rubbing at her still-puffy eyes, gave a slight hum of agreement. "I feel as though I could sleep through an entire winter."

Marie Allamby, arms crossed tightly over her chest, let out a contented sigh as she reached the bottom step of the staircase. "Well, good luck waking me before noon."

Gulielma Maria, who had been uncharacteristically quiet since her mother's departure, merely huffed as she lifted her skirt and ascended the stairs first, as if sleep were a privilege reserved for those of proper breeding.

One by one, the girls trudged up the stairs, some already undoing their clothing, others unpinning their hair, ready to collapse into their beds and reclaim the rest they had been so cruelly robbed of that morning.

But just as the first girl reached the landing, a sharp, unmistakable voice rang through the foyer.

"And where do you all think you're going?"

The blood drained from their faces as they froze mid-step, heads whipping around to see Headmistress Hope Terwilliger standing at the base of the staircase, arms folded across her chest, an expression of pure mischief dancing in her sharp eyes.

A terrible silence followed.

Hope's gaze swept over the sleepy, sluggish mass of girls, her lips twitching as though she were enjoying this moment far too much. Then, in an all-too-cheerful tone, she delivered the final blow:

"I do hope you ladies enjoyed your breakfast. Because we have a hectic morning ahead of us."

Groans and protests erupted immediately.

"Busy morning?" Patience gasped, horrified. "But we just got back!"

"We haven't even slept properly yet!" the Kidd exclaimed, throwing her hands up in disbelief.

"Surely you jest!" Gulielma Maria cried, clutching her chest as if Hope had just announced their immediate transportation to a workhouse.

Hope smiled sweetly, walking up the stairs to the bedrooms. "Oh, I never jest."

She clapped her hands together, the sound snapping through the hall like a whip, making a few girls visibly flinch.

"Upstairs, wash your faces, brush your hair, and make yourselves presentable. Then report to the classroom downstairs within 15 minutes. Any later, and you'll be on kitchen duty for the entire week."

A chorus of protests followed, with some asking, "Kitchen duty? Does that mean cooking or cleaning up?"

Hope arched a brow, tapping her foot against the wooden floor in a way that suggested she would not be moved, answering, "Both."

"What could be so important that it cannot wait until we've had a proper nap?" Marie Allamby groaned.

Hope's grin widened. "Oh, nothing too difficult. Just a bit of morning scripture, a thorough lesson on etiquette, and, if you're fortunate, an introduction to your daily exercise regimen."

Instantly, shock registered on each of their faces.

"Exercise? But we've already walked halfway to Pennsylvania," Gulielma Maria practically shrieked.

"Etiquette? So soon?" said Dorothy Whiting, looking genuinely betrayed.

"Scripture?" Sarah Bradley looked like she might bolt for the door. "Headmistress, we've only just been abandoned by our families, and you think the first thing we need is a sermon?"

Hope beamed. "Oh, I think it's exactly what you need. But think of it more as a reading lesson." Then she stopped to ask, "You all do know how to read?" only to receive blank stares from half their faces.

Hannah spoke up, "I know how to read and write."

Gulielma Maria sighed, "Who doesn't?"

"Hmm," Hope said thoughtfully. "I would like each of you to show me your writings, and I'll be the judge of your abilities."

Hannah recoiled. "But my writing is private."

"Then I'll have to assume you are illiterate until proven otherwise."

There was no point in arguing. With collective groans, the girls turned back toward their rooms, their once-eager ascent now feeling like a weary retreat after a lost battle.

Hope watched them go, her satisfied smirk firmly in place, before calling out one final warning:

"Fifteen minutes before inspection, ladies! Oh, and make your beds properly. Remember, the kitchen is always in need of extra hands if you'd rather not be on time!"

A new urgency filled the girls' steps as they scrambled toward their rooms, coats, shawls, and half-fastened shoes flying in all directions.

When the time was over, Hope climbed the stairs and surveyed the activity.

"That's better," she said, standing in the doorway of the nearest room. "Today, we will learn how to make our beds properly."

"What?" Gulielma Maria protested, but when Hope held up two clamshells wired together and clicked them like castanets, everyone remained quiet and listened.

"So, who here feels they know how to make a bed properly, hmm?" Hope asked.

Boldly, Hannah stepped forward. Gulielma Maria muttered under her breath, so only she and Sarah could hear, "Of course you do—Slave," causing Hannah to elbow her, sending her into a screaming fit of feigned pain.

"What just happened?" Hope demanded, her eyes narrowing.

Gulielma Maria rubbed her arm, complaining, "I don't know, she just hit me for no good reason."

Disapproval flashed on the Headmistress's lips, and she turned her attention to Hannah. "We will discuss this later. Hannah, show everyone how to make a bed."

"But isn't she going to get a clam?" Gulielma Maria complained. "She hurt me really bad. You saw her. Or is she and her sister somehow special?"

"Hannah?" the Headmistress asked, purposefully ignoring the spoiled child's complaint by directing Hannah to make the bed while her focus fixed on Gulielma Maria's besmirching eyes, trying to figure out her game.

Hannah moved swiftly around her bed, tucking in all the corners before finally fluffing the pillow. Hope walked around, nodding her head in approval. Then, with squeals of shock from the other girls, she reached out and pulled off all the blankets and sheets, revealing the crumpled mattress underneath.

"Is this not part of the bed as well?" Hope asked, her voice sharp with disapproval. "The bed is more than what you see on the surface," Hope said, her tone firm. "It is about thoroughness and attention to detail. A properly made bed means every layer is neat and tidy, even the mattress."

"The mattress?" Patience asked with bewilderment.

"Yes. As you sleep throughout the night, or day, as I suspect some of you are used to doing, the feathers inside get pushed around and squashed, causing a trough to form down the middle," she said, running her hand down the furrowed bed.

"That's where I like to snuggle," Maria Allamby said as if there was nothing wrong with a broken-in mattress.

Without discussion, the Headmistress said with authority, "From now on, each time you make your bed, you must fluff the mattress." Moans and groans slid out of each tired mouth until Hope added, "And each Saturday, the entire mattress is to be flipped."

"Oh, no," came the complaints.

Gulielma Maria, trying to lift the corner of the mattress, announced, "I don't think I can even pick one of these things up."

"Then," the Headmistress said, "you will need your friends to help you do it."

Sarah said under her breath, "If you've got any friends."

As soon as she said it, Gulielma Maria pointed her finger at Sarah. "She said I didn't have any friends."

"Tis true," Hope added to everyone's surprise. "Friendship is earned, and so far, I do not see any effort on anyone's part to earn each other's friendship. So get to it and help each other flip the mattress before coming down for our reading lesson." She stopped Sarah by grasping her arm, saying, "You and your sister will help Gulielma Maria flip her mattress and vice versa if you don't mind."

"Of course not," both sisters said before turning to Gulielma Maria's glowering face.

The students stood in silence, absorbing the lesson. Hope's point was clear: half-measures and superficial efforts were not acceptable.

"Now, Hannah," Hope continued. "Show us again, starting from the mattress. Make sure each layer is smooth and properly tucked in."

Hannah nodded and began again, this time making sure the mattress was fully fluffed so that no bumps, dips, or troughs were felt or visible and that every layer was perfect. She smoothed the mattress cover, meticulously tucked in the bottom sheet, spread the top sheet evenly, and finally placed the blanket and pillow with care.

"Much better," Hope said, inspecting the bed closely. "This is the standard we will all follow. Gulielma Maria, you will go next."

Gulielma Maria, still rubbing her arm, said, "I hope I can with my arm aching so." She stepped forward, looking with disdain at Sarah's bed. "But this isn't even my bed," she protested.

"All the beds are the same. This one will be used for you to demonstrate, if you don't mind?"

She moved slowly but carefully, her previous defiance replaced with a grudging determination to avoid further ridicule.

As she finished, Hope inspected her work and nodded approvingly. "Well done. Remember, attention to detail and thoroughness will serve you well, not just here, but in all aspects of life. Now, everyone, let me see you flip and fluff your mattresses."

"Aw," Marie Allamby complained. "It's not even Saturday."

"Well, once you figure out how to best flip a heavy feather mattress, reconvene downstairs for our next lesson."

"Oh my God, these mattresses are heavy," Marie complained.

"I know," the Headmistress laughed anticipating their struggle. "I'll give you a hint on how to do it easily." When all eyes and ears were on her, she said, "Instead of using one hundred percent of your effort to accomplish the task, you can employ ten percent of ten people to do the same job." Without explaining any more, the Headmistress smiled and turned down the stairs.

The students nodded, understanding the broader lesson. They moved on to their tasks, flipping the heavy mattresses as the rooms filled with a renewed sense of diligence, focus, and nervous, struggling laughter.

Hannah glanced at Gulielma Maria, who was still quietly fuming, and whispered to her sister, "Who the hell does she think she is, the Queen of England?"

Sarah nodded, her eyes filled with determination. "Don't let her get to you. This is our school—our home. If she wants it to be hers too, she'll have to prove she belongs."

Hope listened to the interactions just out of sight, pleased to hear the first lesson of the day taking root as mattresses flipped and beds were properly made one by one. The Willow was not just about education but about shaping character and instilling values that would last a lifetime. And on this morning, as the girls learned to make their beds, they were also learning the importance of integrity, perseverance, and mutual respect.

In the days that followed, each morning followed the same routine. The triangular bell would ring, the students would tumble out of bed, get dressed for classes, and make their beds. The Headmistress no longer bothered inspecting their rooms, and no one had to be reminded to be at breakfast on time.

Breakfast was no longer a display of each girl's different lifestyle. No one arrived dressed in nightgowns or robes anymore; everyone was always prepared for a full day's work. Hope always sat back near the pantry, sipping her tea and watching her students' progress.

Now, a week after the girls had waved their goodbyes at the dock, Hope settled into her usual spot and watched as the girls took their usual seats around the table.

Each girl picked up a bowl and held it out for the servant to spoon in a helping of porridge. But this morning, something was different.

"Where's the honey?" Gulielma Maria asked boldly, voicing what a few of the others were also wondering.

"No, honey," Hope said, but she pointed to a small keg nearby. "But you might like this instead."

"I always have honey on my porridge," Gulielma Maria complained, her tone edged with entitlement.

Before she could press further, Marie Allamby, having already dipped a spoonful of the thick liquid from the keg onto her porridge, took a bite.

Her eyes widened in pleasant surprise. "Oh my, this is good. I dare say, better than honey!"

Gulielma Maria forced her way to use the casket next, and when she tasted a finger full, she smiled and poured almost the entire container into her bowl.

"Hey, don't use it all," the others complained.

When, after only two more girls took their turns at the tap, the thick liquid stopped flowing entirely, Hope said, "Well, that's the end of it. I'll have to make a note to get more next time I order supplies—which will be in a week, come Monday."

"Aww," everyone said in a deflated tone, looking at Gulielma Maria's full bowl with a mix of envy and disdain.

"Share and share alike," Hope said firmly.

Hannah followed it up with, "As ye sow, so shall ye reap," causing Hope to groan inwardly, having thought the girls should have already begun to become friends by now.

The girls began eating plain porridge, some reluctantly accepting its bland taste while others picked at the edges with little appetite.

As breakfast continued, Hope addressed the group. "Today's lesson seems to be about resourcefulness and making the best of what you have. Just like with the sweetener, sometimes you won't have what you're used to, but you can find something just as good, if not better."

The girls nodded, some more enthusiastically than others. Gulielma Maria seemed to contemplate Hope's words, her initial defiance waning. She glanced around the table, noticing the envious looks directed at her bowl.

With a sigh, she pushed her bowl towards the center of the table. "Here, everyone can have a little taste."

The room fell silent for a moment before the girls began to murmur in surprise. They took small portions from Gulielma Maria's bowl one by one, sharing the remaining sweetener as Hope walked out of the kitchen to meet Abigail and Eunice at the front door.

"Thank you," Hannah said quietly, acknowledging the gesture. As she reached for a spoon to scoop some of the runny maple syrup into her bowl, Gulielma Maria nodded, a small smile forming on her lips, and said, "It's only fair." However, as Hannah gingerly returned her full spoon to the bowl before her, Gulielma Maria slapped her hand, knocking the spoon to the floor.

Hope returned to the kitchen with Hannah's mother and aunt to watch the interaction with satisfaction. "Remember, girls, this is how we build a community—by sharing and supporting each other—oh, and being completely dressed for breakfast, ready for work."

"Thank you, Headmistress," Gulielma Maria said as the servant picked up the gooey mess and wiped the sticky floor clean.

As the girls finished their breakfast, an unspoken rift between Hannah and GM beginning to surface.. Although oblivious to the underlying tension, Hope felt confident that lessons like these, though simple, would lay the foundation for their growth as individuals and a group.

Hope felt a sense of accomplishment as the girls prepared for all-day reading and writing as expected. Their journey at The Willow was beginning, but already, they were learning the importance of cooperation, empathy, and resilience. Moving to where the chairs were now set up in the classroom, Hope picked up a slate pencil and wrote the name "Sir Isaac Newton" on the large slate board.

As chairs scraped the floor and each girl found a comfortable seat, Hope asked, nodding to Abigail standing in the back next to her sister observing, "Who here has heard of Sir Isaac Newton?"

Everyone looked around until Hannah raised her hand. Gulielma Maria muttered, "Figures. She's probably been told all the answers."

"Gulielma Maria," Hope said, fixing her with a stern look. "Do you have something to say? Who do you think Sir Isaac Newton is?"

Put on the spot, Gulielma Maria said with perfect clarity, "I haven't the foggiest," causing giggles to ripple through the classroom.

"Let this be a lesson to you all," Hope said, clacking her clamshell castanets together to punctuate her meaning. "If you do not have something positive to contribute, do not contribute at all."

"Yes, ma'am," Gulielma Maria begrudgingly said, causing more snickering.

"Now, Hannah," Hope continued. "What do you know about Sir Isaac Newton?"

"I have read his book," Hannah said proudly.

"Ah, you mean this one?" Hope asked, holding up an ordinary brown leatherback book, less than 2 inches thick, before reading the title on the spine aloud, "Isaac Newton's Philosophiæ Naturalis Principia Mathematica, 1689."

"Yes, ma'am. It's my mother's."

"And what do you know about it?"

Hannah reluctantly said, "I read it, but that does not mean I understand. In it, I did find strange and peculiar was his mention of the word 'gravity.'"

"Ah, yes, gravity," Hope said, nodding. "Does anyone besides Hannah have an idea what that means?"

When no one ventured a guess, she held out a bright red apple and promptly dropped it to the floor. After a few seconds, she asked, "Why did that apple fall to the ground instead of shooting off into the sky, never to be seen again?"

The students laughed at her preposterous question.

"Any idea? Any idea at all?"

She probed until Kidd said with a laugh, "Because you dropped it?"

"Yes, that's part of it," Hope said, smiling. "But there's more to it. Gravity is the force that pulls objects towards the Earth. Sir Isaac Newton discovered that everything has a gravitational pull. The ground beneath our feet is considerable, pulling everything towards it—including apples."

The students looked intrigued but confused. Hope continued, "Let me explain further. Gravity is a force we play with all the time. We take for granted that everything falls downward and that our feet stay on the ground, but why isn't it the other way around? Why, when you let go of the apple, did it not float or even fly off into the sky? Gravity pulled it down. This force affects everything: rocks, feathers, cannonballs, musket balls, arrows; everything, including us."

Sarah chimed in on the discussion. "So that's why Hannah's spoon fell to the ground when GM slapped it away so she could not have any maple sugar in her porridge after you left the kitchen?"

"Ah," Gulielma Maria gasped, saying, "Liar." But the look on everyone's face told the truth without a word.

"Hey, GM," Eliza said, pointing to her mouth. "Got something between your teeth."

The prideful girl instinctively reached up and felt a tooth, saying, "It's a stain."

"Oh yeah? It looks like more than a stain to me. It looks like a worm is eating your teeth."

Gulielma Maria frowned and pursed her lips.

Noticing the frown forming on Hope's face, Hannah raised her hand again with a new question. "So, gravity is a 'force' explaining why we stay on the ground and don't float away. But what do you mean by force? How does this work?"

"Excellent question," Hope said, pleased. "Newton's work on gravity helped us understand why things fall, and we will spend a lot of time this year learning about exactly what that means. His discoveries are fundamental to everything we know about science today."

The girls nodded, beginning to grasp that what seemed like a fundamental facet of life was actually a complex concept.

"Now, let's experiment," Hope said, handing out small objects like feathers, stones, and leaves. "Drop these and observe how they fall. Notice the difference in how quickly they reach the ground."

The girls eagerly participated, dropping their objects and watching their movements. They noticed the heavier objects fell faster while the lighter ones drifted slowly to the ground.

"Why do you think that happens?" Hope asked.

"Because some are light and others are not?" the Kidd answered.

"Very astute. That's why if a leaf falls from a tree, it doesn't crush you like a boulder. There's not as much gravity pulling on a leaf as there is on a boulder."

The students were fascinated by this new information. Hope continued, "Remember, learning about these concepts helps us understand the world better. Sir Isaac Newton's discoveries were just the beginning of what we can learn about the natural world. There is much more to come on this."

The Headmistress turned around and, with a wet rag, wiped down the slate board. After waiting a few seconds for it to dry, she wrote on the board the name "Joan of Arc."

"Oh, I've heard of her," Gulielma Maria said with recognition.

"Okay, tell us what you know," Hope prompted her.

"She was from the town of Arc—France, maybe?" Gulielma Maria ventured.

"You are correct about France," Hope said, giving her praise that she heartily accepted with a smile. "However, there is no such place as Arc in France."

"But why is her name Joan of Arc?" Gulielma Maria smirked as she over-emphasized the words, then turned to laugh with the front row.

"Joan of Arc was actually born in a small village in northeastern France called Domrémy, and she was baptized as 'Jeanne,' not Joan," Hope explained.

"Well, that's dumb," Gulielma Maria said in an uncaring fashion.

"Only as dumb as the name Penn," Hope retorted without thinking. The room fell silent, and everyone, including Abigail, frowned at Hope's harsh remark.

"I'm sorry, that didn't come out quite right," Hope said, recovering quickly. "What I meant is that names often have meanings or origins that aren't immediately obvious. 'd'Arc' was her father's surname—just as yours is Penn. Her father was Jacques d'Arc, and in French, 'd'Arc' means 'of Arc.'"

Gulielma Maria's smirk faded as she considered this. "So then... her family didn't come from a place called Arc?"

"Exactly," Hope said, smiling and nodding. "Joan of Arc was Jeanne d'Arc—' daughter of Jacques d'Arc.' It's a way of showing family lineage or geographic origin. Whether a name honors a place or a person usually depends on the context."

She glanced at GM, then continued. "Joan left an extraordinary legacy. She was a young peasant girl who claimed to have visions from God, telling her to support Charles VII and help drive the English from France during the Hundred Years' War."

"She led armies, didn't she?" Hannah asked, clearly intrigued.

"Yes, she did," Hope confirmed. "She played a crucial role in several important battles. Unfortunately, she was captured, tried for heresy, and burned at the stake at the age of 19. But her courage and faith made her a symbol of French unity and nationalism."

"She sounded brave," Dorothy said softly.

"She was incredibly brave," Hope agreed. "Joan of Arc's story is a powerful example of how determination, faith, and courage can change the course of history. It's also a reminder that anyone, regardless of status or gender, can make a significant impact. We will also be learning about courageous figures from history this year."

The girls listened intently, absorbing the lesson. Hope concluded, "So, remember, it's not where you come from or what your name is that defines you, but your actions and your character."

The lesson ended, and the girls prepared for their next activity.

"Now, for our next lesson, which will lead us into our physical exercises for the day," Hope began, and everyone groaned.

"Physical exercises?" Maria Allamby complained as she licked the sweet taste of maple syrup off her finger.

"Yes," Hope confirmed. "We are going to see how combining what we know about Sir Isaac Newton and Joan of Arc can help us in the real world." She turned and picked up what looked like a wooden sword in one hand and a feather duster in the other. She acted as if she were weighing them before saying, "Hannah, Gulielma Maria, come up and pick your weapon."

Before anyone could figure out what she meant, Gulielma Maria jumped up and took the wooden stick from her. Hannah lowered her shoulders and accepted the feather duster with a curious expression.

"This will be a duel to the death — ha — not really," causing nervous laughter, even from Abigail's lips. "But if you let your guard down, you could receive a wicked welt or possibly a tickled nose." Hannah held up the duster like a champion. "Joan of Arc was known for her valiant swordsmanship, and Newton for gravity. Now, let's see which will become victorious, wood or feather," Hope announced as Gulielma Maria held up her weapon in victorious salute to the ruckusing crowd.

Abigail grasped Eunice's arm as she saw the look of exasperation on her daughter's face.

Hope yelled out, "On guard!"

The girls circled each other. Gulielma Maria dragged her wooden sword on the polished floor until Hannah planted her feet with one hand on her hip and the other pointing the duster, ready to fight. Gulielma Maria, feeling superior, swung the wooden sword with enthusiasm, but Hannah used the feather duster with surprising agility, deflecting the thrusts while barely moving her feet.

"Remember, it's not just about strength but also about strategy and understanding your environment," Hope called out, watching the girls closely.

Gulielma Maria, frustrated by Hannah's nimbleness, tried to swing harder. Still, Hannah avoided being hit, gently tickling Gulielma Maria's face with the feather duster each time she passed, which made the classroom laugh at the frustrated girl.

The other girls watched in amusement, some cheering for Hannah's clever deflections and others for Gulielma Maria's determined missed thrusts and gouges. The duel continued for a few more wild volleys until Gulielma Maria, out of breath, stood wavering, lowering her wooden sword.

"Do you concede?" Hannah asked, holding the feather duster to her forehead.

"I don't concede, but I've had enough of this tomfoolery," she said with a frown.

"Excellent," Hope said, clapping her hands. "What did we learn from this exercise?"

Hannah, now playfully twirling the feather duster around in big circles by the rawhide end strap, said, "That sometimes being quick and strategic is more effective than just having a heavy hand."

"And that sometimes, training can be just as powerful," Gulielma Maria added, still catching her breath.

"Precisely," Hope said. "Joan of Arc's courage and strength, combined with Newton's understanding of the world, teach us that a well-rounded approach is often the most effective. Strength and strategy, seriousness and humor—all have their place."

The girls nodded, reflecting on the lesson. Abigail and Eunice exchanged a glance, relieved and pleased to see the girls learning in such an engaging and meaningful way.

Gulielma Maria leaned toward Hannah as the others filtered out of the room. "I would have beaten you," she said with a dramatic toss of her hair, "but I was afraid my hard sword might injure you."

Hannah rolled her eyes and rubbed the feather duster into her own cheek with mock sensuality. "You're hilarious. Show me your winning move, O mighty warrior of linens and lace."

With a grin, she gave another playful swish of the duster under Gulielma Maria's nose. That was all the provocation needed. With a burst of theatrical rage, Gulielma Maria swung her wooden sword in a wide arc toward Hannah's head. But Hannah twisted the shaft of the feather duster like a fencing foil, catching the sword and yanking it sideways—accidentally sending Gulielma Maria spinning off balance and straight into a chair with a spectacular sprawling thunk.

The room rattled with commotion.

Gulielma Maria groaned from the floor, her foot tangled in a petticoat and her pride in ruins. Girls came rushing in from the backdoor like bees to a scandal, gasping and giggling as she tried to sit up, dazed and crying.

The Headmistress burst into the room, skirts swishing, brows furrowed. "What in the Queen's name is happening in here?"

"She assaulted me," Gulielma Maria moaned, pointing at Hannah like an opera heroine in her final act. "She twisted my sword and flung me."

The Headmistress turned to Hannah. "Is that true? Did you fling her?"

Hannah, eyes wide and a feather duster still in hand, said nothing.

"I see," the Headmistress said with a sigh. "And are you injured?" she asked Gulielma Maria.

"My head. And possibly my shoulder. And emotionally? Devastated."

"Well then," the Headmistress said, clapping her hands briskly and giving Hannah a harsh look of disappointment. "If the dueling drama is done, let's get some fresh air and exercise to cool things down." With that, she marched out the door, trailed by the chorus of whispering girls and one limping, smirking swordswoman.

"Exercise! Ah, how come?" Maria Allamby asked as she followed everyone into the garden.

As they moved outside, the girls chatted excitedly about the duel and the lessons learned. But to their surprise, waiting for them were bows and quivers of arrows arranged in a row, with round targets placed off at a distance in front of hay bales.

"What is this?" Gulielma Maria asked, just catching her breath.

"You're not pooped out yet, are you?" Hope teased.

"So what if I am?" Gulielma Maria shot back, holding the side of her head, a hint of defiance in her voice.

Hope shrugged as if she didn't care, turning to address the rest of the class, who had been quiet observers up to this point. "Joan of Arc was also an exceptional archer. Has anyone pulled a bowstring before?"

Both Hannah and Sarah had used a bow and arrow before, but chose to stay quiet and let the others learn first.

"Really?" Hope asked again, shaking her head with disbelief. "My father taught me how to shoot when I was five."

"Well, your father must have wanted to be in your life," Kidd said, her arms folded tightly against her chest.

The comment hung in the air without gravity, and the tension reminded them that they were not all the same. Hope decided to diffuse it with action. "Let's get started. Archery is not just about strength but also about focus and precision. Just like with the duel earlier, it requires a steady hand and a calm mind—and," she said, holding everyone's attention, "gravity."

"Not gravity again," Marie said, looking too tired to participate.

"Yes, gravity. How far can the best archer shoot his arrow?" she asked. Then, with a shrug, she admitted, "I don't know either, but it can't be that far because," she stopped again to listen for an answer until Dorothy retorted, "Gravity."

"Gravity! Yes," she said, picking up an arrow and feeling how heavy it was in her hand. "Not very heavy. Here," she said, handing it off to Lena, who looked at it briefly and passed it on to Mary. Picking up another, the Headmistress held it up and acted like it was flying through the air while still in her fingers. "What if I were to drop it? It would fall to the ground. Not like a boulder or feather, but like a stick. It can't help it because—" She stopped to put her hand to her ear to hear the students around her murmur, "Gravity."

"Precisely. So when you use the bowstring to force it to fly at a target, if you are not close enough to hit it, it is forced to come back to the ground by what?"

"Gravity," everyone moaned.

"So if the arrow is always going to fall after you shoot it, then the trick to shoot it further is to shoot the arrow higher above the target so that gravity pulls it down, it can hit the target on its way down; make sense?" Looking at their blank faces, she picked up the bow, nocked the arrow to the bowstring, aimed the arrowhead higher than the target, and let the arrow fly. The arrow did exactly as Hope had described, hitting the target's center. "See how simple it is. Now watch what would happen if I aimed directly at the target." She repeated the process; this time, the arrow hit the ground yards before the target. "That pesky gravity can cause problems if you don't know it is always there, pulling." She pulled back another arrow and aimed high, planting it right next to the other in the center of the target.

She demonstrated how to hold the bow correctly and nock an arrow onto the string, keeping her two fingers on either side of the feathered shaft, and explained each step clearly. "You want to stand with your feet shoulder-width apart, grip the bow firmly but not too tightly, arms out, and draw the string back smoothly."

The girls watched intently, their initial reluctance turning to curiosity. Hope handed the bow to Gulielma Maria. "Give it a try."

"Why are you picking on me?"

"Because I know you can do it."

Gulielma Maria took the bow, her previous frustration replaced with determination. She mimicked Hope's stance and drew the bowstring back, aiming high, but her first attempt sent the arrow wide of the target, landing harmlessly in the hay bale while popping her wrist with an intense sting.

"Ouch," she cried, making the others more reticent.

"Not bad for a first try," Hope encouraged. "Remember, it's all about control and patience. Hold the bow further away from your body, or it will pop your arm. Now, again."

Gulielma Maria nodded and tried again, this time with a bit more focus. The arrow flew closer to the target, and she grinned, a sense of accomplishment washing over her.

"Who's next?" Hope asked, looking around, but Gulielma Maria wanted to try one more time. She grabbed another arrow, placed it on the bowstring, pulled it back as hard as she could, and shot it high into the air. To everyone's surprise, the arrow soared out of sight over the distant trees.

Hope sighed. "That would have been on target if you were shooting from the top of a castle into a sea of advancing troops. Surely, you would have lucked into hitting someone. But here, it is not wise to shoot uncontrollably. Now, who wants to be next?"

Hannah stepped forward, taking the bow and an arrow with a confident smile. She nocked the arrow, drew back the bowstring, and released smoothly. The arrow hit the target near the center.

"Impressive," Hope said, nodding approvingly. "Clearly, you have some experience."

Sarah followed, her shot equally precise, landing just beside Hannah's.

The other girls took their turns, some struggling at first but gradually improving with Hope's guidance. The girls cheered each other on and celebrated each small victory.

Lena walked up for her turn at the bow and reluctantly pulled on the tight string. "It's stronger than it looks," she muttered. Under the close tutelage of the Headmistress, Lena worked the arrow into position and then struggled to pull back the bowstring. As she let go, the string snapped back, hitting not the side of her arm but the tip of her right breast. Withdrawing quickly to hold herself, she frowned before shouting, "It popped my tit!"

Everyone's faces reacted with a mix of pain and laughter as if they felt her discomfort. Hope quickly said, "That can happen to anyone, women and men alike, if you don't hold the bowstring away from your body. Here, try it again."

"No, I'm good," Lena replied, still wincing.

"If you don't get right back into the game, it will be twice as hard next time and may prevent you from ever trying again," Hope encouraged.

"I'm okay with that," Lena said, trying to hand the bow to the next girl.

Then, to everyone's surprise, Gulielma Maria stepped forward and said, "What's wrong with you? You chicken? You need a boy to do your work for you?"

Striking a chord that no one knew existed, Lena stopped, took back the bow, and loaded an arrow. When she pulled back the string, Gulielma Maria placed her hand over Lena's breast and said, "Out further." Then she commanded, "Fire," still holding her hand in place.

Everyone watched as the arrow flew, missing the top of the target by only inches, and sailed to hit the distant outhouse door with a resounding thud.

"Thanks. That felt better," Lena said, her confidence restored.

Gulielma Maria shrugged, looking uncharacteristically supportive. "It's nothing. Just needed a little adjustment."

The other girls cheered, and Lena felt a surge of pride. With a smile, she handed the bow to the next girl, ready to face the next challenge. The solidarity and unexpected support from Gulielma Maria had turned a painful moment into a triumph.

By the end of the session, the girls were hungry and exhausted, their initial hesitation replaced with enthusiasm and a growing sense of camaraderie. Hope felt a deep sense of fulfillment as they stacked their weapons and headed back inside. The Willow was indeed becoming a place where these girls could grow, learn, and thrive together.

Marie Allamby rejoiced, "My favorite time of the day—dinner!"

Everyone agreed, continually surprised at how well they were fed at The Willow. The long table was laden with typical New England fare: roasted turkey with savory stuffing, cornbread, a medley of root vegetables, clam chowder, apple pie, and freshly churned butter with warm bread.

Hannah sat beside the Kidd, and Gulielma Maria came to her side, asking, "Where did you learn to do all that?"

"What?" Hannah replied, her expression genuinely puzzled.

Gulielma Maria feigned a frown and added, "Sword fighting and archery."

"Oh, you mean dusting?" Hannah said, obviously alluding to Gulielma Maria's previous reference to her being a black slave.

"Ha. I was wrong about you," Gulielma Maria said with a hint of laughter.

"Well, I learned archery from the Mohawk," Hannah said with a laugh, causing Gulielma Maria to walk away in disbelief. Then, swinging her head to the Kidd beside her, Hannah added, "And the sword fighting from your father, Uncle Willie."

The Kidd dropped her spoon, her mouth agape in disbelief, looking at Hannah. Hannah nodded without speaking at first, until the moment became strained. "Yep. We'd sword fight in our backyard all day long. He'd always beat me, but I got in a few whacks with my wooden sword before we graduated to real steel; no sharp blades, of course. My mother wouldn't allow it. She was afraid I would hurt your daddy," she half laughed.

The Kidd blinked a few times, still processing what she heard. "Uncle Willie?"

Hannah grinned. "Well, I suppose there are many things you don't know about him. He was always trying to teach me something new. Said it was important to be skilled in many things."

The Kidd slowly picked up her spoon again with a thoughtful look on her face. "I guess there's a lot I need to learn."

"I can teach you if you want?"

"I want to learn how to fight just like him."

"Then you're going to have to learn how to cheat."

"The Kidd shot her a frown of disapproval until Hannah added, "Uncle Willie always said, 'Cheating's better than dying.'"

The girls shared stories and laughter as the dinner continued, enjoying the sumptuous food and the warmth of each other's company.

Hope watched from the head of the table, feeling a deep sense of satisfaction. She raised her glass of ale and said, "To new beginnings and the lessons we learn from each other."

"To new beginnings!" the girls echoed, clinking their glasses and digging into their delicious meal with renewed enthusiasm.

"Now, this afternoon will be pistols, and maybe even a long gun," Hope said to the now muffled audience. "What? Gravity affects a musket ball, too. Don't look so worried. Tomorrow, we shoot off the cannon!"

Marie Allamy choked on her drink, saying with fear, "cannon?"

"No, not really," the Headmistress gaffed and then lamented, "I haven't got one yet."

But Sarah, unable to contain herself, blurted, "We do." Hannah shook her head in disapproval and began looking around for her mother, hoping she hadn't heard that fact about their backyard.

Gulielma Maria, tired of all the sisters' tall tales, said in a droning voice, "And I suppose you got it off a pirate ship," just as Abigail walked into the kitchen, sipping her tea.

Sarah lowered her eyes, knowing she should not have mentioned it, until Abigail contributed, "You know, I'm not sure where my father got that cannon, now that you mention it—probably left over from the Dutch. My father only shot it off once after cleaning its guts, that I can remember. I think to see where it was aiming by 'testing the thunder.'" She straightened up her back and looked around the table, taking in each of the girls' faces. "You definitely need to take gravity into account before throwing a ball out into the Hudson." Then, as quickly as she strolled in, she strolled out, sipping her tea, looking for her sister for more light conversation.

Gulielma Maria moved back to Hannah's side and said under her breath, "We have Mohawk traveling through our land. Tell me more about them?"

"Maybe later, when we are telling ghost stories," she laughed and turned to Kidd, giving the smartass rich girl her back. "Have you seen a couple of real swords around here?"

The Kidd's wild eyes looked around before asking excitedly, "To practice?"

"Either that—or to show this Pennsylvania girl what a real fight is like," she said, smiling with gritted teeth, causing an indignant scoff from GM's hissing mouth.

Gulielma Maria caught Lena rubbing her bruise and offered, "I know how you feel, except it was my arm and not your—ah."

Hope said, "Breast?" causing the youngest of them to snicker. "You know, legend has it that the Amazonian warrior princesses used to cut off their right breast so it wouldn't get in the way of their bowstring."

"Ooooh," groaned around the table.

"Amazonian?" Hannah asked as her mother strolled back into the dining area to listen.

Hope nodded, saying, "It's from Las Sergas de Esplandián. The Adventures of Esplandián? It's the fifth book in a series of Spanish chivalric romances by Garcí Rodríguez de Montalvo. Written in the days of Cristobal Colon, before Queen Isabella's death? Ah, you'll hear of them more in our history lessons." Then, when she saw more interest in the subject, she added, "It is about an island named California, inhabited only by black warrior Amazon women." She raised her eyebrow and nodded her head, acknowledging the intriguing premise.

Patience asked timidly, "All of these Amazon women cut off one of their breasts?"

"My dear, don't fret. The adventures I speak of are Fiction. You do know what that means?"

Patience sat as still as a mouse, afraid to speak in front of the others. She feared she would say something foolish and be laughed at, especially by Gulielma Maria.

Hirana, one of the group members who never spoke up and was considered by most to be illiterate, offered, "Fiction means fake. It's made-up stories. Most of the myths and legends of the past are Fiction, too. Some say even the Bible is a work of Fiction."

"Oh, my child, hold your tongue," Hope warned. "Talk like that will get you in big trouble around these parts. Someone could prick you as a witch and execute you in the name of the Lord God Almighty for casting aspersions upon the almighty Bible." Then, to turn the subject quickly, she added, "Amazon means different things in different languages. For instance, in the Circassian language, a branch of the Caucasian languages spoken on the Black Sea—it'll be in your geography classes—it meant 'moon-mother' or 'mother of the forest.' But in Greek, which is one of the languages we are to delve into quite heavily when its time comes, 'A' in front of a word means without. And 'mazon' or the plural 'mazos' means breasts. So putting the two together—you'll see how this is done later—you come up with the word 'Amazon,' which means without breast."

"And these Amazon women are—" Hannah asked, being cut off.

"Black?" Gulielma Maria offered, looking at both Hannah and Sarah.

"As it was written in Fiction, yes, and was ruled by the Islamic Queen Calafia. But," she added with a nod to Hirana while holding up one hand to any more questions from the impulsive Gulielma Maria. "Like all male-dominated fictional worlds, in the end, she is defeated and converted to Christianity—just like they are trying to do to the rest of the known world."

Abigail, now standing with Eunice near the kitchen door, turned her head toward her sister with raised eyebrows. "Just when you think you know someone."

"I know. I wonder what might've happened if she'd suggested reading Grandfather's Koran," Eunice whispered with a sly grin. "We'd have a new witch trial before supper—this time with better ale and hors d'oeuvres."

"The book is in the library beside where I keep Newton's book," Hope said for everyone's benefit. "You're welcome to read it, if you know how to read Spanish—ah, another language you will immerse in, in due time."

Hannah stood from the table and stepped out of the kitchen, returning a few moments later with the leather-bound book in her hand.

Gulielma Maria groaned, "Don't tell me you know Spanish as well."

"I did tell you our father is a Spaniard?" Hannah replied with a wry lift of her brow. "Or has that tidbit slipped thy memory like a fish through a torn net?"

"Oh yeah," she replied with an annoyed sigh. "Anyway," Gulielma Maria said, addressing the other girls around the table, "I think I'll keep my breast if you don't mind. I'd feel lopsided without one of them." She grasped both of her own breasts with her hands, eliciting murmurs of strenuous agreement from everyone around the table.

After the noon dinner, everyone was full. True to her word, Hope beckoned everyone outside, and just as she had said, the staff had already replaced all the archery equipment with muskets. Hannah whispered to her sister, "Don't tell anyone about my twins upstairs. My muskets are my secret weapons."

Sarah looked at her with surprise that she had even mentioned it, not having to be reminded, 'Loose lips sink ships.'

Hope raised her arms to get everyone's attention. "Guns are much more deadly than bows and arrows," she began, causing everyone to roll their eyes at the obvious statement.

"We will only place shots in the barrels once you look and act proficient. The first time you pull the trigger is a shock to your system, and I've seen people, even grown men, drop theirs when firing a new weapon for the first time."

Hannah leaned in and told the Kidd, "Not bloody likely."

The Kidd turned and asked, half-breathing, "My Father taught you that as well?" and Hannah nodded with swagger.

Hope continued, "Over the next few days, we are going to immerse ourselves in everything muskets—"

Lena spoke up, cutting her off to ask, "Why are we learning all of this so soon—or at all, for that matter?" She laughed, adding, "Not just because of gravity, I assume."

"Good question," Hope said. She looked around at the innocent faces surrounding her and paused to collect her thoughts. "I teach you today because of

Hannah." Everyone looked at Hannah, and Abigail shook her head, knowing no one knew the Mohican had taken her as a child. "No, not our Hannah, but Hannah Swarton née Joana Hibbard, a New England colonial pioneer who was captured by Abenaki Indians and held prisoner for over five years, first in an Abenaki community and later in the home of a French family in Quebec. She was eventually freed and told her story to the Reverend Cotton Mather of Boston.

"On the 16th of May, in the year of our Lord 1690, English settlers fortified a settlement on Casco Bay—the coast of Maine—in a vain attempt to take the land as their own from the Indians. It was attacked by a war party of some fifty French-Canadian mercenaries led by Jean-Vincent d'Abbadie de Saint-Castin, about fifty Abenaki warriors, a contingent of French militia—sent by the Sun-King, Louis the Fourteenth—led by Joseph-François Hertel de la Fresnière, and three hundred to four hundred Penobscots under the leadership of Madockawando. Fort Loyal was attacked, and about seventy-five men in the Casco settlement fought for four days before surrendering on the twentieth of May on condition of safe passage to the nearest English town. Instead of honoring the conditions of their surrender, most of the men, including John Swarton, were killed, and the surviving settlers were taken captive, including Hannah Swarton and her children, Samuel, Mary, John, and Jasper Swarton. One source says that of over two hundred people in the fort, only ten or twelve survived and were taken into captivity."

The girls listened in silence, absorbing the gravity of the story.

"If that should ever happen to one of you in my lifetime," she stopped to wipe a tear, "I would surely be struck dead with grief." She stopped to compose herself before continuing, "Learning to defend yourselves is not just about preparing for battle; it's about understanding the responsibilities and dangers of our world. The skills you acquire here may one day protect you and your loved ones."

Hannah and Sarah exchanged a serious look, understanding the depth of Hope's words. The other girls nodded, some more resolutely than others, but all with a newfound respect for the lessons they were undertaking.

"Now," Hope said, breaking the tension, "let's start with the basics. We'll begin with how to handle a musket properly. Remember, safety first. Always."

The girls lined up, and under Hope's careful supervision, they began their musket training. The atmosphere was noticeably charged with excitement and seriousness as each girl lifted the heavy weapons and looked down the empty barrels.

"Okay, now that you have handled a musket, who here has actually fired one off?" Hope asked.

No one answered until the Kidd pointed to Hannah. "She has."

Gulielma Maria said out loud, "Why am I not surprised?"

"No," Hannah said with a frown. "You need to try, not me." But the Kid cowed with a look of anguish, casting all eyes from her meekness to Hannah.

"Would you like to demonstrate what a flintlock's flash and bang look and sound like?" Hope asked, turning to Hannah. But when she hesitated, she added, "You don't have to if you feel uncomfortable."

Her words stung Hannah's ears like an open dare. She didn't want to be known as that girl who shied away from challenges among the other impressionable students. She knew that when it came to firing off a musket, she loved the thrill of the bang and the lingering smell of gunpowder that coated her clothing for hours, if not days, after.

She stepped forward, and Hope asked, "What do you want to do? Fire one with or without a musket ball?" She posed the question as she looked out at the targets, still upright against the hay bales.

The gleam in the young woman's eyes, looking at the weapon's half-cocked position to avoid accidental discharge, reflected her unspoken desires. Automatically lining up the needed munitions in front of her, she shook the powder horn, hearing the distinctive soft 'swish-swish' of powder grains shifting within. The sound was pleasing, almost hypnotic, and it reassured her that the powder would run free, unclogged, and true—ready to prime the charge without fouling. All before her evoked images of daring adventures and unbridled independence. Hope, sensing the spark of determination in her, stepped back cautiously, her lips pressed in a small, knowing smile, allowing the young woman to do as she would.

With the calm of practiced ease, Hannah smiled at the Kidd as she tipped a spread of powder across the flash pan and lowered the frizzen to hold it in place. Then, pulling apart a few wadding pieces, she brought them slowly to her nose to smell the oily residue. Gripping the cottony pieces in her teeth, she moved to roll a couple of musket balls with her fingers before sliding out the ramrod. Then, with lightning speed, she placed the powder horn in the barrel, poured a dose, slipped in a ball to forcefully ram the spit-out wadding into place. Without hesitating, as if her life depended on speed, she fully-cocked the hand cannon, pointed it at the arrow target, and blasted off the round. The shock of the deafening, thunderous blast—thick with smoke—hit like lightning striking the yard. The whole effect reverberated in the girls' stomachs, each flinching instinctively, hands flying to cover their ears as their eyes squinted shut against the concussive force.

Before the girls could even catch their breath, Hannah had already primed, loaded, and fired off another round. The sharp crack of the musket echoed through the air as smoke curled around her like a battle-hardened warrior. Panting heavily, she laid the gun on its side, her eyes wild with exhilaration, adrenaline surging through her veins. The ramrod, still clenched between her teeth, gave her the feral appearance of a military General ready to face down an entire battalion.

The other girls stared in awe, their faces a mix of admiration and astonishment. The Kidd broke the silence, shouting, "That was incredible. How did you learn to do that?"

Hannah shrugged, placing the ramrod on the table with a small smile playing on her lips. "Practice. Lots of practice."

Hope stepped forward, her face calm but impressed. "Thank you, Hannah. That was an excellent demonstration. Now, everyone, we're going to break this down into steps—but without the musket balls. It's crucial to get comfortable with the process before we move on to live ammunition—tomorrow," she added, raising her eyebrows. All the students were becoming used to the fact that what she said would come to pass.

"First, knowing the order of how to load a musket is essential." The girls nodded, their excitement to continue their training nearly palpable. Hannah's display had inspired them, and they were eager to learn more.

As the night grew darker and the stars began to twinkle overhead, the girls continued to practice, guided by Hope's patient instruction. Each step they took, each lesson they learned, brought them closer together, forging a bond that would carry them through whatever trials lay ahead.

When the training finally ended, the girls returned to the meeting area, tired but exhilarated. As they began to root out snacks and ale provided by the kitchen staff as their casual supper, the Headmistress announced, "Tonight, we pair off with your new dancing partners to review a few dance steps."

A chorus of complaints circled the room, prompting the Headmistress to add, "We can't have you standing around, not knowing how to dance at the ball."

Every girl's heart fluttered except Mary Allamby, who was clandestinely already married with children. But even with that encumbrance, she felt their excitement rubbing off onto her as everyone's chatter filled the air.

"From time to time, we will practice dance steps with different partners. Hold your hand up if you know how to dance any country dances?"

Unsure, most of the girls frowned and looked to see if anyone else knew of these dance steps.

"No? No one knows the 'Hole in the Wall?'" she asked, showing a footstep or two. "How about the 'Geud Man of Ballangigh' or 'Mr. Beveridge's Maggot?'"

"Ew. I don't want to dance to Mr. Beveridge's Maggot," Mary said with disdain.

"Alrighty then, how about something more eloquent; the Minuet, perhaps?"

Recognizing the dance, Gulielma Marie launched her hand into the air along with several others, including Hannah and Sarah.

"The minuet?" The Kidd chided. "That sounds French. I'm not going to hop around like a French frog."

"Alright, those with your hands up, line up on this side and face those who haven't danced this step before. You have now become our de facto dance instructors."

The Headmistress clapped her hands briskly to attract everyone's attention. Nodding at the obstinate Kidd, she said aloud, "We will practice the slower Germanic Allemande instead. Here, Hannah stand in front of me. You'll be my partner for this demonstration."

Hannah breathed in deeply through her nose and moved to face the determined woman.

"But I'm not as good with the Allemande," she said hesitantly.

"Good, then I will actually be teaching you something," she pronounced before raising her voice to the others. "Before you begin the dance, you and your partner should stand facing each other. The gentleman should offer his hand to the lady, who accepts it lightly. This is more of a ceremonial gesture before you move into the dance. Ah, remember, this is also a form of communication. Loosen up, eyes on his, and a pleasant smile is a requirement." She spoke with raised, smiling eyes at the frigid-looking Hannah. "You will then step forward on the right foot, then the left, keeping the movements smooth and in time with the music 4/4 time."

"Do you hang onto the rascal the whole time? And what is 4/4 time?" the

Kidd asked, and others nodded in agreement.

"Oh dear," the Headmistress gasped at the depth of ignorance in her students. "We'll touch on that later. Next, turn with your partner by gently raising your hands, allowing for graceful movements and interwoven turns." She and Hannah, not so gracefully, turned.

"If we are all on the dance floor at the same time, would we be bumping into each other?" the Kidd said, making the others laugh nervously.

The Headmistress nodded, saying, "We all turn in the same direction, incorporating passing steps by moving past your partner and turning to face them again."

Hannah went through the movements and stopped for further instructions, looking at the Kidd with a mix of confusion and concern.

"Always maintain elegant posture and fluid movements, ending with a bow or curtsy as a sign of respect and conclusion."

Hope looked around at all the perplexed faces and said, "See how easy it is? Now, we add another layer to the movements. I call it skipping and hopping."

After an hour of bumping and sliding and Mary Allamby huffing and puffing around the dance floor, the young women of the Willow looked and felt more secure in their footing. The Headmistress played an accompanying tune on one of the harpsichords while explaining the tempo of the 4/4 pace. As the day's lesson came to a close, Hope addressed the group. "Now that you are an accomplished dancer," she began, causing a rumble of laughter and garish moves, "you are now elevated to be your escort's dance instructor."

"What do you mean?" Mary asked.

"I mean, young men are not expected to know how to dance as well as the ladies. Therefore, you will have to teach them. Part of the evening is devoted to patience and practice. The care and comfort you show will only serve to elevate you in the eyes of the young men, fostering their appreciation."

Hope then clapped her hands together and announced, "This is the end of the day. Let us gather around the library."

Hannah and Sarah looked at each other with satisfaction as they walked, knowing that this long day was just the beginning of their journey at The Willow.

Standing beside the arrow, balancing a clam shell in her hand, Hope said, "It was a good day." Then, as if with a heavy heart, she continued, "But not perfect. Demerits are due." Everyone froze in place as she spoke. "Each night, the day will be tallied up, and demerits will be awarded accordingly. Life is harsh, and you must feel its consequences before you learn from your errors." Without hesitation, she said, "Hannah. One demerit for striking a fellow student, Gulielma Maria. That is intolerable and cannot happen again." She looked down at the clamshell before holding it up over her head to pull off the arrowhead labeled 'HH' and letting the clam slide down to lie beside the next arrow's clamshell labeled 'GM' that Gulielma Maria's mother gave her on the first night for her past transgressions.

Everyone looked on with interested trepidation, knowing that Gulielma Maria had just faked the injuries she had received that morning. Still, Hannah stood and took her demerit without a word in her defense. Then, to everyone's surprise, Sarah stepped forward. On her tiptoes, she pulled off the arrowhead labeled 'SH,' stooped down to pull out a clamshell, and let it drop over the wooden shaft with a sliding thud before replacing the arrowhead. She then turned and faced the astonished group, saying blankly, "That's because she beat me to it."

Then, even more surprisingly, the Kidd came up and did the same thing, announcing to the group, "Mine is because today I was a coward to not volunteer to shoot the musket first." Once the words left her mouth, every other student stood in line to drop a clamshell over their arrow, calling themselves cowards, except Gulielma Maria.

Then Hope sighed, tearing her eyes away from the whole row of clam shells mounted on every arrow. She reached to remove the arrowhead marked 'GM' and began to pull off her lone clam, saying, "Your helping Lena was an act of kindness and deserves the removal of one clam."

When the shell was removed entirely, Gulielma Maria took it from the Headmistress's hand and examined it closely. Then, with a nod of appreciation, she held it high over her head, letting the hefty shell fall back down the arrow shaft into place, saying, "I was not a friend today, and I may not be a friend tomorrow, but one day, I hope all of you call me your friend."

The room fell silent as the girls absorbed Gulielma Maria's words. It was a moment of raw honesty that touched everyone deeply.

Hope nodded, her moist eyes softening. "Growth and friendship take time, and acknowledging your faults is the first step towards improvement. Let this be a lesson to all of you. We are here to support each other, to grow together, and to learn from our mistakes."

The girls nodded solemnly.

As the evening continued, the girls relaxed, chatting quietly among themselves. The atmosphere was one of reflection and quiet determination.

Hannah sat with Sarah and the Kidd, feeling a mixture of emotions. She was grateful for their solidarity but determined to prove herself in the coming days.

As the sisters advanced upstairs, they were interrupted by their mother and Aunt Eunice standing at the front door.

"Hannah, Sarah. I believe your mother wants to speak with you," the Headmistress said with a nod to the door.

The sisters ran to the front door to say their goodnights. "I wish you and Aunt Eunice didn't have to stay down at the Inn."

"Maybe if your mother hadn't invited so many students, there would be room," Eunice remarked.

"Really, I ask you. Which students would you have not accepted to allow room for your snoring aunt and me?"

Eunice frowned, knowing her sister spoke the truth.

"Anyway," Abigail continued, giving each a long, silent hug. "We," she said, looking at her stern sister. "We not only have important family business in Boston—"

"Pirate business," Eunice warned.

"But along the way to Boston, we will try to spend other people's imaginary money."

"Whatever is imaginary money?" Hannah asked.

"It is money someone pledges to give to a cause—the Collegiate School moving to New Haven from Old Saybrook," she said, revealing her mission. "Pledging, but never giving."

"Meaning," Eunice added in a low, grizzly voice as she held open the front door, ready to leave, "their pledges will be fulfilled by laundered pirates' silver instead, and no one will be the wiser."

"But mother?" Sarah asked. "Move the Collegiate School? Whatever for?"

"I have some ideas about concentrating the Connecticut educational system in New Haven," she revealed with a nod.

Both girls gasped.

"And to concentrate Connecticut's eligible young Bachelors as well. How else will we ever find enough dance partners for each class's year-end ball?" Eunice added.

"My dears," Abigail added, her voice tinged with a mix of affection and solemnity. "I am sorry to say we are leaving on tomorrow's tide and may not return for possibly a month. I have an important mission regarding the Collegiate School tutors in a nearby town, and then onto Boston. While I wish I could share more details with you, I am somewhat worried about moving the school to New Haven. So many other towns are in the bidding."

"Yes," Eunice said with a stern voice. "We shall return the wiser." She turned a sly smile to Hannah, then a sterner look to Sarah. "Do endeavor to keep the house as tidy as a church and the gardens less wild than the forest. I trust you to uphold the family's honor – or at least not to dismantle it entirely. We wish we could stay, but alas, duty calls." With a graceful nod to Hannah, she opened the front door, letting in a damp, wind-laced breath of night air that smelled of rain and distant thunder. Abigail followed, watching as the girl stepped into the gloom, already leaving behind her a trail of gentle tears that shimmered like dew in the flickering lantern light.

The young women exchanged concerned glances. It was rare for their mother to embark on such journeys, and the lack of details only heightened their unease.

Abigail stepped through the threshold and made her way down the steps. From the bottom, she turned and added, "Please, take care of each other in my absence," her eyes sweeping over each of her daughters with a loving yet firm gaze. "Remember the lessons you've learned, not just about social graces, but about being mindful, commanding, and supportive of one another." Then she sighed, breathing in the fresh scents of the night's air, and told them, "We will not be sleeping at the inn." A note of finality in her voice as she waved goodbye. "Captain Holloway is waiting to ferry us to the ship," she said, pointing to men standing in the shadowy recesses. "We'll spend the night on the sloop, planning to set sail at first light's tide. Good night, my loves. I miss you already."

The revelation brought a new wave of concern among her daughters. The image of their mother embarking on a journey under the cover of the night added a sense of impulse and mystery to her mission. They knew Captain Holloway to be a reliable and seasoned sailor, which offered some comfort, but the idea of their mother sailing away at dawn without them was still unsettling.

The daughters stood for a moment, watching their mother's figure disappear into the night, each feeling pride and worry. As they slowly retreated into the house, the reality of their mother's absence began to settle in. They knew their mother was strong and capable, but the unknowns of her mission hung heavily in their hearts.

Gulielma Maria walked past Hannah and Sarah's open bedroom door and then stopped, turning back to poke her head in. "Mohawks, huh?"

Sarah looked at Hannah, who shrugged and said, "She's got to see it sometime."

"See what?" Gulielma Maria asked, stepping further into the room.

Hannah rolled up her shirt sleeve, revealing a thunderbird totem tattooed on her forearm. "This," she said, fingering the vivid symbol.

Gulielma Maria's eyes widened in surprise. "What in the world is that?"

"Let's just make a long story short," Hannah began. "I was a child and don't really remember all of it. But yes, that Hannah Swarton story today could have been me or you. I was taken by the Mohicans when I was very young."

Gulielma Maria's expression softened with a mix of shock and sympathy. "I had no idea. So—that is a Mohican symbol?"

Hannah shook her head, her face serious. "No, it's Mohawk. The Mohicans took us, and the Mohawks saved us. It's okay. It's part of who I am now. Sachem Hendrick Tejonihokarawa—"

"Who?" Gulielma Maria asked, laughing at her pronunciation.

"Tee Yee Ho Ga Row A," she said, slowly fingering the ink below the central figure. "He had a False-Face healer named Broken Finger mark my brother and me as children to protect us."

"Us? You too?" Gulielma Maria asked Sarah, who folded her arms, shaking her head slightly.

"No," Sarah said quietly. "Our older brother Jacob."

"Hendrick signed the talisman personally," Hannah said, indicating the symbols below the larger bird figure, "so anyone who saw it would protect us and return us safely to our home. But to answer your first question, yes, the Mohawks taught me many things, and I bear this tattoo as a reminder of my time with them and the lessons I learned later when we visited their villages to pay them tribute."

"What is that supposed to be, ah, a signature?"

"A wolf. For the Wolf clan," Hannah emphasized.

"Wolf? It's the skinniest dog I've ever seen."

"Yes, to me as well, but I concluded that if it were fatter, it might appear rounded, like the Turtle or possibly the Bear clan. They are warriors, not artists."

Sarah added, "What Hope said today about learning skills for survival is true. The natives are, first and foremost, warriors. So take advantage of everything you learn from The Willow. One day, it may very well save your life and the lives of your loved ones."

Gulielma Maria took a deep breath, absorbing their words. "I guess there's much more to this place than I realized."

Hannah smiled gently. "We all have our stories and our reasons for being here. The important thing is that we learn and grow together."

Gulielma Maria nodded, her eyes filled with a new sense of respect and understanding. "Thanks for sharing that with me."

Hannah rolled her sleeve back down. "No problem. Ah, please keep it to yourself. We're all sisters in this together, but that doesn't mean we still can't have our secrets."

As Gulielma Maria left the room, she looked more uplifted and confident. Hannah watched Gulielma Maria walk across the hall and into the room where the Kidd was staying. As she turned to shut the door, Gulielma Marie smiled briskly back.

In their room, Sarah looked at Hannah. "That was strange. Gulielma Marie went into the Kidd's room and shut the door."

"Oh, she rooms with the Kidd now. It seems Gulielma Marie couldn't stand Lena's quiet demeanor, and the Kidd didn't like Allamby's snoring."

Hannah laughed, "I wonder how long the Kidd will put up with GM's high-falutin nonsense."

"So you think she'll be okay with knowing?"

"Knowing what?"

"GM?" Sarah said, darting her eyes to her sister's arm, indicating her thunderbird tattoo.

Hannah nodded. "I think so. She's tough and starting to see that we're all here to support each other."

"I hope you're right. Now, I think our mission is to help the Headmistress concentrate on the shy ones in the class. I believe they have more to offer than just googling eyes," she laughed.

"Yes, and also Sarah Bradley."

"The Kidd? But why do you refer to her as such? You know she doesn't like being called Sarah."

"I know. Sarah can't go by that ridiculous nickname forever. I've been telling her about her father, Uncle Willie."

"Are you sure that is a good idea? Mother said she just learned she is the step-daughter of the infamous Captain William Kidd. This was what sent her into her rebellious spirit."

"I think once I share with her all the things he taught us—"

"Sword fighting and how to shoot muskets?" Sarah asked. "Ha, I must say, I think you were showing off, especially when you reloaded and fired another shot before everyone had a chance to recoil from your first blast. You could have at least asked if everyone was ready before beginning."

"You know, the funny thing is that it felt so natural and exhilarating; I only wanted to keep shooting until all my shots were spent."

"I know, everyone could see the crazed look in your eyes."

The sisters settled into their beds, the day's events weighing on their minds but also filling them with hope. The faint scent of extinguished tallow lingered as the rhythmic chirp of crickets seeped through the shutters.

"You know," Hannah said, lying awake, rolling to her side. "This bed does feel better with the mattress flipped."

CHAPTER 20

Leaving for Boston, 09/1715

THE MORNING SUN, resembling a large, piercing, bloodshot eye on the horizon, cast a brilliant hue over the sloop as the vessel gently made its way towards the quaint town of Branford, just east of New Haven. Abigail and Eunice, having risen with the early red dawn, were eager to commence the day's endeavors. The previous evening, Captain Holloway had shared with the women news of his discoveries during his visit to the Collegiate School in Saybrook, and the discussion had lent new vigor to their mission. Branford, they had decided, was the next critical stop.

Abigail, dressed for the day's activities, stepped out onto the ship's deck, welcomed by the fresh breeze of the open sea. The distant outline of Branford's harbor was coming into view, its peaceful demeanor belying the bustling activity that awaited them.

Captain Holloway, a figure of quiet authority and seasoned experience, approached Abigail. "We can get closer to the town's edge," he said, eyes scanning the approaching landscape. "A short journey up the Great River, and we can anchor off the bridge known locally as Cart Point."

He was familiar with these waters and their nuances. The bridge at Cart Point was a well-known landmark among the locals, marking a convergence of various paths and trade routes. Anchoring there would place them in an ideal position for their visit to Branford.

Captain Holloway explained that from Cart Point, they would enjoy a leisurely walk along Town Street, which led straight into the heart of Branford. Their destination was the corner of Pig Lane, where the Reverend Samuel Russell resided. More than a respected clergyman, Russell was a key trustee of the Collegiate School and possibly held vital information that could influence their efforts. His insights—or discretion—might prove pivotal to the success of their plans.

As the sloop navigated up the Great River, the serene beauty of the surrounding landscape unfolded. The river's banks were lined with stiff saltwater marshes, and the gentle flow of the water provided a soothing backdrop to their anticipations and plans.

Upon reaching Cart Point, the crew skillfully anchored the vessel. The bridge loomed ahead, a sturdy structure that connected not just two banks of the river but also the people and their lives.

Abigail and Eunice, now poised to disembark, gazed towards Branford with a blend of determination and curiosity. The quaint town lay ahead, its secrets veiled in the blowing noon mist, beckoning them with the promise of adventure and intrigue. Captain Holloway began to follow as they prepared to step off the boat into the dinghy, but Abigail halted him with a gentle yet firm hand. "I think it's prudent for you to stay aboard," she advised, her voice steady and commanding. Her eyes, sharp and discerning like a cat's, swept over the rugged crew as if assessing their loyalty and intent.

"But Ms. Abigail," Holloway protested, his brow furrowed with concern. "No matter the quaintness of a town, there can be an unsuspecting lurker with other plans than welcome."

"Yes, indeed, Captain," Abigail replied, her tone laced with a hint of irony. "And if your memory serves you well, the same goes for a ship's crew with desirable cargo aboard." Her words were a subtle reminder of the delicate balance of trust and caution they must maintain when carrying chests of silver.

Holloway paused, his gaze shifting back to his men, marked by a frown of contemplation. Then, with a nod of understanding, he turned and ordered the dinghy cast off. "I read your message, loud and clear, ma'am," he said, his voice carrying a mix of respect and resignation. Recognizing the depth of her strategy and the roles they each must play, he added, looking up, "Best make haste. The weather is changing."

As the dinghy drifted away, they could hear the Captain keeping his men busy, shouting out, "I feel the weather changing in my bones. Make sure your coats have a good smear of oil, or you'll be as good as a drowning rat when the sky opens over your heads."

Abigail and Eunice stepped onto the dock, their hearts beating in unison with the rhythm of their unfolding plan. The town of Branford awaited them, its sleepy streets holding the key to the next moves in the grand chess game they'd hoped to play and win.

The walk from Cart Point towards the Reverend's residence in Branford proved to be as straightforward as Captain Holloway had described. The path was clear and the distance short, but, as the Captain had warned, they remained cautious and attentive to their surroundings.

Branford, built on its Puritan foundations, had a welcoming aura. With its neat houses and well-tended gardens, the town reflected the disciplined yet harmonious life its residents led. Abigail and Eunice, while walking through the streets, could sense a subtle blend of strict Puritan values and the more pragmatic aspects of daily life in a colonial town.

The half-mile journey was invigorating, with the fresh brisk breeze and the gentle sounds of the townsfolk's commerice adding to their sense of anticipation. They passed by workmen toiling at their day's work, some stopping to offer a polite nod or a curious glance towards the newcomers.

As they came into view of Reverend Samuel Russell's house, they noted it was a quaint, well-kept abode. It was a modest structure with a detached barn, keeping with the Puritan ethos of simplicity and functionality. The house backed up to a green space, a common area that likely served as a gathering place for various community activities.

The Reverend's house, located near this central communal space, indicated his involvement and status within the town. For Abigail and Eunice, its proximity was an encouraging sign, suggesting he was a respected and influential figure in the colony.

As they approached the property, Eunice, ever observant, noted the hurried movements of a man fastening the buckles of his traveling cloak just outside. A sturdy, gray-haired figure, whom they assumed was Reverend Samuel Russell, seemed preoccupied and began to stride toward the waiting carriage as he adjusted his gloves.

Before he climbed in to make his exit, Abigail called out with friendly insistence.

"Reverend Russell?"

He turned, startled but polite, offering a brief nod. "Ah, a pleasure, but I must say, you've caught me at an inconvenient moment."

"We won't keep you long," Abigail assured him, her tone honeyed with feigned intent. "This is Eunice Fowler, and I am Abigail Huntington. We were passing through and thought it prudent to inquire about the Collegiate School. We have concerns... and wish to know how we might help."

The Reverend, already turning back toward his carriage, paused mid-step. He studied Abigail with an expression both weary and amused, before exhaling heavily.

"Concerns?" he repeated, removing his gloves and hat and tucking them under his arm. "Well, you would not be the first to voice concerns. The school has had a rocky existence since its inception."

He nodded toward the carriage, then gestured toward the house. "Come in, quickly. I can spare a moment. It's not that my urgency will accomplish a miracle."

Inside, the modest parlor was sparse but well-kept, its wooden walls lined with shelves of theological texts. A single chair at a writing desk stood near the hearth, papers strewn about, evidence of a hurried departure.

The women followed his outstretched hand and settled into a cluster of high-backed chairs, their cushions faded and embroidered with scenes of pastoral virtue. The wood creaked slightly beneath them, echoing the room's quiet formality. Reverend Russell set down his hat and gloves but remained standing, his bony fingers tapping a restless rhythm against the carved top rail of another chair, as if time—or perhaps patience—were slipping from his grasp.

"To lay it bare," he began, "the Collegiate School suffers because its very foundation—the Puritan Old Dissenter Laws—was flawed. The laws condemned 'Satan's influence' over the illiterate. The school was enacted through an ad hoc committee more concerned with appeasement than with proper planning."

Eunice leaned forward slightly. "Appeasement? To whom?"

Russell let out a short laugh. "To the factions that could not agree on where to place it! The General Court of Connecticut granted its charter in 1701, driven by urgency rather than wisdom. They did not establish a permanent home for the school, nor did they secure adequate funding. Ha, these are the same spineless people who could not agree on the placement of Connecticut's capital and, in their compromise, made Hartford and New Haven co-capitals; how absurd. Instead, the same indecision left the school's fate to the trustees' even more indecisive hands to figure out."

Abigail exchanged a knowing glance with Eunice, asking, "And these trustees are?"

Russell sighed. "The Reverend James Pierpont leads them, along with Abraham Pierson, Thomas Buckingham, and Samuel Mather, among others."

"Wait, Samuel Mather, not Cotton?" Eunice asked with poorly concealed disdain.

Russell nodded as if she should already know the answer. "Cotton Mather's uncle Samuel?" Then in a shifting stance, he added. "While I am convinced the trustees are all men of faith, they are not men of teaching. They aimed to be on par with their alma mater, Harvard, but how? The school has no true infrastructure—only borrowed rooms in various homes. The students are scattered, traveling daily to poorly planned lessons that consist of nothing more than reading and writing from the scriptures."

Eunice frowned. "And the tutors?"

Russell gave a wry chuckle. "Ah, yes, the tutors. Most of them are Harvard men—men who failed to secure ministries of their own and landed here out of necessity, not skill. They lack proper education, training, and, in many cases, the passion to teach."

Abigail folded her hands in her lap, considering his words carefully before tilting her head to ask, "And how many students are we talking about?"

"And where do they all come from?" Eunice added.

The Reverend placed his hand on his chin and paused to think about the question before coming up with an acceptable answer. "Each class typically ranges from five to ten students, depending on how many are in the area at any point in time. The majority of the students were from Connecticut towns, but some traveled from Massachusetts, where some Puritans believe Harvard had become too liberal. I suppose more students could be accommodated from further away, other colonies perhaps, if only the school were more organized and had a larger, more permanent facility."

"It seems to me," Abigail said smoothly, "that the school lacks a foundation—both in infrastructure and in method. If a central location were established, where students could live and study without the burden of daily travel, then perhaps the curriculum could be refined into a more harmonious platform of learning."

Reverend Russell lifted his gaze, and for the first time, the frustration in his furrowed brow seemed to soften. Beneath his bushy eyebrows, the Reverend's small, deep-set eyes sparkled with an alert interest that belied his years.

"You are not wrong, Mrs. Huntington," he admitted. "A proper home for the school would solidify its reputation and give it the stability it so desperately needs."

Abigail smiled. "Then perhaps it is time to rally support for such a change."

Russell's agreement was wholehearted, but his urgency returned as he checked the longcase clock in the corner.

"A discussion for another day," he said, moving to retrieve his gloves and hat. "I must hitch my carriage and ride to Old Saybrook this afternoon for school matters and to teach my courses."

Eunice smirked. "So, you are both a trustee and a tutor?"

Russell gave her a knowing grin. "When there are too few heads, one must wear many hats."

As they followed him to the door, Abigail placed a gentle hand on his sleeve. "I hope your journey is smooth, Reverend. And when you return, I'd be most interested in speaking further about the school's future."

Russell gave a firm nod, tipping his hat as they stepped out toward his waiting carriage, leaving Abigail and Eunice to watch from the front pathway as he rode off toward the uncertain future of the Collegiate School.

Despite the brevity of their conversation, Abigail felt the sincerity of the exchange was remarkable; his words had carried the weight of deep concern and commitment to the cause.

Walking away from the meeting, Eunice commented, "The Reverend was quite a pleasant fellow. He was level-headed and to the point. Men of the cloth always look like they are in a hurry to do something, making you feel as though you owe them for their time." Her words carried a hint of amusement.

"Indeed," Abigail agreed. "In this case, we should have dropped off a large donation. His forthcoming was quite enlightening, to say the least."

As the waiting crewman rowed Abigail and Eunice back to the sloop, the small boat rocked gently on the water. The rhythmic sound of oars dipping into the water and the distant call of seabirds filled the air, creating a serene atmosphere. Each sister was lost in her thoughts, reflecting on the day's events and conversations, their minds a whirlwind of contemplation and strategy.

Breaking the silence, Eunice's voice carried a note of concern. "It sounded like the Collegiate School in Old Saybrook is breaking apart."

Abigail nodded, her gaze fixed on the approaching sloop. "Yes, however, the students seem not to find it hard to attend classes where the tutors live, be it Wethersfield, Guilford, Milford, or Hartford."

"Not to mention Old Saybrook or Killingworth," Eunice offered.

"Or New Haven," Abigail added, her eyebrows raised in speculation. "The Reverend did mention that it's up to the Connecticut Assembly, which alternates between Hartford and New Haven each year for its sessions, to fund the Collegiate School. He called the two towns 'co-capitals'—I wonder, dear sister, what would happen if the struggling school suddenly became too expensive to support in Old Saybrook?"

"Then they would have to look elsewhere," Eunice replied, her tone contemplative.

"Exactly."

The boat continued its steady course, the conversation giving way once more to thoughtful silence as they pondered the future of the Collegiate School amidst the changing tides.

The dinghy slowed over the water and gently struck the sloop with a soft thud of resolve. Captain Holloway, leaning over the side, observed the two women struggling to board the ship.

"Shall we make our way to Boston?" he suggested, as the women grappled with the swaying rope ladder—skirts bunched, gloved hands grasping damp hemp, boots slipping on the slick rungs. Eunice let out a small grunt of effort, pulling herself upward onto the deck with determination. At the same time, Abigail, one foot braced against the gunwale, paused to steady herself before climbing after her.

The Captain grasped each of their shoulders and drew them close. "I fear the cargo in our hull is adding too much ballast. If a gale should catch us in open waters, we may be forced to relieve ourselves of some weight, to the detriment of our cargo."

"How much did you bring?" Abigail asked, carefully avoiding any explicit mention of silver in their hold.

The Captain leaned in, lowering his voice. "As you instructed. We're carrying the last of the treasure from the Ganj-i-Sawai—the Mughal of India's so-called 'floating mountain' of coins."

"How apropos that it marks the end of Henry Avery's stash," Eunice said into her sister's ear, exchanging a knowing smirk with the Captain.

"Eight large chests are heavy enough," the Captain replied in a low whispering growl, "but you're right. All that booty isn't doing any good lying fallow beneath your house, ma'am. And its unusual strike draws suspicion as currency." His low tone underscored the gravity of their situation.

"Just an efficient use of product, Captain," Abigail whispered with her face and eyes cast downward.

Eunice laughed, "There's nothing like the weight of a solid coin in your hand. When someone gives me a paper note, I ask, 'Where's the weight of a pound in that?'"

"Remember, silver is not just for trade, but it is a work of art in itself,"

Abigail agreed, trying to temper down her sister's words. "Heavens forbid Jeremiah Dummer be without something to smith, laundering our investor's treasure by smelting it into works of art and paying us back in our new King George's African gold. I never thought I'd say I am glad Queen Anne is dead. She inflated the price of coin currency so high that it became impractical to show it in public. Although paper money is easier to carry and trace, it is also easy to forge or incinerate. Reducing alchemy's attempts to turn lead into gold a futile sport," she added with a sly glance at her sister.

"I do so love gold and silver more than gems," Eunice proclaimed.

"I as well," Abigail agreed. "If only an alchemist could transform diamonds, rubies, and emeralds into an equal value of silver and gold. Gems are so hard to get their true value back, even after being used to make garish jewelry, ostentatious religious adornments, pompous royal metals, and fanciful tiaras for would-be princesses. Ha, it's no wonder they are piled up inside chests for pirates to steal."

"Maybe we should try selling them back to the Mughal of India," Eunice quipped.

"Would that not be convenient for all?" Abigail lamented.

Captain Holloway's past pirate's lust shimmered in his eyes briefly before his face grew more serious and he gestured out over the water. "I feel the weather changing, ma'am."

"Very well, Captain. Proceed to Boston with haste. I fear leaving the Willow for too long."

Eunice put a gentle hand on her sister's arm. "Hannah is a good lass and will undoubtedly guide Hope's curriculum on a steady course."

"Yes, but I fear for Sarah," Abigail said, frowning. "She has never been left to her own devices. How I wish I were there to watch over her burgeoning education."

"Like our mother was there for you?" Eunice asked, deepening her sister's frown.

CHAPTER 21

Mr. Reginald Lightfoot

THE NEXT DAY, the girls at The Willow Finishing School sat fidgeting in their seats, eagerly awaiting the arrival of their first guest lecturer. Word had spread quickly among the students: Reginald Lightfoot, the esteemed mathematician and astronomer, was about to make his grand entrance. His fortune was to have one of the only telescopes in Connecticut, and the Headmistress herself had practically swooned when announcing his upcoming visit.

"I am thrilled to present to you, young ladies, a true scholar of the celestial sciences," the Headmistress had declared with dramatic flair. "Mr. Lightfoot is well-versed in navigation and cartography. Over the next few months, he will undoubtedly broaden your understanding of the world and, perhaps, the very stars above."

The door to the classroom creaked open, and Reginald Lightfoot swept in. He wore an outrageously tall, plum-colored hat adorned with a single, rather bedraggled feather, which seemed to dip in time with his every nod. His long coat, embroidered with a peculiar pattern of constellations, swept the floor as he walked, his steps purposeful yet oddly theatrical. He looked every bit the eccentric intellectual he was reputed to be.

Lightfoot cleared his throat dramatically, raising one bushy eyebrow as he surveyed the class. His other hand clutched what looked like the school's copy of Sir Isaac Newton's Philosophiæ Naturalis Principia Mathematica, and his eyes darted back to the book as if it were his one true love.

"Ladies," he announced, his voice tinged with an aristocratic flair. "I am Reginald Lightfoot. Mathematician, astronomer, navigator, and cartographer—though I am certain my accomplishments speak for themselves," he said, bowing deeply with his hat in hand.

The students exchanged amused glances, whispering behind their gloved hands. Lightfoot, evidently undeterred by their giggles, continued.

"It is my great privilege to impart to you the secrets of the heavens. Few in Connecticut—nay, perhaps few in the entire colonies—possess the knowledge

I bear. And fewer still have laid hands upon this, the most exquisite volume ever penned." He held up Newton's book reverently, as if presenting a rare relic from Jesus Christ himself to an awestruck congregation.

The Headmistress cleared her throat, eager to focus on the lesson. "Yes, well, Mr. Lightfoot. I am glad you enjoyed reading our book." She stepped closer to recover the book from his hands, and he momentarily resisted before relinquishing it with a sigh. "Mr. Lightfoot also possesses a telescope. A rare instrument, as you may know."

Lightfoot puffed up like a rooster. "Yes, indeed! My telescope, crafted in London, is the finest money can buy. It allows me to peer deep into the fabric of the aether, to see sights that would blind lesser minds with their brilliance."

He gestured grandly to the girls. "Have you ever gazed upon the craters of the Moon?" He placed his hand to his heart and exclaimed, "I have." Then he continued, "The moons of Jupiter? I have. The rings of Saturn? I have. Or perhaps even the Great Nebula in Orion?"

"No!" the Kidd said with mocking astonishment. Her comment drew a look of ire from the Headmistress, who hesitated to click her clamshells to not distract from the lecture.

"No?" he exclaimed, frowning. "I didn't think so," he added, smirking.

The girls shook their heads, some stifling laughter. They were certainly captivated, though perhaps not in the way he intended.

"And navigation!" Lightfoot continued, adjusting his spectacles with an exaggerated flourish. "Should you ever find yourselves adrift upon the high seas, men of my expertise could guide you safely back to shore." He knowingly tapped the side of his nose as though revealing a hidden secret. "With the stars and a compass, I could lead you to the ends of the earth."

Eliza raised her hand with a cheeky grin and asked, "Mr. Lightfoot, have you... Ever actually been to the ends of the Earth?" The class laughed out loud.

Then Kidd asked, "If you lost your compass while there at the ends of the Earth, could you find your way back?"

The Headmistress realized the class was getting out of hand, so she redirected the conversation. "Mr. Lightfoot. With your telescope, how far can you spot a ship coming to New Haven?"

"Hundreds of miles!" he quickly declared with an enormous smile.

Shocked by his quick, inaccurate response, she asked fearfully, "But what of the curvature of the Earth?"

The learned man of science stopped to think, adjusting his thick glasses before answering, "You know. I don't think I've ever used my enormous telescope to look at something as mundane as a ship on the horizon." Lightfoot blinked, momentarily thrown off. "And, young ladies, a man of my caliber does not need to traverse the globe to understand its secrets physically. I have traversed the realms of knowledge, which is far more impressive than mere physical distance."

The class tittered, and Lightfoot's eyes returned, almost magnetically, to Newton's book, sitting on a small table next to him. He stroked the cover with a reverence usually reserved for the divine.

"Ah, Sir Isaac Newton," he sighed, almost dreamily. "A mind so vast, so beyond comprehension, it's as if he were made of stardust himself. I admit, I spend most nights under the heavens, studying the stars—but also studying the words of Newton, who unlocked the secrets of motion and—"

"Gravity?" Gulielma Marie blurted out, putting a look of shock on Lightfoot's face.

"Mr. Lightfoot," asked Kidd, attempting to stifle a smile. "If you love Newton so much, why don't you just… marry him?"

The classroom burst into laughter. Even the Headmistress had to cover her mouth to hide a grin.

Lightfoot looked scandalized, clinging to the book to his chest as though it were his dearest friend. "Why, young lady! Such irreverence! Marriage to a man's intellect—especially one as towering as Newton's—is a sacred bond beyond the understanding of mere mortals."

He adjusted his glasses, clearly flustered, and turned his attention to the two men who had just entered the classroom. They were struggling to carry a meter-long telescope and set it up on the floor. "Now, let us return to the matter at hand! I will teach you how to observe the cosmos with this magnificent instrument."

He tapped the telescope lovingly. "Observe, ladies, as I align it with the heavens... though, given that we are indoors, you'll have to use your imaginations. On the other hand, my house has a large window looking out to the heavens."

"Oh, I've seen your house," Hannah said. "It's not far from here. Large front window?"

He nodded as Hirana, trying to be helpful, suggested, "Perhaps we could take it outside, Mr. Lightfoot?"

Reginald Lightfoot froze as though struck by a sudden revelation. "Yes... yes! An outdoor lesson! How wonderfully revolutionary." He sniffed, signaling with his eyes for the men to put the instrument outside while trying to regain his composure. "Follow along, ladies!" he said haughtily, as though heading outdoors had been his idea all along.

The class gathered their shawls and bonnets and filed outside, eagerly awaiting their turn to look through the esteemed telescope. But as they clustered around, they noticed Lightfoot standing near the doorway, fixated on the copy of Newton's book again, muttering phrases like, "Ah, pure genius," and, "If only others could grasp the immensity of his wisdom."

After the two men set up the apparatus, the girls stood in line, one by one, ready to peer through the telescope.

"I don't see anything," Lena said, being allowed first in line by the obliging young men.

The Headmistress led Mr. Lightfoot by the arm to the telescope, and he picked up on Lena's question. "Yes, it is daytime. All the stars and planets cannot be seen during the daytime."

"Why?" Hirana asked.

"Why? Because of the Sun."

"My father said that each person has a guiding star. And when you die, the star falls out of the sky," Dorothy said.

"Guiding star? Don't be ridiculous. What does your father do for a living?" he laughed.

"He's a preacher."

Mr. Lightfoot looked as though his foot was now heavy in his mouth as he reflexively said, "Oh."

Then Gulielma Marie added, "She's the granddaughter of Samuel Goodyear, the former Deputy Governor of Connecticut?"

"Yes, well. Science and religion don't always meet eye-to-eye."

"So you are saying science is right and religion is—"

"No! No, no, no. I mean, that's not what I am saying." He looked to the Headmistress for help.

"What he is trying to say—I think— is when the sun comes up each day, its light is so bright, it blots out all other specks of light in the heavens, save the moon."

"Yes! Yes, yes, yes. Save the Moon," he gasped, looking up. "And today, we cannot even see the moon, um."

"So what are we going to look at?" Eliza asked.

"Oh, let's see," he said, glancing around. "Ah," he murmured, shifting the telescope away from the lone willow tree draping over the barren pond. Instead, he directed it across the backyard, past the neighbor's trees, toward a distant house. "Here we are. This house must be at least a thousand meters away. Look!" He gestured for the students to line up and take a turn at the telescope.

But when Lena looked into the eyepiece, she saw something that made her blush and turn her head away, saying, "Oh my. I don't think it is proper to look."

"What?" Kidd said, moving to view it next. In the viewfinder, she found the house with a large window. Through the window, a man could be seen standing above a tub, taking a sponge bath. "Say, I think I've seen this guy around town?"

The Headmistress moved to see next, and when she did, she quickly pushed the instrument, redirecting it with a frown of dissatisfaction toward the students' surprised faces. Then, to Mr. Lightfoot, she said, "This has all been most illuminating."

"I'll say," the Kidd exclaimed.

The Headmistress raised a calming hand to all the audible protests. "Let us all go back inside and thank Mr. Lightfoot for a most pleasant first lecture in astronomy. His next will be in mathematics, where we hope he will be just as studious—"

"And illuminating," the Kidd laughed.

Lightfoot was lost in his own world, eyes darting back and forth, muttering, "Yes, yes… the laws of motion… undeniably illuminating."

As Mr. Lightfoot and his men carefully packed up the telescope, bustling with exaggerated care, they shuffled out the door in a chorus of grunts and muffled complaints about the "delicate instrument." The door swung shut behind them with a final creak, leaving the classroom filled with a lingering sense of bewilderment and half-suppressed giggles.

Headmistress Terwilliger, who now stood near the front of the room with a patient yet slightly exasperated expression, clapped her clam shells briskly to regain the students' attention. With a firm nod, she moved toward the large slate board that had been brought out for her lesson.

"Now, ladies," she began, her tone steady and clear. "Let us focus on understanding some of the concepts Mr. Lightfoot was, shall we say, attempting to convey." There was a soft murmur of laughter, but her look silenced it quickly. "While Mr. Lightfoot may have dazzled us with tales of his telescope, let's see if we can understand these celestial principles in simpler terms."

She picked up a piece of chalk and, with swift, practiced strokes, drew a small circle on the board. "Here," she said as she labeled with care, "is the Sun. As we know, this is the center of our solar system."

Gulielma Marie laughed playfully. "But I always thought I was the center of the solar system," she said, gasping and slapping her hand to her forehead.

The classroom laughed out loud, and Kidd stood up and said, "How can that be if I am the center of the solar system?"

The Headmistress comically clacked her clam shells at first to all the ruckus and then turned to a sterner expression when her gentle nudging didn't suffice.

Once the class sat back in their seats beside the figure of the Sun, she sketched another smaller sphere and labeled it 'Earth.' Peering over the classroom to check for bad behavior, she drew an even smaller one next to the Earth and labeled it the 'Moon.' "This, of course, represents our Earth, and here we have the Moon. And beyond, the Sun and the stars." She gestured to the chalk dust lightly scattered around as if each speck were a distant star.

Headmistress Terwilliger stepped back slightly and smiled at her students' attentive faces, clearly excited to learn. "Now, you see," she continued, pointing to each body in turn. "The Sun has a gravitational pull much greater than the Earth. The Earth, in turn, exerts a stronger gravitational pull than the Moon. This gravitational force keeps each of these bodies in motion, holding them in balance so they would not fly apart out into —well, who knows where."

She drew a circular path around the Sun and labeled it the Earth's orbit.' "The orbit is simply a pathway the earth takes by drifting through the aether around the Sun under the influence of—"

She held her hand to her ear to hear the class moan in unison, "Graaaa-vit-y" as she traced her finger around the Sun.

Hope nodded her approval and asked, "At the same time, the Moon revolves around the Earth on a similar path, due to—"

"'Graaaa-vit-y" the class repeated with the same monotone as she drew yet another smaller circular path around the Earth, showing the Moon's orbit.

Her hand moved gracefully across the board, chalk dust floating like tiny stars in the faint light filtering through the windows. "Each of these bodies," she continued, her voice taking on a reverent tone. "Drifts in the vastness between the stars, known as the aether."

Patience looked thoughtful. "So… are we, ah, I mean, the Earth just floating in this, what you call aether? That's kinda creepy, isn't it?"

Headmistress Terwilliger nodded. "In a manner of speaking, yes. We are indeed drifting in aether, along with the Sun, Moon, and stars. But thanks to gravity, we remain tethered to our world, stable and secure. It's what holds everything together in this delicate balance."

Marie Allamby timidly gathered the courage to ask, "Is there also gravity between a man and a woman?"

A wave of surprised gasps rippled through the classroom, hands flying up to cover amused smiles. Eyes darted from Marie to the Headmistress, anticipation evident in every glance.

"Of course," she mused. "But that is a gravity of a different kind, I think. We will discuss that one in a different class, taught by Dr. Ignatius Snodgrass."

Fearing the mention of a physician as a teacher, the girls were silent, each contemplating this newfound perspective of the heavens. The Headmistress made the grand mysteries of the cosmos seem clear, almost as if they could reach out and touch them.

"Now," she said, her tone lighter as she capped off the lesson. "If we were to travel beyond the influence of Earth's gravity, or even the Sun's, we would drift, just like those stars. But even they remain fixed, presumably by?"

"Gravity," each student mindlessly said with the reflexive fervor they delivered an 'amen' at church.

"But here on Earth, we are part of this grand, celestial dance," she concluded.

The students exchanged glances, some smiling, others deep in thought. The Headmistress had taken Lightfoot's convoluted explanations and brought them down to Earth—or, instead, to a more understandable orbit.

"And," Headmistress Terwilliger added with a knowing look. "It is important to remember that while men like Mr. Lightfoot may proclaim grand titles and complex terms, the heart of understanding lies in simplicity." She gave a soft chuckle, which the students shared, remembering Lightfoot's theatrics with amusement.

The Headmistress took one final look at the chalkboard, with its elegant orbits and labels. In her own quiet way, she had brought the stars down into the classroom, casting her students not as mere spectators but as participants in the grand, cosmic dance.

"So, my dear students," she said, setting the chalk aside. "Remember this: while we may be small, we are part of something far grander than we can see—a testament to the wonder of the world and the vastness of God's creation."

With that, she dismissed the class, and the girls left with a spark of curiosity and wonderment. They filed out of the classroom, ready to share their newfound knowledge and perhaps, one day, even challenge the grand ideas of men like Reginald Lightfoot.

CHAPTER 22

Storm

IN OPEN WATERS, the wind turned stiff out of the East, challenging the sloop's sails with its unyielding force. By the time, the sea, previously a picture of tranquillity, was transforming into a restless entity, its waves growing in size and strength. Abigail and Eunice, unaccustomed to the roughness of the sea, clung to the railings, their eyes wide with a mix of fear and awe. The raw power of nature, so evident in the churning waters and the relentless wind, was both terrifying and exhilarating. The open sea, with its unpredictable temperament, reminded them of their vessel's smallness in the vastness of the world.

As the sloop's sails billowed in the gusty wind, Captain Holloway shouted out orders with a voice that cut through the howling wind. "Keep a keen watch on your footing, lads!" he bellowed, his eyes scanning the horizon and then falling on his crew. The men, seasoned by countless voyages, moved with practised agility, their bodies swaying in rhythm with the vessel's motions. "Be prepared to drop the main sail if'n we keel over!" as his shouts of pending dire straights strengthened everyone's resolve.

The deck became a flurry of activity as the crew hustled to adjust the sails, ensuring the sloop harnessed the wind's power efficiently without tearing under the increasing strain. Each man knew his role, their movements swift and precise, a demonstration of their experience and the captain's leadership.

The sloop's stem heaved and dipped, riding the waves with a vigour that matched the ocean's mood. The captain, ever vigilant, kept a steady hand on the helm, guiding the vessel with an expertise born of years at sea. His orders continued to ring out, a guiding beacon amidst the cacophony of wind and waves.

"As I had suspected, Ma'am," Captain Holloway shouted over the roar of the wind when Abigail made her way to the helm, gripping the rail tightly for support. His face was set, eyes squinting against the spray of the sea, as he steered the sloop with unwavering focus. "I suggest we make for Old Saybrook lest the storm ravages our sails and set us adrift in this tempest." His voice carried a sense of urgency. Abigail, her hair whipping around her face, nodded in agreement. The wisdom in the captain's words was clear. With its sheltered harbour, the seaside town offered a haven from the burgeoning storm. It was a detour, but it was necessary to ensure the safety of the vessel and all on board.

The captain barked new orders to the crew, his command cutting through the storm's chaos. The men sprang into action, adjusting the sails and changing course with harrowing efficiency. As the sloop turned, cutting through the waves towards Old Saybrook, Abigail held fast, her eyes fixed on the roaming horizon. The decision to seek refuge was wise, but she couldn't help but wonder about the delay it would cause in their plans. She had hoped to reach Boston in just a few days to launder pirated silver, yet, in the face of nature's fury, such concerns were unimportant. Survival was paramount, and they had a fighting chance in Captain Holloway's capable hands.

"As you will, Captain," Abigail responded, her voice steady despite the tumult around them.

She turned, bracing herself against the boat's sway as she made her way back to the small cabin. The sloop pitched and rolled on the waves, proof of the storm's growing intensity. Each step was cautious and measured as she navigated the heaving deck.

Upon reaching the cabin, Abigail found Eunice sitting stiffly on the edge of the narrow bunk, her hands clasped tightly in her lap, eyes fixed on the wooden door as if trying to bore through it. The modest, cramped quarters offered a semblance of shelter from the chaos outside, its damp dimness wrapping her in uneasy quiet. Eunice looked up as Abigail entered, her face still drawn but lifting slightly, her eyes searching her sister's for reassurance.

"We're heading to Old Saybrook," Abigail announced, settling down beside her sister. "The captain believes it's our best chance against the storm."

Eunice nodded, understanding the necessity of the decision. The sisters sat huddled in the cabin's close quarters as the storm raged outside. For now, Old Saybrook was their beacon of hope, a safe harbour amid the tempest.

After enduring an hour or two of the constant crashing of the hull against the angry waves, the storm outside seemed to subside momentarily. Abigail and Eunice rose from their shared secured spot on the bunk and began to stretch their cramped limbs. The brief respite, however, quickly gave way to a more jarring sensation. Suddenly, there was a solid feeling of complete stoppage, and the cabin heaved violently, tilting onto its side and thrusting the women against each other on the cabin wall.

"What has happened?" Eunice shouted, her voice laced with panic, as Abigail landed on top of her.

"I believe we have gone aground," Abigail replied gravely, her tone a mix of fear and realisation. The abruptness of their situation was disorienting; the once horizontal floor of the cabin was now a vertical barrier against which they were pressed. In the cramped and dishevelled cabin, Abigail and Eunice clung to each other, their minds racing with questions about their safety and the fate of their ship.

Though the storm had slightly abated, it continued to churn the sea around them. The sound of Captain Holloway shouting orders and the crew scrambling on deck could be heard over the howl of the wind, as could the threatening creak of the ship's strained timbers.

After an a several tenuous minutes, the door to the cabin creaked open, and Captain Holloway looked in, his face etched with the fatigue of the day's trials. He cast a discerning eye over the cabin, ensuring the safety of its occupants. Abigail immediately voiced her concern. "What has happened? The silver?"

"Aye, Ms Abigail, we are listing on the Saybrook sandbar," the captain replied, his voice steady despite the circumstances. "Safe and sound for the moment, ma'am, but the storm is still shifting to the nor'east. With any luck, it may blow us off into deeper water. If not, we will at least see the shape of the hull for any indications that we need to cork and careen. Aye, as far as the silver goes. It is still in the hold, but the question remains: is it still in their chests?"

Despite the tension of the situation, Abigail couldn't help but smile at the captain's words. "Captain, I've always enjoyed your unyielding optimism."

The captain offered a weary but genuine smile in return. "Optimism, Ms Abigail, is sometimes all a sailor has in times like these."

The cramped and tilted cabin felt slightly more bearable after the captain's parting words. Even in the face of adversity, his confidence was a comforting balm to the sisters' frayed nerves.

Outside, the night stretched on, the storm continuing its relentless tango around them. Inside the cabin, they settled in for the night, each lost in their own thoughts but united in their hope for the morning's light and the chance of rescue from their precarious perch on the Old Saybrook sandbar.

The night seemed endless, the sloop held in a tense, tilted stillness. For Abigail and Eunice, morning could not come fast enough; each minute in the cramped cabin dragged like an hour. The storm passed, but its uncertainty lingered.

At dawn, hope arrived with the light. The crew was already moving, voices and boots thudding across the deck as they assessed the damage. Abigail and Eunice emerged stiff and weary, climbing carefully to the slanted deck.

The sloop lay stranded on the Saybrook sandbar, her hull canted, the sea rushing around her quickly with indifference.

Stripped to their essentials, the men waded into the cold shallows, sounding the seabed with poles, calling depths, searching for a way to get free. Holloway directed them steadily, his voice cutting clean through the rippling surf. Abigail and Eunice watched, knowing their fate rested with these men and the tide.

Then rowboats appeared.

Relief flickered across Abigail's face. "Rescue," she murmured.

Captain Holloway's eyes narrowed. "Not always."

The boats circled like sharks. "Come ashore!" the men called, voices slick with false concern.

"We are not in danger," Holloway shouted back. "Help tow the bow to deeper water, or be on your way."

One called out, "Your hull's breached! She'll sink!"

"Our vessel is sound," Holloway replied coolly. Turning to Abigail, he said low, "They want us off the ship to plunder our cargo as salvage."

"What do we do?" she asked.

"We wait—or signal that ship at anchor to help tow us into deeper waters," he said with a flick of his eyes to the distant ship. "Better still, let the river do the work. Floodwaters will lift us free."

"Floods?"

"How do you think the sand got here? Look—we're already half a foot higher than we were five minutes ago."

Abigail looked past the captain and was surprised to see the crew climbing aboard in the swirling water. The sloop creaked, timbers groaning as water pressed beneath her. The salvagers grew restless, cursing as their prize slipped away.

Then the river surged.

The sloop lurched. The mast straightened. The hull shifted free.

Holloway watched the looters with grim satisfaction. "Looks like the sea favors the patient."

"Trim the sails!" he barked. "We're not clear yet."

As the sloop drifted into deeper water, Holloway turned to Abigail. "We still need to check for leaks."

"Do what you must," she said. "We trust you."

The salvagers scattered. The bilge was pumped, the hull sound. Holloway even wrung their stolen flotsam back from the would-be pirates—for a few coins of silver.

By afternoon they were underway, rounding Cape Cod toward Boston. The sea was calm, the wind kind.

"We were fortunate not to ground off Provincetown," Holloway said. "She'd have been smashed to kindling."

Eunice smiled. "Still time for that yet."

"I plan to avoid it," he replied, eyes fixed ahead.

The sloop cut cleanly through the water. Abigail watched the shoreline recede, relief washing over her. The danger had not passed—but they were afloat, intact, and moving forward once more.

CHAPTER 23

The Disappearing Book

THE MORNING SUN had barely risen above the horizon when the Willow girls were already bustling about, tidying their beds and gathering in the kitchen for breakfast. Today was to be a day steeped in the French way of life—language, customs, cuisine, and, much to the dismay of one particular student, the minuet.

As breakfast ended, the dance lessons began. With her ever-keen eye, the Headmistress noticed that the Kidd was not participating with the usual grace expected. Instead, she was hopping around the room like a French frog. Her lips pursed in mock concentration. Her exaggerated leaps and haphazard arm movements bore little resemblance to the delicate steps of the minuet they were all supposed to be learning.

"Kidd!" the Headmistress called sharply, clacking a pair of clamshell castanets she kept in her pocket precisely for moments like these. The sharp, percussive sound echoed through the room, halting Kidd's amphibious antics.

"Settle down at once!" she commanded, her voice like a snap of cold winter air. "The minuet is not a dance for jesters but a refined art that speaks of dignity and poise. You are to float, not flail!"

The Kidd muttered under her breath but complied, settling into her movements with a begrudging respect, though a mischievous gleam lingered in her eye.

As the lesson continued, the conversation shifted from graceful movements to weighty ideas, naturally drifting to Sir Isaac Newton and his theories on gravity. It was, after all, a matter of gravity that kept their feet anchored to the floor, allowing them to execute their steps precisely — the Headmistress explained.

Hannah, ever the curious one, raised her hand. "If we're learning about gravity, shouldn't we have Newton's book? Possibly name a new step of the Kidd in his honor?" she asked, glancing toward the school's small but well-loved library.

"An excellent suggestion," the Headmistress replied with a nod. "It would be useful to have his work on hand. Why don't you fetch it for us, Hannah?"

Eager to delve into Newton's words, Hannah dashed to the library, trying to remember a quote from the 'Great Thinker' she thought would be apropos in teaching. She scanned the shelves, her fingers brushing along the spines of well-worn books, each holding a world of knowledge within its covers. But as she looked under 'N' for Newton and then on every other shelf just in case it had been misplaced, she found no trace of the book.

With a slight frown, she searched again, methodically checking each row. When that failed, she began to ask her classmates if they'd seen it. They shook their heads one by one, each as perplexed as she was.

"Has anyone borrowed it?" Hannah asked, her voice carrying a note of urgency.

"I haven't seen it," Hirana responded, shrugging her shoulders.

"Perhaps it's in someone's room?" Lena suggested.

Hannah's quest soon turned into a full investigation as she went from room to room, looking to see if the book was lying around. By now, whispers were starting to spread. The esteemed book by Sir Isaac Newton, the great mind of their age, had gone missing!

Finally, Hannah approached the Headmistress with a furrowed brow. "Headmistress, I can't find the book anywhere. I've checked every shelf, and no one seems to have it."

The Headmistress considered this news for a moment. "Very well," she replied, though a glint of worry appeared in her eyes. "We must not take this lightly. Sir Isaac's work is invaluable, not only to our studies but to science itself. I shall send word to Mr. Lightfoot at once. Perhaps he inadvertently picked it up when he departed yesterday."

A swift message was dispatched to Mr. Lightfoot, inquiring if he might have mistakenly taken the prized volume home. Meanwhile, the students continued their lessons with an unspoken tension filling the air. The missing book had become a topic of fervent speculation.

"What if Mr. Lightfoot took it to sell?" whispered Patience, her eyes wide with scandalous thoughts.

"Nonsense! He wouldn't do that!" Mary replied, though she sounded a bit unsure of herself.

The Headmistress overheard and silenced the room with a single look. "Let us not engage in wild conjectures. If he does have it, I am certain it is merely a misunderstanding."

The day dragged on, each hour stretching longer as the mystery of the missing book gnawed at everyone's minds finally, as the sun began to set, a message returned from Mr. Lightfoot.

He had checked his belongings thoroughly and assured them he did not have the book. He even suggested that perhaps they had misplaced it themselves, though the tone of his note hinted at his own annoyance at being troubled over what he called "such trivial matters."

"Trivial matters?" the Headmistress muttered, her lips pressed into a thin line. "He, above all, would say Sir Isaac Newton's writings are hardly trivial."

The girls shared uneasy glances. The book was nowhere to be found, and now it seemed as though their esteemed visitor needed to learn its whereabouts, too.

As the evening drew close, the Headmistress gathered the students for one final address. "Until we locate this book, I must ask each of you to remain vigilant. Come to me immediately if anyone sees or hears anything that might help us in our search."

The girls nodded, each whispering among themselves as they left, hoping the mystery would soon resolve itself. As they headed off to bed, they exchanged theories about what might have happened. Perhaps one of them had borrowed it without realizing the importance of returning it.

"Or perhaps," suggested the Kidd, the class's most imaginative student, "it vanished on its own, spirited away by the unseen forces of gravity."

Hannah and Sarah lay in bed that night, their minds racing. Sarah couldn't shake the feeling that the book's disappearance was more than mere carelessness, a suggestion that Hannah had already suspected.

"I think Mr. Lightfoot stole the book away to be his own."

"I agree, but what are we to do?" Hannah asked.

Then, as if thinking the same thing, they sat on the side of the bed and began putting on their clothing.

Hannah looked up at her sister for her reaction as she stowed her muskets in her belt under her shawl. When Sarah responded by lifting the edge of her shawl to reveal an inch of shiny, sharp metal, Hannah added, "If we take the book back by force, would that make us pirates?"

Sarah smiled, patting her knife, saying, "I hope so. After all, if Sir Isaac Newton could uncover the laws of the universe with his instruments, surely we could find a single book with ours."

They moved past the Kidd's open door as they stole out of their room. To their chagrin, they heard the familiar voices of both the Kidd and Guiliana Marie talking about Captain William Kidd.

"Whoa, where are you two going?" The Kidd said, seeing them pass, drawing Gulielma Marie's attention.

"This is none of your business. Now get back to bed," Hannah said firmly, but Gulielma Marie stepped forward, her curiosity piqued.

"You two aren't sneaking out, are you?" she queried.

Hannah and Sarah exchanged a glance but said nothing, prompting the Kidd to chime in, "Does this have something to do with the missing book?"

When silence was their only answer, the Kidd's eyes lit up with determination. "Wait. I'm going with you," she declared.

Without hesitation, she pulled a metal sword from under her bed and gave it a theatrical swish through the air, startling everyone in the room.

"No. You can't go. If we are caught, there will not be enough clamshells in Connecticut to cover our arrows. It will mean expulsion for sure."

"Good, then I'm going with you, too," Gulielma Marie said, and they all stood silently, trying to figure out what to do next.

"I tell you what. Both of you stay here and watch our backs coming back in—"

"No," Gulielma Marie said emphatically. "If we don't go, no one goes. That's the deal. I'd hate for a loud noise to attract the attention of the Headmistress—coming from your room, perhaps?"

"You wouldn't?" Sarah scolded, but the look on her face said otherwise.

Slipping out the back into the moonlit yard, the four young women tiptoed around the side of the house and out into the street.

"Do you know where we are going?" the Kidd asked, and Gulielma Marie shrugged.

Hannah said, "I know where it is," and Sarah asked, "Where?"

"You know. We walked by it several times, looking for a place to purchase. It's a funny-looking house with a big front window." Then the realization hit her, "Oh, sorry. You weren't with us the first time when we were looking for a place for the Willow."

"Yes," Sarah hissed. "And why wasn't I included the first time?"

"Ah, not sure. You'll have to ask mother?" she said trying to deflect the question.

"The large window is where he puts his telescope. It's not far."

Trying not to be spotted wandering around at night, the girls ran from tree to shrub like Indians on the hunt. Gulielma Marie bruised her arm running into a tree limb and was shushed into submission when she cried out.

The Kidd said harshly, holding up her sword like a crazed pirate, "There's no crying. Not tonight!"

When they reached the house, they slipped around the back and found the door unlocked. "Hah," Sarah said. "There's not even a lock on the door."

"He'll reconsider that after tonight," Gulielma Marie chortled.

Each girl slid inside, leaving the door partially open for a quick getaway. As they moved slowly through the house, the moonlight shining through the windows helped them navigate the labyrinth of misplaced clothing, books, and worn-out furniture. They all froze when they heard a creaking of the overhead flooring.

Hannah whispered, "He must be up looking at something through his telescope." She then pointed for Kidd and Gulielma Marie to stay behind, but they would not listen as each moved quietly up the narrow stairs. Halfway up, the old boards began squeaking under the weight, causing them to freeze. Hearing shuffling feet, their worst nightmare sounded out.

"Hello? Is someone there?"

Hannah looked down the stairs at all the people with her and could think of only one thing to do. "Hello, Mr. Lightfoot. It's ah, Carol from the Willow," she lied, hoping he didn't remember her name. "You told us to come over and look through your telescope." She spoke with what each of the girls hoped was the sound of innocence.

The surprised man moved quickly to a candle to look down at them as they came up the stairs. "Did I really?"

He looked perplexed as each trotted up the stairs and into his observatory. "Did I really tell all of you to come?"

"No, not really," Kidd said, pulling out her sword and pointing it at his gut. "We came by to get Sir Isaac Newton's book back. We know you took it."

The man's eyes shot to the side of the room. He reached out to grasp the dull sword and said, "But I don't have it."

Gulielma Marie, already moving to where he looked, spotted the book and shouted, "Here it is!"

Mr. Lightfoot moved quickly, pulling the sword from Kidd's hand and pointing it at Gulielma Marie, before shouting, "Get back."

Seeing the Kidd's rash decision, Hannah moved to the side of the room to observe. When the tides turned, she cocked a musket and pointed it at him, saying, "A sword in a gunfight? Mr. Lightfoot, I thought you were smarter than that. We don't want any trouble—just the book back."

Mr. Lightfoot laughed, "Those little things aren't even real."

Hannah cocked her second pistol, saying, "That's not what the pirate who tried to steal from my mother thought when I blew his brains out on the deck. Now, give her the sword back and sit down before you get into more trouble."

"More trouble?"

"Seriously? You shot someone?" Gulielma Marie gasped, and Sarah and the Kidd shrugged.

"Yes. More trouble, like when you invited us over tonight, you touched her breast," Hannah said, slyly pointing a pistol in Gulielma Marie's general direction.

"He did?" she asked, confused.

"I did?" he asked, equally confused.

Hannah looked at her with exasperation, wanting her to play along. Once Gulielma Marie received the message, she said, "Yes, keep your hands to yourself," and reached out to slap the man's already surprised face.

"I'm going to call the constable," he replied, rubbing his cheek. "It's your word against mine. Who will believe a gang of self-appointed girls over a renowned man of science? Did you learn nothing from the Salem Witch Trials?"

"Indeed, starry-eyed Sam," Gulielma Marie said. "You mean who is not going to believe the granddaughter of William Penn, the founder of Pennsylvania, over a fickle Lunar Larry with the predilection for touching young women inappropriately?"

"Who? What?" the man of science sputtered, casting his eyes around the dark room, feeling outnumbered and outsmarted. "Look, I only wanted to borrow the book," he cried out in a defensive, conciliatory confession.

"Then why did you suggest we lost it at the Willow, Cosmic Caleb?" Gulielma Marie grilled.

"Oh, yes," he said, caught in a lie. "That was a delay tactic—to give me more time with the precious book." Looking back and forth at the young ladies and the confiscated book while rubbing his red cheek, he sheepishly asked, "What do we do next?"

The next morning, bright and early, Mr. Lightfoot knocked briskly on the front door of The Willow, his expression a blend of false urgency and poorly masked nerves. He fidgeted incessantly, adjusting the cuffs of his coat and clearing his throat as though rehearsing lines in his head. When the house servant opened the door, he pushed his head forward, craning to see who might be present within.

"Good day, sir," the servant greeted, quirking a brow. "May I inquire about your business here?"

Mr. Lightfoot barely registered the words. "Yes, yes, my business. Is the Headmistress about?" he stammered, his voice teetering on the edge of frantic. He shuffled nervously on the porch, smoothing his queue and tugging at his coat as though his composure hung by a thread.

Moments later, the Headmistress appeared, her eyes sharp with morning clarity. "Mr. Lightfoot," she greeted him, a bit surprised to see him unannounced. "What brings you here so early?"

He bowed awkwardly, nearly toppling forward in his eagerness. "Madam Headmistress, I was… well, I was in the neighborhood and, er, thought I might inquire—have you, by chance, located Sir Isaac Newton's book? The one we discussed?"

Before the Headmistress could answer, the sound of thunderous footsteps on the staircase behind her interrupted their conversation. Hannah, Sarah, The Kidd, and Gulielma Marie appeared, seemingly drawn to the commotion at the door. Gulielma Marie held the book triumphantly in her hand, her face alight with mock surprise.

"Look what I found when I flipped the mattress!" she exclaimed, her tone dripping with innocent excitement, and one of her signature smirks curling her lips.

Mr. Lightfoot froze at the sight of the girls, his face draining of color before flushing an alarming shade of crimson. But as he locked onto the familiar leather-bound volume in Gulielma Marie's hands, his eyes widened in relief.

"Oh my goodness!" the Headmistress exclaimed, her face lighting up. "Thank heavens it's been found!"

"Good!" Mr. Lightfoot blurted out, his voice breaking as he attempted to feign relief. "Wonderful news! Absolutely splendid!" He nodded so vigorously it seemed his head might detach.

Hannah stepped forward, her expression deceptively sweet. "Thank you for your concern, Mr. Lightfoot," she said smoothly. "Would you like to borrow it again?"

Mr. Lightfoot recoiled as though the book were a venomous serpent. "Oh! Oh no, no, no, I couldn't possibly impose," he stammered, waving his hands frantically. "I wouldn't dream of it. I… I've remembered an urgent errand I must attend to. Mustn't dally. Farewell, ladies, farewell!"

He backed away from the door with the grace of a drunkard trying to navigate a tightrope, nearly tripping over the threshold before whirling around and fleeing down the path. The girls watched him retreat, stifling giggles until the door shut behind him.

Unable to contain themselves any longer, they erupted into laughter, collapsing onto one another in shared glee. "Did you see his face? I thought he was going to faint!" Sarah howled, clutching her stomach.

"Oh, I can't wait to hear his next lecture!" Gulielma Marie said with a mischievous gleam in her eye.

The Headmistress, however, frowned, her eyes narrowing slightly. "Quite," she said curtly, her tone edged with suspicion. She looked between the girls, her instincts tingling, but said nothing further. Instead, she turned toward the library with the book in hand, muttering something about securing it in a locked case this time.

CHAPTER 24

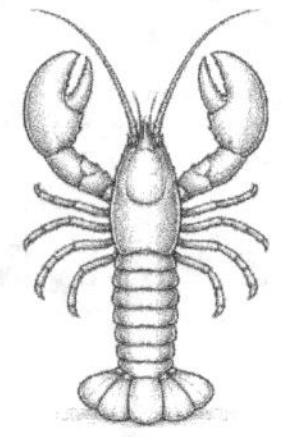

Boston

AS THE SLOOP DREW CLOSER to Boston, the sight of ships lining the docks, packed tightly like herring in a net, came into view. To avoid the congestion of the city docks, Captain Holloway skillfully steered the vessel north, sailing into the mouth of the Charles River past Hudson's Point. Their destination was Gee's Shipyard, known for its quality craftsmanship and reliable service.

As they navigated the bustling waterway, Captain Holloway approached Abigail and Eunice, curiosity evident in his expression. "You've never told me how you met this Joshua Gee fellow," he said.

Eunice laughed, her eyes sparkling with joy. "The shipwright Gee? Goodness, who knows? How did we meet you?" she teased. Leaning into her sister and cupping her lips, she added, "I do believe he is in between wives at the moment. Oh, dear. Do you believe that since both his previous wives were named Elizabeth, this puts me at a disadvantage?"

Gazing at the lively town of Boston, Abigail gathered her thoughts before responding. "It was my mother, Annica, who knew him first." She paused, reflecting on the story she had never told. "Joshua Gee was quite the adventurous spirit back in his younger days. According to my mother, he traded far and wide, which included the Mediterranean. As with many merchants who dared pass through Gibraltar's Pillars of Hercules, he was captured and enslaved by Barbary Pirates out of Algeria."

The captain groaned at the mention. "Moorish devils," he muttered.

"Well, it wasn't as bad as all that," Abigail continued. "He was a clever fellow and a good shipbuilder. Soon, he gained the trust of his slave master, and one day, he hitched a ride back to Manhattan on my great Uncle Phillip's ship, the La Grace."

She smiled, recalling the way her mother always spoke of Gee. "Mother saw his worth and invested capital in him, setting him up in Boston, where he soon opened a shipyard on the Charles River. He has been a close friend of the family, and we visit him whenever we have business in Boston."

Holloway nodded, a look of respect in his eyes. "Well, he has the reputation of a highly skilled craftsman. I'll be glad for him to give our hull a once over," he said.

Abigail smiled reassuringly, confident in Gee's abilities. "He's the best in Boston," she affirmed.

As they finally came alongside Gee's Shipyard, they found it bustling with activity, and to their dismay, there were no slips available. Captain Holloway, demonstrating his skill at the helm, maneuvered the sloop to double-moor alongside a frigate undergoing a re-rigging, its yardarms and sails meticulously worked on.

As they secured their ship against the larger vessel, a sudden commotion erupted, shattering the relative calm. Shouts of anger reverberated across the deck, creating a cacophony of discord. The frigate's captain, his face flushed with indignation, loudly protested, vehemently opposing their unexpected encroachment.

"Slash those lines free!" the frigate captain barked at a lone seaman.

However, before the situation could escalate further, Abigail acted with remarkable swiftness. She leaped onto the larger ship, her movements embodying a blend of determination and grace. She strolled across the deck, her presence commanding yet unobtrusive, exuding quiet authority. Without uttering a word, she then disembarked down the gangplank that reached from the frigate to the dock.

Captain Holloway watched as Abigail disappeared from view before shouting, "Hear ye, matey," his voice booming across the divide to the crewman on the other ship. "Ye need not do this, son." But the seaman, caught in the grips of fear from his captain's stern command, clearly felt he had no choice but to obey and took his knife to the lines. Each fell into the water, letting the sloop adrift.

The frigate's captain, momentarily taken aback by Abigail's bold yet composed demeanor, resumed watching the floundering vessel with satisfaction. His hand was held firmly on the hilt of his cutlass as if waiting for more action against his boat.

The crew of the sloop, taking their cue from Captain Holloway, resumed their work with renewed focus, ensuring their drifting vessel stayed close enough to the yard.

Gesturing around the sloop's deck to indicate Abigail's absence, Captain Holloway remarked to Eunice, "Well, leaving without a word is one way to handle a disagreement."

Before responding, Eunice caught sight of her sister in the distance, approaching the shipyard's main office. "Seems like Abigail can defuse any argument without a single phrase," she said.

The frigate's captain, still standing with the cutlass in hand, watched them for a moment longer before sheathing his weapon and returning to his ship's business.

When Abigail came back into sight, she was not alone. Accompanying her was an older man, his thinning gray hair and lean frame giving him a distinguished appearance. They moved swiftly down the path from the main office. The man's expression was scowling, yet his eyes held a determined and commanding presence. As they approached the ship that had refused to allow the sloop to double dock, the man's demeanor shifted to visible anger.

Stepping onto the gangplank with Abigail at his side, the older man shouted, his voice carrying across the harbor with such force that spittle flew from his mouth. "Where is the captain of this scowl?" he demanded, his tone brooking no argument.

The captain of the frigate, taken aback by the sudden confrontation, emerged on deck. The older man wasted no time. "What is the meaning of your cutting the sloop free?" he questioned sternly.

The frigate's captain, with an air of arrogance, replied, "Ah, Mr. Gee. I don't allow such practices on my ship. It's not good to share the dock with another who could be pirates, traversing my deck day and night looking for things to steal."

Gee, undeterred, informed him, "This sloop is trustworthy."

But the frigate's captain remained obstinate, refusing to reconsider.

"Aye," he scoffed. "A pirate's trustworthy—right up until he pinches your spyglass, drinks your rum ration, or lifts the pipe tobacco from your coat. And if he can't find something worth stealing, he'll stick you with a blade just for the trouble."

"I see," said Mr. Gee, his voice laced with disappointment. He turned to one of the shoremen working the vessel and gave instructions. Then, giving the frigate's captain one last look of disapproval, he and Abigail exited the gangplank.

From his post at the helm of the sloop, Holloway eased the tiller in short, deliberate motions, letting the current nudge the vessel sideways while trimming the sails just enough to keep her steady. He was careful to maintain his position near the dock, holding her in place with slight shifts of the rudder so he could slip neatly into a berth as soon as it was vacated. From there, he watched with quiet curiosity as the man produced a bottle of rum from his pocket, and he and Abigail broke into a cheerful, light-hearted exchange, laughing as they took turns raising it to their lips.

Before long, the crew who had been working on the frigate's sails descended the shrouds and ladders to assemble on deck, confirming their orders. Then, without hesitation, they began to cut the frigate loose from the dock. The frigate's captain, realizing he was alone with only one other man while his ship's crew was on shore leave, began to shout and protest. His voice, however, seemed to fall on deaf ears.

As the frigate drifted away on the Charles River, the captain's screams of dire straits echoed, ignored by everyone, save the poor, lone crewman who was receiving orders from the fuming captain that he could not accomplish alone. Meanwhile, Captain Holloway, seeing the scene unfold, seized the opportunity. He skillfully maneuvered the sloop into the now-abandoned slip.

Abigail watched the scene with relief and gratitude as Captain Holloway assisted her sister to the pier after their swift landing. "Well, that's one way to solve a docking dispute," she remarked to her sister, who nodded in agreement.

"Indeed, Ms. Abigail," Holloway replied, his eyes on the task at hand. "Sometimes the sea delivers justice in its own unique way."

Abigail looked out in the channel and quipped, "I hope they do not become a navigational hazard."

Mr. Gee gestured with a shrug, saying, "If they are, it's their fault. The crew should have tied their line better, departing for shore leave."

"Quite," Abigail chuckled.

As the sloop sat in its berth, the crew secured the vessel, stowing the sails and dressing the deck. The morning drama had come to a satisfying resolution. For Abigail, Eunice, and Captain Holloway, it was a reminder that the unexpected was always around the corner in the world of seafaring.

CHAPTER 25

Joshua Gee

THE BUSTLING ACTIVITY AT THE DOCK continued as a stout horse-drawn cart pulled up alongside the sloop. The crew, under Captain Holloway's vigilant supervision, began unloading the cargo hold. With coordinated effort, they hoisted out the chests of silver, still intact despite the arduous journey, and carefully loaded them onto the cart.

Once the job was complete, Joshua Gee, overseeing the operation with a keen eye, instructed his crew to examine the sloop's hull and rigging, ensuring everything was in shipshape condition. His attention to detail and commitment to quality work were evident in his every command.

Turning to Abigail, Gee extended his hand with a familiar twinkle in his eye. "Miss Abigail, Eunice, your rooms at my house are just as you left them—always at your service," he said warmly, slapping the large cork back into the nearly empty rum bottle. "No need for ceremony. We can polish this off later."

Abigail nodded in appreciation. "Thank you, Joshua. We're grateful for your hospitality."

As they made their way through the streets of Boston, the mansion loomed into view, an impressive structure just past Copp's Hill Cemetery. The journey down Prince Street offered a glimpse into the bustling city's daily life.

Eunice noticed the old windmill on the hill, its sails at a standstill. "Looks like the storm did some damage here as well?" she remarked, her gaze fixed on the motionless structure.

"Indeed," Gee replied, his tone reflective. "Storms may tear a ship to splinters, but they keep the yards and craftsmen busy mending what's broken. Destruction for some, opportunity for others—that's the way of it."

As they drew near the mansion, its stately elegance revealed itself in full. The crunch of gravel beneath the carriage wheels mingled with the clatter of hooves, and the air carried the briny tang of the harbor mixed with the faint sweetness of fresh-cut hay stored in nearby barns. Sunlight glinted off the tall windows, catching on polished panes and casting sharp flashes across the lawn. The white clapboards shone bright against the clear sky, their neat lines framed by tidy hedgerows and the vivid green of summer grass. For Abigail and Eunice, the great house rose as an emblem of Gee's prosperity and standing in the community. Still, more than that, it offered the reassurance of comfort and security after the hardships of their recent voyage at sea.

As they stepped inside, they were enveloped by the warmth and luxury of the mansion, a welcome change from the confines of the sloop. The sisters shared an approving look, silently acknowledging the new phase of their adventure, now unfolding in the heart of Boston and within the walls of Joshua Gee's impressive home.

Once the silver was safely stored within the confines of the Gee mansion, Abigail took the initiative to request a meeting with the renowned silversmith Jeremiah Dummer. She had not lost sight of the significance of their cargo and its potential transformation under Dummer's skilled hands.

That evening, their host treated them to a magnificent meal. The spread was lavish, a feast that spoke not only of New England's bounty but also of Gee's far-reaching community ties. At the center of the table was a roasted goose dressed with sage and thyme, its golden skin glistening in the candlelight. Though the house lacked a lady's hand since Gee had been widowed, he prided himself on providing for guests as if none were absent. What he could not offer in domestic refinements, he made up for with hearty abundance—platters of boiled cod with mustard sauce, trenchers of squash and beans, and imported Madeira poured freely.

Abigail, touched by the effort, lowered her gaze to her plate. "It must be a lonely thing," she said softly, "to set such a table without her." Sorrow flickered in her eyes, for she knew too well what it meant to lose a spouse and to keep on living for those who remained—though in her case, the loss was not by death but by geography.

Gee's bony fingers drummed once against the table before he folded his hands. "You honor her memory by speaking so, Abigail," he said, voice even but edged with weariness. "But my days of marriage are behind me. The sea and the yard still keep me occupied enough, and my son gives me joy where I need it. What's gone is gone."

Abigail leaned forward. "And your son, Reverend Gee—how fares he? I heard he has taken on some weighty responsibilities in Boston."

A flicker of pride lit the shipbuilder's weathered face. "Aye. Joshua is working closely with Cotton Mather now. A rising man among the ministers. He shoulders his charge well."

At the mention of Mather, Eunice twitched her face in a way that made her disapproval plain, though she smoothed it over quickly with a bright smile, rubbing her nose as if to suppress a sneeze. "How proud you must be, sir," she said, her voice laced with a playful note. "To have your son laboring with such a man—Boston must already be a safer and holier place for it!" Her tone walked the fine line between jest and courtesy, leaving the table unsure whether to laugh or nod.

Gee chuckled, shaking his head at her slyness. "Proud, aye—but Boston is a restless city. One man, even my son, cannot keep all its spirits in check."

Eunice, unwilling to let the moment drown in gloom, leaned back with her usual candor. "If you serve lobster this delicious every night, then surely your house cannot feel so empty or lonely—even without a wife in it. Any grandchildren?" Her remark drew a ripple of laughter that eased the heaviness, though Abigail still caught the shadow that lingered in their host's eyes.

"Grandchildren come only after marriage, or so they say," Gee said with a shrug.

Platters of venison haunch sat beside bowls of buttered lobster, cod stewed with onions, and a tureen of creamy clam chowder. Corn puddings, brown bread sweetened with molasses, and pumpkins baked in their shells paid homage to the land they stood upon.

Yet intermingled with the local fare were luxuries that only a man of means could provide. Dishes of candied oranges and citron gleamed alongside plates of preserved figs and raisins shipped from the Mediterranean—bowls of sugar, white as snow and costly as coin, flavored delicate syllabubs. There was chocolate from the West Indies, spiced with cinnamon, and tea from the Orient poured into porcelain cups.

Tankards of cider and strong New England ale mingled with the more cosmopolitan offerings—Madeira wine glowing ruby in the glass, and rum punch laced with nutmeg and lime. The food was not mere sustenance but a pageant of plenty, each dish a reminder of Gee's prosperity and the far-flung web of trade that bound Boston to the edges of the known world. For Abigail and Eunice, weary from sea and storm, the table was both comfort and spectacle—a sign that their host's house was as secure as it was opulent.

Eunice, her gaze sweeping across the laden table, shook her head with a small, rueful smile. "Mr. Gee," she said softly, "you needn't have gone to such expense on our account. A simpler fare would have been more than enough."

Gee threw back his shoulders, a gleam in his eye as he lifted his glass high. "Simpler fare?" he barked with a laugh, the sound booming yet warm. "Madam, the sea feeds us hardtack and brine, but under my roof you'll eat like governors and kings. Nothing less will do. What's coin or cargo compared to the honor of such a company?"

He gestured broadly to the feast, the silver dishes gleaming like plunder newly taken, and then inclined his head with merchant's polish. "No, ladies—nothing in my larder, nor in all Boston's markets, could be too fine for you." With that, he drank deep, the bravado of a seafarer twinned with the poise of a man well-seated among the city's elite.

Following the meal and several glasses of cognac from the Charente and Charente-Maritime départements of France, Abigail and Eunice went their separate ways for luxurious hot baths. For each, the experience was rejuvenating, washing away the fatigue and stress of their recent adventures. A change of clothing allowed them to shed the last remnants of their voyage and settle into the comfort and normalcy of life on land.

The following morning, Abigail and Eunice were welcomed with a sumptuous breakfast, the table groaning under an array of dishes that promised both nourishment and delight for the day ahead. As they indulged in the feast, they seized the opportunity to immerse themselves in the world news, a luxury they had been deprived of since their departure from Manhattan.

Mr. Gee, known for collecting newspapers from around the globe, had amassed an impressive array of international publications. Although some editions needed updating, this collection offered the most current insights from distant lands. The sisters eagerly delved into the papers, their eyes scanning the printed words that connected them back to the broader world.

The conversation around the breakfast table was vibrant and engaging, brimming with discussion of the latest political developments, societal changes, and the activities of notable figures from around the globe. Each story and report felt connected to broader global events.

During a lull in the conversation, Eunice, with a twinkle in her eye, decided to share a story from one of the newspapers. She cleared her throat theatrically and began, "So, there's this tale about a Dutch captain named Peter Jansen Wessel, or 'Tordenskjold' as they nickname him. Now, this chap found himself in quite the pickle during a naval skirmish."

Abigail, intrigued, leaned in. "Do tell," she urged.

"This Wessel fellow, he's out there off the coast of Norway, sailing under a Dutch flag — and who does he bump into? A British ship flying Swedish colors, the De Olbing Galley, commanded by this Englishman, Captain Bactmann."

She paused for effect, then went on, "At first, they are all cautious, eyeing each other up. But when the British hoist their true flag, all hell breaks loose, and they're firing cannons like there's no tomorrow. They go at it all day, and the English try to sneak off when night falls."

Eunice leaned back, mimicking a ship's captain with an exaggerated pose. "But come morning, they're at it again! Fourteen hours of cannon fire, back and forth, and both ships are getting quite the battering."

Abigail, now thoroughly entertained, prompted, "And then?"

"Well, here's the kicker," Eunice said with a chuckle. "Wessel's ship is running out of gunpowder. So what does he do? He sends a boat over to the English with a white flag. The Englishman thinks, 'Aha, they're surrendering!' But no, Wessel's man says, 'Excuse me, sir, but could we borrow some gunpowder and cannonballs? We'd like to continue shooting at you properly.'"

The absurdity of the request left Abigail in stitches. "You're jesting!"

"No, as true as I sit here!" Eunice insisted, laughing. "Imagine the look on that English captain's face, being asked to supply his enemy with the means to keep fighting him!"

Joshua Gee grinned broadly, amused by the women's collective burst of laughter. As Abigail and Eunice both regained their composure, he took a knowing sip of tea before saying with an arch of his eyebrow, "Don't believe everything you read in those papers. If they only wrote down what actually had happened, then no one would care to learn how to read."

Abigail, her eyes still scanning the last lines of an article she had just read, turned to Eunice with an expression of surprise and intrigue. "Eunice, listen to this," she began, her voice tinged with excitement. "I've just read about a school founded by Archbishop Thomas Tenison. It's possibly the first mixed school in the country, established for ten poor boys," she paused for effect and then added with emphasis, "and ten poor girls. Quite progressive, don't you think?"

Eunice, her interest piqued, leaned closer. "Really? How do they manage that in the heart of England?"

"Apparently, simply enough. The pupils at Tenison's are organized in a typical British school manner, with a house system. Each house influences the color of the miters on their school ties. From years 7 to 10, they're deeply involved in this system, competing, for all things, in House Points."

Eunice folded her paper down to listen more carefully. "Whatever are house points?"

"I suppose some demerit system of give and take, just as Headmistress Hope has employed at the Willow with those clamshells and feathers. Don't you suppose she had already read about this? This issue dates back to last year."

"Interesting. I can see Hannah's face when the Headmistress issued her a clamshell for not making her bed properly."

"Or Hannah's face for burning the porridge." Abigail laughed as she read further and reported, "And there seems to be something called the Inter-House Cup, which I believe is a sporting competition."

"That sounds quite engaging," Eunice remarked, clearly impressed.

"It's fascinating. Should we consider incorporating sports into our curriculum?

Eunice thought for a moment before responding. "Perhaps we could. Maybe introduce something like that Iroquoian game, La Crosse? Mohawk customs and traditions could be an interesting addition, as the women are usually in charge of their clans. Toughing up those prissy lassies with a rough-and-tumble sport would not hurt. After all, they are learning to shoot muskets and fight with a sword." Then she chuckled, "Maybe Kidd would benefit from such gaming activities—especially if she was told Hannah learned it from her very own father, Captain William Kidd."

"Ha, Uncle Willie never played La Crosse," Abigail admonished.

"Yes, but Kidd would not know that."

Abigail nodded in agreement, her mind already exploring the possibilities. "Yes, indeed. Introducing La Crosse would add a physical dimension to our curriculum and allow engaging with and appreciate different cultural practices. I like it."

"We could contact Sachem Hendrick to assemble a squad of his young Mohawk braves to come down and teach it to them?" Eunice ventured.

"Oh my. Now, wouldn't that be a complete scandal? The townsfolk would probably call up the militia," Abigail said, snorting a laugh while sipping her tea.

"Speaking of scandals," Eunice added. "I do hope Hannah and Sarah are behaving themselves. They can be proud of their opinions."

"Indeed," Abigail agreed, before addressing their host, the master shipbuilder. "Will our ship be fit for the voyage home?"

"Ah, not to worry. I have already spoken to my foremen this morning on the matter. Everything is shipshape, considering crashing into a sandbar amidst that storm," he said with a nod. He bit off the cork on the nearest bottle of rum and took a satisfying swig. "I've put you next in line for careening and corking the hull just to ensure oakum and pitch fill every nook and cranny, lessen your springs a leak at sea, havin' to bail the bilge to reach the shore."

"Wouldn't want to do that," Eunice said with reassurance.

"Aye, 'tis the same reply from ye captain," he said with a nod of satisfaction.

"And this will add to our stay?" Abigail asked.

"Fortnight, I spect. Tides willing."

CHAPTER 26

Captain John Cornelius Prout

THE STUDENTS HAD SCARCELY SHAKEN off the dazzle of their astronomy lesson—sun, moon, and stars still lingering in their thoughts, the lost Newton book still the subject of hushed debate—when a new distraction stole their attention—from the kitchen drifted an aromatic aroma, sharper and richer than the usual morning fare, curling through the corridors like a summons of its own.

Before they could speculate further, the firm rap of a knock echoed at the front door. Headmistress Terwilliger rose, her presence commanding instant silence, and called the young women to order in the classroom. Chairs scraped, hems rustled, and voices hushed as all stood poised. Another guest had arrived, and with them, another lesson was about to begin.

With a flourish of her hand, she introduced Captain Cornelius Prout, the self-proclaimed "seasoned businessman," who strutted into the classroom with his wiry frame, moth-eaten coat, and a grin that looked like he'd just tricked a fox out of its dinner.

Following him was his son, John Prout—a young man with a gentler, if somewhat world-weary, demeanor. Hannah's face lit up as she recognized him. Upon their arrival in New Haven, she had met John down at the docks, where he graciously showed her the way to the inn her mother and aunt frequented. Additionally, he had subtly guided Hannah to the shadier dockside establishments when she was investigating the whereabouts of the now distinguished Headmistress. He was a polite and courteous distraction—a refreshing contrast to his eccentric father—and now, it seemed, he was here to assist with today's lecture.

"John Prout? So good to see you today. This is your father? You said he's in the fur trade?" Hannah asked with sparkling, raised eyes.

"Ya-yes, ma'am. And many other ventures, too many to recount."

"Oh, I see. I don't think we have formally met. I am Hannah—"

"And I am her sister, Sarah," Sarah said, rifling her hand into the conversation. But when he didn't know how to respond, Sarah grasped his hand and shook it with a magnetic smile that locked each in a timeless trance.

"Ahem," Hannah cut in. "John, what are you doing here?"

"Oh, I'm here to help my father with his latest endeavor. Would you like to help me this time?" He held out his hand to the kitchen while directing his question toward Hannah, but Sarah quickly answered, "Of course," grasping his arm and following his lead.

Captain Prout attracted attention, jingling a change purse tied to his belt with one hand while waving the other hand with a flamboyant flap, nearly knocking over a candelabra sitting on one of the harpsichords. "Ladies, I have brought something truly extraordinary for you today! You may have already noticed the aroma from the kitchen of a new beverage that will change the world! Forget tea from the Orient—this is the drink of the future, straight from Arabia! And soon to be planted in the Caribbean and South America." He reached into a burlap sack with exaggerated flair, paused for dramatic effect, then pulled out a small tin canister and held it aloft. "Coffee!" he exclaimed.

The students murmured with curiosity as Captain Prout poured several roundish, flat beans onto a classroom table. As the rich aroma wafted through the room, some of the girls wrinkled their noses while others looked intrigued.

Captain Prout, ever the showman, cleared his throat, took a dramatic stance, and launched into a monologue. "Coffee! A beverage born in the ancient lands of Ethiopia and the Arabian Peninsula, cherished in the Ottoman Empire, is now finding its way to our humble shores. Allow me to regale you with its storied origins."

He leaned in conspiratorially, eyes twinkling, clearly savoring his audience's attention. "According to legend," he continued, "coffee was first discovered in the ninth century by an Ethiopian goat herder named Kaldi. As the tale goes, Kaldi noticed his goats acting particularly spirited after munching on some red berries from a certain tree. Intrigued, he sampled the berries himself, and lo and behold! He experienced a newfound vigor and energy."

Captain Prout gestured grandly as though channeling Kaldi's astonishment. "Kaldi then took these miraculous berries to a nearby monastery. The monks, skeptical at first, soon discovered that a drink brewed from the harder beans within the soft red berries helped them stay awake through long hours of prayer. It was a revelation!"

The Captain glanced around the room, savoring the captivated expressions of his audience. "Now, mind you," he smirked, "there's no real historical evidence to back up this charming tale. It may be more fable than fact, a story embellished over time. The monastery was most likely a mosque, and sheep were just as likely to have eaten the berries as goats. But isn't it marvelous all the same?"

He straightened, holding his audience rapt. "From those humble beginnings, coffee journeyed through the Arabian Peninsula, revered by Sufi mystics, embraced by the Ottoman Empire, and now, finally, it reaches us here! Mark my words, my friends—coffee will one day supplant tea as the favored drink of the discerning palate, body, and mind!"

His eyes gleamed as he surveyed his audience, who looked caught between fascination and amusement at his theatrical grandiosity. He was sure he had painted a vivid picture of coffee's mystique and allure, leaving them all intrigued about this exotic beverage.

Seeing the students' curiosity piqued, Captain Prout launched into a grand explanation of the coffee business. "Now, let me enlighten you on how a product like this reaches your hands! It begins with the farmers—the humble souls who cultivate the coffee plants. If these farmers don't have a market for their crops, their hard work amounts to naught. They must receive fair compensation for their labors, for, you see, even farmers in deep dark Africa and the holy lands of Arabica have to eat and drink!"

He leaned in, extended his hand with a finger-wag of conviction, nearly poking poor Marie Allamby in the nose. "Then come the entrepreneurs, the brave souls who invest their capital to buy the raw product from the farmers. These entrepreneurs must understand how to manufacture the coffee beans with as little waste as possible, lest they squander their funds. It's all about efficiency!"

"Coffee beans?" Patience asked. "Not leaves like tea?"

He coughed—another one of his compulsions making an appearance, signaling the telltale sign that he was building up to the lecture's grand finale. "No, my dear. Coffee, as you can see before you, is not a leaf, but a bean," he said with slight irritation before scrutinizing the coffee bean and conceding its odd shape by adding, with a shrug, "Of sorts. Not like peas or other beans, but bean-looking nonetheless."

In the kitchen, John rolled his eyes discreetly at Sarah. He was clearly accustomed to his father's flair for the dramatic. With practiced efficiency, he directed the kitchen help to wrap the previously roasted beans in cheesecloth, pound them into particles with a blunt mallet, and then throw them into a pot of boiling water to steep.

The Captain continued in the classroom, "Once the coffee beans are picked by hand, they are stripped of the outer softer covering, dried, and packaged for shipment."

"Are you referring to the pod?" Patience asked.

"No pod," he said with a smile, gritting his teeth. "Just a soft red outer covering, discarded and fed to the happy little goats. Merchants sell their wares to wholesalers like me to spread this joyful product worldwide to fine people such as yourselves." His voice seemed to swell with forced pride.

"For what price? It's not exorbitant like black peppercorns, is it?" Hannah asked, examining a small, hard bean.

Captain Prout pursed his lips and said with a slight squint, "Well, as you put it, somewhat the same. A shilling or two per pound?"

"A shilling or two per pound?" Hirana gasped. "Is this to be something only consumed during the holiday season—at someone else's home?"

"If you would like, yes. But for most, the middlemen wholesalers—" he paused and bent forward in a bow, claiming the position—will sell the product for everyday use to retailers, who then sell it to consumers, such as yourselves! The more you like the coffee, the more demand there is at retail, and thus, the more we must produce on the farm, or the price of demand will cause the price to soar out of sight, to say, three to six shillings per pound and up, driving down any goodwill interest created in the first place."

From the side of the classroom, the Headmistress moved briskly to the front, her hands smoothing her gown with absent-minded precision. Her eyes flicked toward the open door leading to the kitchen, where the aroma was wafting stronger by the minute, then back to the students waiting expectantly.

She cleared her throat, a half-smile tugging at her lips despite the distraction. "Actually, my dear Hirana, that is not a bad price, I dare say." Her words carried enough warmth to be encouraging. "As I have come to appreciate, tea leaves run more than thrice that of this coffee bean," she said emphatically. "Although—" She smiled, holding a few beans in her hand as if feeling their weight. "You would get more tea leaves than coffee beans for your money because of—?" She paused, looking at all the inquisitive students' faces, including the Captain's, for an answer. Then, when no one ventured a guess, she announced to a room full of moans, "Gravity."

Hannah appreciated the Headmistress's sly comment but was eager for the visiting tutor to continue—genuinely interested in understanding his logic.

"But Captain Prout," Hannah said, "won't the wholesalers run out eventually if this coffee product begins to have a higher demand than tea?"

"Ah, a sharp question!" the man beamed, his chest puffing up as if he'd taught her everything she knew. "Yes! Higher retail demand will indeed strain the wholesaler's supply, thus placing a greater demand on manufacturing, which, in turn, places a greater demand on the farmers to grow more raw coffee beans."

With a soft chuckle, John was suddenly at Hannah's side, handing her a small cup. Hannah took a cautious sip and raised an eyebrow in surprise, saying, "Tis different. A bit bitter perhaps, but not in a bad way." She turned to Sarah, who was accepting her own cup from John with a shy smile, and said nonchalantly, "I like this. We should purchase a few beans. Don't you think?"

Sarah watched John as he continued making his way around the room, handing a small cup to each girl from a tea tray containing cream and sugar, and didn't respond.

Hannah, after sipping thoughtfully some more, abruptly exclaimed, "So the key to all of this is—money!" She shot her sister a grin, feeling quite pleased with herself for deciphering the underlying message. Still, her revelation fell on deaf ears, as all of Sarah's attention was on the young man distributing the intriguing beverages.

Captain Prout's eyes twinkled with pride as he nodded, grasping his small coin pouch and giving it a little jingle—his infamous 'Coin Tinkle' making him look and sound affluent. "Precisely, young lady! It all comes down to commerce, trade, and the flow of coins from hand to hand. And, of course, to the men brave enough to sell it to the world! After all, there are pirates between us and this culinary treasure."

Now looking slightly exasperated, John chimed in gently, "Father, perhaps they'd like to hear a bit more about the taste of the coffee rather than the economics of it?"

Captain Prout laughed heartily, giving his son a good-natured slap on the back. "Ah, always the pragmatist, my boy! Very well, ladies, how do you find the taste?"

Some of the girls took cautious sips, exchanging uncertain glances. A few seemed to enjoy it, while others looked like they were politely forcing it down.

The more timid girls glanced over to see if Marie Allamby would try it. She merely sniffed it with a scrunched-up nose, not indicating approval. They'd already learned that if she wouldn't eat something, it was surely awful.

Hannah whispered loudly to Sarah, "It tastes like burnt beans… but in a good way?" causing a ripple of giggles to pass through the class.

Catching wind of the laughter, Captain Prout put on a grand air of mock offense. "Burnt beans? I'll have you know, ladies, that this is a sophisticated taste, one acquired only by the most refined of palates!" Then, after tasting a cup, he said, "I like mine like I drink my tea—sugar and cream if you please." He strode over to where John had been working, scooped a hefty spoonful of sugar, and then drizzled a sizable portion of cream. As he stirred the concoction, he added, "It is best drunk quickly, lest it cools and becomes less palatable—something in common with tea."

Marie Allamby, more interested in the sugar and cream, scooped in two spoonfuls of sugar and topped off her cup with cream before drinking it down with satisfaction. The other girls followed suit, showing similar signs of approval. "I should show this to my father in Barbados to see if he'd like to grow it." This was the first time Marie had mentioned to anyone where her family lived, and Hannah made a mental note to write it down in her journal.

The Headmistress, who had been observing the spectacle with a bemused expression, stepped in to wrap up the lesson. "Thank you, Captain Prout, for this enlightening and… flavorful explanation of bringing a new commodity into the marketplace. We shall certainly consider coffee's potential as a rival to tea in the future."

The Captain perked up with delight. "I would be happy to set up the school with regular deliveries—according to supply and demand, of course."

"Yes, but no, I think," she said with a sad bow of her head. "The school has a limited budget, and if I were to spend it extravagantly on coffee, we must go without other things, such as tea and maple syrup."

Moans of displeasure reverberated around the classroom until Hannah said with a wink to her sister, Sarah. "I say we try it for a few weeks. At least until my mother returns."

To Hannah and the Headmistress's surprise, Sarah declared, "Yes! It would help if you could show my mother a sample of this when she returns from Boston. She has a taste for the exotic."

"And I will be glad to deliver it when you are running low," John inserted enthusiastically, causing both women to raise their eyebrows as Sarah's smile widened.

"Alright. Make it so. But just until Abigail can approve the budget increase," the Headmistress said with a nod to the delighted face of Captain

Cornelius Prout, Businessman, Extraordinaire.

As the class prepared to file out, John approached Hannah with a small notepad in his hand. Sarah, stepping to John's side close enough for her shoulder to press against his, smiled like Mr. McDermot on fish day. The young man's face reddened with Sarah's touch, but he maintained his businesslike tone as he said to Hannah, "If you'd like, I can bring more coffee anytime. I'd love to—" He paused, and his eyes went to Sarah at his side. "-—see you ladies take to it."

Hannah nodded at her sister's captivated expression of adulation. "I'd like that. Perhaps it's an acquired taste?"

John chuckled as he turned to smile at Sarah, holding his arm. "Indeed. Much like the Prout style of business."

As they left the room, Captain Prout puffed up his chest one last time, giving the students a final overzealous bow that nearly knocked over the candelabra on the Harpsichord.

"Ladies, remember this day when coffee becomes the drink of choice for the colonies! You'll be able to tell your grandchildren that you were among the first to taste it!"

With that, he and John took their leave, leaving the girls smiling over their cups, unsure whether they were more impressed by the dark drink or by the sugar and cream added to it.

"Headmistress, are we going to have a dance lesson today?" the Kidd asked with some agitated irregularity.

Hope, slightly taken aback by the enthusiasm of the query, was about to respond when Kidd held up a hand to stop her. "But first," the young woman said sharply, "I need to freshen up. Please excuse me for a moment." She turned and walked urgently out the back door. Through the open doorway, Kidd could be seen grasping a handful of grass and a few leaves along the way to the outhouse. Within seconds, several other girls moved swiftly toward the back.

"Yes," Marie Allamby exclaimed. "I feel like dancing as well." This response to the more slothlike of the girls surprised everyone.

"I suppose we could fit it into our schedule before dinner," the Headmistress concurred. "Or perhaps this afternoon, when we will be immersing ourselves in all things Greek?"

Instead of responding, Marie's expression shifted to urgency, and she abruptly excused herself before dashing out the backdoor.

The Headmistress walked to the back door and noticed a line forming at the outhouse, each student holding something nervously in their hands from the yard to use as Marie pushed her way to the front of the line.

"Excuse me. Pardon me," Marie said loudly as she passed by the stricken faces until she reached the front of the line.

"Marie! Wait your turn," shouted Mary.

"Yes, Marie. We all have to go!" Patience growled.

But undeterred, Marie flung open the door, grabbed a leaf from Hirana's hands, and shouted with dire distress at Kidd's puckered face, still hovering over the drop with her dress bunched up, "Aren't you finished yet?"

That evening, the girls practiced their Greek alphabet and recited multiplication tables as everyone settled into their beds until the hush of sleep dissolved over the house. The Headmistress finished reviewing Hannah's writings in the kitchen and patted her on the back, saying, "Better, but there is room for improvement. Try to express what you want the readers to see in their own minds, not by simply telling dry facts, and you will be a more convincing writer," she said. "Now, I believe that's enough for tonight." The candlelight flickered against the wood-paneled walls of the schoolroom as Headmistress Terwilliger set aside the quill and parchment, nodding at her assessment of Hannah's writings. The air smelled of ink, wax, and the lingering scent of old books, and outside, the wind rattled the branches against the glass panes.

Hope stood, stretching her back slightly before lifting the three-branched candlestick from the desk. The shadows in the corners of the room deepened, and the wavering glow of the flames made the furniture seem to shift and breathe. She turned toward the back of the room, her sharp eyes scanning the darkened space near the back door chair.

A soft shape, barely distinguishable in the dim light, caught her attention. Someone lay curled up and motionless in the chair.

Hope furrowed her brow. "Marie?" she called, stepping forward.

The girl did not stir.

Hannah, standing by the stairs, turned her head, watching the glowing shadowy figure of Hope cross the floor. A cold feeling slid down her spine. The room, which had been warm with learning and conversation earlier, now felt different—thicker, heavier.

Hope stepped forward cautiously, her skirts whispering against the polished floor, and reached out, her fingers hovering just above Marie's slumped shoulder.

"Marie?" she repeated softly.

The instant her hand grazed the wool of Marie's shawl, the girl jerked awake and sat bolt upright with a scream.

Marie's breath came in short, panicked gasps. The candlelight cast shifting shadows across her pale face, her lips trembling as though she had just seen a specter.

Hope shivered at her side, her own heartbeat quickening at Marie's frantic expression, forced her to put down the candle holder on a nearby table.

Marie, now fully alert, raised a shaking hand and pointed toward the window, her fingers rigid with fear.

"I saw her," she whispered hoarsely.

Hannah moved to Hope's side following Marie's gaze. Through the old, wavy glass of the window, the distorted reflection of candlelight flickered against the blackness outside, twisting shapes into eerie, unearthly forms.

Hannah swallowed. "Saw who?"

Marie's voice was barely above a breath. "My grandmother. She was looking right at me."

Hannah's stomach tightened. A gust of wind rattled the windowpane just then, making the distorted image in the glass quiver as if it were alive.

Hope, though composed, exhaled slowly before picking up the candleholder to gaze out the window.

"There she is again!" Marie shouted, and both Hannah and Hope leaned forward to see more clearly.

"You must have had a bad dream, Marie. The mind plays tricks when it is tired."

Marie's tear-streaked face turned toward her, desperate for reassurance. "It was her, Headmistress. I swear it. She was right there, in the glass. Watching me."

"What did she look like?' Hannah asked.

"She looked like me. My mother always said she looked exactly like me."

Hannah's own arms prickled with gooseflesh at the certainty in Marie's voice.

"Come," Hope said, her voice calm but firm, "Let's get you to bed. You've frightened yourself, but nothing lingers here except the night."

Hannah hesitated for a moment before placing a steadying hand beneath Marie's elbow. "I'll help you upstairs."

Marie sniffed and nodded, allowing Hannah to pull her up from the chair.

As they turned toward the stairs, the floorboards creaked beneath their feet, the house settling with the wind.

As Hannah led Marie up the staircase, the candle flames flickered. She couldn't help but glance back over her shoulder, the wavy glass remained empty—yet her chest tightened as she half-expected a pale face to be waiting there, pressed against the warped pane, watching. She quickened her pace, silently praying they would reach the landing before some phantom hand rapped against the glass—or worse, before a shadowed face pressed itself into view and haunted their night with the persistent presence of a dreadful apparition.

A lingering chill followed them. The staircase creaked beneath their weight as Hannah guided Marie up to the bedrooms, the candlelight in her hand casting elongated shadows on the walls. The night air felt heavier now, as if the chill had settled into their bones. Marie's breathing was uneven, but she said nothing as they reached her door.

"Here we are," Hannah murmured, nudging it open.

Marie hesitated, glancing back down the hallway, her eyes still filled with the lingering fear of what she had seen—or thought she had seen.

Hannah gave her a gentle squeeze on the arm. "Try to get some rest. Morning will make all of this seem much less dreadful."

Marie nodded weakly and slipped inside, closing the door behind her.

Hannah's feet felt unnaturally loud as she walked toward her own room, the candle's glow barely cutting through the gloom. When she pushed open her door, she found Sarah seated at her writing desk, the tip of her quill idly tapping against parchment, seemingly in a quandary over how to complete a writing assignment.

Sarah glanced up, her eyes unnaturally bright in the dim glow. "Well? How did Hope like your writing?"

Hannah hesitated before only saying, "I am improving," but the words stuck in her throat, still haunted by the moment in the downstairs study.

"Oh. Well, maybe she will not have such criticism or such high expectations for what I write?" Sarah said, pushing her writing aside with a frown.

Hannah exhaled slowly, the sound barely louder than the creak of the floorboards settling beneath the wind's long fingers. Without a word, she dropped her journal onto the desk with more force than necessary.

The sharp slap of leather against wood echoed in the stillness. "Sarah," she began carefully, "do you believe in ghosts?"

Sarah's brows lifted, her curiosity piqued. "Ghosts?" she repeated, the single word sending an eerie ripple through the hush that had settled over the room. "I thought you were writing about pirates, not ghosts. Why do you ask?"

Hannah pressed her lips together, as if afraid that saying too much might call forth whatever had followed them from below. But the memory of Marie's wide, terrified eyes and the way she had trembled at the window refused to be buried.

She swallowed. "Marie… she swears she saw her dead grandmother tonight."

Sarah's fingers, once idly tapping against the wood of her desk, stilled.

Hannah's voice dropped to a whisper. "She woke up startled, pointed to the window, and said she saw her staring back at her through the glass."

A gust of wind rattled their room's windowpane, making the old, wavy glass quiver and distort. For a fleeting moment, the reflection in the dark pane seemed to move, shift—watch.

Sarah's frown deepened, but there was no amusement, no easy dismissal in her expression now.

"And you?" she asked quietly. "Do you believe her?"

Hannah rubbed at her arms, trying in vain to chase away the chill skittering down her spine. The candlelight quivered again, and she was suddenly aware of how dark the room's corners had become, how they seemed to stretch deeper than they should.

"I don't know," she admitted, though her voice was less confident than she would have liked.

Sarah regarded her for a long moment before shifting in her chair, her own gaze drifting toward the darkened window. The silence between them thickened, heavy, expectant.

Then, she shrugged, but there was no lightness to it.

"If ghosts do walk among us," she said, her voice barely above a breath, "I suppose this is as good a place as any for them to linger."

A faint, hollow creak echoed from the hallway beyond their door.

Hannah shivered, her fingers curling into the fabric of her dress, her heartbeat quickening despite herself.

The silence stretched taut, like a thread pulled to the breaking point. Hannah knew if she let herself think too long about Marie's ashen face, about the way the glass had seemed to breathe, she would find herself staring into their upstairs window, waiting—dreading—what she might see staring back.

She needed a distraction.

With a sigh, she flopped herself onto the bed, pressing her palms into the mattress as she turned toward her sister, forcing her thoughts elsewhere.

Her frustration—first at Hope's critique of her writing, then at Marie's terror—began to soften.

She tilted her head toward Sarah, her voice teasing, her words meant to pull them both away from the unnerving stillness that had settled around them.

"Your John…" she said, letting his name drift into the darkness.

Sarah turned sharply, but Hannah caught the small smile tugging at the corner of her mouth, betraying whatever nonchalance she wished to feign.

"What of him?" Sarah asked, though her voice was quieter now, the night's unease still lurking in the room's shadows.

Hannah smirked. "He seems to be a brutishly handsome, level-headed young man."

Sarah scoffed as she moved to her bed, but Hannah saw the faraway look settle into her sister's gaze. For a moment, the tension in the room seemed to fade, but just as the air grew lighter, Sarah spoke again, her voice hesitant, uncertain.

"Hannah… you don't think any of Mrs. Clark's nine children died in the old house we demolished to build this one, do you?"

Hannah's mouth tightened as she turned to gaze across the small, shadowed room, her eyes drifting toward the candle flickering in the blackened window. The faint glimmer of moonlight caught on the distant trees, and for a moment she seemed spellbound by the night beyond. Sarah followed her sister's gaze, distracted by the darkness outside.

That was all the time Hannah needed. With quiet, careful steps, she slipped from her bed, padding across the floorboards to the other twin. She crouched low, biting back a grin as she leaned close, her voice dropping into a ghostly whisper.

"And now they wander this house… searching for their beds, and their tiny stuffed dolls and—BOO!"

As she shouted the word, Hannah gave Sarah's shoulders a sudden, violent shake. Sarah let out a startled shriek, her body jerking away as she instinctively swung her hand, aiming to slap at Hannah's arm and shove her aside.

"Stop that! You are NOT funny!" she snapped, her voice high with lingering fright.

Hannah collapsed onto her back, laughing, while Sarah frowned, holding her hand to her chest, willing her heart rate to slow down. After a moment, Hannah's laughter quieted into a soft giggle, and both settled into a contemplative silence. They listened as the wind howled through the eaves—when something in the darkened house went bump.

Sarah's breath hitched. She froze, her heart still hammering against her ribs.

Her wide eyes darted toward Hannah, who had gone perfectly still, the last of her laughter dying in her throat.

In a hushed voice, Sarah asked, "How many children do you think died in the Clark house?"

The words landed like a chill, settling deep into the marrow of the night.

Hannah hesitated, her fingers twitching slightly where they lay against the quilt. The flickering candle cast wavering shadows across her face, making her expression unreadable.

"I don't know," she admitted at last.

Then, after a pause, her voice dropped even lower.

"But her oldest—Thomas, I believe his name was—when he looked at you, you could swear there was a demon behind his eyes."

The room plunged into silence. A new, weighty stillness crept in—one heavier than before.

Outside, the wind pressed against the house, making the walls groan. The candle sputtered, its flame dipping for just a second.

Neither girl moved.

Somewhere in the distance, a floorboard creaked. Outside, the wind whispered against the window, and in the depths of the dark glass, the candlelight trembled more.

Hannah smirked, letting her words float into the darkness, redirecting the subject once again. "John *is* brutishly handsome."

Sarah rolled her eyes, though her expression softened in a way that told Hannah she was not far off the mark.

"Brutishly handsome? You make him sound like a pirate."

Hannah chuckled. "Perhaps a gentleman pirate, then."

Sarah shook her head as if the idea was a silly one, but Hannah caught the faraway look that settled into her sister's gaze—the kind that spoke of hidden thoughts and unspoken dreams.

For the moment, the unease of Marie's fright and the ghostly presence she claimed to have seen was replaced by something warmer, more familiar—the whisper of love and longing, tucked away in the quiet of the night.

When Sarah spoke again, her voice was tinged with intrigue. "He's from old money—I believe he is related, through an aunt, to Theophilus Eaton, the first governor of New Haven Colony. His father, once a captain under Colonel Benjamin Church against the French and Wabanaki forces in Acadia, distinguished himself in the infamous raid on Grand Pré in 1704. Now, he invests mainly in the fur trade out of Hartford, though I believe coffee and other such commodities have become his true passion."

"I see," Hannah said thoughtfully, rolling over to face her sister. "Were you talking or interviewing him?"

"Oh, I know. I hope I didn't scare him off. It's just that if I show any interest in him, our mother will want to know," she complained. "And if I don't supply acceptable answers—well, it's as good as over. I've seen how she has treated you and Jacob."

The moonlight streaming through the window cast a gentle glow on her face, reflecting her contemplative mood. "Will you see him again?" Hannah coaxed.

Sarah's heart fluttered at the thought, a mix of anticipation and uncertainty. "I'm not sure. I want to. He said his father is leaving for Hartford within a fortnight." Then, after a long pause, Sarah asked softly, "What of your John? — Mr. MacCreedy?"

The room fell silent again, the sisters lost in their own thoughts. The possibility of a budding romance for Sarah, the excitement of new connections, and the uncertainty of the future all hung in the night like a delicate mist.

"I'm not certain. Ha, I once thought of sabotaging the stair banisters so that he'd have to come and repair them. But alas, they are as stout as he is strong and would not budge." Then, after a long silence, Hannah said, "Mother once told me of Andreas: Men are not trusted to be loyal to one woman. They always have an agenda that doesn't include you.'"

"How can she say that? What of father?" Sarah countered.

"She also revealed Father has another family in Albany."

"What?" Sarah asked, sitting up in bed to see if she was teasing.

"And she was married before she married Father."

"No. You are not making this up?"

"And—"

"No. You'd better be truthful with me, or I will never believe you again."

"Jacob, our older brother's real father, is named Jan Aersen van der Bilt. He owned the van der Bilt Brewery on Wall Street."

After a long, silent pause, Sarah asked, on the verge of tears, "Why are you telling me all of this now?"

"I guess so, your heart is not broken after being pierced by Cupid's arrow."

Outside, the world was at peace, the stars twinkling in the vast sky, each one a silent witness to the young women's dreams and hopes. Inside, Hannah and Sarah lay awake for a while, their minds adrift in a sea of thoughts and possibilities, before the gentle embrace of sleep finally took them into its comforting arms.

CHAPTER 27

Garden

THE RISING SUN CAST A GENTLE GLOW through the window of the Willow's kitchen eating area, where the scent of warm porridge and coffee filled the air. The events of the previous evening still lingered in the sisters' minds as they gathered for breakfast, each lost in her own thoughts.

Amidst this scene, Sarah leaned closer to her sister, her voice low but tinged with curiosity. "What do you think Mother is up to? Sometimes, I think she leads a secret life outside our own."

Hannah half-laughed at her sister's comment. "Like our father?" she quipped, and Sarah frowned, expression turned grim, and her eyes reflected a deeper understanding of their complex family histories.

In a hushed and speculative tone, Hannah whispered, "I believe our mother is just as enigmatic as our unfaithful father." Sarah's eyes widened as though her sister had just said something blasphemous. Hannah nodded somberly. "To me, Abigail Spragg is as layered and torturous as the lives of the pirates she is connected to." With that, the edge of Hannah's mouth turned up with a half-grin, and she shifted her attention to her warm bowl of porridge and the conversations surrounding them, leaving Sarah contemplative.

Once it appeared that everyone had finished breakfast and had a second and a few third cups of coffee, Hope stood up, commanding the room's attention. "It is a most beautiful day, and it would be a shame to let it go to waste. Please dress in your gardening attire and meet me back in the yard. There is a great deal to attend to if—" She paused and arched an eyebrow. "—if this yard is to become the envy of the community."

As soon as the words left her mouth, a wave of complaints erupted, led by Gulielma Marie. "What? Where I come from, we have servants and slaves to do such things as that."

The Headmistress disregarded the protests and addressed the room thoughtfully. "Besides," she said. "When you are sitting at the table, relishing the 'Three Sisters'—corn, beans, and squash—you will have a greater appreciation for what it took to deliver God's bounty to your plate."

Then the Headmistress smiled at Gulielma Marie, nodding as if acknowledging a known truth. "What Gulielma Marie just said is true for most of you here. And, although you can successfully navigate the rest of your lives without getting your hands dirty or tilling the soil, you will also miss out on the pride of accomplishment. Imagine, later in life, standing next to a tree or shrub that you had personally planted in your youth. And when you visit someone else's property, possibly a man of your liking, you will have just that much more to talk about. Men today don't simply want the flower, but the fruit to bear him seeds."

Gulielma Marie pouted, pulling a book from the nearby shelf, then reclined at the window, saying, "Today, I do not feel like sowing seeds for anyone."

"Suit yourself," the Headmistress said. Her words, spoken with a mix of firmness and encouragement, aimed to instill a sense of responsibility and the value of hard work, even in those unaccustomed to it. Her firm attitude was vanquished when she saw workers gathering in the backyard. The Headmistress understood the importance of these young women experiencing all aspects of life, not just those within their usual realm of comfort and privilege, but she would not hold up the class for one spoiled child.

"Ladies, gather your bonnets and work gloves. We are moving outside for the next lesson," she announced.

As the students gathered around the Spartan backyard pond, their attention was immediately drawn to the activity on the side of the house. There, attended by several workers, in neatly organized rows, were a variety of plants, their roots carefully wrapped in burlap and sorted into groups based on species and size. The array presented as the color of paint, each plant a brushstroke waiting to contribute to the landscape's overall beauty.

The Headmistress, with a discerning eye and a tone imbued with both challenge and opportunity, addressed the eager assembly. "These plants, currently uprooted and awaiting your touch, are yours to transform this space as you see fit," she began, her voice resonating with a blend of instruction and inspiration. "I will provide you with insights into their full-grown splendor, and then, it will be up to you to decide their placement. Be mindful in your choices, for once these plants find their new home in the earth, relocating them could spell their demise."

Lena's voice trembled with apprehension as she surveyed the overwhelming assortment of plants. "How are we ever going to plant all these ourselves?"

The task before them loomed large, far beyond the delicate work of embroidery or polite conversation.

"Ew. Is that a pile of horse droppings?" Eliza wrinkled her nose and pointed at the pungent mound nearby.

The Headmistress, ever composed, flashed a knowing smile. "Indeed, but fear not. It's been composted." She sniffed the breeze with a wrinkled nose of her own. "I am here to cultivate young ladies, not backyard brutes," she said, folding her hands primly. With a graceful gesture toward the group of workers unloading implements, she continued, "These gentlemen are here to assist. You will choose where each plant goes, and they will handle the labor—digging the holes, placing the plants, and ensuring they are properly settled."

Then, with a mischievous glint in her eye, she added, "And yes, they will also add ordures to the holes to nourish the plants so they grow strong and fast."

Hirana blinked. "Ordures?"

"Yeah," Kidd chimed in with a smirk. "Road apples, stable leavings, muck, dung—it's all the same when it comes out of a horse's rear."

Patience gagged. "Lovely. Our flowers will smell just wonderful."

After the group displayed revulsion, Eliza couldn't help but laugh, casting a glance back toward the house. "I think she thought we were going to dig with our hands like a peasant Bostonian," she said with a chuckle, referring to Gulielma Marie, who was peering out the window from behind her book.

"I don't think it is all that," Lena said. "I think it's because she has her own flowering at present."

"Does she?" Hope asked, and Lena nodded, rubbing her lower waist.

"She asked me if I could afford her cotton pads. She seems to have forgotten to pack any."

"She asked me too, but I haven't had to use them yet," Kidd said with a worried frown.

"I see," Hope replied. "I have a complete stock in the kitchen if anyone is in need."

Lena quickly added. "I gave her mine—along with fennel seeds to chew on. They always helped my cramping."

"Fennel?" asked Eliza. "My mother used warm compresses of rose and lavender on me."

"Ever heard of motherwort?" the Headmistress asked. Her eyebrows raised when no one acknowledged hearing of it.

"Motherwort? Ew, I don't want worts," Eliza exclaimed.

The group shared a light-hearted moment, their laughter ringing in the morning air.

As their laughter reached the house, Gulielma Marie ducked her head back into her book, sensing the collective gaze upon her. Her action was swift, almost comical, as if the laughter and the attention it brought were too much for her to bear.

At that moment, Hope thought the poor girl was becoming an enigma to the group, a solitary figure juxtaposed against the backdrop of camaraderie and teamwork unfolding in the yard. Her retreat into the pages of her book was a silent statement, a barrier that kept her safely ensconced in a world of her choosing, away from the uncertainties and challenges of the task at hand.

The Headmistress gestured toward the workers, bringing the group's attention back to the task at hand. "This is not just a lesson in horticulture but a test of foresight and teamwork. Years from now, your collective vision and effort will be evident when you return, perhaps for a reunion or when future classes wander these grounds. Let's hope they see a well-thought-out masterpiece rather than a chaotic jumble they feel compelled to replace."

The cool air was abuzz with the students' animated discussions. They crouched in small clusters, sketching plans into the dirt with sticks, each recalling the gardens they had known from home.

Patience described her family's plot in Rhode Island, where rows of beans and cabbage crowded against the stone walls, catching the sun's warmth. Marie brightened at the memory of her mother's herb bed in Barbados, filled with sage, thyme, and lavender, their scents clinging to her skirts on summer days. Eliza recalled apple trees heavy with fruit in autumn, the boughs so laden they needed propping with sticks.

Hirana laughed as she traced the shape of tall corn stalks, remembering how pumpkins sprawled at their feet, the vines curling in a tangled embrace. Dorothy, more wistful, told of roses climbing along a fence and marigolds edging the path—her grandmother's way of keeping pests at bay. Lena recalled carrots and turnips, staples from her father's kitchen garden, suitable for keeping through winter in a root cellar.

The chatter of their voices mingled with the chirp of crickets from the neighboring hedgerow. For a moment, it felt as though all their gardens—apple orchards, pumpkin patches, herb beds, and flower borders—had been planted side by side here at The Willow, each memory taking root in the ordinary soil of New Haven.

Hannah and Sarah, with their rich heritage of tending to the lush, expansive gardens that adorned their family's estate along the Hudson River, possessed a deep, almost innate understanding of horticulture. Their childhood was woven with countless hours spent among the verdant rows of meticulously cared-for plants and flowers. This experience had imbued them with a keen eye for botanical beauty and an appreciation for nature's delicate balance. As they stood back in the schoolyard, their gaze swept over the scene with nostalgia and keen interest. They observed their peers with a gentle, knowing look, understanding the excitement and challenges of envisioning and creating a serene garden space.

The Headmistress finally gathered the group around her to unravel the garden's mysteries in an educational and enchanting way. "We are not simply planting a garden for food, but an environment complete with tall trees and bushes in a pleasing and thought-provoking pattern." Her hands moved around gracefully, each gesture bringing the potential and grandeur of the small plants before them to life.

"Imagine," she began, her voice rich with passion and experience. "When fully grown, these saplings will stand like sentinels, their branches stretching towards the heavens." She pointed towards the sky, her fingers tracing the imaginary canopy of leaves. Beneath these towering guardians, a secret world of shade will emerge. It's a world where the sun plays hide and seek, dappling the ground with patterns of light and shadow."

Her words conjured images of a mystical garden, where each plant had its role and story. "In these shaded enclaves, we must think carefully about our plant choices," she continued. "Some plants revel in the sun's embrace, basking in its warmth and light. Others, however, find solace in the cool, gentle shadows, thriving in the protection offered by their taller companions."

At this moment, the Headmistress was not just teaching her students about plants; she was imparting wisdom about life itself. She was showing them how diversity and balance are vital to a garden's success and essential to the life of the world around them. The students, each absorbed in Hope's words, were beginning to see the garden not just as a collection of plants but as a living, breathing ecosystem, a microcosm of the world at large.

Noting the position of the old weeping willow tree already established alongside the backyard oval pond, Hope gently wove a more profound metaphor into her lesson that mirrored the students themselves. Just as the plants in their garden will vary, with some destined to grow tall and proud, reaching for the sky, while others would remain small, providing shelter and support at the base, so too were the students different. Like the plants, each of them had its own potential and path to growth. Some might rise to heights in society, while others might find strength and purpose in a more sheltered, supportive role. Much like the garden, the beauty of their future lay in this diversity and the interdependence of their roles.

The students approached the open space in the backyard surrounding the small pond with a clear sense of purpose. They meticulously measured and marked out the spaces for each tree, understanding that they were not merely planting trees but creating a future haven. Their actions were thoughtful, recognizing the need for each tree to have ample room to expand and for sunlight to weave through the branches, nurturing the plants below.

As the students engaged in a lively debate over the placement of each plant, bush, and tree in their burgeoning garden, a spirited argument arose concerning the arrangement of the flowering bushes. With a keen eye for variety, Lena proposed planting two different types of bushes in an alternating pattern. In contrast, Kidd suggested a pattern where every fourth bush would be different, creating a rhythm of repetition and artistic flair in the garden's design.

The discussion was in full swing, with each student passionately advocating for their vision, when suddenly, a clear, unexpected voice cut through the chatter. "I think similar bushes should be planted together as one unit; that way, they will all grow together and stand as one united front." The group turned in unison, surprised to find the source of this new perspective.

There stood Gulielma Marie, no longer the detached observer from behind the window. She had stepped into the fray, her sleeves rolled up, ready to engage. Her clean hands, previously occupied with the pages of her book, were now bare and poised for action. "If you intersperse the different plants in a line, one type of bush will surely outgrow the other and block the light, causing the other to fade away," she explained with a confidence that resonated with her peers.

Gulielma Marie, who had initially distanced herself from the activity, was now an integral part of the team, contributing her insights and ideas. Her transition from a solitary figure behind a book to an active participant in garden planning demonstrated the power of community and collaboration. It was a reminder that sometimes, stepping out of one's comfort zone and engaging with others can lead to meaningful contributions and a sense of belonging.

CHAPTER 28

Dr. Ignatius Snodgrass

THE MORNING SUN cast a warm glow over The Willow, its golden rays streaming through the windows as the young ladies gathered in the main hall, chattering excitedly after their now-regular morning constitution of coffee and outhouse. Sarah held a cup of coffee in her hand, feeling especially exhilarated about the start of a new day—a new day that might mean another visit from John.

Today, they were to meet a new instructor—a certain Dr. Ignatius Snodgrass, a man of impeccable reputation and known for his "modern" approach to medicine. Word had spread quickly that he was not only a skilled physician but also, as a passing note added by the Headmistress, "quite a handsome fellow." This last detail, of course, had sparked whispers and fits of giggles among the students as they nursed their own cup of coffee.

But no one was prepared for the man who strode confidently into the room with an air of authority and a jawline that looked like it had been chiseled from marble. He was tall, with a shock of dark hair, piercing blue eyes, and an unsettlingly charming smile that revealed dazzling white teeth. His attire was impeccably tailored—dark coat, waistcoat, and a pristine cravat. And though he appeared every bit the gentleman, something in his gaze suggested he was more interested in practical matters than polite company.

Headmistress Terwilliger stepped forward, clearing her throat. "Young ladies," she began, raising her voice to cut through the giggles, "I present to you Dr. Ignatius Snodgrass, a respected physician who will be teaching a series of weekly classes on family health and first aid, among other important topics."

Dr. Snodgrass gave a slight bow, his eyes sweeping over the assembled young ladies. "Good morning, ladies," he said in a rich, baritone voice that made several girls gasp and fan themselves discreetly.

"Doctor?" the Headmistress inquired. "Would you like a cup of tea—or perhaps—a cup of coffee?"

At the mention of the exotic drink, the doctor's eyes sparkled with gratitude."Yes," he announced, "I'll try a cup of coffee if you do not mind."

Pleased with his acceptance, she took the doctor's hand and entered the kitchen, where the servant poured the remaining coffee from the stove through a cheesecloth, catching the grinds.

"Sugar and cream?" she asked, and he nodded with acceptance, holding out one finger to stop her at only one teaspoon.

"I don't want to overwhelm the flavor on my first taste."

"Oh, you have never had a cup before?"

"No," he said and slurped. The doctor savored the taste and aroma before adding, "And I dare say, I hope it is not my last."

After finishing his cup, he turned and walked into the classroom, where the students eagerly awaited him. Resuming his prideful stance, he announced, "I am here to instruct you over the next few months on a number of topics vital to the well-being of family life. As an overview today, we will be covering everything from common diseases to first aid, quarantine protocols to matters of feminine hygiene."

An audible gasp rippled through the room at that last phrase, and several girls' cheeks turned pink. The Headmistress herself looked momentarily taken aback but maintained her composure.

"Now," Dr. Snodgrass continued, seemingly invigorated by the collective discomfort. "Let us begin with the fundamentals of first aid. Imagine, if you will, that a family member has suffered a fall and injured themselves. It is essential to know how to dress a wound and prevent complications."

He straightened his posture, his eyes glinting with an almost unnatural enthusiasm. "Ah, I must say, I feel quite energized discussing such practical knowledge. The mind sharpens when engaged in matters of urgency, does it not?"

Sarah leaned toward her sister, Hannah, and whispered, "It's probably the coffee."

As he spoke, he reached into his medical bag, pulled out a wooden carving that looked like a child's arm, and set it on the table. Next, he withdrew a jar of a strange, thick, yellowish substance and held it up for everyone to see. "This is a salve," he explained. "Made from honey, beeswax, and a little bit of bear grease. An excellent remedy for minor cuts and bruises."

"Bear grease?" the Kidd whispered, wide-eyed.

"Indeed!" Dr. Snodgrass said, overhearing her. "Bear grease is a staple of frontier medicine. Many remedies involve ingredients that might seem, well, unconventional. Now, who would like to assist me in applying the salve to this mannequin's wound?" The doctor took out a long knife and stabbed it brutally into the wooden effigy of a child's arm.

A hesitant hand rose from the back of the room. It was Eliza, known for her curiosity. She approached, clearly nervous but intrigued.

Dr. Snodgrass guided her hands as she applied the salve, explaining each step in a matter-of-fact tone. "Gentle pressure to stop bleeding, like so. And remember, removing any foreign debris is paramount to avoid the formation of yellow bile." He said the last word with such gravitas that a few girls shuddered, picturing all manner of gruesome things.

"Next," he announced, "we shall discuss the topic of quarantine."

The girls exchanged glances. "Quarantine?" Patience murmured.

"Yes," Dr. Snodgrass said, his expression serious. "If someone in your household contracts an illness, it is imperative to separate them from others to prevent the spread of disease. A small room, preferably well-ventilated to prevent the accumulation of harmful fumes, should be set aside for the sick individual. And under no circumstances should they share a bed with anyone else."

He took a step closer, raising an eyebrow. "Think of it like keeping a particularly naughty cat in a separate room so it doesn't scratch the rest of you."

That prompted a few titters of laughter, and even Headmistress Terwilliger's lips twitched in amusement.

But then, as Dr. Snodgrass moved to the next topic, the atmosphere shifted once more. "Ladies," he began, with a stern and gentle tone. There is another matter that we must address, though it may be delicate: the subject of women's health."

The room went completely silent. One could almost hear the collective intake of breath.

"In particular," he continued, "we shall discuss hygiene... during a lady's monthly courses. Are all of you experiencing this cycle?"

Sideways looks ricocheted around the room with no one brave enough to answer his embarrassing question.

"I assume so. Then, is anyone experiencing any symptoms today?"

All eyes shot to Gulielma Maria, but she frowned and shook her head as if she had no idea why they were looking at her. A few girls' faces turned beet red, and they squirmed in their chairs as if they needed to excuse themselves. Patience looked as if she might faint. Headmistress Terwilliger cleared her throat, looking almost as flustered as the students, but she nodded for him to proceed.

"Now, I understand that this may be a source of discomfort for some," Dr. Snodgrass said, addressing the girls with a calm, almost fatherly gaze. "But knowing how to manage this natural part of life is essential. Cleanliness and proper care are paramount. One should use cotton cloth pads, wash daily— albeit some more than once per day— and, if possible, boil the soiled cloths in hot water to maintain their freshness."

"Boiled the used pads?" Hirana squeaked, horrified.

"Indeed," he replied with a grave nod. "Boiling ensures that all impurities are removed. And remember, ladies, this is nothing to be ashamed of. It is as natural as the changing of the tides or rising of a full moon."

By now, the students were shifting uncomfortably, as if they were all experiencing those same symptoms. Some looked out the back door, some hid their faces discreetly behind their hands. But Dr. Snodgrass pressed on as though utterly oblivious to the room's embarrassment.

"Now, let us move to pestilence and diseases and their symptoms, shall we?" he asked, reaching back into his medical bag and pulling out a set of somewhat alarming-looking diagrams. He held up a crude picture of a person with red spots all over their face.

"Smallpox," he declared with dramatic flair, his eyes sweeping over the girls. "Has anyone here had the pox?"

Slowly, Eliza and Marie Allamby raised their hands.

"Can you tell us about it?"

"My mother said I was lucky and had a mild case," Marie said, rolling up her sleeve to show a few pox scars. "My older brother was off across the island apprenticing for a rum maker when he died."

"Of the pox?" Hannah gasped.

Marie only nodded.

Eliza raised her hand and said, "Three of my friends died. My mother moved the family out into the country when it first started to show up."

The doctor nodded solemnly, adding, "It begins with a high fever, followed by these pustules that generally form first on the tonsillar pillars and corners of the mouth and nose." He pulled out a flattened wooden stick and said to the nearest girl, the Kidd, "Open your mouth and stick out your tongue and say 'awe'." When she did, he looked carefully, holding down her tongue to say, "Unremarkable," before pulling out the stick, wiping it a few times on his sleeve, and replacing it in his inner coat pocket. "If you see anyone with such symptoms, it is imperative to isolate their miasmas in a quarantined area immediately, such as what your mother did by moving you to the country's fresh air," he said with a nod to Eliza. "Only the most vigilant care can prevent the spread. And only those who have survived this scourge may care for this illness, or they may find themselves in the grave as well."

The Kidd looked as if she wanted to ask how one could find oneself in a grave, but she was too distracted by a scratched tongue to ask, so she choked out, "Miasmas?"

"Bad air," he responded with a grave expression, shifting his eyes around the room, looking for a possible source of such noxious vapors.

The girls stared, both fascinated and horrified, as he flipped through diagrams of various diseases, each more dreadful than the last: typhoid, dysentery, consumption, measles, diphtheria—all laid out before them in vivid detail.

"Which of these is the 'Purple Death?'" Hannah asked, holding onto her sister's hand for comfort.

"Ah, yes. A layman's term," he acknowledged. "It could mean many things, from diphtheria to the grippe. Each is as deadly as the other and is treated similarly: Drinking water or ale. Rest, warmth, and—," he added with what appeared to be fatherly advice, "—a double portion of love."

"Love?" Patience asked.

"If all else fails, love is all you have left to offer the dying."

Finally, he turned to the last topic. "Ladies, as future caretakers of families, you may one day be tasked with assisting in or experiencing yourselves... childbirth."

A collective gasp filled the room.

"Yes, yes," he said, holding up a hand to quell their shock. "It is no easy task, and I won't go into detail here. We will go through the basics later: warm towels, hot water, and a steady hand. And if the baby does not cry upon entry to this world, a gentle tap to its feet or pinch of a nipple often does the trick."

"I saw the doctor pick up my baby brother and smack his little bottom until it glowed like a forest fire to make him cry," Eliza said, receiving frightful sideways glances from all the shocked faces.

Dorothy looked as if she might faint, and Mary covered her mouth in shock. Though maintaining her composure, the expression on the Headmistress's face made it clear she had started to regret her decision to invite Dr. Snodgrass for this lesson.

After what felt like an eternity, he finally closed his medical bag, snapping it shut with a triumphant grin. "And there you have it, ladies! I will teach you a comprehensive overview of the essentials of family health once a week for your time here at the Willow."

Several of the young women quietly gasped, and all stared at him with expressions of awe, horror, and confusion.

Dr. Snodgrass gave a satisfied nod. "If there is one thing I hope you take away from today's lesson, it is this: knowledge is power. And with a little courage and cleanliness, you shall be well-prepared for whatever life brings you. There is nothing worse when you have a sick child than not knowing what to do."

After looking around at all the petrified faces, he said, "Now, if you will excuse me, I have a baby to deliver." Then, slightly hesitantly, he asked, "Would anyone want to go along and assist?" Nearly everyone's mouth had gone agape at the offer when the unexpected happened.

"I will go with you," Marie Allamby said from the back of the room with her hand held up. "I like babies."

The doctor fixed his eyes on her innocent face and then accepted her assistance with a nod. But before he asked her name, he looked to the Headmistress's shocked face for approval. "May she, ah—"

"Marie. Her name is Marie."

"Ah, Marie is French, isn't it?"

Marie could only muster a smile of ignorance.

"French for 'wished-for child,' how apropos." Then he looked again for approval, and the Headmistress reluctantly smiled and gave her permission.

"Good. It is this woman's eighth child so it won't take all night. I'll bring her back as soon as it is safely over."

"I'd like to go, too. I like babies. Two assistants are better than one," burst from Eliza's lips, turning everyone's head.

"Eliza?" the Headmistress questioned.

"Eliza is short for Elizabeth, is it not?" the doctor asked, receiving her stupified nod. "Hebrew, meaning 'God is my oath.'"

The girl shrugged with blank happiness as if she hadn't ever known what her name meant until today.

The Headmistress nodded again, moving to both girls' sides. "If you feel uncomfortable and need to come back early, send word, and I will come fetch you."

"It'll be alright, ma'am," Marie said, holding Eliza's hands. "I've seen babies born before. It's not as bad as it sounds, lest someone dies. Then it's just a lot of crying."

With that astonishing revelation, the doctor ushered the girls out the door, courteously bowing to everyone as he tipped his hat.

The door clicked shut, leaving stunned silence in its wake. The girls slowly turned to each other, still processing the shocking yet strangely enlightening encounter. The Kidd, finally breaking the silence, whispered, "Well… I believe it is imperative that I do not think of honey, beeswax, or bear grease the same way again."

And with that, the room erupted into nervous, relieved laughter, the girls sharing a newfound camaraderie over their first unforgettable encounter with the enigmatic Dr. Ignatius Snodgrass.

CHAPTER 29

Green Dragon Tavern, Boston

The noonday sun cast a bright blue sky over Prince Street as Abigail and Eunice prepared for an essential meeting near Dock Square. They had received word that they would meet with the renowned silversmith Jeremiah Dummer to discuss laundering their pirated silver. Mr. Gee, ever the gracious host, had offered to lend his carriage for their journey, but they declined, feeling the walk would do them both good.

As they stepped out into the Back Street that circled the Mill Pond, Abigail remarked, "It was quite generous of Mr. Gee to lend us his carriage."

Eunice nodded in agreement. "Indeed. Isn't it funny to think that almost thirty years ago, our Great Uncle Phillip was offering Mr. Gee a ride from Algeria back to America, where he was a slave? But I am glad we are walking. Seeing how we are not transporting our cargo, what would we look like arriving at a pub in such a fancy cart?" When her sister didn't venture to say, Eunice added, "Old Maids."

The brisk journey on Hanover Street was picturesque, leaving them to watch the high tide rush past on its way to fill the pond and work the distant mill paddles. The rhythmic clop of the horses' hooves blended with the vibrant city's sounds. The sisters, arm in arm, observed the lively scenes of Boston life unfolding around them.

As the tavern came into view, Abigail shrugged to her sister and, with a yawn, said, "Well, it isn't my Manhattan."

Upon arriving at Dock Square, they found the Green Dragon Tavern alight with activity, the perfect public venue for conducting secretive pirate business. As they walked through the door, they noticed Jeremiah Dummer sitting at a table, already engaged in conversation with whom they supposed was his politically influential son, Jeremiah Dummer Junior.

Dummer Senior stood up as they approached, his keen eyes appraising the sisters. "Ah, you must be the young ladies I was told to expect."

"Yes, Mr. Dummer," Abigail replied, extending her hand and playing the part of the new acquaintance to the eavesdropping tables spread about them. "We're here regarding a matter of commerce."

A gentleman of keen wit and sagacious political insight, Dummer Junior inclined his head with decorum, with a more notable Boston accent. "And I stand before you as his progeny. 'Tis a genuine delight to make your acquaintance. My sire hath oft extolled the virtues of your ventures."

Eunice smiled. "We're grateful for your assistance in this matter. The shipment's provenance is delicate, to say the least."

Jeremiah Dummer Senior let forth a gentle chortle. "Delicate, verily. Yet be at ease, for my prowess in subtlety is equally matched by my reticence." Then, calm and subdued, he murmured, "And those of your special patronage remain securely ensconced between my lips."

Feeling reassured, Abigail added, "We're looking forward to seeing how you transform these pieces in your workshop."

Dummer Senior then gestured towards a more reserved, quiet corner table that just opened. "Shall we discuss the details over a pint?"

Soon, Abigail and Eunice were sequestered in a dimly lit corner with Jeremiah Dummer and his son. That this was a hub of whispered conversations and clandestine meetings was becoming more evident to the ladies. The atmosphere was lively yet subdued, with the murmur of patrons blending into the background.

Abigail began leading the conversation, "Mr. Dummer, we have eight full parcels awaiting your inspection."

Dummer Senior waved his hand dismissively as the robust barmaid placed the mugs around the table with a slight smile on her face. "No inspection is necessary, Miss Abigail. I trust the quality of what you bring. Payment will be made upon receipt of the goods. Your supply is much anticipated and in great demand, especially for chocolate pots."

"I like chocolate; who doesn't? Perhaps one day, chocolate will be added to ale," Eunice exclaimed with a toast to the smoothness of their transaction. "It's a relief to hear that Boston is still a sweet place to do business. I remember the day when your Puritan founders considered chocolate a decadent sin. We aim to ensure everything is in order on our end."

"As do I. As do I," he said, tampering off his thoughts with a firm smile.

Abigail directed her attention to Dummer Junior, who had been listening attentively. "I understand you're the appointed agent for the Province of Massachusetts Bay and the Colony of Connecticut," she said.

"Yes, that's correct," Dummer Junior replied, his tone reflecting a sense of responsibility.

"Then you must know about the Collegiate College in Old Saybrook and its imminent needs?"

After taking a sip of ale and wiping off the froth from his chin, he answered, "I am. How are the school's needs a concern of yours?"

Not wanting to seem too eager, she sipped her ale before explaining. "Oh, I'd heard of its difficulties from a certain trustee, who indicated that if a more central location for the school is not secured soon, it may experience an irreconcilable splintering." She let her words settle before adding, "That means the tutors and students will find it hard to come together."

"Ms Abigail, it is not my place to establish a meeting place for the students, nor is it my job to monitor the tutors. But you have not explained why you are so concerned—"

"My son Jacob needs a good education," she quickly interjected.

"I see. Have you not considered Harvard?" When the table remained quiet, he added, "I could give him a reference that would guarantee his admission. I am both an active alumnus and donor."

"That would be greatly appreciated, but my Jacob, for his own reasons, mind you, refuses to go to Harvard. Something to do with his opinion of others who have matriculated from there recently, I think."

"Oh, and whom might they be?"

"I'm not sure. I'll have to ask him when I see him next," Abigail said with a thoughtful frown.

"I see," he exclaimed." I am well aware of the difficulties facing the Collegiate College in Saybrook. How may I offer my help?"

Eunice, sensing an opportunity, leaned in. "The college could certainly use support, especially now. It's struggling to maintain its operations."

Dummer Junior nodded thoughtfully. "Education is vital for our society's growth. I believe in supporting institutions that foster learning and development. I'll ask the legislature what can be done to aid the college."

Impressed by his commitment, Abigail said, "That's very commendable, Mr. Dummer. The college would greatly benefit from any assistance you can provide."

The Green Dragon Tavern served as a cradle of nascence, absorbing the weight of their words and hinting at a pivotal role the tavern would play in their relations for years to come. The clinking of ale mugs and the low murmur of conversations provided a lively yet discreet backdrop as if the very essence of the place encouraged the exchange of ideas and the birth of initiatives that could shape the future.

Abigail pushed the subject further by saying, "If books could be given to the school, it would greatly enhance the students' educational experiences."

Dummer, intrigued by the idea, revealed, "I have written many books myself and have a few other scores stored away that I could divulge from my library."

Abigail saw her opportunity. "I know of a certain Elihu Yale," she said, "a native of New Haven, who could donate a large quantity of books in short order."

"Indeed, I have heard of this former Governor of India."

Abigail nodded, glad he knew of Yale to avoid bogging down the conversation with more explanation.

"Yes, indeed, Fort George, India, to be precise. His hometown connection may leave room in his heart for philanthropy?"

"Books, you say? But does Old Saybrook have the facilities for such niceties?" Dummer asked with concern. "I fear for the life of my own books becoming wet and worm-ridden."

"Perhaps not in Old Saybrook," Abigail postured. "That is why I propose the school be moved to New Haven."

"New Haven? Why not Hartford? It is closer to Harvard, making it easier to share the faculty if necessary in the school's infancy."

"Perhaps," Abigail said. She refreshed herself with another sip of ale before mentioning the most critical factor. "But will Hartford pledge enough money to make the school solvent? And might their proximity be a detriment to both student bodies? After all, why go to Harvard when you can just as easily matriculate from Hartford?"

"Yes, excellent point," he conceded. "So you are suggesting New Haven would be a better location?"

"Indeed. It would be more accessible to the other colonies by water. I have already heard of a sum of some two thousand pounds, possibly more if needed, being discussed amongst the principal landowners—Davenport and Easton, to name a few," she said, causing both men to raise an eyebrow.

"Davenport, you say? I do believe Cotton Mather has a Davenport aunt who is still living in New Haven. Ah, married a Warham Mather, Cotton Mather's cousin."

"Small world; good to know," she said with a smile of assurance. Then she added, "And perhaps Sir Isaac Newton could donate one of his books to the cause?"

"Newton?" the Junior exclaimed with shock in his voice. "However, could that be arranged?"

"If you write to both him and Yale, I can have one of my agents in London deliver the letters. Londoners are quite taken with anything from the New World, and a word carried from here carries weight."

"In that case, it would be greatly appreciated if he could donate one of his books to Harvard as well?"

"I'll see what I can do," Abigail said with a sly smile that appeased them all.

"Well, gentleman. It has been most stimulating indeed," Eunice said, sensing her sister had already overstepped her bounds and that their business was now concluded.

"Yes, it has indeed been stimulating," the Senior Dummer said, standing and bowing as the ladies begged their farewells.

"We will wait at Joshua Gee's mansion—"

"Yes, as usual, I will be by to secure the product," he affirmed.

"And we will be expecting those letters for Yale and Newton you pledged," Abigail said to the Junior, who, alerted to his task at hand, gave a nod to the ladies, and then a reluctant one to his frowning father.

"I fear my letters alone will be of little consequence," he said hesitantly. "It is not my position to ask for books and other supplies for the school. Perhaps I can implore Cotton Mather to write such a letter addressing those needs?"

"Of course, do as you see fit. I trust your judgment. However, we will be leaving soon for Manhattan and hope to include your letters sent with one of our regular shipments to London, as the matter of education is slipping through the fingers of knowledge as we speak," Abigail said in parting.

"It will be done," he said with reassurance, amidst the stress evident from his father's frowning face.

Waiting until they had left the tavern behind, Eunice said in a questioning voice of surprise, "Sir Isaac Newton and Elihu Yale. Whatever has birthed your illusions of grandeur?"

"Oh, my dearest sister," Abigail said, looking back over her shoulder to see if anyone was near enough to overhear. "Whatever happened to your pirate spirit? I may not have told you that I have come across, well, found on my doorsteps, really, a large quantity of books. Including the one written by

Newton in our school's library."

"Oh. You mean forcefully rerouted to your back door steps," Eunice said. "And you are alluding to this Yale character as a potential donor because he is Hope's estranged uncle?"

"Precisely. Poetic justice, don't you think?" Abigail said, seeming quite pleased with herself. "Besides, how else can we explain the existence of a rare book such as Sir Isaac Newton's Philosophiæ Naturalis Principia Mathematica showing up on our shores?"

"And those foolish, highfalutin men will never know where or who gave the books and will inevitably not rebuke credit for doing so themselves. One of the many benefits of living so far away from jolly old England," Eunice mused. "Perhaps they will one day name the school after you—Spragg College!" she declared to the surrounding trees with a lofty wave of her hand.

"Good lord, no! Van Salee would suit me," she sneered, indicating their great-grandfather, the pirating Governor of Salé. "But of course, Dummer College would be even more apropos, I think."

But then Eunice asked quizzically, "Isn't Dummer College an oxymoron?" Making them both laugh out loud.

As they ambled back towards Hanover Street, Eunice turned to her sister with a curious glint in her eye. "So, Abigail, where to next?"

Abigail hesitated momentarily before responding, "To a place nearer our current abode, but I feared to mention it earlier for worrying you might blunder over the fact while we were talking in the tavern."

Eunice's brow furrowed, slightly perturbed by the notion. "Blunder? I hardly think I blunder," she retorted with a hint of defensiveness.

"Cotton Mather," Abigail said gently, souring her sister's face. "We are going to pay him a visit as well."

After a moment of quiet, Eunice's disgusted expression shifted as realization dawned. "Ah, I might have indeed had a comment or two about that infuriating soul," she admitted reluctantly. "And why, in heaven's name, are we going to that sanctimonious man's house?" Eunice inquired, brushing off her blouse, curiosity piqued despite her reservations.

Abigail outlined her plan with strategic flair. "To ask him to also write letters to Yale and Newton, of course. If we were to ask him out of the blue, so to speak, I presume he might not comply. But, on the other hand, Dummer asks him to do the same thing right after we ask him. Well, this may be too much for the minister to resist. He is, after all, a very verbose writer."

Eunice considered this for a moment, then chuckled.

Abigail added, "And then I thought, while we're there, we could ask him to come and teach at our little school."

Eunice's laughter filled the calm neighborhood. "But naturally, for a suitable fee," she added, her amusement evident.

Abigail nodded in agreement, a smile playing on her lips. "Precisely, for a suitable fee. It's an audacious plan, but it just might work and help put our little school on the map, closer to being on par with Harvard."

As they continued over Mill Pond Creek through the streets of Boston, the sisters strolled in contemplative silence, each considering the potential of their bold strategy and the unlikely partnership they were about to propose to one of the colony's most prominent figures.

The women walked a block past their turn on Prince Street to the corner of Fleet Street, where they approached a modest dwelling, its structure unassuming yet dignified. Abigail pulled a piece of parchment from her pocket and, after scrutinizing the written words, looked up and confirmed, "This is indeed Cotton Mather's residence. See the family crest charged with three Lionel ramparts next to the door?" They opened the small gate and entered the garden, where they noticed a black man attentively tending to rows of plants.

Approaching him, they asked, "Excuse us. May we know your name? Is Reverend Mather at home?"

The man straightened up and replied, "I am Onesimus, and no, the Reverend is not here; he's currently at the church."

Abigail's gaze drew to some plants with sacks covering their stems. "Onesimus? Does that mean you are useful or profitable to the Reverend?" But before he could answer, she asked, "What, pray tell, are you doing to these spent plants?"

Onesimus looked at the hanging sacks and explained, "I'm collecting seeds. The Reverend wishes to see if they grow differently come spring."

"Different? In what way?" Abigail asked, her interest evident.

Onesimus answered, "Different colors. He believes he might see new colors from the old ones. He's quite good at it, even with corn."

"Different colors of corn, you say?" Eunice interjected, her interest now fully engaged.

"Yes, he's good at that too," Onesimus proudly confirmed.

The women stood for a moment, intrigued by the notion of changing colors. Abigail, remembering their primary mission, then asked for directions to the church.

They thanked him warmly before setting off, their minds abuzz with the day's revelations and the prospect of meeting the ominous man of God.

Their journey took them down Fleet Street, the cobblestones beneath their feet echoing the rhythm of their thoughts. Turning onto Garden Court, they were soon greeted by the sight of Clark Square, a serene enclave north of the city's hustle. The Square was dominated by the church, its spire reaching skyward, a testament to faith and the fear of God.

Eunice's eyes were drawn to a large, intricately carved wooden sign as they approached the Square. The sisters paused beneath it, their mouths agape as they read the inscriptions. The names and dates seemed to whisper stories of the past, drawing them into contemplation.

Eunice broke the silence, her voice filled with wonder. "Do you think the Clarks of New Haven are related?"

When Abigail remained silent, lost in her thoughts, Eunice added, "I do recall that Mrs. Clark's son, Thomas Clark, was a merchant from Boston."

"There's got to be more than a few Clarks running around this colony, no doubt," Abigail finally replied, a note of pragmatism in her voice. She gently nudged her sister, urging them towards the church.

Entering the Square, the church loomed before them, its doors open as if welcoming seekers of knowledge and faith alike. The sisters exchanged a glance, their shared sense of purpose evident. Today was not just about meeting Cotton Mather, but about delving deeper into the interconnected threads of their world, where faith, science, and the pursuit of knowledge intertwined in a system of discovery.

Eunice leaned in close to Abigail's ear. "You know what Hope said about his involvement in the Witch Trials," she said in a hushed voice. "He sentenced those poor girls to death, for what?"

Abigail, always the pragmatist, responded, "The community was behind him."

Eunice huffed, her disapproval evident. "He's also renowned for being quick with the whip. Every little tit-for-tat received no less than ten lashes. Are you sure you want to subject your daughters to that chance?"

Abigail laughed, a sharp, almost defiant sound. "Ha, Hannah's muskets would put a quick end to that nonsense," she said, just as they chanced upon the Reverend himself coming briskly out of the church, his expression one of urgent purpose.

"Ah, Reverend Mather?" Abigail called out, her voice strong and clear.

"Yes, 'tis I. May I be of service?"

"I am Mrs. Abigail Huntington, and this is my sister Eunice. We have come a long way from New Haven to speak with you."

"Ah, yes, New Haven. I'll be going there soon. What a coincidence." Mather paused, his eyes narrowing slightly to scrutinize the women before him, before a look of resolution crossed his face. "Mrs. Huntington, Miss Eunice, what brings you to my church this day?" he asked, his voice a blend of curiosity and authority.

Eunice and Abigail exchanged glances, their determination reaffirmed. "We seek your assistance in a matter of education," Abigail began, her tone respectful but firm. "We are hoping you might write a letter to a certain Elihu Yale, in London, endorsing the idea of expanding the library at the Old Saybrook Collegiate School."

"Elihu Yale, in London? Whatever for?"

Abigail feigned misunderstanding and inquired, "You do know the man?"

The Reverend narrowed his bushy eyebrows as if concentrating before asking, "Remind me."

"Elihu was born in Boston to David Yale, a Boston merchant and attorney to Robert Rich, second Earl of Warwick."

"Robert Rich, second Earl of Warwick?" Mather asked, still needing to become more familiar.

"Why yes, while in London, Elihu's father was the attorney not only to the Earl but also to Ursula Knight," Abigail said as if Knight's name were recognition enough. She saw that her tactic of confusion was working on the pompous Mather, who nodded as he looked up, as if he had possibly heard of the woman and her significance. "Oh, did I mention," Abigail asked, tapping on her sister's shoulder for her recollection, "Both Elihu's grandfather and uncle were Chancellors of— Oh, my goodness, I can't remember, but they were a correspondent of Elizabeth Tudor?"

"Tudor?" he asked, blinking his eyes with wonder.

"Yes, Queen Elizabeth."

The Reverend shook his head to clear it, asking, "And what of this expansion you mentioned? A certain Collegiate School in Old Saybrook?"

"Yes, of course. How silly of me to confuse you with all the names of Elihu's illustrious pedigree. Anywho, Theophilus's son, London merchant Thomas Yale the second, married the daughter of Bishop George Lloyd of

Chester. After his death and her remarriage to Governor Theophilus Eaton, she and her children emigrated to America as a reconstituted family."

After hearing Eaton's recognizable name, Mather perked up, saying, "Yes indeed. Theophilus Eaton. My cousin Warham lives in New Haven and is quite well acquainted with the Eaton family."

"Ah, you see. What a small world we live in. And that is the connection between Elihu Yale and New Haven." Abigail looked at her sister again with worried eyes before saying, "Did I mention that Elihu was the former President of the East India Company out of Fort St. George, India? Upon his recent return, he is now considered one of the richest men in England, rivaling even the King."

"Oh dear. This is knowledge I did not know."

"I am certain if such a prominent figure as yourself were to ask for a donation, his secretaries would, without hesitation, oblige your request forthwith," Abigail said, forcing a smile and holding up her outstretched hands as if in admiration of the now dumbfounded Reverend.

"But, how could I even correspond with such a man as Elihu Yale?"

"Oh, you can leave it up to me, Reverend sir. We are staying at the Gee mansion—"

"Yes, indeed. Joshua Gee lives near my residency, and his son, Reverend Joshua Gee Jr., is one of my proteges."

"Really?" Abigail said, tapping her sister on the shoulder to remind her of this interesting fact.

Mather's eyebrows lifted slightly. "And this expansion, you say? What purpose would this serve?"

Eunice stepped forward, her voice steady, "Books, kind sir. In your correspondence, if you were to ask for books, the students would be enriched far beyond their tutors' knowledge of subjects."

Abigail slapped her sister's shoulder, saying, "Did I mention Elihu's brother Nathaniel Eaton, Harvard's first Headmaster and President designate, was present at the founding of Harvard?"

"I myself matriculated from Harvard."

"You don't say," Abigail answered, slapping her sister, causing Eunice to push her away with an over-animated smile of disapproval.

For a moment, Mather was silent, weighing their request. Finally, he nodded. "Very well. I will put all of this into thought and prayer. I am expected in New Haven as a character witness. An illustrious acquaintance — ah, whose family this Square is named for." He pointed discreetly to the prominent marquee with the name 'Clark' written upon it. "Someone took advantage of his senile mother and purchased her home right from beneath her. Pushing her out into the streets. Only through the kindness of her son Thomas' heart was she saved from destitution."

Eunice gasped. "How diabolical," she uttered.

"Ah, yes, don't you bother yourself with the facts. An eldest son's inheritance must be upheld, or the colony will soon fall into the hands of pirates. Now, if you will excuse me, I have an urgent matter to discuss with Governor Dummer." He obviously dropped the name Dummer to impress the ladies with his connections and community stature.

"Oh, one more thing," Abigail said, interrupting his leaving. "We have a school in New Haven and would greatly appreciate it if you spent some time tutoring when you are visiting." When the man of the cloth hesitated to commit, Abigail added, as if an afterthought, "We have budgeted a thirty pounds stipend—"

"It would be my pleasure. Boys can never get enough of the word of God while they are young and impressionable."

"Indeed," she said with a harsh glance at her sister's sour face.

CHAPTER 30

Mr. Warbleworth and Mr. Tinkletune

AS THE DAWNING SUN GLANCED across the windowpanes, the morning air in The Willow carried the scent of warm bread and freshly boiled coffee. The girls lingered at the breakfast table, sipping from their cups, chatter breaking into bursts of laughter that quickly hushed whenever someone mentioned singing. Nervous excitement sparked in their eyes—today was their first music session—but beneath the brightness ran an undercurrent of unease. For some, the chance to discover hidden talent felt thrilling; for others, the fear of being found wanting weighed heavier than the scales they would soon be asked to play.

When the kitchen servant began clearing the dishes, the young ladies drifted into the classroom in a flurry of rustling skirts and hushed whispers, each taking her seat with a mix of composure and fidgeting nerves. Patience smoothed her sleeves and adjusted her linen mob cap, while Marie Allamby stole anxious glances at the harpsichords waiting like sentinels at either side of the library.

Just as the room settled into a sprinkling of gossip, a firm knock at the great oak front door echoed in the foyer. The sound startled the girls into an upright posture, spines stiffening as every head turned. Headmistress Hope, her brow lifting with calm authority, strode across the classroom and out toward the foyer. The girls could hear their Headmistress drawing back the latch, followed by a man's voice filling the entryway.

A moment later, with her hands clasped before her—and a rare glint of amusement lighting her eyes—Hope reappeared in the doorway of the classroom with two men at her side and addressed the spellbound class. "Ladies, today we are honored to welcome two esteemed musicians who will guide you in the arts of voice and Harpsichord. Please extend your welcome to Mr. Cornelius Warbleworth, your voice instructor, and Mr. Basil Tinkletune, your harpsichord master."

The class politely clapped. Cornelius Warbleworth was tall and thin, with a mop of frizzy hair that seemed to have a life of its own, bouncing and swaying as he moved. He wore thick spectacles that made his eyes look as round as saucers, and he had long and spindly fingers clasped tightly together as if he were restraining them. Warbleworth's face was set in a permanent expression of awe, as though he had just encountered the world's most magnificent sight—an expression that, unfortunately, would never leave his face, no matter the quality of the singing he was about to endure.

Beside him was Basil Tinkletune, a stout little man whose round frame and rosy cheeks gave him the air of a well-fed cherub. Basil scanned the girls' faces, commenting appreciatively on his alert, fascinated audience. His sizable, bulbous nose dominated his face, while an unruly mustache all but swallowed his mouth, twitching with every muffled word he spoke. When he puffed out his chin—as he seemed to do for emphasis—it gave him the look of a bullfrog preparing to croak.

His fingers, though plump and dimpled, moved with surprising quickness: one hand forever raking absently through his tousled facial hair, while the other toyed with a curious necklace of flageolets, whistles of differing musical tones, that hung about his neck.

They began moving toward the front of the room. Tinkletune's gait had a curious bounce to it, his short legs pumping with the rhythm of a man half his girth. Every step carried a certain merriment, as though he marched to a tune that only he could hear. Altogether, he was an odd spectacle for a harpsichordist: part jester, part showman, and entirely unforgettable.

Before either man made it very far, the Headmistress asked brightly from the doorway, "Would either of you gentlemen care for a refreshment before the lesson—perhaps tea or a cup of coffee?"

At once, their eyes lit up. "Coffee?" Basil Tinkletune gasped, clutching his ample stomach as though salvation had just been offered. "Madam, you've said the holiest word since 'Amen.'"

With a graceful wave, she motioned for them to follow her.

In the kitchen, the servant was already pouring steaming cups. The rich aroma filled the air, and Basil seized his with both hands, inhaling as if it were rare perfume.

"Ahh, roasted beans! This is the true fruit of Eden. Apple? Pah! Eve would have taken this instead."

Warbleworth took a cautious sip, then coughed into his sleeve. "Strong as a Roman gladiator—and twice as tempting," he croaked, before softening his voice as the kitchen girl giggled. "Yes, yes, delightful indeed!"

Basil, having drained his cup, smacked his lips with a satisfied pop and thrust it forward as though refills were his birthright. "Another?"

The Headmistress folded her arms. "Gentlemen, the young ladies await your instructions."

Both men sighed in disappointment, setting down their cups like boys denied a second helping of cake. As they shuffled toward the classroom, Basil leaned toward his friend and muttered—loud enough for the kitchen girl to hear—"Mark my words, if this lesson founders, it'll be for want of another cup."

"Ladies!" Mr. Warbleworth exclaimed as he stepped into the room, clapping his hands with a resounding smack that startled half the class. "Today, you shall embark on a most wondrous journey! A journey of the voice!" He gestured with wild enthusiasm with every word, and his voice seemed to climb several octaves with each syllable, creating an effect that left the girls blinking in mild astonishment.

"And," added Mr. Tinkletune, rubbing his hands together with glee, "you shall learn to coax beauty from the noble harpsichord, one of the finest instruments ever to grace the hands of a musician." He patted a nearby harpsichord as if it were an old pet, causing it to emit drumming that sounded rather like an over-ripened gourd.

The girls exchanged glances, a few stifling nervous giggles, as Mr. Warbleworth straightened his spectacles and peered at them with great interest.

"Now," he intoned in a booming and trembling voice. "Who shall be the first to grace us with their… natural talents?"

There was a moment of silence as the girls looked at each other, unsure who would be brave enough to volunteer. Finally, Gulielma Marie, who was always a bit of a braggart, raised her hand. Warbleworth's face lit up.

"Splendid! Step forward, my dear. And which song would you like to entertain?" he asked, gesturing grandly.

"I believe it will be Over the Hill and Far Away."

"Ah, an excellent choice. Proceed."

Gulielma Marie cleared her throat, stood straight, and breathed deeply. Nodding to Mr. Tinkletune to commence the accompaniment, she began to sing, or at least she tried to sing, "When I was young, I used to court a lass, But I was foolish, and I let her pass. I'd win her now if I could play the part, To ask for her with all my heart." What came out sounded more like a prowling cat caught in a rainstorm—a series of warbling pitches that rose and fell unpredictably. Warbleworth's expression remained rapturous, though one of his eyes twitched behind his thick spectacles.

"Marvelous! Marvelous!" he proclaimed, though his voice cracked ever so slightly. "A truly… unique voice, my dear. A natural, unrefined quality, one that we shall—mold."

Sarah leaned in and whispered to Hannah, "It's probably the coffee," eliciting an involuntary burst of laughter from her usually stoic sister.

He cleared his throat and asked, "Now, who wants to continue with the chorus, umm?" When no one wanted to follow her dire performance, he insisted, "Please, anyone?" He began humming and clapping the beat to the chorus, adding a word here and there to fill in the tune, "Humm, humm, over the hills, humm, humm, and far away, humm, Where duty leads me I will stray. Through mountains high or valleys low, Over the hills and far away." Then, as if shocked, his face sprang into a bright expression, asking, "Does no one know the rest of the song enough to sing?"

"I do," Gulielma Marie answered.

"No?" he concluded, shaking his head with a forced smile.

He turned to the other girls, who were doing their best to keep straight faces. "Who should I pick to join us in our celestial choir?"

Eliza raised her hand to volunteer, emboldened by Gulielma Marie's bravery, and stepped forward, gracefully holding out her hands and taking a deep breath. She opened her mouth, and what came out was not the sweetness of a young maiden's soprano but a sound that resembled a foghorn echoing across a harbor. Mr. Warbleworth's smile remained plastered to his face, though his left eyebrow appeared to quiver an octave higher.

"Ah, such power!" he exclaimed, clapping his hands together. "A voice that could shake the very heavens. We shall, hum, soften it, just a touch."

The other girls, unable to contain themselves, dissolved into a fit of giggles, but the Headmistress quickly silenced them with a stern look and threatened a clack.

Meanwhile, Mr. Tinkletune sat at the Harpsichord, cracking his knuckles with an intense look of concentration. "Now, ladies, allow me to demonstrate the elegance of the harpsichord," he said, his fingers poised dramatically over the keys.

He played a delicate trill, his sausage fingers dancing across the keys with surprising grace for a man of his round stature. The sound emanated was bright and cheerful, filling the room with a lively melody that made the girls' eyes widen in admiration.

"Who would like to try?" he asked, looking up with a twinkle in his eye.

Eliza, always eager to learn something new, raised her hand. She approached the Harpsichord and placed her fingers on the keys, but as she began to play, it became painfully clear that she had no sense of rhythm. Her fingers pounded the keys at irregular intervals, creating a cacophony that sounded less like music and more like a herd of elephants stomping through a china shop.

"She made a better sound with a musket," hissed Gulielma Marie.

"Excellent, excellent," Tinkletune said, nodding encouragingly as though the auditory equivalent of an avalanche hadn't just assaulted him. "A bit... spirited, perhaps, but enthusiasm is a good start!"

Next came the Kidd, who, in her usual rebellious fashion, approached the Harpsichord with a determined scowl. She jabbed at the keys as if they had personally offended her, producing a discordant jangle that made several girls wince. But Tinkletune merely nodded approvingly.

"A forceful touch!" he declared. "We shall work on... finesse."

As the session continued, it became evident that none of the girls who tried their hand were particularly musically inclined. Voices clashed, pitches wavered, and the Harpsichord endured more abuse than it likely had in its entire existence. Mr. Warbleworth, despite his twitching eye and gradually paling complexion, continued to applaud each attempt with unwavering enthusiasm.

"Marvelous! Simply marvelous!" he declared after each girl had her turn, though by the end, his voice had become slightly hollow. "You are all... works in progress, but what a joy to behold!"

Hannah whispered to Sarah, "Most definitely the coffee."

By the time the lesson ended, the girls were exhausted from laughing, Mr. Warbleworth looked as if he needed a lie-down, and Mr. Tinkletune's mustache drooped from sheer exertion. As they packed up their things, the Headmistress gave the students a small smile, clearly amused.

"Thank you, Mr. Warbleworth, Mr. Tinkletune," she said, nodding graciously. "I'm sure the girls have learned much today."

"Indeed," Warbleworth replied, his voice a bit hoarse. "It is... an experience I shall not soon forget. I want to invite you and your students to sing in our congregational Center Church on the Green's choir — the First Congregational Church?"

"Oh? Is Reverend Warham Mather still preaching there?" the Headmistress responded with surprise.

"Why no," he said with the sound of dread in his voice. "The Reverand has left the pulpit. Moved onto the practice of law." Both Mr. Warbleworth and Mr. Tinkletune looked relieved not to be associated with such an ominous figure as Mather.

Feigning not already knowing of Mather's fate, Hope replied with thanks, "What a gracious offer. However, the class is previously engaged at the much smaller, more needy Trinity Church associated with the orphanage."

"Orphanage? Yes, quite a noble cause," he said, bowing his head to leave. "And thank you for the coffee. It was an unexpected pleasure, to be sure. We will look forward to another cup during our next lesson. Will it be in a week?"

"To be sure, and I thank you for your due diligence today."

As the two men exited the room, the girls burst into laughter again, exchanging stories of their musical mishaps. Though they may not have learned to sing or play particularly well, they had undoubtedly gained a memorable lesson in the art of humility—and perhaps, a newfound respect for those who could make music sound as lovely as Mr. Warbleworth and Mr. Tinkletune.

As the students shuffled around the classroom, still chuckling to themselves, Headmistress Terwilliger could only shake her head in amusement.

"Gather around. Come sit," she said, waving her hands as she sat at the nearest of two harpsichords, waiting for the class's full attention. I want to sing you now a song that is near and dear to my heart: The Unfortunate Rake."

"Oh, I know that one," Hannah said, feeling spirited, and Sarah beside her nodded enthusiastically, saying she did, too.

"Then maybe you will accompany me on the chorus?" she said as she hummed a few chords to start singing:

As I was a-walking down by St. James's Hospital,
I was walking down there one day,
What should I spy but one of my comrades,
All wrapped up in flannel, though warm was the day.

Everyone's eyes gleamed with surprise at the eerie beauty of her voice as it blended seamlessly with the keys. Hannah and Sarah softly joined in the chorus, singing in solemn harmony as the Headmistress played the tune:

Oh, had she but told me when she disordered me,
Had she but told me of it at the time,
I might have gotten pills and salts of white mercury,
But now I'm cut down in the height of my prime.

The Headmistress stopped playing to acknowledge the sister's voices. "My, that was beautiful. How long have you two been singing together?" she asked.

Sarah spoke up after looking at her sister for an answer, "For as long as I can remember, we were expected to entertain guests at our house."

"And are you equally versed in playing?" Hope asked, standing and presenting the Harpsichord bench to them to take over.

The two reluctantly looked around at all the expectant faces. Gulielma Marie crossed her arms and glared at the two as they rose from their seats and crossed the room. Each sat at one of the twin harpsichords and ran their fingers over the keys, playing a few chords to familiarize themselves with the instruments.

"What do you have for us to hear?"

Hannah shyly looked over at her sister, and Sarah slumped her shoulders. "Grabgesang?" Sarah asked.

"Oh?" Hope perked up. "I'm not familiar."

Sarah informed, "Heinrich Schwemmer? He's German." Then, with a teasing voice, she added, "Andreas liked to sing it in German, but no one knew what he was singing—" quickly receiving a sharp look from her sister. Sarah's face gaffed with shock before she looked back down at the keys.

"And whom might this Andreas be?" Gulielma Marie mused. "Someone of your liking, perhaps?"

Proudly, Hannah retorted, "Yes, as a matter of fact. A past boyfriend, although no one, I dare say, would have called him a boy." She wiggled her head while looking up, signaling he was a full-grown man. "Something you may experience in the very distant future, perhaps?"

In the brooding silence that followed, the sisters concentrated on the keys. Slowly, each pressed one finger, then another, until the Harpsichord's melody rang out in an eerily haunting tune. The steady, slow tempo created a contemplative, solemn mood befitting a funeral setting. The girl's harmonies intertwined in a way that brought warmth and depth, allowing one to blend while still highlighting individual melodic lines. Hannah began to sing with a beautifully smooth voice:

O, how blessed you are, you righteous ones,
Who has come to God through death!
You have escaped the torment and suffering.
That still holds us captive here.

Sarah followed with the next verse, in an equally melodic voice:
You have reached the shore; we still sail the sea,
We are still tossed about by waves and storms,
While you rest in peace and security,
You have reached the safe harbor.

When they finished the last three verses together, no one had words for its beauty. The Headmistress rubbed her eyes and wiped her nose before sniffing to look at all the awed faces, wanting more.

"I dare say," she said. "I would be eternally satisfied to hear you play in my heart until the day that I die."

Then, to break up the mood, Hannah began to pound out the notes for the popular and lively song Lilliburlero. The Kidd jumped to her feet and started doing a quick-stepping jig that morphed into a marching dance around the room, eliciting others to join in the laughter and improvising movements along the way.

Hope watched the joviality with a satisfied smile. This, she knew, was precisely the sort of lesson they would remember far longer than any note or tune.

Later that evening, as if on cue, like a well-timed cuckoo clock, John Prout knocked on the front door, bearing a sack of coffee beans for the morning meal. Sarah answered expectantly, her heart fluttering slightly at the sight of him standing there in the dim evening light, his face softened by the lantern he held. When she reached out to take the beans, her hand lingered on his a moment longer than usual as she said, "Would you like to stay and have a cup?"

"A cup of coffee? No, I dare not," he replied with a slight chuckle, though his eyes had a warmth that matched her own. "Coffee at this hour would render me sleepless for half the night, robbing me of my dreams."

"Dreams?" she asked, emboldened by the moment. "What is it that you dream of?"

The question seemed to catch him off guard, and in his reluctance to answer truthfully, he smiled, his expression softening. "Many things," he murmured, "but perhaps tonight, I'd prefer dreams in the waking hours."

Blushing, Sarah stepped aside to let him enter. They walked together into the kitchen, the silence between them filled with a gentle warmth as if neither wanted to spoil the moment with too many words. She could hear the Headmistress in the other room, shushing the giggles and whispers of curious students who were clearly eager to eavesdrop on the handsome visitor. Sarah busied herself with preparing the tea, her fingers trembling ever so slightly as she reached for a container.

"Chamomile?" she asked softly, glancing at him.

He nodded, his gaze never leaving her. "Yes, please. Something gentle for the evening."

As she poured the hot water over the leaves, her hand brushed against his arm. She felt a subtle yet undeniable spark, and she noticed he did not pull away. Instead, he placed his hand over hers, steadying her slightly trembling fingers as she extended the cup for him to take and drink. They shared a look that lingered, a silent acknowledgment of the connection that was forming between them.

They took their tea to a small kitchen corner, speaking in hushed tones about simple things—the moon outside, the chill in the air, the promise of spring around the corner. Their conversation was easy and comfortable, but their hands touched every so often as they gestured or passed the teacups, each brush of skin lingering a little longer, carrying an innocent yet growing affection.

As the evening wore on, John reached over to gently tuck a stray lock of Sarah's hair behind her ear, his fingers grazing her cheek. She blushed but did not pull away, her hand resting on his arm, feeling the warmth through the fabric of his sleeve.

When it was finally time for him to leave, neither seemed eager to part. Standing by the door, he held her hand a moment longer, his thumb lightly brushing across her knuckles.

"Thank you for the tea," he murmured, his voice soft.

"And thank you... for the company," she replied, her heart pounding as he gently squeezed her hand before letting go.

As he stepped back into the night illuminated by his lantern, Sarah closed the door, leaning against it for a moment, her cheeks flushed and her heart full. She knew that something had changed that evening, something precious and promising, and she couldn't wait to see where it would lead.

CHAPTER 31

Mutton McCleaver

A KNOCK AT THE FRONT DOOR caught the Headmistress's attention as she and several students finished breakfast. She frowned and rose. "Is that the other girls? They should just let themselves in."

"Ooh, Sarah, maybe it's John," Kidd said with a knowing smile as Hope left the kitchen.

But when Hope opened the front door, she found a woman standing awkwardly, flushed and smiling, clutching a basket, with a young girl by her side. The Headmistress immediately recognized them—the baker's wife and daughter, whom she had seen around town before. In a flash, she recalled this same woman clucking her tongue and briskly steering her daughter away in obvious disapproval when the school opened.

"Hello, how may I be of service?" the Headmistress asked, forcing a polite tone.

The woman gave a flustered nod. "Hello, Headmistress Terwilliger, is it?"

"Yes, I am she. And you are...?"

"Oh! Yes, well," the woman stammered, extending her basket hesitantly. "We are the baker's family—Mrs. Bunty Dougharty, this is my daughter, Dolly. I, uh, had a rather enlightening conversation with a Mr. Tinkletune about your little school. Ha," she said, cupping her hand to her mouth, hoping to hide her attempt at spreading gossip, but could not help herself. "You do know, his real name isn't Tinkletune. It's Croker. It was said that at his last church, he was teased relentlessly, so he decided to change his name."

"Really? And Tinkletune was his best choice?"

"I know. What woman would want to take such a name?" she laughed.

The Headmistress frowned and then, with a revelation, looked up at the swaying trees and said, "Maybe that is the point."

"Pardon me?"

"Oh, nothing."

"I thought it would be neighborly to stop by and introduce ourselves. And to, um, bring a basket of fresh-baked bread, of course."

"Oh, my! How very kind of you. That is most welcome," the Headmistress said, nodding.

The Headmistress took a step backward and gestured for the pair to enter just as the lively group of Hannah, Hirana, Patience, and Gulielma Marie appeared outside the gate, their laughter echoing through the crisp morning air.

Hope and Mrs. Dougharty couldn't help but watch as the girls approached the house.

"That was so funny," Hirana giggled, nudging Hannah. "The look on that woman's face when you showed her your purse—I don't think she thought you were serious until her eyes nearly popped out of her head!"

Another round of laughter erupted as the girls relived the moment, their joy infectious.

Mrs. Dougharty raised a brow, glancing at the Headmistress. "Looks like this is a fun place to go to school," she mused, shifting her basket as she moved aside to let the girls pass.

As the students stepped through the doorway, their mirth only slightly subdued in the presence of a guest, they nodded respectfully to Mrs. Dougharty and her daughter.

"Good day, ma'am," Hannah said with a polite curtsy.

"Oh, Hannah? Did you find maple syrup?" the Headmistress asked.

"Oh, yes, ma'am," she said, looking down into her basket.

"That, and chocolate," Gillema Marie laughed.

"And a scented candle—lavender," Hannah added before turning her attention to the girl standing shyly beside her mother. "And what's your name?"

Dolly, wide-eyed with curiosity, hesitated before answering, "Dolly Dougharty."

"Well, welcome, Dolly," Patience chimed in with a friendly smile before the group swept inside, their conversation about the market picking up right where they had left off.

"And then—oh, you won't believe what she said next—"

Their voices faded into the depths of the school, leaving Mrs. Dougharty chuckling softly as she turned back to the Headmistress. "Lively bunch you've got here," she said. "That's good. A school ought to be full of life, don't you think?"

The Headmistress smiled knowingly. "Indeed, Mrs. Dougharty. Indeed."

They stood exchanging smiles that felt more awkward than warm, until the Headmistress finally nodded toward the kitchen. "Would you care to come in for a cup of tea?"

Mrs. Dougharty hesitated, her face uncertain, until the Headmistress added, "Or perhaps... a cup of coffee?"

Mrs. Dougharty's face lit up with sudden enthusiasm at the mention of coffee, as if she had been waiting to hear those exact words. "Yes, please!" she exclaimed, perhaps a bit too loudly. She eagerly followed the Headmistress toward the kitchen, her daughter trailing shyly behind.

As she passed, she offered the customary nods to the kitchen staff—small, practiced gestures that required no words. A glance toward the hearth, a tilt of the head, a faint lift of the brow. The message was understood at once.

Mugs were set out. Coffee followed, dark and steaming.

Only then did the Headmistress turn back to her guests, a measured smile settling into place. "Please," she said gently, "make yourselves comfortable. Cream and sugar?"

Mrs. Dougharty and her young daughter sipped tentatively at cups of coffee, each with a spoonful of sugar and a generous splash of cream. The Headmistress observed them with amusement. "Have you ever had coffee before?" she asked.

The two shook their heads in unison, smiling as they took another cautious sip.

"Do you like it?" Hope asked, raising an eyebrow.

They both nodded, this time with broader smiles and perhaps a hint of newfound fondness for the exotic brew. Just then, Sarah came into the kitchen, drawn by the aroma of fresh bread.

"Yes, we've been brought some delicious bread," the Headmistress said, noticing where Sarah's attention was focused. She took the opportunity to introduce Sarah to their guests. After a polite exchange, she suggested that Sarah take Dolly and show her around so that she could meet the other students.

The main hall was bustling with activity as each girl pursued her interests. Some gathered around the harpsichord, their fingers fumbling over the keys, while a few tried to sing along, often out of tune. In the corner, the Kidd and Hirana were engaged in an intense mock sword fight, wooden blades clashing with exaggerated swishes and dramatic stances. A handful of others lounged lazily by the windows, absorbed in their books, occasionally glancing up to watch the lively scene unfold.

Dolly was immediately swept into the eclectic mix of girls. The Kidd showed her how to hold a practice sword, enthusiastically demonstrating a few basic moves before Dolly was whisked away to join the group around the harpsichord. The girls welcomed her with open arms, and soon, Dolly was giggling, attempting to sing along to their chaotic melody, clearly enjoying the camaraderie.

"What happened in the market that was so funny?" Sarah asked, curiosity lighting up her face.

"Oh, you should have been there," Patience laughed, still breathless from the memory. "We were inquiring about having a dress made for Hirana—she has nothing for the year-end ball."

Hirana jumped in, "A group of old ladies was standing around, poring over bolts of fabric, when Hannah asked about making me a ball gown. Ha! That one woman with the wart on her nose—"

"The one whose face looked perpetually puckered, like she'd just sucked on a pickle?" Patience interjected, barely containing her giggles.

Hannah smirked. "Did you see her running her fingers along every seam, huffing like she was personally offended by the stitching?"

"That must be Mrs. Boykin," Dolly eagerly added, instantly recognizing the culprit. "She's a seamstress."

"Boykin? What a funny name for a seamstress," Marie Allamby said, pulling her dress tightly around her pear-shaped figure.

"I think they were all seamstresses, the way they acted," Hannah laughed.

"When the whole shop realized we were from The Willow and that we were holding a formal ball, the one built like a teapot muttered about 'today's disgraceful youth' while aggressively tugging at her sleeves as they'd suddenly shrunk."

Gulielma Marie puckered her lips in mock disapproval. "She actually demanded to know, 'Who in their right mind would have a girls' school here in New Haven?'"

Dolly, absently tapping her fingers on the harpsichord keys, nodded. "That sounds like Mrs. Potts. She complains to my mother about the price of bread every single week. It's just what she does—you get used to it. Some people knit to pass the time. Mrs. Potts complains."

"Well, I left them with something to chew on," Gulielma Marie said with a wicked grin.

"Sure did," Hirana snorted, barely containing her laughter.

Sarah leaned in, intrigued. "Prey tell?"

Gulielma Marie puffed up with pride. "I told them the school was here to stay. That a new class would arrive each year, and every single one of them would need a proper ball gown. Then, I ever so sweetly suggested that any seamstress clever enough to establish herself as a high-end dressmaker would make a handsome profit."

Patience clapped her hands. "You should have seen their eyes widen at the thought! Like they'd just found a silver coin in their porridge." She raised her brows in mock exaggeration, earning a chorus of laughter.

Hannah, however, suddenly turned serious. She looked at Dolly and asked, "Why do people in this town dislike our school so much? Everywhere we go, people either turn their backs on us or give us an earful about how we shouldn't be here."

Dolly hesitated, then shrugged. "I don't know. Maybe they're just set in their ways. It's how they were taught—it's all they know, and they're afraid of change." She sighed, her fingers pressing random notes on the keys. "I'd love to come to this school, but my father can't afford it. Maybe that's part of it. People don't like things they can't have—especially when it's something they secretly want for their own daughters."

By the time Mrs. Dougharty had overstayed her welcome and was making her exit, Dolly was dragging her feet, clearly reluctant to leave. Her mother, sensing her hesitation, let out a long-suffering sigh—one filled with equal parts pride and resignation.

"My Dolly, when she comes of age, would truly flourish in such a place," she admitted with a wistful look. Then, with a courteous but firm tone, she added, "But alas, we could never afford such an education for her." She took Dolly by the arm and guided her toward the door, leaving behind a room full of girls who wished things could be different.

With parting smiles and warm goodbyes, Mrs. Dougharty and Dolly finally left, Dolly casting wistful glances over her shoulder as she was led out the door. Headmistress Hope stood in the empty hallway as the door closed, frowning slightly. She couldn't shake the thought that Dolly would have thrived within the Willow's walls, and it saddened her that such a promising young girl might not have the chance to enjoy any learning environment, save a bakery.

After an entire morning of free time, the enticing aroma of roasted meat, vegetables, and warm desserts filled The Willow, drawing the girls to the kitchen like moths to a flame. They lined up to take their seats, plates in hand and mouths watering at the sight of platters of lamb and salt-cured pork, their glistening skins crackling beside a trencher of rich brown gravy.

Curiously—but hardly noticed—all the food had been pushed to the far side of the long oak table, as though space had been reserved for something else yet to come. Still, the distraction of buttered rolls steaming beside bowls of mashed turnips and honeyed carrots was enough to occupy their senses, while a tureen of thick clam chowder perfumed the air with the briny scent of the nearby sea.

At the center sat a golden suet pudding, still warm, flanked by baked apples swimming in syrup and cream. The air shimmered with the mingled scents of cinnamon, nutmeg, and roasted fat — a feast fit for both scholar and sailor alike. The Headmistress clacked her clam-shell castanets, drawing the chatter to a halt.

"Ladies," she announced with a mischievous twinkle in her eye. "Before you indulge in today's feast, I have arranged a special lesson. Today, we welcome Mutton McCleaver, the town's esteemed butcher, to provide you with — a Bite of Knowledge."

A hush fell over the room as a burly man lumbered in, whom the Headmistress let into the foyer after all the girls entered the kitchen. The man looked more like a bear than a mere mortal with a sizable bloody sack slung over his shoulder. His apron, once white, was now a map of old bloodstains and smears, giving him the appearance of a battle-worn warrior fresh from some meat-based crusade. He carried a massive cleaver and a large, glistening knife in one hand. On his broad belt, he hung what appeared to be a long, greyish stone in a pocket of a well-worn, sparsely haired animal skin. As he surveyed the room with his ruddy, whiskered face, he looked like he was deciding which of the girls to carve up first.

"Good afternoon, lasses!" he bellowed, waving his cleaver in a friendly yet terrifying salute. "Today, I'll be showing ye the fine art of butchery. Now don't be shy, ladies—this knowledge could be mighty useful someday!"

He turned, and after carefully delivering his sharpening stone to the table, he slammed a hefty leg of lamb out of his sack onto the empty side of the table, mere inches away from the prepared feast. The thud sent a shockwave through the room, causing the girls to flinch and even a few to gasp. Almost instantly, their appetites wavered as they eyed the hulking butcher standing over his 'bloody class material.'

"See here," he said, bringing his massive knife up to point at the lamb, then swinging it wildly to emphasize his point. Rather than use his finger like an average person, McCleaver had the peculiar habit of punctuating his words with his blade. Whether he was directing someone to the lamb chops laid out on a platter or making a rhetorical point, the knife would gleam and gleam, drawing the girls' attention to the blade rather than his words. The students instinctively leaned back in their seats, wondering if they'd make it through the lesson with all their fingers intact.

"Now, ye have to approach yer meat with respect," he lectured, his eyes narrowing as he glared down at the leg of lamb as if it had personally offended him. "Ye don't just go hackin' and slashing willy-nilly. Ye give it a good stare down first, make it know who's boss." With that, he leaned close to the haunch of lamb, squinting as though daring it to talk back. The girls exchanged uneasy glances as he began what they would later call his 'Carcass Glare,' a moment of silent contemplation in which he locked eyes with the meat as if having a private argument with it.

After a dramatic pause, he gave a satisfied nod and muttered, "Aye, you'll make a fine meal," before bringing down his cleaver with a mighty whack! The sound echoed around the room, and several girls jumped in their seats. To their horror and amazement, a pesky fly that had been buzzing around the meat met its untimely demise under McCleaver's blade, perfectly bisected in a single chop.

Without missing a beat, he grinned devilishly, leaned closer to the girls, and said, "Ah, yes, a secret spice of mine. Adds a bit of flavor, ye see." The girls stared at him, their faces a mixture of horror and fascination, while he proceeded to slice up the lamb as if nothing out of the ordinary had happened.

As he continued to chop, McCleaver became more animated, his 'Chop and Talk' habit in full swing. Each point he made about proper slicing technique was punctuated by a vigorous chop, sending small bits of lamb flying here and there. "Ye want clean cuts, sharp edges. No one likes a mangled piece of meat!" he proclaimed, all while bits of fat and muscle splattered across the table.

"Now, pay close attention, lasses," he said, pointing with his knife yet again, this time dangerously close to Hirana's nose. She recoiled, unsure whether to laugh or faint. "If ye cut along the bone here," he said, demonstrating with a flourish of swipes, "ye get a cleaner, juicier slice!"

He brought the knife down again, slicing expertly through a particularly stubborn gristle. "There! Just like magic," he announced, looking extremely pleased with himself.

"Remember, ladies," he continued, wiping his blade absentmindedly on his blood-stained apron. "It's all in the wrists! You have to coax the meat into falling apart. Just like handling unruly livestock or persuading a rooster not to crow before dawn!"

The girls were now visibly queasy, and several looked over at the plate of roasted lamb, almost touching the bloody leg carcass with a mixture of dread and resignation. The savory meal suddenly seemed far less appetizing after watching McCleaver perform his "surgery" with such gusto.

As he finished chopping the last of the raw meat, he stood back, admiring his handiwork. Then, with a sweeping gesture, he pressed his belly on the carved meat to stab a sliver of the roasted dish that had been so lovingly prepared for the meal. "Now, here's the true art of butchery: serving it up with pride!" He took a deep, exaggerated sniff of the skewered morsel and closed his eyes as if he'd just inhaled the scent of paradise. Satisfied with what he tasted, he carved another small chunk of meat with his bloodied knife, picked it up with his fingers, and displayed his darkly stained teeth and white-coated tongue as he chewed, gnawed, and slurped down the meat with a satisfied moan. He finished by licking his fingers, burping, and commenting, "Aye, a bit too well done for my taste, but still delicious."

The girls shifted uncomfortably, their appetites thoroughly extinguished. Sarah leaned over to Hannah and whispered, "I think I'll be sticking to the vegetables today."

Finally, McCleaver finished his demonstration, wiping his bloody, greasy hands and blade on his apron one last time and giving the lamb leg a parting pat. "A job well done, if I say so myself. Now, don't be shy, ladies—dig in! There's no better way to appreciate the art of butchery than by enjoyin' the spoils!"

Just as the girls thought they were free from the horrors of the "Bite of Knowledge," he cleared his throat and raised his cleaver once more, capturing their attention with a gleam in his eye that was both thrilling and unnerving.

"Now, ladies, don't think we're finished here! Next session, I'll be teachin' ye the proper ways to kill livestock—aye, there's an art to it if ye want the best flavors. And let's not forget the delicate craft of spicing collected blood for makin' blood sausages," he announced with a proud grin as if he were offering them the secrets of delicate prose.

The room fell silent, each girl's face a palette of horror, intrigue, and barely contained nausea. The thought of preparing "spiced blood" was almost too much to bear, yet none of them dared to look away from the man who seemed to find poetry in butchery. With a final, hearty moo-snort and a wave of his cleaver, McCleaver folded his knives across his chest with satisfaction, leaving the girls wide-eyed and clutching their napkins as if they might faint on the spot.

The Headmistress let out a long, quiet breath and offered the butcher a cup of coffee.

Snapping his head, the large, burly man looked as though he was going to cry with appreciation. "Why, I heard of coffee but never have I tasted it," he said, showing a kinder, softer side to his brawny semblance.

"Kidd. Would you serve Mr. McCleaver a cup, please?"

"With pleasure, ma'am." She fetched a cup from the cupboard, carefully wrapped the handle with a towel, then picked up the boiling pot with coffee steeping inside and poured him a cup, filtering it through a cheesecloth. After setting the heavy pot on the table, she quickly snapped her rag against his arm, stunning a fly that flipped onto the table right next to his drink. Kidd glanced at the fly and then offered, "Would you like cream and sugar—or perhaps a bit of your 'special spice,'" she said, nodding to the fly, "in your coffee?"

"Aye, you're a wiry little cuss, ain't ye?" he said. He drank his down black before slamming his cup on the table with a satisfied gasp and proclaiming, "I like it."

Kidd smirked, "Your first name isn't Mutton, is it?"

The grisly man smiled with his stained teeth.

"What is it?" she questioned, moving closer to pick up his cup.

"Beauregard," he said, leaning in so only she could hear.

Kidd stood absorbing his name before gesturing with a shrug, "It'll be our little secret."

As the door swung shut behind him, the Headmistress sighed, her gaze sweeping over the equally shocked faces of her students. The last of the flies, which had attempted to alight on his backside, managed to escape with him, leaving the room in uneasy silence.

"Well, ladies," the Headmistress began, attempting to inject some levity. "It appears we're in for quite the education. This knowledge will undoubtedly be a valuable tool for the comfort of your future family meals. Let us hope, however, that you'll be just as skilled at sheltering this activity from your own children. We wouldn't want to turn them all into plant eaters."

The young ladies, who had been eagerly awaiting this meal just an hour earlier, now looked at the food with barely concealed dread. Their forks remained untouched, and a few cast wary glances at the roast meat as though expecting it to rise and perform its own grisly demonstration. More than one appeared to be seriously contemplating a shift to vegetarianism.

Sensing the waning enthusiasm, Headmistress Terwilliger clapped her hands to gain their attention, signaling it was healthy to skip a meal occasionally. "Well, ladies, wasn't that enlightening? I do hope you gained valuable insight today. And now, if you choose, enjoy our meal?"

Marie Allamby picked up her plate and began to fill it with all manner of meat and vegetables, saying when she saw everyone's fearful faces, "What? I've butchered goats and pigs before. At least he didn't show you how the entrails are harvested to pack with leftover spiced sausage meat scraps."

The room was silent as the girls exchanged glances, each waiting for someone else to take the first bite. The only sound was Kidd mocking McCleaver's 'moo-snort' after he exited the room, but the class was too queasy to laugh. Clearly, the lesson left a trail of butchered appetites, saddened vegetables, and thoroughly unsettled stomachs in its wake.

"I hope he isn't going to come every week to ruin our appetites," Patience remarked.

"No, not so often. Next week, this spot in the schedule will be Mrs. Silence Stitcher, teaching us how to darn socks and hem up dresses. She will likely show you how to make a bonnet from your favorite cloth."

Also feeling squeamish from the day's brutal demonstration, the Kidd pushed her plate away and said, "Bread and cheese it is, then." The others quickly followed suit, their minds haunted by the unforgettable sight of Mutton McCleaver, his gleaming knives, and the "secret spice" of his eccentric butchery.

CHAPTER 32

John

THE MORNING AIR BUZZED with anticipation as Headmistress Hope gathered the students in the classroom after breakfast and waited for everyone's attention. "Ladies," she said, clapping her hands together to gather the chatty girls' attention. Her composed yet encouraging smile revealed that she had an announcement of some importance.

"On Wednesday evenings before long," she began, hands folded before her. "The esteemed Reverend Morton, who you know is head of the orphanage, will be leading a Bible class, and this shall be an excellent opportunity for you to meet and greet the fair people of New Haven and the surrounding communities."

Grumbles from the students about how 'fair' the townsfolk had been to them murmured across the room until the Headmistress said, "The Baker Dougharty will provide cakes and pastries, and John Prout will supply the coffee," lightening up the mood substantially.

"Maybe he'll bring his newest addition, a Hazelnut coffee blend," Sarah suggested, raising everyone's eyebrows with delight.

Before she could say another word, the Kidd called out eagerly, "Is Dolly coming too?" standing on her tiptoes to be heard above the crowd.

Headmistress Hope's lips twitched with amusement as she replied, "I certainly hope so."

Excitement spread among the students. For many, this was the first formal event where they would not only represent the school but also interact with the broader community. This community had not always welcomed them warmly.

The day proved to be long, filled with rigorous lessons in reading, writing, and arithmetic that tested the girls' stamina. Quill pens scratched against parchment as sums were painstakingly worked out, and verses were copied in foreign languages with diligent effort. The scent of ink and candle wax mingled with the occasional frustrated groan from weary students.

The lovely Lena let out an exaggerated sigh, pausing mid-sentence to rub her aching wrist. "No one would dare come to visit this school, Bible class or not, for fear of being cast into the local den of iniquity," she muttered under her breath, just loud enough for those around her to hear.

A few girls stifled giggles, while others smirked knowingly. Her sentiment wasn't entirely untrue.

Over the preceding weeks, most of the students had overheard sharp words in the marketplace—hushed voices complaining that the school was a disgrace, meddling with the natural order. Some shopkeepers barely concealed their disapproval, offering curt service or suspicious glances when the girls pooled their coins for necessary purchases. Others turned their backs, as if ignoring the school's existence might somehow make it vanish.

As late afternoon approached and the sun dipped below the horizon, Sarah eagerly awaited John's delivery of coffee beans. His daily visits and the couple's subsequent rendezvous in the parlor had quickly become a cherished routine, and their conversations deepened with every meeting. The other girls also looked forward to his arrival, their excitement adding a vibrant buzz to the household.

As John and Sarah sat in the parlor, their heads close together in quiet conversation, Hannah stood at the base of the stairs, watching them. She saw the way John looked at Sarah with genuine affection and admiration, and couldn't help but smile when she saw her sister throw on her greatcoat and lead John out the back door into the garden. She resolved to support her sister, even if it meant stepping back and allowing Sarah to navigate this new territory on her own. After all, the garden outside, though touched by autumn's fading, was beautiful—nurtured by their collective efforts and illuminated by the reluctant light of the waning moon. Perhaps Sarah's heart, too, would flourish under John's gentle care.

As Hannah began to climb the grand stairway, retiring to her room, she glanced out the window and saw the huddled couple strolling through the quiet backyard. The moon's soft glow bathed the garden in silvery light, casting a serene and almost magical atmosphere over the scene.

Hannah's heart swelled with a mix of emotions. She knew that sharing the garden, a place of beauty and hard work, was a significant step in Sarah and John's relationship. It was a gesture of trust and intimacy, just as it had been with her and Andreas when she showed him their family garden on the Hudson River all those years ago.

She could still remember how Andreas' face lit up with admiration as he marveled at the lush greenery and vibrant flowers. It was a memory she cherished, even though it had ended in heartache.

The next morning, Hannah awoke early to the gentle light of dawn filtering through her window. She rolled over to face her sister, asking as she turned, "What time did you finally come to bed?"

Even when she received no reply, it took a moment for Hannah to realize Sarah's bed sat untouched, the sheets neatly in place from the day before. A wave of panic washed over her. Throwing on her robe, she hurried out of the room, her mind racing with worry.

Hannah flew down the stairs, trying to suppress the urge to shout out her sister's name. She dashed into the kitchen, hoping to find Sarah there, perhaps preparing an early breakfast or drinking coffee with the other girls. But the kitchen servants shook their heads, looking around the empty table with blank stares, only heightening her anxiety.

Struggling to maintain her composure, Hannah made her way to the backyard, her eyes scanning every corner for any sign of her sister. The garden was eerily quiet. Nothing could be seen among the spent flowers and frost-covered foliage.

Reluctant to disclose her fears openly, Hannah discreetly approached Hope, who was in the classroom attending to some morning tasks before the students awakened—Hannah's look of unmistakable dread caught Hope's attention immediately.

"What is it?" Hope asked, her voice calm but filled with concern.

"It's Sarah," Hannah cried, her voice trembling. "She didn't come back last night, and I can't find her anywhere."

The blood ran from her face as Hope's expression shifted from concern to determination. "Stay calm, Hannah," she instructed gently. "We'll find her. She can't have gone far."

Quickly drawing the attention of one of the housekeepers who was on her way to work, she explained the situation with calm authority, which helped steady Hannah's nerves. They fanned out, thoroughly searching the house and grounds.

Hannah and Hope returned to the garden, retracing Sarah and John's steps from the previous evening. They reached the secluded corner where Hannah last saw Sarah sharing her laughter with John, but there was no sign of either of them.

Just as despair began to settle in, a rustling sound came from behind a large hedge. Hannah's heart leaped into her throat as she rushed towards the noise, Hope close behind.

To their immense relief, they found Sarah and John, both looking a bit disheveled but safe, emerging from a small hidden alcove where they had apparently fallen asleep.

"Sarah!" Hannah cried, half in relief and half with exasperation.

Sarah looked sheepish, her face flushed. "I'm so sorry, Hannah. John and I lost track of time talking and must have dozed off."

Hope, though relieved, fixed them with a stern but understanding look. "You gave us quite a scare, Sarah. It's important to let someone know where you are, especially at night."

John, equally embarrassed, nodded. "I apologize, Headmistress. It was irresponsible of us."

Hannah, still shaking with relief, hugged her sister tightly. "Promise me you won't disappear like that again."

Sarah nodded, her eyes sincere. "I promise, Hannah."

"I now know what Mother felt when the Mohican took Jacob and me," she said, bursting into tears and hugging her sister while looking sternly at John's sorrowful face.

The Headmistress's attention focused on John. "John, what will your father say about you?"

"He will not know. He's in Hartford. Besides, I frequently spend the night in my dinghy fishing off the docks."

Then the Headmistress focused on Sarah, saying, "It will be left up to you to explain why your arrow received not one, but two demerits—one for each of you."

With the crisis averted, they all returned to the house, where the other girls had begun descending the stairs in search of their morning coffee.

Throughout the rest of the day, Sarah behaved differently toward her sister. She appeared distant, quiet, and visibly irritated. Concerned about the sudden change, Hannah eventually confronted her. "What's wrong, Sarah?" she asked, but Sarah remained silent. Frustrated, Hannah pressed for an answer.

"I am the one who was worried sick this morning because of your irresponsibility. Why are you being cold to me?" At this, Sarah broke down in tears. Amidst her sobbing, Hannah managed to make out what she was saying.

"During our time together, John asked for my hand in marriage."

Hannah was taken aback but not entirely surprised. "You said no, I presume?" she inquired. "You cannot get married now! What would mother say?"

Sarah looked at Hannah, trying to control her sobs, and shook her head.

Hannah asked cautiously, feeling a sense of dread, "That's all that happened? You said 'no.' Right? Then lost track of time and fell asleep?"

To her dismay, Sarah shook her head again but remained silent. Hannah gasped, struggling to compose herself. "You mean to say that you—"

"We bundled," Sarah cried out. "I love him—and he loves me. He plans to secure a bond for our marriage and seek his father's blessings in Hartford. His father is trying to secure a land patent from the Mohican."

"Oh my, Sarah. What do you think Mother will do when she hears about this?" Hannah asked, her voice filled with concern.

"I don't know," Sarah replied, wiping away her tears. "Hopefully, by then, it will be too late for her to intervene."

"You do realize that once he secures the marriage bond, you'll be legally married," Hannah reminded her.

Sarah nodded and smiled, filling Hannah's heart with hope and pride for her sister's future with John.

Seeing Sarah's joy, Hannah couldn't help but feel a mix of emotions—she wanted her sister to be happy, yet she worried about the challenges ahead.

"Promise me you won't do anything rash. Getting married so young means facing more than just love's uncertainties," Hannah said softly. "There'll be the struggle of starting a household—whether here in New Haven or back in Manhattan—the whispers of propriety from the townsfolk, and the uncertainty of Mother's blessing. Not to mention waiting for Father's word to reach us all the way from Albany before any vows can be spoken."

Sarah hugged her back, strengthening the bond between them. "I promise, Hannah. I promise."

The rest of the day passed as the sisters shared their hopes and fears and planned for the future, a mix of trepidation and excitement. Despite the uncertainty, they both felt a new chapter unfolding.

As night fell, the garden outside seemed to whisper its blessings, with a sprinkling of fresh snow bowing the heads of the wilted flowers and covering the trees, which stood as silent witnesses to the bond and love that would soon unite Sarah and John. The cloudy grey skies above shielded the young lovers' new path through the stars, while the sisters found solace in each other, ready to face whatever the future held.

CHAPTER 33

Cotton Mather

THE SOUND OF CARRIAGE WHEELS crunching over the cobblestones drew the girls' attention through the cracked-open window to the street. The air carried that distinct October bite—cool, damp, and edged with the promise of frost on the pumpkin. Hannah was the first to spot the familiar silhouettes through the wavering glass. "It's them—it's Mother and Aunt Eunice!" she cried, leaping to her feet.

Chairs scraped, and skirts rustled as she and Sarah scrambled from the table to the front door. From outside came the clatter of hooves and the rising sound of voices—two, distinctly feminine, clearly at odds. Even before the footman reached the latch, they could tell Abigail and Eunice were quarreling about something that had perturbed them on the ride from the docks to the school.

"I told you the upper road was the better way!" Eunice's voice carried ahead of her.

"And I told you that road is always half-washed from storms!" Abigail shot back.

Before another word could pass, Sarah threw open the door herself. A rush of crisp autumn air swept inside, tinged with salt from the harbor and the scent of fallen leaves. Abigail and Eunice stood on the walk, cloaks billowing, cheeks flushed—not just from the chill, but from their spirited dispute.

"Mother! Aunt Eunice!" Sarah cried, hurrying forward. Whatever grievance had divided the sisters dissolved as Sarah flew into her mother's arms, clinging to her with a sob of joy and sorrow mingled. "Oh, Mother..." she whispered, her words dissolving against Abigail's shoulder.

Seeing her sister's distress, Hannah gently placed a hand on Sarah's back, guiding them both through the front foyer, away from the kitchen full of students, through the classroom, and out into the garden, away from curious eyes. There, among the curling vines and withering blooms, she turned to face her mother and Aunt.

"A great deal has happened since you left," Hannah began, her voice calm but tinged with emotion. "In a way, I wished you were here—but in another, I'm glad you were not."

Abigail exchanged a glance with Eunice, a quiet dread tightening in her chest. Hannah drew a slow breath, her eyes scanning the thinning garden as if searching for courage in the last of its color. "Sarah met a young man named John. Do you remember him? He liked to fish?"

Abigail stiffened at the mention of the opposite sex, holding her sobbing daughter tightly. "Yes," she replied, her voice wary.

"Well," Hannah continued. "They fell in love."

Abigail chortled, a mix of disbelief and anxiety in her laugh. "Fell in love?"

Sarah pushed back from her mother, exclaiming, "I love him!" before collapsing into her mother's arms, overwhelmed by her emotions.

Hannah took a steadying breath and announced, "John secured a bond for their marriage, and Sarah stole off to sign it."

Eunice gasped, placing one hand over her mouth and the other comforting hand on her sister's shoulder. "You are—" She paused, struggling to say the word, before pushing out, "Married?"

Abigail's eyes widened in shock. "Where is the boy now?" she demanded, her voice a mixture of fear and anger.

Neither Hannah nor Sarah spoke; the silence stretched unbearably until finally, Hannah said softly and slowly, "John is gone."

Sarah's wail of sorrow cut through the garden, causing Abigail to hold onto her daughter even tighter, trying to extinguish the burning flames of horror that consumed her.

Abigail's face turned pale as she tried to process the news. "How did this happen?" she asked, her voice barely more than a whisper.

Hannah, fighting back her own tears, explained, "He went to Hartford to secure his father's blessing — and hasn't returned."

"Well, that doesn't mean anything," Abigail reassured.

Hannah spoke for her distraught sister. "It's been weeks since we last saw him. His Aunt has delivered the coffee—"

"Coffee?" Eunice asked, blinking around like a hen who'd just forgotten where she laid her egg.

Hannah shook her head, waving her hand dismissively. "Later," she said, brushing the coffee off for now. "His Aunt said it didn't go well with the Mohican, who refused to recognize the title after the Pequot sold the land to his father. Apparently, the purchase stirred a great deal of trouble between the tribes—old grievances reignited over borders and hunting rights—and John's father somehow found himself caught in the middle of it. There was a serious fight, and both he and John were involved."

"Oh, was anyone hurt?" Abigail asked.

"His Aunt didn't know all the details. She'd only received a terse correspondence asking for more money. From that, she suspected it didn't go well because John had not returned." Hannah stopped and looked at her sister.

More wails of sorrow cut through the garden, causing Abigail to hold her daughter even tighter as she tried to extinguish the burning flames of horror consuming her. She looked stoically at Hannah's thunderbird tattoo, remembering their last encounter with the Mohican—when they had stolen her and her brother Jacob as children.

Eunice stepped closer, wrapping an arm around the crying Hannah for support. Abigail held Sarah, her heart breaking for her daughter's sorrow. "Oh, my sweet girl," she murmured, gently rocking Sarah. "I'm so sorry. His father may have had other plans for his son."

"You mean as you have for me?" Sarah murmured.

Abigail recoiled and looked at Hannah with suspicion.

"Yes, Mother," Sarah confessed with her face still buried in her mother's bosom. "Hannah told me you were married before Father. About your mother annulling the marriage, and then the arranged marriage to Father."

"What else did she tell you?" she said, her steely green eyes still fixed on her oldest daughter.

Sarah straightened, her face blotchy but steady. She drew a quiet breath, brushed a tear from her cheek, and lifted her chin—a small act of courage that made her look older than her years. "You mean about Jacob?" she asked, causing her mother to roll her eyes with irritation. "Everything," she said, falling back into her mother's arms with deep sorrow.

Once a place of joy and hope, the garden now felt like a stage for their collective grief. The frozen, spent flowers seemed to bow under the weight of their sorrow, the vibrant colors long muted by the season's heaviness.

As mother and daughter sat, united in their pain, Abigail took a deep breath and let out a soft sigh. "We will get through this. You'll see. He'll show up when you least expect it; I'm sure of it," she said with reverent determination. "Together, we will find a way to heal."

Sarah, still clinging to her mother, nodded weakly. "I don't know how I can go on without him. I'll never love again," she whispered, her voice raw with anguish.

"You are strong, Sarah," Abigail replied gently. "And you are not alone. We are here for you every step of the way."

Once again, the garden would become a place of healing and renewal. Together, they would find a way to move forward through these darkest times. As the sun set, casting a golden glow over the land, they held onto each other, drawing strength from their shared love and the unbreakable family bond.

As days turned into weeks, Abigail went out of her way to comfort her troubled daughter, Sarah, offering solace and companionship at every opportunity. However, this intense focus came to the detriment of Hannah, who felt increasingly neglected. Seeking distraction and perhaps a sense of belonging, Hannah began pushing the envelope in her relationships with the other girls, often engaging in mischievous antics and testing the boundaries of their camaraderie, collecting shell demerits along the way.

During this stormy period, the school received unexpected news: none other than Cotton Mather would be visiting The Willow. The announcement sent ripples of excitement and anxiety through the school. When she heard the news, Abigail seemed particularly out of sorts, her usually composed demeanor slipping. Hope, elated at the prospect of such a distinguished visitor elevating their status, couldn't help but notice Abigail's unease.

"Why do you seem so troubled, Abigail?" Hope asked gently, her curiosity piqued.

Abigail sighed, a look of concern etched on her face. "I did invite him to tutor the students, yes. But I withheld one crucial detail: that this is a girls' school. Cotton Mather is known for his rigid views on women's roles. He may be more inclined to lecture us on our wayward ways, citing that a woman's place is in the kitchen and not at the head of a family or an educational institution."

Hope furrowed her brow with confusion. "Well, surely when you invited him, you wanted him to accept?"

"Yes, of course," Abigail said, her smile thinning. "But I confess, I never expected him to accept. I thought it would be one of those invitations that everyone is too polite to answer. Now it seems my charm has become my curse—and I've invited a fox to critique the henhouse."

Hope's face softened with understanding. "I have to admit, I share in your apprehension. If he were to recognize me from my past pricking, he may reveal my complicity in his cousin's Witch Trials—a past I would rather expunge forever."

Contrite, Abigail said, "We must prepare for his visit then and ensure that our purpose and dedication are clear. We cannot let his opinions undermine what we have built here."

Hope nodded, still worried but bolstered by Abigail's resolve. "I fear he will try to impose his beliefs on our institution. We need to be ready to defend our mission and our progress."

Hannah, standing around the corner out of sight, bristled at the notion that this Reverend wielded such power over the more gentle gender. She felt a surge of determination rise within her. If this man came and went with prejudice against the school, ill will might spread and poison the institution of higher learning for all those who would follow. With a devious conviction, she decided to take matters into her own hands.

She slipped away discreetly and gathered the other girls in a secluded garden corner. The excitement and mischief in her eyes quickly captured their attention.

The day of Cotton Mather's arrival at The Willow had finally come. All the girls were still upstairs, hurriedly dressed and preparing for class, when Abigail and Eunice heard the sound of his carriage coming to a stop in front of the house. The classroom had been meticulously transformed, complete with an altar where the orchestra once sat in the library, creating a solemn, spiritually intellectual atmosphere.

Eunice and Abigail opened the front door and stood on the porch to greet Mather, who was letting himself through the gate with a stern, almost repugnant expression. Hope had already recused herself because she feared he would recognize her. As he approached the sisters, the air was thick with tension, and without a preamble, he set the mood with his opening words.

"Why didn't you tell me—"

Abigail braced herself, knowing she had to explain to him why she had invited him to a girls' school. But Mather continued, surprising her.

"This is the very property Thomas Clark accused of being unlawfully purchased from his senile mother. It had been in his family for decades."

Abigail's eyes widened in realization, and she quickly composed herself. "I am truly sorry for the misunderstanding, Reverend Mather. But I assure you, the misunderstanding was on his part, not ours."

Mather's stern expression softened slightly. "Yes, as it seems. His mother was most persuasive that she was in sound mind and heart. She insisted that you purchased the property fair and square at what many in the courtroom said was decent and equitable, if not exorbitantly priced. You are—" He hesitated before finishing with, "to be commended."

Mather's eyes rose, and he took in the sight of the building before continuing. "When his father's Last Will and Testament was reviewed and judged a legal document, Thomas Clark begrudgingly acquiesced, setting free your title to the land. However, I fear his contempt has not been extinguished completely. Indeed, his vile and vinegar would have led me to send a pricker after him in days past."

Eunice, who had been quietly observing, raised her eyebrows and interjected, "Maybe his heart would be set straight with a good whipping; ten lashes perhaps?"

Mather's eyes sparkled at the notion, but he shook his head regretfully. "Thomas Clark is an outstanding citizen of Boston and should not be treated otherwise. Now, please show me your school. I only have an hour to spare."

With that, Abigail and Eunice led him inside, their hearts pounding with a mix of relief and anxiety. They moved through the grand foyer, finally arriving at the epicenter of the Willow.

"This is our classroom, Reverend Mather," Abigail began, gesturing to the well-arranged room and its altar. "Our students are ready to demonstrate their knowledge and skills."

"Students? I don't see any students," he said just as a cluster of figures appeared at the top of the stairway.

Hope stood out of sight, gazing upon the scene, mortified, while Eunice bit her knuckles to hold back her laughter. Standing at the front of the group, at the top of the stairs, were Hannah and Sarah, dressed as young men.

As they began descending the stairs, it became evident that all the girls had transformed their appearances with remarkable ingenuity, yet the effect was both convincing and comical. They wore woolen breeches that reached just below the knee, with tucked-in stockings that looked slightly too big. Their linen shirts, typically worn as both undergarment and outer layer, were loosely tucked into their belted trousers. Still, the shirts were a tad too large, giving them a somewhat billowy appearance over their tightly wrapped breasts. Over their shirts, they wore sleeveless waistcoats, long and somber dark fabric, adding an air of seriousness to their otherwise humorous disguise.

Their hair, usually styled in the elaborate fashions of the time, was hidden beneath wigs and tricorn hats, which they had tilted at jaunty angles. They had even darkened their eyebrows with soot and smeared charcoal on their faces to mimic stubble, though the effect was more smudgy than rugged.

Hannah's usually vibrant, expressive eyes were narrowed with determination, her jaw jutted forward, and her posture was rigid as she tried to embody the demeanor of a young gentleman. Sarah, more petite, stood with her shoulders squared, attempting to appear broader and more imposing, though she looked more like a squirrel trying to puff itself up as she rearranged something stuffed into her crotch.

Abigail and Eunice exchanged horrified glances, unsure whether to laugh or cry. The overall effect was undeniably amusing, and they could barely contain themselves, with their shoulders shaking with silent laughter.

As the girls, disguised as young men, descended the stairwell, Sarah mumbled to no one in particular, "God, I wish I didn't drink that third cup of coffee."

Cotton Mather's eyes lit up with keen interest as he saw the student parading down to meet him. "What a fine and handsome class of students," he remarked, clearly impressed. "Come, sit while I learn more about what you know."

The "students" filed down the stairs, trying to mimic the mannerisms of young men. They dug and scratched at various parts of their bodies, trying to appear nonchalant, though some couldn't suppress the occasional uncontrollable smile. Mather, misinterpreting their amusement, took it as a compliment to his presence and beamed with excitement.

"Well, it is a pleasure to see you all today," he said, emphatically nodding. "It is encouraging to witness such a group eager to learn."

The disguised girls took their seats, exchanging furtive glances and stifled giggles as Mather began his lecture. He launched into a practice dissertation, his voice rising and falling with the fervor of a seasoned orator. He spoke passionately about the goods and evils of the world around them in the colonies, emphasizing the importance of moral fortitude.

"And most especially," he intoned about men's pirating nature. "Such acts are not only a crime against the crown but a crime against God Himself. The very land we live on must be respected and cared for."

Maintaining their serious expressions, the girls listened intently, occasionally nodding their heads in agreement. The intermittent snicker slipped through, but Mather, ever eager to believe in his audience's earnestness, mistook these as signs of engagement and enthusiasm.

Sitting at the front, Hannah scratched her chin thoughtfully, a gesture she had seen many men use when contemplating serious matters. "Reverend Mather," she said, deepening her voice, "What do you believe is the greatest threat to our colonies today?"

Mather's eyes sparkled with approval. "A fine question, young man, and your name?" he asked with beaming eyes of pleasure.

"Ah," Hannah said, taken aback, unprepared to answer such a question. Her mind fluttered momentarily before saying, "Johanan, but you may call me Hans."

Mather nodded and said, "Hans, our greatest threat is eroding our moral values. We must stand firm against the temptations that threaten to lead us astray, be it through piracy, greed, or the neglect of our divine duties. Family values are, above all, the moral compass we must all follow, with the man being the head of the household."

"Yes, but what should a woman do if her husband is lost during their marriage?" Hannah added, causing her mother and Aunt to feel nauseated, and Sarah to squirm in her seat.

"Good question," he said, coughing into his hand. "You should accept the fact that your widow—ah, that sounds a bit morbid, but the truth—should, with haste, find another man to take her as a wife by any means at her disposal."

Abigail and Eunice stood in the background, biting their nails, hoping and praying that this conversation would pass without incident.

Hannah rubbed her chin, catching her sister's glaring eyes, and asked, "What means are at her disposal? What exactly does that mean?"

Mather froze at the blunt question while looking to his side to the women standing in the foyer before swallowing hard to say, "I don't think you will have to worry about that; after all, you'd be dead."

Hannah followed his regard to see her mother's eyes practically bulging out of her head, before saying, "Good point," and letting him off the hook.

As Mather continued, the disguised girls nodded solemnly, their attempts to suppress their mirth becoming more challenging. Yet, their ruse held, and Mather remained none the wiser.

After thoroughly exploring his topics, Mather concluded his lecture by complimenting the class: "I am heartened to see such bright and attentive young minds. You give me hope for the future of our colonies."

He then nodded curtly, his eyes scanning the room with critical interest, and invited the students to ask questions. The girls, despite their nerves, held their composure. Each one took turns asking and answering questions, engaging in discussions, showcasing their intelligence and depth of understanding.

The skepticism with which Mather had entered the school entirely disappeared. He observed their decorum and depth of knowledge with a growing, albeit reluctant, respect. The student's performance was flawless, each one playing their part to perfection.

Finally, as the hour drew to a close, Mather addressed Abigail and Eunice. "Your students are quite... remarkable," he said, an inscrutable expression on his face. "I must say, they have a surprising depth of knowledge and civility."

The girls, relieved that the lecture had ended, exchanged quick smiles of triumph. As Mather gathered his notes, Abigail stepped forward, her face a mask of professionalism. "Thank you, Reverend Mather, for your enlightening discourse. Our students have learned much from your visit."

Mather nodded, clearly pleased. "It has been my pleasure, Mrs. Huntington. Continue your good work here. I hope you do not mind if I stop by from time to time?"

Hesitantly, she answered, "Of course not. You are always welcome, with suitable notice. We provide our students with many field trips, some of them overnight."

"Of course, and thank you. Oh, one more question," he said, chancing another gaze back at the handsome students. His eyes focused on Gulielma Marie's posture and mannerisms. She had refused to wrap her breasts because of the acute discomfort she was experiencing as of late and instead chose to add girth around her abdomen, giving her a rich, rather lumpy-looking obesity. Everyone held their breath, hoping he hadn't seen through their ruse. "Was my letter to Elihu Yale met with your satisfaction?"

Abigail let out the breath she'd been holding. "Very much so, and I thank you again most emphatically. The fruits of your labor will hopefully be seen on the next few tides."

"Excellent," he said with a look of anticipation and one hand extended in a contingent yet expectant fashion.

"Oh, forgive me. I had almost forgotten. I had become so engrossed in your marvelous lecture," Abigail said, handing him a small leather pouch of silver from a dress pocket.

The look of greed spread across the man's face like a ravenous rash. He weighed its content in his meaty fingers before bowing to say, "Oh my, thank you, madame. Not necessary, but greatly appreciated."

The students stayed in their seats while Abigail and Eunice walked Mather to the front door and waved him off. As his carriage departed, the girls let out a collective sigh of relief, their spirits buoyed by the success of their daring plan. Hope joined Abigail at the window, both women watching as the Reverend's carriage disappeared down the lane. The silence he left behind was almost holy. Abigail exhaled, long and shaky, pressing a hand to her chest as though releasing the weight of hours of restraint.

"Well," she said, half laughing, half gasping, "if he'd stayed a moment longer, I might've confessed to witchcraft just to send him running sooner."

Hope chuckled, coming from the kitchen, relief softening the lines around her mouth. "You and the girls handled him beautifully."

Abigail gave a wry smile. "Handled him, yes—but next time I invite a man like that, remind me to catch the pox instead."

Later that evening, as the girls gathered in their rooms, they recounted the day's events with uncontrollable laughter. Hannah, still dressed in her disguised trousers, grinned broadly as she changed into her nightshirt. "We did it," she said, the pride in her voice unmistakable.

Abigail and Hope, though still reeling from the day's unexpected twist, couldn't help but join in the laughter. The Willow had stood the test of time, albeit deceitfully, showing the capabilities and potential of young women, even under the guise of young men. The school remained a beacon of hope and progress in an uncertain world, ready to face challenges with resilience, ingenuity, and a good sense of humor.

CHAPTER 34

Springing the Trap

AS THE EVENING FOLLOWING Cotton Mather's visit drew to a close, the halls of the Willow Finishing School grew quiet. The flickering light of lanterns illuminated the girls' cozy bedroom, where Abigail and Eunice had gathered with the girls to say good night. The room was filled with the scent of fresh ink and well-worn leather bindings, a space dedicated to ideas and learning. Tonight, however, the atmosphere held a sense of mystery and purpose.

Abigail cleared her throat, drawing attention. "Girls," she began, her voice calm but serious. "We wanted to speak with you about a trip we must take in the morning. Captain Holloway has just returned from Manhattan on our sloop, the Atlas, and Eunice and I will be heading to the neighboring town of Old Saybrook on a matter concerning the future of our school."

"Leaving us again. Oh, Mother, I fear what will happen in your absence," Sarah said, her voice trembling with a mix of affection and apprehension.

Hannah nodded, her brow furrowed. "Old Saybrook? Is something the matter, Mother?"

Eunice placed a comforting hand on her niece's shoulder. "No, my dear, nothing's wrong. But the Collegiate School's current quarters may not remain suitable for long. With increasing collaboration from certain influential men, we're exploring the possibility of finally moving it to a more secure—and open-minded—place, perhaps even here in New Haven."

Hannah glanced between them, sensing the weight beneath Eunice's calm tone. "Is that what kept you so long the last time you went away?"

Abigail hesitated, sharing a quick look with her sister before answering with a faint, almost guilty smile. "Indirectly," she admitted.

Sarah, still flushed from emotion, folded her arms and sighed. "Well, I can't say I'm not glad to have you home. It's been... easier, having you here." Her voice softened, her following words quieter. "After John, the house felt so empty."

Abigail drew her daughter into a gentle embrace, pressing a kiss to her hair. "Then I'll make the most of every moment before I leave again. But, my dear, what we're working toward—this school, this future—it's all so that young women like you might have the freedom to choose your path, not just follow one set for you."

Eunice nodded, her tone lightening the moment. "And if all goes well in Saybrook, perhaps the next time we leave, it'll be to welcome an entire college into your backyard."

The following morning, the salty breeze of the New Haven harbor carried a scent of the sea as Abigail and Eunice approached the bustling docks. Their skirts swished against their ankles, and Abigail pulled her shawl tighter against the crisp morning air. The rising sun glared over the scene, where sailors barked orders and carts rumbled over warped and missing planks. Captain Holloway stood at the end of the pier, his figure a striking silhouette against the backdrop of his sloop.

As they drew closer, the sisters were greeted by a surprising sight—the sloop's deck was a veritable mountain of crates and tarps stacked precariously high. The smell of aged leather and parchment mingled with the brine of the harbor, and Abigail's sharp eye caught a crate with a corner pried open, revealing neatly bound books within.

Captain Holloway tipped his hat and flashed a grin, though his expression showed a hint of exasperation. "Ladies," he greeted with a sweeping bow. "Welcome aboard the finest library ever to set sail. Apologies in advance for the accommodations—or, rather, the lack thereof."

Eunice's brow arched as she took in the towering piles. "Captain," she quipped, hands planted firmly on her hips, "I didn't realize you were running a bookshop."

"Not just books," Holloway replied with a chuckle, gesturing toward the disorder. "Almost two thousand bound volumes destined for Old Saybrook. If I were a gambling man, I'd wager this might be the finest collection the Colony has ever seen—though I dare say, it has made your cabin... somewhat impassable."

Abigail sighed, glancing toward the sloop. "Let me guess," she said, her tone dry. "Even the galley has been overtaken?"

"Every nook and cranny," Holloway admitted, scratching the back of his neck. "It's a tight fit, but books are less likely to complain than passengers, so I count myself lucky."

Eunice rolled her eyes but couldn't hide her amusement. "At least it's a short excursion," she quipped. "No need for my beauty to sleep."

"Beauty sleep, ma'am, is overrated when traveling with such fine literary company," Holloway countered with a wink, gesturing toward the nearest crate. "And if you'd like, you're more than welcome to read through them as we sail."

Abigail stepped closer to inspect the one open crate, pulling back the tarp. "These look more expensive than I would have anticipated," she murmured, tracing her finger over the gilded lettering on a visible spine. She straightened up and turned to face the Captain with an arched eyebrow. "And whose collection are you transporting?" she asked, rehearsing the presentation she planned to convey to the tutors and residents of Old Saybrook when the books were delivered.

"Oh," Holloway replied cryptically, clearing his throat as a grin tugged wider across his face. He began to recite his prepared response. "Elihu Yale, ma'am. Fresh from London. These books are in need of a more… charitable home."

Eunice gave a soft, skeptical snort. "How philanthropic of this Mr. Yale. And of you, my dear Captain, for ferrying such treasures in the name of mankind's enlightenment."

Holloway tipped his hat with mock gravity. "Aye, madam — I do what I can for the cause of enlightenment… especially when it pays by the crate."

As the crew scurried about, Abigail turned back to Holloway. "And where are we supposed to sit?"

"Anywhere you can find space," he replied with a shrug. "Though I'd suggest the bow. It's the least cluttered spot on this floating library."

Eunice grumbled good-naturedly but took Abigail's arm, leading her to find their place. "Come, sister. Let's see if we can find a perch that doesn't involve straddling a stack of religious doctrine. I wouldn't want to aggravate my rheumatism."

As the two women carefully stepped, maneuvering around crates and sailors, Holloway watched them with a smirk. "You know," he called after them, "with all these books around, you might find a tome on how to enjoy a cramped voyage."

Abigail paused mid-step and turned to glare at him. "Captain," she said coolly, "if I find such a book, I'll gladly lend it to you. You clearly need it more than I do."

Eunice stifled a laugh as the sisters continued their way forward, leaving Holloway chuckling behind them. The sloop creaked and swayed in the gentle morning tide. The journey to Old Saybrook promised to be one for the books—quite literally.

When the afternoon arrived, Abigail and Eunice knew it was time to spring their trap on the Collegiate School in Old Saybrook. The meticulously crafted plan was unfolding even more smoothly than Abigail had dared to hope, as the ship's cargo was ferried around the sandbar and into the town center—no less by the very scoundrels who had tried to claim salvage rights when the sloop lay stranded on the sandbar. The schoolhouse, small and ill-equipped, stood in stark contrast to the sheer volume of books being delivered. Along with the books were several bundles of goods and a grandly painted portrait of the German-born, sausage-eating King George the First.

At first, the Collegiate School tutors were positively ecstatic, their eyes wide as crate after crate of books was unloaded from the ship's hold. Each title that emerged seemed more precious than the last—Plato, Milton, Bacon—a veritable kingdom of learning delivered to their humble doorstep. "A gift from Providence itself!" exclaimed one tutor, his powdered wig nearly toppling as he craned to read the gilded spines.

Abigail and Eunice stood at a respectful distance, watching the excitement with polite smiles and private amusement. It was as though they were witnessing a band of children unwrapping toys they did not yet know how to play with.

But as the mountain of crates continued to grow, the mood began to shift. "That's the twelfth case," muttered another tutor, looking from the stack to the sagging shelves within their little schoolhouse. "Wait. Or perhaps the fifteenth—blast it, I've lost count!"

By the time the last crate hit the dock, the air of reverence had dissolved into confusion. The tutors huddled together, fretting.

"There's no room in the house," one said, tugging anxiously at his cravat.

"Nor in the rectory," added another. "The very walls will burst from the weight of wisdom."

"Maybe we might build a new wing!" shouted a third, only to be met with horrified stares from townsfolk who had been drawn to the dock by the excitement and now stood in whispering clusters watching the dramatic unloading. Talk of local building projects always elicited pushback; such suggestions required funds, and funds required meetings, and meetings meant dealing with Trustees.

The chaos swelled until a younger tutor, red-faced and sweating, cried, "Gentlemen, for the love of heaven, if we cannot house them, at least cover them before the sea air eats through the bindings!" He grabbed a sheet of canvas and threw it clumsily over the nearest stack.

Eunice leaned toward her sister, her voice dry. "There's no more coming, of course—but oh, I do want to tell that jumpy fellow we've another ship due next week. I'd wager his wig would leap clean off."

Abigail's eyes sparkled with mischief. "No, that would be too much. We want to overwhelm, not drive them away," she murmured. "Let enlightenment dawn slowly. Too much illumination all at once might blind them all."

One of the Collegiate tutors, clearly flustered, shouted, "Don't hang that rascal's picture! We need the wall space to stack books!"

Eager to sow further chaos, Abigail nodded and pushed for even more room as more books came ashore. "It seems evident that you need to raise sufficient funds to build a much larger library to accommodate these wonderful gifts."

The gathered townspeople, having agreed to adopt the Collegiate School, now faced the orphaned religious histories, dramas, and scientific manuscripts—most beyond their understanding—and began to murmur uneasily. Some flinched at the notion of housing the excess books in their homes, as though the bindings might breathe foreign thoughts into their souls and taint their Puritan values. Many shook their heads, rejecting Abigail's suggestion of expansion outright, claiming emphatically that they had no money to spare on a frivolous endeavor like a school, especially when it was clear that none of their children would qualify for a leisurely life of reading and writing. The idea of investing in a larger, unprofitable school couldn't have been less appealing. Distancing themselves from the escalating situation, they began to drift back to their homes, leaving the tutors and the school to grapple with the overwhelming influx of books.

Standing by Abigail, Eunice couldn't help but smirk at the unfolding chaos. "It seems our plan is working perfectly," she whispered.

Abigail nodded, her eyes twinkling with satisfaction. "Indeed. With the townspeople unwilling to support the expansion, it will be only a matter of time before they reconsider the school's location."

As the sun set over Old Saybrook, the once-ordered town had an air of disarray, with crates piled high at the school and in the surrounding homes. The tutors, their initial excitement replaced with mounting frustration, continued to struggle with the logistics of protecting their newfound treasure trove.

In the days that followed, the town found itself at a crossroads. The sheer volume of books had proven to be a double-edged sword, raising difficult questions about the institution's future. During this tumultuous time, Abigail and Eunice stayed in the local inn, each working to promote the school's expansion—using estimated numbers so high they made many pucker and cringe at their mere mention. When the sisters met in private, they shared knowing looks and quiet observations, pleased to see their plan to overwhelm the school and town unfolding exactly as they had envisioned.

On a misty Tuesday morning, Abigail and Eunice sat alone in a secluded corner of the inn next to the crackling fireplace. Steam rose gently from the teapot as Eunice poured, her steady hand belying the mischief in her eyes. "So," she began, her lips muffled by the edge of her cup. "Our grand scheme to bury Old Saybrook under a mountain of unread books seems to have worked. I hear the tutors are near weeping."

Abigail smiled faintly, stirring her tea with slow precision. "We gave them knowledge in abundance—how they choose to drown in it is hardly our fault."

Eunice leaned closer, her voice dropping. "And now the legislature's ears are pricked. Dummer himself will get his ear full of the 'crisis of learning' in Saybrook."

"Good," Abigail said, setting down her spoon with quiet finality. "It will force their hand. New Haven will be the obvious savior, and The Willow will blossom beside it."

Eunice raised an eyebrow. "And the two thousand pounds you pledged? I do hope that wasn't yours."

Abigail's lips curved. "Not mine, exactly. Negotiated contributions. Pirate coin spends the same when melted into charity."

Eunice laughed, nearly spilling her tea. "Everyone involved would have apoplexy if they only knew where the funds really came from."

"Let each choke on his own piety," Abigail replied dryly. Then, softening, she added, "By the time the trustees realize what we've done, the Collegiate School will have moved—and our young women will have their education enriched."

"With a steady flow of eligible bachelors," Eunice added with a grin, swirling the last of her tea in her cup to the low crackle of the fire. "You realize, of course, that if our plan works, New Haven will be crawling with bright young men desperate for education and direction."

Abigail looked up with an arch of her brow. "And we just happen to have a house full of bright young women desperate for opportunity and purpose."

Eunice grinned. "Opportunity and purpose—such genteel words for matchmaking."

"Call it what you will," Abigail replied, a sly smile curving her lips. "Society thrives on balance. For every scholar, a muse. For every sermon, a song."

Eunice chuckled and set down her cup. "Then may our muses be well-funded and our scholars well-groomed."

They both laughed softly, the sort of laughter that carried the weight of victory disguised as modest conversation.

Eunice reached for the teapot and poured them each another splash before leaning back, swirling the amber liquid in her cup. "Let the girls continue to study in peace while we do all the ungenteel labor," she quipped, her lips curling into a mischievous grin. "They are already learning to curtsy, parry, and compose their moral essays. Maybe we should teach them how to plot, negotiate, and charm half the Colony?"

Abigail arched a brow over her teacup. "Parry?"

Eunice smirked. "A well-timed curtsy may soften an insult, but a steady hand with a sword—or a musket—settles most disputes far quicker."

Abigail laughed, shaking her head. "Heaven help New Haven."

"Better that than helpless," Eunice said with a shrug. "Charm wins the drawing room, but a good aim keeps one alive long enough to enjoy it."

Abigail gave a knowing smile. "A fair division of duties, I'd say."

Eunice nodded sagely, then added with a glint in her eye, "And as for the men of the Collegiate School—well, they'll soon have lessons of their own to master. Let's see how those lofty scholars manage their Greek declensions while surrounded by clever young women with a keen eye for a prosperous match."

Abigail chuckled, setting down her cup. "Heaven help them. I fear the poor boys won't know whether they're reciting the Psalms or composing sonnets."

"Either way," Eunice said, raising her tea in mock salute, "education in New Haven will take a most practical turn."

Abigail raised her cup in a quiet toast. "To education—of every sort."

"Precisely," Eunice replied, clinking her cup against her sister's. "And to the fine art of knowing just how to teach it."

They each sipped—a conspiratorial toast between sisters who were quietly redrawing the map of Connecticut, one pot of tea at a time.

CHAPTER 35

Talitha Cumi

THE SUN HAD BEGUN TO SINK, casting long amber strokes across the windows as preparations for the evening Bible study neared completion. At long last, tonight was the night Reverend Morton—head of the New Haven Church and the orphanage—would lead a public Bible class at The Willow. Invitations had been sent throughout New Haven and the surrounding countryside, though neither Hope nor the girls expected unfamiliar faces to appear. Aside from tutors and the occasional vendor delivering goods, the townsfolk still maintained a careful distance from the school.

However, Hope had instructed everyone at The Willow to—as always—prepare for all eventualities. The cakes and pastries had arrived earlier that afternoon, their warm, spiced aromas drifting through the building and rendering the girls nearly useless with anticipation.

Several had already been caught "accidentally" wandering through the kitchen—Marie Allamby claiming she'd misplaced a handkerchief three times, and Lena insisting she needed to "check on the spoons." When one bold student attempted to slice the tiniest sliver imaginable off a spice cake, she was marched out by the kitchen staff, cheeks flushed and crumbs betraying her guilt like feathers on a fox's whiskers.

Hannah sighed dramatically as she straightened her skirt's waist. "I do wish Mother and Aunt Eunice would return. When the Reverend begins his lesson, we'll be made to sit in the very front. I'd much rather stand with them in the back."

Sarah leaned close, lowering her voice. "Perhaps it is better they are not here yet. Mother would start whispering questions, and Aunt Eunice would start answering them, and before long—"

"—We'd be debating theology while the rest were learning the Psalms," Hannah finished.

Sarah nodded solemnly. "And then Aunt Eunice would say something like, 'Well, our dear grandfather's Koran says—'"

Hannah's eyes widened. "Sarah! Reverend Morton would flip his wig."

A firm knock at the front door broke the soft hum of girlish chatter. When Hope opened it, Reverend Morton stood waiting—tall, solemn, and dusted with New England's autumn chill as though the wind itself had ushered him to the schoolhouse.

"Reverend Morton," Hope greeted with a respectful bow. "We are honored by your presence. Please, come in."

He stepped across the threshold, removing his hat and coat and letting the Headmistress hang them in the coat rack. Hope led him toward the classroom, where the girls straightened as though commanded by an invisible rod of propriety.

As he entered, Reverend Morton paused to take in the unfamiliar sight—rows of chairs, harpsichords gleaming near the well-stocked library, lace-collared girls holding their breath, attempting to appear studious and angelic all at once. His brows lifted, unsure whether to be impressed, unsettled, or both.

Hope offered a gentle smile. "Reverend, would you prefer tea or perhaps a cup of coffee?"

Morton exhaled a long, conflicted sigh. "Ah, coffee… I admire it far too much to trust it. Surely any drink that stirs such devotion must carry a snare for the soul. Best you bring me tea, Mistress Terwilliger, lest I fall prey to temptation before the Scriptures are opened."

A few girls bit their lips to stifle their own coffee-induced giggles.

Hope nodded dutifully and slipped toward the kitchen. As soon as she disappeared, the girls exhaled in relief and rustled into their seats. Marie glanced toward the well-stocked refreshment table—cakes untouched, extra chairs lining the walls like soldiers awaiting inspection.

"All those chairs dragged from our chambers," she whispered to Lena, "and no one to sit in them but one trembling teacup."

Lena smothered a smile. "And cakes enough to feed a Davenport wedding—but alas, only righteousness for company."

Before they could dissolve into further mischief, Hope returned with a steaming cup. Reverend Morton accepted it with a grave nod, settling himself.

He had barely lifted the cup from the saucer when—KNOCK-KNOCK.

Every girl stiffened.

Sarah stood, heart fluttering. "I shall attend with you, Mistress," she murmured, slipping to Hope's side.

They opened the door—

"Dolly!"

Dolly Dougharty burst in with a grin, parents behind her bearing baskets fragrant with spices and butter, whipped icing.

"Good afternoon!" Dolly chimed. "Mother feared you might faint from hunger before the lesson, so we brought salvation by pastry."

Sarah laughed, hugging her. Dolly bounded ahead and into the classroom like a sunbeam, where she began arranging sweet buns and rolls and whispering greetings to friends.

Hope was showing Dolly's parents where they might sit when—KNOCK-KNOCK.

She froze mid-step, then composed herself, smoothing her apron with forced calm.

"I shall fetch the next miracle," she murmured, eyes bright with controlled hope.

The girls exchanged wide, excited looks.

Those chairs may not remain empty after all.

At first, they trickled in—curious neighbors, skeptical townsfolk, and a few churchgoers lured by the promise of coffee. Then the trickle turned into a steady stream. More than just an audience for a Bible lesson, this had become an event.

Women in modest cloaks, men still dusted with the evidence of a day's work, even a few older daughters who had dragged their suspicious parents along—all filled the classroom. Some brought additional cakes and pies, supplementing the generous spread, while others stood, unsure of what to expect—but didn't dare miss out on the unprecedented event.

The kitchen staff scrambled to keep up. Every available pot was filled with water to brew coffee, and soon, the rich, exotic aroma of the dark beverage mingled with the warm scent of hazelnut and the rare, costly spices of cinnamon and nutmeg. The enticing blend drew in even those stand-offs who had arrived out of mere curiosity.

Reverend Morton, a man not easily impressed, took in the sight before him with a bemused expression.

"I daresay there are more souls here tonight than at my Easter service," he remarked dryly, casting a glance at the Headmistress. "Perhaps this should become a regular event."

Hope, holding a steaming cup of coffee, raised it slightly in approval, the flickering candlelight reflecting in her knowing smile.

To gather everyone's attention, the Reverend took a moment to acknowledge the school's previous esteemed guest, Reverend Cotton Mather, who had graced The Willow with a lesson that left the students both awed and contemplative. Each student smiled at the astonished faces surrounding them as a murmur swept through the room, but before the moment could settle, Reverend Morton cleared his throat and, with a wry smile, muttered just loud enough to be heard by all, "Reverend Mather is a most enlightening lecture, I'm sure—though, curiously, I seem to have been left off the list of attendees." His remark, delivered with the perfect blend of feigned offense and dry humor, prompted a ripple of laughter from the more skeptical members of the audience. A few knowing smirks passed between them, silently acknowledging that if Cotton Mather approved of this institution, there might be more to The Willow than many had initially presumed.

With the crowd settled, Reverend Morton took his place at the front of the classroom where the altar stood erected.

Clearing his throat, he lifted his well-worn Bible and addressed the assembly.

"Tonight, I shall read from the Gospel of Mark, Chapter 5, Verse 41. But before I do, let us consider the time in which these words were written."

He began to pace slowly, hands clasped behind his back, his voice rich and deliberate.

"At this time, the land was under Roman rule, a rule that saw fit to divide men and women into separate stations. Women, especially, had little say in their own lives, and education was a luxury afforded only to a select few. Yet, Christ came not to uphold these divisions, but to transcend them—to bring knowledge, healing, and truth to all who would receive it."

A few people looked back and forth with confusion to see how the others were reacting to this unconventional sermon.

"Mark tells us of a ruler of the synagogue named Jairus, whose daughter lay dying. This was a man of status, of influence. And yet, he humbled himself to seek out Jesus, for even the wealthiest man in the world could not buy his daughter's life."

He let the weight of that truth settle before continuing.

"When Jesus arrived at the house, the mourners had already begun their wailing. They had declared the child dead. But Christ turned to them and said,

'The child is not dead but sleeping.' They laughed at Him."

The Reverend's voice dropped, his tone serious.

"But Christ was not deterred. He took the girl by the hand and said, 'Talitha Cumi'—which means, 'Little girl, I say unto thee, arise.' And she rose."

A hush fell over the room.

Reverend Morton let the moment settle, then exhaled.

"Now, why do I share this story with you tonight?" His gaze swept across the crowd, lingering on the young women of The Willow.

"Because Christ did not see this girl as lesser. He did not see her as unworthy of life, unworthy of learning, unworthy of His time. He called her to rise—to learn, to live."

Murmurs of agreement rippled through the gathering.

"Education is no different. Ignorance is not what God desires for His children. If we keep young women from learning, are we not like those mourners who scoffed, who dismissed the girl's potential before she even had the chance to awaken?"

The question hung in the air.

"Let us not be like those who laughed," he implored. "Let us be the hands that lift, the voices that encourage, the minds that seek knowledge. For in learning, we do not just better ourselves—we answer the call of Talitha Cumi."

Hope, who had long since given away her seat and was standing in the back of the room, felt her throat tighten with emotion and her eyes well with tears at the Reverend's words. As she pulled a handkerchief to dab at the corners of her eyes, she realized that women all around her were doing the same. Even some of the men looked moved, exchanging glances and looking thoughtful.

She scanned the room more thoroughly, feeling her heart race slightly with excitement. A shift was occurring, she could see. The school, long met with suspicion and doubt, was finding its foothold.

And as the evening wore on, conversations grew warmer, and the once-skeptical townsfolk lingered, refilling cups of coffee, savoring slices of pie. The girls, Hope was pleased to see, were not clustered off in their own group but instead had branched out to engage with different locals. Moving gracefully from one conversation to the next, Hope was almost overwhelmed with the sense that, for the first time, the people of New Haven were seeing The Willow not as a threat—but as a part of their community.

CHAPTER 36

Samuel Sewall, 12/1715

A SHARP, AUTHORITATIVE KNOCK rapped on the heavy wooden door. Sarah, who had been in the middle of sorting the week's laundry into neat piles—petticoats here, stockings there—froze for the briefest moment. Her heart leapt, foolish and hopeful, before she could stop it. Then, straightening her apron as though steadying herself, she hurried toward the door, a fragile spark of what if it's John… flickering in her chest. Although she had finally managed to fold her sorrow neatly away like a keepsake in a drawer, untouched but never forgotten, her hope that he would reappear on the doorstep never dissipated. After nearly a month, she still spent the nights tossing in a restless half-sleep, John's image vivid in her mind.

She pulled open the door with a bright smile, only to have it falter slightly as she took in the figure before her. The man was aged and dignified, dressed in a simple, well-tailored coat that spoke of respectability and restraint. His face was stern, and his eyes were sharp but not unkind.

"Hello, I am Samuel Sewall," he announced, his voice polite yet carrying an unmistakable weight of authority. "I hope you find my intrusion palatable?"

Recovering from her surprise, Sarah offered a graceful curtsy, letting years of practiced etiquette take over. "Yes, sir, you are most welcome," she replied, raising her hand in a gesture of hospitality. "Would you care for a cup of tea—or perhaps coffee?"

Samuel Sewall's expression softened slightly, and he nodded with a faint smile. "Coffee would suit me well, thank you."

She stepped back, allowing him to enter the dimly lit foyer. As he took in the surroundings, Sarah led him toward the parlor, where morning light filtered through the heavy curtains, casting a warm glow across the room.

"I hope your journey was comfortable, Mr. Sewall?" Sarah asked, her voice steady though her curiosity simmered beneath the surface.

"Yes, as comfortable as one might expect in these times," he replied, his tone measured. "I understand that Cotton Mather was here just last month?"

Sarah hesitated before answering, a faint shadow crossing her face. In the weeks after his visit, Cotton Mather's lecture hung in the air like the stubborn curls of smoke rising from the embers of a festival swine roast—heavy, greasy, and reluctant to drift away even with the morning breeze.

"Yes, he was," Sarah said. "His lecture was… rather memorable." She could feel the weight of Sewell's gaze upon her and sensed he was testing her, perhaps measuring her reaction to the mention of Mather's name.

"Indeed, I would expect nothing less of Cotton," Sewall replied, nodding slowly. "The man has a way of leaving an impression, particularly regarding matters of faith and morality."

Sarah inclined her head, choosing her words carefully. "He certainly has his convictions, though at times they can be… challenging for some of us."

Sewall's eyes flickered with interest, and he allowed himself a faint smile. "It is precisely his convictions and those of my cousin that bring me here today, Miss…" He paused, waiting for her to supply her name.

"Sarah, ah, Huntington," she answered, taking the opportunity to pour him a cup of coffee, the steam rising gently as she handed it to him.

"Thank you, Miss Huntington," he said, taking the cup with a nod of gratitude. "I am here on behalf of some of our more concerned citizens. I was here presiding over the matter of this, ah, property," he began, pausing to sip his coffee with a pucker.

"Sugar? Cream?" she offered, and he waved his hand, declining. "I like it black, thank you."

"They were worried over the legality of the purchase, and about the," he paused… "Ideas of a School—"

Sarah felt her stomach twitching, her pulse quickening, and she was relieved when the Headmistress strolled into the parlor.

"Ah," Sarah said, turning to the man with her hand extended, beginning her introduction. "Ah, Mr. Samuel Sewall. May I introduce you to Headmistress Terwilliger?"

The man stood and took Hope's extended hand, both of them focusing on each other with a recognition of memory.

"Yes, Mr. Sewall?" Hope resisted curling her lip in disgust as she said the man's name. "Did I overhear something about the legality of the purchase? I thought that was already settled? Can we be of further service?"

"Tis true, the property was judged to be purchased squarely, indeed. However, the complainant, Thomas Clark, I am afraid, still sees it as a gross injustice. He is not a man to quarrel with and definitely one who cries over spilt milk."

The man's gaze went to the doorway as a group of girls strolled past, looking in with sweet smiles and nods. "I understand, from speaking with Reverend Mather and again to my cousin Jeremiah Dummer, that The Willow is a place of progress, a sanctuary for young—" He stopped to clear his throat, seeing lovely Lena walking past. "Can grow beyond the strict societal constraints placed upon them."

Hope stood still, her face darkened with circulating heat, and could only nod and listen.

"Mather's visit," he continued, "stirred my interest and my aspirations to see how you ran such a ship-shape school. Maybe we could even emulate it in some fashion if we follow my cousin's recommendations to move the Collegiate School from Old Saybrook to New Haven."

"Your Honor," Hope said abruptly, drawing a look of surprise from Sarah and extinguishing the pretense that she didn't know the man sitting in the school's parlor.

"Ah, do you know of me?" he asked, slurping his cup and raising his eyebrows.

Hope's heart raced with the thoughts that he may remember her as well, as the once witch pricker. "I believe many in this region remember you as the presiding Judge at the—" she began calmly, as if the information was common knowledge.

He held up his hand, stifling her from speaking further. "I would rather not hear those words for as long as I live. It shames me to think of it. Let us all feel comfort in repentance and the mercy of God to help heal the weary mind by forgetting chapters in our lives that have become unsavory to our souls."

Hope was taken aback by his response, and then relieved. The tension in her jaw began to dissolve, and she offered a slight but genuine smile. "Forgotten, but not repeating? Mr. Sewall," she said, steadying her voice. "I can assure you, we strive to guide students in ways that align with both virtue and intellect. Their education here is not meant to challenge authority but to prepare them to be thoughtful and capable members of society."

Sewall nodded thoughtfully, setting his coffee cup down. "I don't doubt your intentions, Headmistress Terwilliger," he replied. "However, it is difficult to deny that education, especially for the, ah, gentile," he said with a frown at the Kidd walking by swinging a sword. "Can sometimes lead to… unintended consequences. A sharp mind, while commendable, must also be guided carefully, lest it stray from the path of righteousness."

The Headmistress held his gaze, unflinching. "A sharp mind can be a force for good, Mr. Sewall. The students are taught to think, yes, but also to understand and respect the values of our community. Consider how, in the Gospel of Mark, Chapter five, Verse forty-one, Jesus resurrects a deceased girl." She paused and then recited: "And Jesus took the child by the hand, and said unto her, 'Talitha Cumi,' which is by interpretation, 'Maiden, I say unto thee, arise.'"

"Talitha Cumi," the Judge repeated with a nod. His expression softened, and he turned his probing gaze away from Hope and onto the younger girl. "Tell me, Miss Huntington, as we were just discussing, are you familiar with the events in Salem and other places from years ago?"

Sarah's breath caught. The question was unexpected, prompting a sudden glance at the Headmistress, which sharpened the conversation; then she nodded slowly. "I am aware, yes."

Sewall took a deep breath, his voice dropping to a softer tone. "I was there, you now know. I played my part in those trials." His eyes grew distant as if he were staring back through the years. "It is a burden I carry, for terrible mistakes were made in the name of faith. I have since dedicated myself to a quieter, more considered view of justice."

Hope's guardedness continued to soften as she saw genuine regret in the Judge's face. "I appreciate your honesty, Mr. Sewall. And I hope you understand that the Willow is committed to justice in its own way. The students are not merely taught knowledge; they are also taught empathy, compassion, and the strength to discern right from wrong."

"Right from wrong," he repeated, regarding her with newfound respect. "You may be right, Headmistress Terwilliger. Perhaps I am merely haunted by shadows of the past. But remember," he said, rising to leave. "There are still those who believe that teaching an impressionable mind to think for herself is—" He stopped to let gravity settle around them before finishing his thought. "Well, thinking is the first step toward acceptance. But defiance of their virtues, as they see it, is a dangerous thing."

The Headmistress met his gaze firmly, her voice steady. "Then let them think as they will. We believe that thought and virtue are allies, not enemies."

The man of justice stopped and looked the Headmistress straight in the eyes with a knowing look. "Which brings me to ask, how did you get the Reverend Mather to teach—"

"To teach at a girl's finishing school?" she added.

He nodded.

"Maybe the Holy man was finally transformed by the true love of God."

A quiet, smirking smile touched Sewall's lips as he nodded, then, with a final bow, he left the parlor, his footsteps echoing in the foyer. As Hope closed the door, he said, "We all have our pricker. But it's how we use it that sets us apart."

Closing the door, a sense of resolve bloomed within her. This was her path—and no shadow from the past could darken the light of her purpose.

CHAPTER 37

Day of Grand Ball

ABIGAIL AND EUNICE RODE UP the long Fleet Street from New Haven's harbor inn in a coach. Their ball gowns—the finest money could buy in Boston—were tucked around them, making them feel trapped with nowhere to move. Sitting prominently beside Abigail, in large, colorful boxes lay gowns of equal elegance—a surprise gift, one for each of her daughters and one each for Hope and her daughter, Ursula.

Cramped and frustrated, Eunice chided, "If we had given these dresses to everyone before, Captain Holloway would have had more room for those books, and we would not be so—" she shook her head with annoyance at the cramped coach cabin, "Incommodious."

"But that would have spoiled the surprise," she said, adjusting in her seat. "You remember being surprised—once?"

"Surprises are overrated."

Abigail ignored her sister's incessant whining as she looked out the small coach window. "The inception of The Willow has certainly not been without its challenges." She watched the same townsfolk walking past, who had been staunch protestors when the school first opened. "I wonder what they are thinking now? That letter from Sarah was quite telling."

Eunice nodded as she looked around the streets for the conspicuous Constable Zachariah Hullabee, hoping to find the chance to show off her magnificent Ball gown incidentally. "Yes," she said after a moment. "Just think back to how, in the beginning, an unease hung thickly over the town, settling like a damp fog that crept into every corner of our burgeoning school."

Abigail looked at her sister with mock surprise. "Listen to you, waxing so poetically."

Eunice rolled her eyes. "I'm serious. You could feel the town's silent disapproval in every restrained nod and carefully averted gaze. All of them whisper their undeniable rejection. Frowns, whispers, and even outright confrontations. The idea of a formal education for women was not just novel but, to many, preposterous," she finished with a snort.

Yet, they both knew that the cloak of disapproval began to fray at the edges as the months rolled on. Local merchants started to experience the undeniable benefits of the school's presence. The necessity for food, textiles, and services for The Willow's extracurricular and daily operations meant that reliable and substantial coins began to flow into tills that might otherwise have remained worryingly empty.

Abigail and Eunice stepped carefully out of the coach, each carrying one of the colorful boxes adorned with satin ribbons. As they entered the foyer, they could hear Hope in the kitchen giving the girls last-minute reminders. Abigail shushed her sister, then peeked around the corner, watching and listening silently from the foyer.

"Ladies," Hope addressed the students, her voice steady yet kind. "I think we've not yet spoken about a key element of tonight's gathering. Remember what I said in preparation for this event? It wasn't solely about who garnered the most admiration from the gentlemen."

The room fell silent, all eyes on her.

Hope lifted her chin, her tone turning solemn with purpose. "The art of conversation," she began, "is a discipline far more powerful than a fluttered lash or a charming smile. It holds weight where mere beauty fails, and can win allies where silence breeds invisibility." She swept her gaze across the room, and the girls straightened instinctively beneath it. "Over these past months, you have practiced social grace in the company of our tutors and the occasional caller. But tonight—" her voice dropped, almost conspiratorial, "tonight demands more of you. A cultivated poise. A mind ready to meet another and not shrink. You are not simply observers—you are hostesses, expected to command a room, to draw conversation forth and keep it alive."

A ripple of poorly contained titters fluttered through the ranks at the mention of male visitors. Hope's eyes narrowed—just enough to silence the giggling in an instant.

"You may laugh now," she continued, voice cool as steel, "but understand this—conversation is a power. And tonight, you shall learn whether you are prepared to wield it."

"For instance, a polite greeting is the first step in engaging someone's interest." She nodded towards Lena, adding, "A smile, as lovely as it may be, is just the beginning. It's important to draw people into your sphere with words.

A 'Good evening' or a simple 'Hello', and most importantly, by looking them straight in the eyes."

Lena lifted her gaze, meeting Hope's eyes with a newfound understanding.

"If a man does not return your gaze," Hope said, "it tells you more about his character than any pretty words he might later utter. You can choose to move on, or if you feel there's something worth pursuing, try a bit harder to catch his attention. But always, always in a civilized manner."

The room was quiet now, each young woman reflecting on Hope's words.

"You're right," Eliza finally said, breaking the silence. "It's not just about catching a man's eye. It's about engaging his mind and his respect."

The others nodded in agreement. Hope, sensing her audience's receptive mood, continued in a gentle yet instructive tone. "And remember, if you haven't met the gentleman before, it's crucial to introduce yourself. A brief, clear introduction sets the stage for a meaningful interaction. For instance, 'I'm Eliza. How do you do?

She paused, a hint of a smile playing on her lips. "Keep in mind, a young man's mind can sometimes be like a fog, filled with all sorts of thoughts and concerns. You may need to remind him of your name, even if he shows a genuine interest in you. It's not necessarily a sign of an ignoramus, but rather that he may be preoccupied with many complexities, making it harder for him to remember the simpler things."

Dorothy, who had been quiet for most of the conversation, spoke up, her voice soft yet clear. "So, it's not just about making an impression, but also about understanding and navigating the complexities of conversations and social cues."

"Exactly, Dorothy," Hope replied, pleased. "It's about creating a connection that goes beyond surface-level interactions. It's about engaging respectfully, thoughtfully, and considerately with both parties involved, no matter whether you look like a goddess or a goat. The goddess in you may catch the eye, but the goat in you provides milk, meat, and a warm pelt to warm your babies throughout the winter."

She walked over to the kitchen door, gesturing across the classroom, which had now turned into a beautiful ballroom. "A safe and effective way to start a conversation is to make a neutral comment about the event."

She turned back to face the group, her expression earnest. "For instance, you might say, 'Isn't this a lovely Ball?' or 'I've really been looking forward to this evening.' Such remarks are non-threatening and open-ended, inviting the other person to share their thoughts and feelings."

"It's like offering a conversational bridge," offered Hannah, "and if they're interested, they'll walk across it."

"Exactly, Hannah," Hope replied with an approving nod. "From there, the conversation can naturally progress to other topics, allowing both of you to learn more about each other in a relaxed and respectful manner. Oh, and Kidd. Sword fighting is not your typical conversation."

The Kidd slapped her hand against her forehead comically, saying, "Now, what am I going to talk about?" Eunice snickered in the foyer, and Abigail waved her hand for her to be quiet.

Hope grinned and continued. "Once you've initiated the conversation and encouraged the other person to share about themselves, the next step is to show genuine interest in what they are saying."

Eliza nodded eagerly. "It's not just about the words we use but also about how we physically respond to the conversation," she offered.

"Absolutely, Eliza. Your body language speaks volumes," Hope replied. She began to demonstrate as she spoke, her eyes bright and attentive. "By maintaining eye contact, you convey your focus and interest. Nodding shows that you are following along, and relevant responses or questions indicate that you are actively processing what the other person is saying."

Patience, who had been practicing nodding and maintaining eye contact, added, "It's like the conversation is a dance, and these actions are the steps that keep it flowing smoothly."

"That's a beautiful way to put it, Patience," Hope said with a smile. "A conversation is indeed like a dance, where both participants take turns leading and following, ensuring that the interaction is harmonious and mutually enjoyable."

Lena, who had been quietly absorbing the conversation, spoke up. "What about non-verbal cues? In a formal setting, how do we manage them? I find that some men can be quite aggressive, almost insulting with their eyes. It's as if they're examining you for the first time, like a prized milk cow at the fair."

Her comment struck a chord, and a brief, uncomfortable silence followed. Gulielma Marie, known for her crass approach to life, broke the nervousness with a laugh. "Well, they may look at you that way, Lena, but for the rest of us, they appreciate our intellect."

"Really?" Lena snapped back. "I thought it was your family's money, property, and possessions that they were interested in, not your homely looks. I bet you drop your family's name within the first seconds of meeting someone. You'll have him half convinced you own Philadelphia before the first dance ends." Her tone was tinged with bitterness.

"I would not do that if I were you," Patience said. "Your family's fame may become an overwhelming impediment to a naive young man's aspirations."

Hope stepped in. "Lena brings up an important point about non-verbal cues. Maintaining a respectful distance, avoiding overly animated gestures, and being mindful of the other person's comfort and personal space are crucial. This applies to both parties in a conversation."

She looked at Lena with a sympathetic yet firm gaze. "Lena, while it's true that some may have less-than-honorable intentions, it's important for us to hold our ground with dignity and not jump to conclusions about everyone. We can use our judgment and intuition to discern their intentions and respond accordingly."

Turning to Gulielma Marie, she added, "And while humor is a wonderful tool to lighten the mood, we must also acknowledge the genuine concerns our friends may have. It's about finding a balance between understanding the reality of our social environment and not letting it taint our interactions with cynicism."

The room fell into thoughtful silence as the girls pondered Hope's words. "Alright," the Headmistress said with a clap of her hands. "Finish with your preparations. Time is now of the essence."

As they left the kitchen, Deborah casually remarked, "I just hope no one is with child after tonight."

Headmistress Hope, taken aback by the comment, clapped her hands together more loudly for them to stop. "And why would that be a concern, Deborah?"

Deborah spoke with a look of trepidation, "My mother told me that you could become pregnant if you get too close to a man during certain phases of the moon."

Others laughed, and Patience, one of the least vocal, said, "I heard that bathing in water where the opposite sex had bathed could do it."

Lena added, "And wearing the clothing of the opposite sex can impact fertility or the likelihood of expecting."

Gulielma Marie said, "Extreme emotions or physical states, like being startled or experiencing a sudden shock, can sometimes lead to an interesting condition."

The room was filled with murmurs of agreement and disbelief when Eliza, with a serious expression, said, "Gazing on beasts in their coupling can bring a lass to a state of increase. A mere look can stir the body's courses."

This last comment caught everyone off guard with a gasp. Sensing their disbelief, Eliza elaborated, "My mother always blamed Apollo for my little brother."

"Apollo?" Hope inquired, puzzled.

"Yes, Apollo is our dog. His coupling with the neighbor's dog, Pleasant, next door, caused her to become quick with child," Eliza explained.

Hirana grinned and loudly said, "My mother said bundling in bed or even perhaps on a sofa with a man sends more children into the country without fathers or mothers to own them than are born among those properly married."

Hannah's eyes gazed sharply at her sister, who shook her head with a questioning look as her hands smoothed her lower abdomen.

Hope cautiously asked, "Hirana, have you ever been bundled with a man?"

The room fell deathly silent, eagerly waiting to hear her answer.

"Not by many, unless there weren't enough beds to go around. But if need be, I can make room for one of these New Haveners I danced with tonight."

"I, too, have bundled with travelers when beds were scarce," Eliza added, seemingly unconcerned.

Gasps of surprise gushed from everyone's mouth as Hope waved her hands to quiet them. "I do not believe your parents would consent to you bundling with anyone here at the Willow, be it male or female," she said firmly.

"Bundle with a female? What's the fun in that?" Hirana laughed, reaching out to touch the candelabra in the middle of the table with a winking smile. Everyone looked perplexed before the whole room erupted in laughter and astonishment. Realizing the extent of misinformation and superstitions surrounding pregnancy, Headmistress Hope saw an opportunity for a vital teaching moment, but indeed, time was too tight.

Several of the girls darted out of the kitchen, some clutching strands of pearls, others balancing slippers or hairpins in their hands. Their eyes wide with excitement as they prepared for the evening's ball, they took no notice of the two older women standing quietly in the hallway. As Abigail and Eunice entered the kitchen, Abigail spotted her daughters, Hannah and Sarah. Their faces lit up as they saw her, and the three embraced tightly, their joy mingled with unspoken sorrows. Finally, Abigail pulled back, studying her daughters' faces. "Sarah, have you heard any word… about John?"

Sarah shook her head, her expression shadowed. "Nothing yet, Mother. It's as if he's vanished without a trace, leaving a hole in my heart."

Abigail squeezed her hand, a quiet promise that they'd keep searching. Then, with a glimmer in her eye, she asked the girls to wait a moment while she and Eunice retrieved the colorful boxes stacked in the foyer.

"Now," Abigail said as the women returned with full arms, "I have a little something that might bring you some happiness tonight, dears."

Sarah and Hannah each opened a box to find a splendid dress in hues of sapphire, emerald, and rose, the finest fabrics twinkling in the candlelight.

"They've come all the way from Boston," Eunice announced with a warm, triumphant smile. "So you'd best hurry—time is very much of the essence."

The girls gasped, eyes wide with delight. Each offered a curtsy, then another, and then dissolved into grateful embraces—one after another—before clutching their treasured parcels to their chests and racing upstairs in a flurry of petticoats and breathless excitement.

"Mind you don't faint from joy before you lace your stays!" Eunice called after them, chuckling as their delighted squeals faded up the banisters.

"Hope, my dear," Abigail said, catching her eye. As she approached, Abigail handed her two boxes. "A gift—for you and for Ursula," she said, looking around. "Where is Ursula?"

Hope opened the lid, her hands trembling as she revealed an elegant ball gown, the fabric flowing in waves of silver-blue. Her eyes filled with tears as she ran her fingers over the dress. "Oh, Abigail… this is beautiful. I don't know how to thank you."

Abigail placed a gentle hand on her shoulder. "You needn't thank me. This is for all you've done for these girls and for the school."

Hope hesitated, her expression turning somber. "As much as we appreciate this, I'm afraid Ursula won't be able to attend. She's tending to sniveling children at the orphanage. But you've made our hearts full with your thoughtfulness, truly."

Abigail nodded in understanding and cast her gaze across the room, catching sight of Kidd standing alone by the staircase in a plain-looking dress. "Then, if you do not mind that the dress not go to waste," she beckoned Kidd over, a sly smile on her lips.

When Kidd approached, Abigail looked to Hope for approval before handing the formal box to her. "This is for you, my dear," Abigail said, her voice soft with emotion. "Your father would have loved to see you wearing something so fine."

Kidd's mouth fell open as she lifted the dress from the box, a rich burgundy with delicate lacework ideally suited to her. Her cheeks flushed with delight, and she gasped, barely able to contain her excitement. "Thank you, Mrs. Spragg! This is… It's the loveliest thing I've ever seen!"

"Good. Now run upstairs and let Hannah and Sarah help you get it on." Abigail nodded encouragingly, and in the next moment, Kidd gave her a massive hug before squealing in delight. She pounded upstairs, taking the steps two and three at a time. They could hear their laughter and playful shrieks echoing through the building as the girls dashed from room to room, trying on the new dresses.

The anticipation at The Willow was almost uncontrollable, akin to the vibrant energy that precedes the first blooms of spring. Tonight was the night of their first official social event, a grand ball, where the hallways and chambers of the now esteemed institution would transform into a dazzling arena of social interplay. The young women, adorned in their finest gowns, whispered excitedly among themselves, their eyes sparkling with a mix of nervousness and exhilaration. For the first time, The Willow would open its doors to the local eligible bachelors, young men of repute and promise, inviting them to mingle and dance under the chandeliers' soft glow. This ball was not just a dance but a rite of passage, a foray into the delicate art of social interaction, where each word and glance carried the weight of potential futures. For the students of The Willow, it was a chance to showcase their grace, wit, and charm, to step out of the shadows of their books and into the light of societal engagement. The heavens were singing with dreams and possibilities as each young lady prepared to take her place during social intercourse on a night that promised to be etched in the annals of The Willow's history.

"It seems we've become a necessary thread in the fabric of the town," Hope remarked to Abigail, her voice laced with a hint of irony as she watched a local farmer deliver a barrel of hard cider to the school's kitchen, setting it next to the baker's bread, pies, pastries, and cakes. The enticing smell of roasted meat from Mutton McCleaver's shop wafted throughout the building, mingling with the faint aroma of freshly churned butter and cheese from the dairy farmer's cart. Beeswax candles, crafted by the town's candlemaker, illuminated every corner of the rooms, their warm glow adding elegance to the festivities. Courtesy of the town's garden club, bouquets of fragrant lavender, herbs, and flowers adorned the tables, adding a touch of natural refinement to the occasion.

"However," Hope said with sorrow, "there are still holdouts amongst the community. The deeply religious and wickedly jealous who hope to see us fail in our endeavors as they have undoubtedly done with their sad, miserable lives."

As the young ladies of The Willow adorned themselves with meticulous care for the evening's ball, a flurry of activity transformed the classroom-turned-ballroom into a scene of enchanting elegance. In one corner, a small makeshift orchestra assembled by none other than Mr. Warbleworth conducting and Mr. Tinkletune on one of the harpsichords, taking control of the ensemble of instruments gleaming under the soft light, tuning and poised to fill the room with melodious harmonies.

Nearby, hired servants moved with practiced efficiency, arranging an array of sumptuous foods and drinks by the kitchen entrance. Each enticing tidbit was a work of culinary art, casting a spell of delight and appetite over the setting. They promised an evening that would awaken all the senses in a celebration of beauty and camaraderie.

"Walk with me," Abigail said, grasping Hope's hand and leading her outside. They walked toward the back garden pond where they sat in silence, comforted by the swaying bare willow branches. In the comfortably cool backyard, a breeze moved through the fallen leaves, whispering the secrets of days to come. "Hope," Abigail began, her tone far more solemn than the firm confidence that was her hallmark. "I've meant to discuss something important with you since returning from New Haven, but alas, the time has not been right until now."

Hope's brow furrowed slightly, her posture stiffening in anticipation. She had always considered herself a steward to Abigail's vision, a trusted lieutenant, never more than that, so she sat giving her her utmost attention.

"You see, when I started this," Abigail gestured broadly to encompass the grandeur of The Willow. "It was a dream, an ambition of your benefactor, Henry Every. But now..." She paused, searching for the right words. "Now, I see it is time for The Willow to go to seed if you will. It has become more than a personal endeavor—it's a legacy you must inherit to complete the circle."

Hope looked at Abigail with a furrowed brow. "That I must inherit? I don't understand."

Abigail said nothing, gazing at the pond and waiting for comprehension to hit the Headmistress.

Hope's eyes widened in disbelief, her heart fluttering like a trapped bird against her rib cage. "But Abigail," she stammered, "this school, this vision—it's yours. I merely walked the path you laid."

Abigail's lips curved into a knowing smile. "And now, I wish for you to pave new paths with it. I have already transferred the title to the land, the building, their responsibilities, and the promises they hold. You are now truly the Captain of this endeavor."

Hope's voice was barely a whisper, her usual resolve dissolving. "I am… afraid. The weight of such a role and the expectations of those high-bred families are daunting. And who will take care of the orphanage?"

"You could let the Reverend and the townsfolk handle that. You and your daughter have already given more than your fair share to this community," Abigail reassured her.

"My daughter will not leave the children."

"Then, when she is ready, she can begin her studies."

"She's been home-schooled. All that will be teaching these girls will be a boring review."

"Then the orphanage is truly blessed by your daughter. Now it is time to spread your blessings elsewhere," Abigail said, placing her hand on Hope's arm, exuding a kind mother's touch.

Hope began to say, "I fear—"

But it was then that Eunice—ever the quiet shadow at Abigail's side—startled them both with her sudden appearance, cutting in with her characteristic wit.

"Fear is the spice that makes the pot boil, my dear," she murmured, lips quirking. "You've been stewing long enough. Time to serve the meal."

Despite the turmoil within, a light laugh escaped Hope's lips, and she felt a sliver of courage wedge into her heart.

Abigail's hand found Hope's again, her grip firm and reassuring. "You will not be alone. We will stand by you, support you when you waver, and cheer you on when you triumph," she said, standing. Abigail walked to Eunice with a nod, leaving the Headmistress alone to contemplate her position. As Abigail pivoted to walk inside, she turned with a stern expression and said, "We will not let you fail."

Sarah sashayed out, holding her dress up, shouting to the Headmistress,

"Mother!" but then quickly withdrew with embarrassment, covering her mouth with one hand and holding up her plunging neckline before smiling and laughing about her accidentally calling the Headmistress 'Mother.' "We have our first escorts arriving," she said, recovering.

Hope looked at Sarah with expectant duties ahead and said, "Thus begins your journey. Now, help me get dressed, or this beautiful ball gown will have to wait for next year's activities."

CHAPTER 38

The Willow Grand Ball

THE ATMOSPHERE BUZZED with a vibrant anticipation and the scent of groundbreaking change as The Willow prepared for the year-end Ball. This evening, Abigail believed, had the potential to redefine the school's place in the town's social echelon. Everyone's 'respond if you please' invitations were more than mere attendance; they were endorsements, a quiet recognition of the school's ascending prominence as a hub of influential ties and a marker of social distinction. Within these revered walls, the most esteemed family trees would converge and knit together, charting the course for a prosperous horizon.

Abigail's cheeks warmed with a soft, rosy glow as she stepped in from the garden, the faint perfume of dried herbs trailing behind her like a whispered promise of spring. With an elegant, nearly imperceptible nod, she signaled to Mr. Warbleworth. He lifted his baton and tapped it lightly against the music stand, prompting the musician cradling the bass violin in the small ensemble to begin.

At the cue, the bow met the string, and a low, sonorous note unfurled through the room—rich and steady—casting a dignified yet welcoming spell over the gathering.

She next swept her hands through the air, calling the girls into the classroom, now dazzling as a magnificent ballroom. Giggles echoed off the walls, and eyes sparkled with excitement as they eagerly shot glances toward the front door, where their expected escorts for the evening were arriving. The room hummed with energy, the thrill of the evening building with every passing second.

At 5 o'clock exactly, as Hope was emerging from her room behind the library in her radiant gown, there was a knock at the front door. She opened the door to find a dozen young men stacked up on the front porch and spilling down the small steps onto the ground, each of them brimming with anticipation and nerves. The Headmistress assumed her role with a poised demeanor and invited them into the oversized foyer. She warmly accepted their invitations, her voice soft yet clear as she introduced the rapidly gathering escorts to one another.

Then, with Hope's gentle instruction, one by one, they began to enter the ballroom, the atmosphere growing more decadent as the mingling of music and the quiet buzz of expectant conversation filled the air. A maidservant stood with a tray of hard cider for each young man to enjoy until the last guest had arrived.

As each young man entered, he awkwardly moved to join the cluster of like-minded, nervous smiles. These were the sons of New Haven's most distinguished families, the offspring of innovative legislators, inheritors of sprawling lands, and scions of colonial pioneers and land pirates, all symbolizing a brave leap into a fresh epoch for The Willow.

The elegant space surrounding them was both intimidating and enchanting. The young ladies of The Willow, in their flowing gowns, shimmered like candlelight in motion. Initially, the young men said very little, hands ringing nervously.

Nathaniel Trowbridge leaned toward his companion, voice barely above a whisper. "Merciful heavens, Josiah—are they all this pretty, or is the candlelight playing tricks?"

"I know," Josiah answered. "Do we bow or surrender?" Josiah Baldwin, whose father owned much of the harbor wharfage, then chuckled under his breath, eyes darting across the room. "I'd sooner face my father's accounts ledger than try to keep step with one of these fair maidens," he muttered.

Nathaniel smirked, attempting bravado. "You think numbers are hard? Try keeping your tongue straight when every pair of eyes in the room is looking at you."

Josiah rolled his shoulders, feigning calm, though the stiff set of his jaw betrayed him. "Then let's pray they are kind. Because, my friend, I've a feeling we're the evening's entertainment."

Their uneasy laughter mingled with the hum of the bass violin, the sound of silk, and whispers filling the air. Both men drew a steadying breath as the Headmistress appeared. The final young gentleman had arrived and, ready or not, the dance of manners had begun.

The Headmistress clapped her hands gently to command the room's attention. "Young ladies and gentlemen," she announced with composed authority, "welcome to the inaugural formal ball of The Willow Finishing School."

Adorned in their elegant gowns, the young ladies clapped politely with their gloved hands. The young men's applause grew louder as they exchanged approving nods and discreet smiles.

Headmistress Terwilliger commenced the formal introductions between the young gentlemen and ladies. Each introduction was to be executed with the precision of a courtly dance, balancing grace and restraint.

"Mr. Nathaniel Trowbridge," she announced, "son of Judge Elnathan Trowbridge of New Haven—may I present Miss Patience Carr?"

Nathaniel stepped forward and bowed neatly, his nervous eyes fixed on her shoes. "Miss Carr," he said, his voice low but steady. Then, lifting his gaze to meet hers, he added softly, "An honor."

Patience dipped into a delicate curtsy, her curls catching the candlelight. "The pleasure is mine, Mr. Trowbridge."

For a heartbeat, neither moved. Then the young man offered a shy smile, and Patience's lips curved in response, the air between them faintly charged with the awkward promise of first acquaintance.

Hope continued in this manner until every young lady and gentleman had been introduced, the room gradually relaxing into a soft murmur of polite conversation and stolen glances.

As the group gathered in the ballroom, awkward bows were exchanged, with each instance of eye contact resembling chickens pecking at spilled grain. Stilted greetings followed, their voices betraying the jitters fluttering in their stomachs. The men's practiced grace, taught to them at home by their doting parents, seemed to crumble under the weight of genuine interaction. They were like sailors in unfamiliar waters, navigating the currents of polite conversation, laughter, and the subtle art of extending a dance invitation—while adrift on a cannonball-holed ship, fast trying not to sink into deep, dark waters.

When the music shifted, the room came alive with the rustle of silk and the murmur of voices. Guests meandered between dances, switching partners cordially, savoring an array of delicate hors d'oeuvres, their laughter light and expectant as they sipped sparkling hard cider.

The polished floors gleamed in the candlelight as the harpsichord struck up a lively country air. The girls, curtseying in measured rhythm, paired off with their assigned partners under the Headmistress's watchful eye.

Gulielma Maria found herself facing a fair-haired young man with impeccable posture, and the hesitant confidence of someone recently reminded to mind his manners.

He bowed smartly. "Your name is Penn, is it not?" he asked, voice carrying just enough to be heard over the music. "Are you, by chance, related to the Pennsylvania Penns?"

For a heartbeat, Gulielma Maria froze—her chin lifted, the perfect answer already forming on her tongue. But then, standing nearby, she caught Lena's knowing smirk. Earlier that afternoon, Lena had teased, "You'll have him half convinced you own Philadelphia before the first dance ends."

The memory burned hotter than the candles. Gulielma's expression faltered, slipping from polished superiority into something tighter, almost sheepish.

"Why?" she said at last, her tone clipped but airy. "Penn is quite a common Welsh name, sir."

Before he could press the matter, she turned briskly, taking his hand as the dance began. The silk of her gown whispered against the floor as she moved with sudden determination, her eyes fixed anywhere but Lena's gloating face.

The atmosphere brimmed with a blend of sophistication and eagerness, setting the stage for an evening where the rhythms of the Pavane and Allemande would guide the night. But a spontaneous transformation unfolded as the heart of the evening began to beat in rhythm with the modest orchestra's strings. Once a stage of uncertainty, the room blossomed into a haven of genuine connection. Laughter flowed more freely, conversations became more fluid, and the focus shifted from the mechanics of the steps to the simple joy of the moment.

For these young men, the Ball was no longer a test of societal acumen but a celebration of maturity and potential. In the shining eyes of their dance partners, they discovered not just peers but kindred spirits, each embarking on a journey of self-discovery and mutual respect.

To everyone's surprise, Lena and her strikingly handsome escort stepped confidently into the center of the dance floor, commanding the room's attention. The orchestra hesitated briefly before resuming, their music weaving seamlessly with the couple's fluid movements.

Lena's radiant smile met her partner's adoring gaze as he guided her effortlessly through the steps. Their connection was palpable, their gazes locked in a silent conversation that left onlookers in awe. Her dress twirled gracefully as he spun her, drawing soft gasps from the crowd.

Whispers rippled through the room, young ladies sighing and gentlemen nodding in admiration. Even the cynical Gulielma Maria watched with softened eyes as the pair danced with such elegance and chemistry that it seemed as though the moment belonged to them alone.

While the room watched the stunning young couple, Abigail looked around her. The ballroom, aglow with the light of countless candles, held within its walls a new narrative. It was a tale of first encounters, the delicate drift between tradition and the yearning for duality, a story of young hearts learning the timeless tune of social harmony.

As the music swelled to its crescendo, Lena and her escort ended with a perfect dip, her head resting near his chest, their eyes still locked. Applause erupted, but they barely noticed, lost in their private world. When they finally bowed and stepped back into the crowd, the room buzzed with excitement, their performance leaving an indelible mark on the evening.

A few of the girls watching began to gather, their chatter softening into breathy whispers. Shoulders brushed as they leaned close, eyes darting between the dancers and each other, the air alive with the quiet hum of envy, admiration, and speculation. A stifled giggle broke out, quickly swallowed by the hush that followed, as if they feared their voices might shatter the fragile grace unfolding before them.

Gulielma Maria, usually so sure of her poise, found herself shrinking beside her partner.

Hannah smiled faintly, proud and a little envious, as her partner—a rather portly fellow more interested in sampling the cuisine than in dancing—excused himself for yet a third heaping plate of hors d'oeuvres and another mug of hard cider. Her eyes wandered in search of her sister, last seen heading to the garden with her escort—she assumed either taking in the evening air or avoiding the dance among the other clearly incompatible couples.

Hope, observing Lena from the edge of the room, allowed herself the smallest sigh of satisfaction; this was precisely what she had hoped The Willow would inspire.

Kidd, standing just outside the circle of dancers, felt a rush of something like courage. The bravery and beauty of her friend Lena seemed to spark a fire in her chest. She turned toward the young man who had been hovering awkwardly nearby—her assigned partner, Nathaniel—and caught his eye with a mischievous half-smile.

He blinked in surprise. Then, with a nervous grin of his own, he extended his hand. Kidd took it without hesitation. The harpsichord struck up a new air—a lively jig that made even the most hesitant feet itch to move. Nathaniel led her onto the floor, his hand finding the small of her back with tentative confidence.

Kidd opened her mouth to say something witty, but the only thing that escaped her lips—and to the utter confusion of the poor young man—was, "Have you ever practiced with a sword?"

"A sword? Well, I, uh—" the young man began.

But before he could stammer out a reply, the sound of the front door bursting open with a deafening crash echoed from the foyer. A blast of cold night air swept into the ballroom, fluttering candles and ruffling both ribbons and composure alike.

A distant voice shouted through the din—raw, urgent, and unmistakable.

The music died mid-note. Every head turned toward the door as the scent of smoke crept in, rushing into the building like a dark omen.

CHAPTER 39

Fire

A MAN STAGGERED into the ballroom, his face pale, his clothes worn and dust-covered. With eyes wide and haunted, he took in the unexpected sight of flickering candlelight and girls swirling in colorful gowns. It was Sarah's John!

"FIRE!" he bellowed, his voice cracking with urgency.

For a moment, stunned silence took hold. Then, as if a spell had broken, the reality of his words took hold, and chaos erupted.

Shrieks pierced the air as the girls in their ball gowns clutched at one another, eyes wide with terror, their faces frozen in fear. The horrifying thought that every colonist harbored—the terror of being attacked by flames in the night—spread like wildfire.

Abigail and Hannah, closest to the ballroom door, rushed forward as John turned and moved swiftly back out the front door.

"John! What happened?" Abigail cried, stumbling into the front yard as the cold night air—now strangely heated by the furious blaze—washed over her. Abigail seized John's arm, pulling him close enough to look him in the eye, but his gaze was locked behind her. She spun toward the school, her breath catching as she beheld the horror behind her. The bottom left side of the building was ablaze—flames creeping up through the clapboards, rising hungrily toward the roof, casting violent orange light across the lawn. Sparks shot upward like furious fireflies, and the heat pulsed against her face even from the yard, a terrible vision of an inferno spreading fast.

"I saw them," he gasped, struggling for breath. "They threw a firebomb at the house—then ran toward the harbor!"

Abigail's eyes blazed with fury and focus. "Hannah!" she barked. "Get your twins and follow us down to the docks!"

Without waiting for further words, Hannah dashed to her room, threw open the chest, grasping a musket in each hand, then turned to run as fast as her rustling dress would allow to catch up, not bothering to tuck her twin weapons out of sight.

Downstairs, the Headmistress, her face taut with terror, issued commands to the panicked students. "Sarah," she ordered, seeing her coming from the garden. "Form a line! We need a bucket brigade! Get water from the pond! Go, go!"

Girls in their ball gowns and the men in their silk and velvet suits ran toward the backyard, lifting skirts and shedding tight waistcoats. In the dark, they scanned the garden grounds to gather any vessel for scooping water, from garden buckets used to water plants to spare chamber pots stored by the outhouse, their fear transforming into grim determination.

The distant clamor of alarm bells continued to roll across New Haven—though they had not been rung at first by the watch or the clergy, but by a handful of curious onlookers drawn by the promise of gossip as the most significant event in New Haven in months unfolded before their eyes. It was they—wide-eyed and hungry for spectacle—who first raised the alarm, shrieking for neighbors and sending boys sprinting up the street to hammer on doors and rouse the rest of the town.

Now lanterns bobbed along the road—first a few, then dozens—as true aid surged forth. From the front yard, Hope could see the silhouettes gathering momentum, the first of them still tying on cloaks or wiping crumbs from their mouths as they ran. Others came more purposefully: families with buckets in hand, tradesmen with wet sacks, mothers clutching shawls as they hurried toward the blaze.

As the first group reached the front gate, the kitchen wing lit the garden like a hellish dawn. Flames licked hungrily up the clapboards, devouring their way toward the eaves. Smoke curled thickly into the sky, turning the stars to smears of trembling light. The townsfolk paused only a heartbeat—just long enough for fear to pinch their faces—before vaulting the low fence, rattling the gate latch, or slipping between the hedge break to reach the blaze from all sides. Some carried buckets filled from backyard wells; others hauled blankets, cloaks, or anything they could use to beat back the flames.

Hope, standing rooted near the front door, felt her knees weaken—not from terror alone, but from the shock of seeing people who she thought scarcely believed in them running toward the fire rather than away. Her breath hitched as she watched Lena dragging her soiled skirt to carry a sloshing bucket and fling it at the top of the flames, while Kidd shouted orders like a militia captain rallying troops on how to extinguish the inferno. Even quiet, bookish

Patience pressed a damp cloth to her mouth and joined the bucket line forming down the path circling the side of the house.

Gulielma Maria gripped Marie Allamby's arm as the wave of aid surged closer, her eyes wide not with fear now—but gratitude. "They came," she whispered, astonished. "Heavens save us… they came."

Sarah nodded, tears streaking the soot on her cheeks as townsfolk swarmed into the backyard to slosh buckets into the pond, amplifying the bucket brigade tenfold. "We're not alone," she breathed. "Not anymore."

Clambering down the cobblestone road toward the harbor docks, Abigail turned to John as they ran. "Where have you been?" she demanded, out of breath. "Sarah has been sick with worry."

John's face twisted with grief. "My father… was taken by the Mohican. I barely escaped with my life." His voice cracked as he spoke, and Abigail pressed her lips together, nodding, understanding that now was not the time for sympathy.

"We'll handle that later," she said firmly. "Right now, we have our own battle."

They ran down to the harbor, the muddy ground wet underfoot, the sharp smell of salt and smoke filling the air. The harbor stretched before them, dark and foreboding. On the deck of a nearby vessel, Abigail could see figures scrambling aboard, casting off lines and unfurling sails in a fever, ready to set sail.

"There!" John pointed, his hand shaking as he gestured at the figures scurrying on the ship.

Before their eyes, shouting orders for their men to set sail, was the Widow Clark's son, Thomas. Abigail knew immediately that the crafty devil had taken his revenge for her buying his ancestral home, which he thought was unjustly taken from him.

Abigail ran past the ship and spotted her sloop moored a short distance away in the harbor. She turned to John, catching his eye. "Where's your dinghy? We must get to my sloop before they leave the harbor."

"This way!" he led them to a small rowboat tucked beneath the dock, ready to launch.

At that moment, Hannah caught up to them, her face flushed, eyes filled with both fear and relief at seeing John alive. "John! Where have you been all this time?"

Abigail waved a hand to silence her. "Time for pleasantries later," she declared, her voice brooking no argument. "Right now, we need speed."

They pulled the dinghy from under the dock. As Abigail and John settled into their places, rainwater sloshed over their shoes in the bottom of the neglected boat, a familiar voice arose in the dark.

"What have we here?" It was Constable Jenkins, his brows raised as he took in the scene, his gaze flickering from Abigail to John's haggard face just as Hannah nudged him from the back, sending him head over heels into the small boat.

"Whoa! Wait? I can't swim," he exclaimed, trying to right his wet bottom in the boat. Hannah jumped down onto his back, sloshing the bilgewater. "This boat's sinking!"

With a ferocious face, Abigail seized him by the arm and hauled his face close to hers, catching him off guard. "Row like your life depends on it! Thomas Clark cannot get away with burning our school," she commanded, her voice steely with urgency.

"And you!" she growled at Hannah. "Start bailing. We're too low in the water to pick up speed."

Jenkins gaped at her, momentarily stunned — but the fire raging behind them snapped him back to action. The glow lit the black water in frantic flashes as he and John pulled hard at the oars, muscles straining, the dinghy slicing through the dark toward the waiting sloop. Hannah, soaked to the elbows, rearranged her belted muskets before bailing water in a desperate rhythm, her breath sharp and quick.

At the bow, Abigail sat poised, eyes narrowed and unflinching, surveying the waters like an admiral in battle — calm amid chaos, commanding the storm itself.

As they approached the sloop, she ordered John, telling him with the sternest of expressions, "When we board, move your boat safely away."

Abigail's eyes met the dark outline of her ship. It was a vessel of both comfort and purpose, and Captain Holloway, her steadfast commander and former dreaded pirate, was as much a part of her as the timber and tar that held her together. "Holloway will know what to do," she shouted.

The skiff crashed against the hull, and Abigail ascended the rope ladder with an agility that belied the layers of her gown. The deck was quiet, and the sleepy night watch nodded to her with a mix of surprise and respect as she rushed past.

"Captain Holloway!" she called out as she ran to his quarters, her voice slicing through the silence.

The door opened, and there stood the Captain tucking his nightshirt into his belted trousers, his features etched with concern at the sight of her unannounced visit.

"Ms Abigail?" he inquired, the question hanging between them like the mist that clung to the water's surface.

"It's the widow Clark's son," she said, the words spilling out, the urgency in her voice mirroring the rapid beat of her heart as she pointed to the deep orange glow over the town. "He retaliated for the purchase of his mother's home by setting fire to our schoolhouse. I need your help to ensure he doesn't flee justice on the tide."

Captain Holloway's eyes hardened at the news, the potency of the situation reflected in his deep-set gaze.

"Consider it done," he said with a resolute intensity as Abigail pointed out his vessel, trying to slip out against the tide. "We'll make certain the scoundrel answers for his crime."

Abigail looked at the Constable as Hannah came to her side with a frown, but Jenkins could only hold up his hands in protest, admitting, "I have authority to do nothing."

The moonlit night was full of worry and the tang of sea salt. Abigail's urgent words had barely left her lips before the Captain, a man whose past was as shadowed as the waters they sailed, sprang into action. The sloop, once still and silent in the embrace of the night, came alive with the flurry of sailors at the Captain's command.

As the crew busied themselves, Abigail's eyes fell upon John, whom she ordered away from the sloop and now stood somewhat awkwardly on deck. "What are you doing here?" she began, her question trailing off into the night.

"Ma'am, I thought you might need a ride back to the docks after," he said with a timid yet determined look in his eyes.

Before she could respond, the Captain's booming voice filled the air, cutting through the night with an authority that spoke of his pirate legacy. "Display the cannons!" he roared.

The deck was a hive of motion as sailors scrambled, hauling two swivel cannons out from their hidden compartments. The guns were hoisted with practiced ease and mounted to the sides of the ship, one pointing out into the darkness of the port side and the other to starboard.

"Make sure we have plenty of powder and balls," the Captain ordered, slapping the young John on the back as if he were part of the crew. "Go to my cabin and collect my musket and blade," his voice growled, signaling an impending confrontation. "This ship may want to put up a fight."

"But I'm just a fisherman," he declared with fear.

"Not today, boy. Today ye be a pirate hunter."

Abigail watched as the seasoned sailors hustled, raising the anchor, loading the cannons and adjusting the sails with a speed that belied the sea's facade. The mood had shifted; the night now held a promise of conflict, of justice riding on the crest of the tide.

The Captain turned to her, his eyes hard as flint, as John returned with his implements. "We'll intercept him before he reaches open water," he assured her, his hands gripping the hilt of his cutlass and musket with old, familiar ease as he slid them into his belt, looking every bit a bloodthirsty pirate. "He won't escape the tide—or our cannons."

In the distance, the silhouette of the fleeing vessel loomed, a shadow against the lesser dark of the burning town. The sloop, under the Captain's expert command, began to move in the water, a predator in pursuit of its prey, with cannons ready and a crew steeled for whatever lay ahead.

"No! We are too close to shore. You might miss and hit something else," ripped from Abigail's lips, sharp and commanding, slicing through the rush of preparations and halting the Captain preparing the cannons in his tracks. The Captain, a man more accustomed to giving orders than receiving them, stopped and turned, the muscles in his jaw working as he clenched his teeth.

Her words stopped him. They could indeed overshoot the target and hit another ship or, worse, hit a house with cannon fire, which stopped all their preparations. His plan to fire upon the vessel evaporated like mist at dawn; now he was forced to take a more direct, yet risky, approach.

"Full speed ahead," the Captain barked, the frustration evident in his tone. "We'll have to ram 'em as they come about."

Abigail's heart pounded against her ribs as she approached the Captain. "Do you think the prow can stand it?" she asked, her voice a mix of concern and doubt.

The Captain's eyes were fixed on the dark expanse of water ahead, his hands steady on the wheel. "We'll be seeing soon enough if Mr. Gee was right about her being ship-shape," he grunted, his attention unwavering.

The sloop surged forward, powered by the ambivalent sea breeze caught in her sails, by the urgency of their mission, and by their resolve, strengthened. The vessel they pursued was now in plain sight, its sails billowing as it attempted to maneuver. But the sloop, with its seasoned Captain and determined crew, gained steadily, the gap between predator and prey closing with every heartbeat.

Abigail moved from the bow to wrap her arms securely in the sail shrouds with her daughter securely in her grips, locking her eyes on the other ship. The night seemed to hold its breath, waiting for the moment of impact. She could only hope that the man they sought would realize resistance was futile, surrendering before the need to force a collision became reality.

The angst was palpable, like a coil wound too tight, as the sloop bore down on its quarry with increasing speed. There would be no turning back; they were committed to the chase and to the hope that justice would prevail without the cost of innocent lives.

The two ships met with a resounding slam, reminiscent of two colossal rams locking horns in a fierce battle for territory out in an open field of hay. At the moment of collision, there was a violent smashing, wood screaming as Abigail's sloop impaled the other vessel, the momentum pushing it back toward the dock in a long, agonizing symphony of crashing boards and popping lines. As the ships groaned and tilted, the Captain unleashed his fury with the rawness of his pirate past, ordering his men to board the vessel and secure its crew: "Grapples up, ye sea-dogs! Lash her tight 'fore she slips away! Board 'er, ye sons of thunder—blades out and tongues shut! Any man standin' be spared if he drops steel and bends the knee—else run 'em through!"

In moments that stretched and ached with intensity, the unarmed crew of the other ship was subdued, pinned down by the crew now commandeering their deck. The Widow Clark's son, the Captain of the injured vessel, flustered and bristling with anger, demanded an explanation for what he saw as a reckless blunder at sea.

Then, from the chaos emerged Abigail, transitioning between the vessels with a sailor's agility. Her presence was a specter of authority, her smile chilling as she confronted the Widow's son, eye to eye. "I have come to claim your ship in recompense for burning my schoolhouse," she declared, her voice slicing like a cutlass.

The man met her accusation with a scornful spit upon the deck. "You cannot prove anything," he hissed, a twisted smirk playing on his lips. "It is you who will pay for the damage to my ship and my crew."

Abigail stood her ground, her heart pounding with a certainty that collided against the absence of any tangible proof. The man's mocking laughter, sharp and bitter, rang out like a victorious battle cry, cutting deep into her resolve. At that moment, a cold realization settled into her bones—the same sensation men must feel when injustice backs them into a corner, leaving them no choice but to seize the law with their own hands. She could sense the threshold before her, the very one that transformed men into pirates. The thin line between right and wrong began to blur, and for the first time, she understood how desperation could harden into rebellion. She tasted lawlessness on her lips and felt the pull of it in her blood, knowing full well that once crossing the line of the law, there was no turning back.

But an unexpected figure emerged before she could speak and give in to the tempest raging within her. Young yet fierce, John's hand shook as he pointed at Thomas Clark.

"You!" he cried, his voice a storm of fury and courage aimed at the heartless Captain. "You did it! I saw you and your crew set fire to the schoolhouse!" His eyes seemed wild with rage as he recounted witnessing the treachery. "I saw you and your crew set the fire and then flee the arson in haste."

"No, you didn't," the combative Captain said, defiantly spitting on the deck.

"You stood, laughing, and watched the fire take hold with joy in your eyes," John continued, anger wracking his frame. "And then you commanded your men to flee before justice could find its way to you. You are a coward. A criminal of the worst kind."

The final act of condemnation sent him into a rage. "You will believe this boy over the captain of this ship?" the erupting man spat out at the absurdity with a laughing taunt.

Standing tall amidst the wreckage in this lawless moment, Abigail shouted, "You have been caught and will pay for your sins most egregiously."

The deck thrummed with tension, and silent anticipation was etched on every face as Constable Jenkins stepped forward. His posture was steadfast, a stark contrast to the militant scene around him. "Thomas Clark," he announced, his voice slicing through the noise with undeniable authority. You are under arrest for arson." Pausing, he added, as if an afterthought, "I always suspected you were trouble from the beginning."

"What is this madness?" Captain Clark erupted in defiance. "You've no right to arrest me. Not here, nor anywhere. We've left New Haven behind—we're on the high seas now."

Standing resolute, Abigail faced off against the smug Captain. "Indeed, we are on the high seas," she countered. "In the domain of the Admiralty, not under the jurisdiction of a mere constable."

Clark sneered, his arrogance unwavering. "You don't intimidate me."

"What?" Abigail quipped, arching an eyebrow. "You mean the Admiralty? By landing your ship, setting fire to part of the town out of greed and vengeance, you have made yourself and your crew"—she paused, her gaze piercing as it swept over the sailors, who stood frozen in fear and trepidation—"nothing less than pirates."

Shock flickered across Clark's face, mirrored in the expressions of his men, before quickly morphing into desperation.

Abigail's voice rang with unwavering authority. "If any man does not accept this judgment and wishes to testify against his Captain, step aside now. Otherwise, let it be known that the Pirate Captain Thomas Clark is hereby remanded into custody by the Constable until the Admiralty intervenes."

The crew stood paralyzed. Clark sneered with pride, convinced that his men would fight by his side.

Abigail stepped forward, her tone dark and foreboding. "I need not remind you—the Admiralty is keen to hang pirates until they are severely dead. Then, their corpses are rolled in hot pitch and tar before being caged in a gibbet, left to rot at the harbor's mouth as a warning to anyone who dares bring their treachery to New Haven's shores."

The whites of every sailor's eyes shone stark in the dim moonlight.

Mutiny unfolded in the heavy silence. One by one, the crew shifted their allegiance, stepping away in a slow, silent betrayal. Their boots scraped softly against the wooden deck, each movement an unspoken confession.

Captain Clark stood alone, surrounded not by loyal men but by the weight of his unraveling command. With every step his crew took away from him, it was as if pieces of his authority, his world, and his very essence were eroding into the void of accusatory desertion.

The upright and resolute Pirate Clark was encircled by treachery, distanced from the cowering silhouettes of those he once called comrades. His voice, a whirlwind of fury and incredulity, pierced the unsettling quiet as he growled ferociously, "No!" This was not merely a rejection of his destiny but the defiant cry of a spirit refusing to be engulfed by the shadows of rebellion.

In a sudden, desperate motion, Captain Clark yanked a dagger from his belt with one hand and lifted a musket with the other. The blade caught what little light there was, its gleam sharp and dangerous—more a flash of wounded pride than resolve. For an instant, the steel reflected the loneliness that had crept over him, the final proof that the bond between him and his crew had shattered.

The men moved in to restrain him, but he slashed wildly, forcing them back. His eyes searched their faces for one last trace of loyalty—anything that said he was still their Captain. Instead, he found only hardened stares and the grim certainty that he stood alone.

Cornered and stripped of command, Clark made his final stand. It wasn't a fight for victory—only a last, furious attempt to cling to the dignity slipping from him. The deck that had once been his realm now bore witness to his downfall, the stage of a captain battling the inevitable end of his own authority.

Observing his defiance, Captain Holloway, who innumerable skirmishes had tempered through his long career, remained undeterred. With the grace of a seasoned hunter, he drew his musket smoothly from his belt. The wooden planks underfoot resonated with his fierce resolve, echoing the raucous roar of the ocean during a tempest. But before Holloway could aim, Clark pointed his weapon straight at the vulnerable Abigail and bellowed with the ferocity of the devil, "Lay down ye weapon, or I'll cut her down."

Holloway's stance stiffened, and his eyes shifted to the side. He saw the woman of the ship standing out in the open. Then, without hesitation, he let the musket bounce across the decking, holding up his hands in submission.

With a glint of triumph in his eyes, Clark leveled the aim of his cocked musket at the one target he despised most. His gaze narrowed with the crazed contempt only the most notorious pirate captains could summon.

John didn't think—he moved.

He had caught the shift in Clark's stance, the murderous intention sharpening in his eyes, and lunged on instinct. He collided with Abigail, shoving her sideways and down before she could register the danger.

The shot exploded in a brutal double-crack, the flash blinding, the smoke blooming like a ghost across the deck. The violent recoil drove Clark backward, the musket clattering from his hands.

Clark stood frozen, momentarily stunned, as the acrid smoke swirled around him and Holloway. His grimace mutated to astonishment as his gaze shifted from Holloway's dropped weapon to the sprawling woman until the pain shifted his numb hand to the bleeding hole in his chest. His knees weak-ened, and the once-shrewd merchant captain turned pirate swayed unsteadily, unable to suppress his bloody cough.

Then, with a sudden shift of his stance, Clark's gaze lifted—and froze. Standing behind Holloway was Hannah's slender figure, both hands gripping pistols. One pointed directly at him, and the other lowered slightly, its barrel streaming smoke, its purpose already fulfilled. The steely determination in the girl's eyes was a silent witness to the shot she had just fired.

With Clark standing stunned, his knife blade outstretched. Holloway unsheathed his mighty cutlass—unyielding and swift. With a single, decisive slash across the neck, he cut the bleeding man down, overpowering the feeble dagger and sending it clattering across the deck. The sound of the blade was accompanied by the sickening spray of blood from Clark's mouth, neck, and chest—a grotesque mockery of laughter, heralding the vengeful arsonist's ignominious defeat.

Triumphant, the Captain turned to Hannah, his face split by a victorious grin. Replacing his bloodied cutlass into his belt, he looked to see Abigail alive, regaining her footing before exclaiming to the Constable, "Ms. Hannah's always got our backs."

John slowly leaned back and slid down to the deck, leaving a dark streak of blood on the mast. Abigail moved quickly to his side, gathering him in her arms, her voice breaking as she cried, "John!" He coughed, blood bubbling from his mouth, his gaze flickering as he looked up at her.

With a weak, sputtering breath, he managed a faint smile. "Ma'am," he whispered, his words punctuated by shallow gasps. "I'd like to ask—" grimacing with pain. "Sarah's hand."

Hannah fell to her knees beside them, tears streaming down her face as she fumbled to open his shirt, her hands trembling as she tried to see if there was anything she could do. Her desperate gaze met her mother's, both women's eyes wide and wet with grief.

John began to lose focus, his breathing slowing. His lips opened, but he couldn't form words. Frowning, he grimaced to slurp in a short breath, letting it out in a slow warbling, "I love her with all my—" His stare glazed over, leaving the distant, lifeless look of death in its place. His body slackened, and his head tilted as his cheeks grew still.

Abigail held him close and looked at Hannah, whose face was twisted in despair. Bowing her head to the lifeless body, Abigail forced a whisper, "I give you my blessing, my son."

The chaos ebbed, leaving only the ripple of water brushing the hull and the crew murmuring in shaken, clipped whispers. The women's loss hung in the silence like a weight no one dared to name.

CHAPTER 40

Sarah's Sorrow

ABIGAIL AND HANNAH STRODE BACK to the smoldering schoolhouse, flanked by Constable Jenkins. The moonlit sky cast a soft, gray light over the grounds, illuminating charred wood and wisps of lingering smoke. As they approached, the extent of the damage became clear: only a small section of the building had been affected. Thanks to the swift action of the students and their escorts, the community's overwhelming support, and the addition of the expensive, well-placed brickwork—insisted upon and personally funded by Abigail—the flames had been effectively contained. The school had been spared complete devastation.

Hannah looked up at her mother, her face pale and weary. "What will we tell Sarah? What if—we said nothing? I don't know if she even realized it was John who came to alert us. She was out in the garden when he appeared." Her voice was a whisper, as if even speaking it aloud would bring more sorrow. "I don't think anybody recognized him."

Abigail paused, considering the merciful option of sparing Sarah from yet another heartbreak. But she turned to Hannah and asked gently, "Would you want to know the truth?"

Hannah lowered her gaze, knowing her mother was right. In painful silence, they walked into the building, where students and townsfolk still bustled about, helping to remove burnt, smoldering wood and offering comfort and support.

Finally, they found Sarah and Eunice in the school's parlor. As soon as they entered, all four women fell into each other's arms, overcome with the relief of being together, and Hannah broke down, her shoulders heaving with quiet sobs.

Sarah, her voice steady despite the night's horrors, wrapped an arm around her sister. "Don't worry, Hannah. Your Mr. MacCreedy will have this ship shape in no time," she said with a brave smile. But Hannah's tears only grew more intense, unable to keep the sorrow locked away.

Abigail, her voice low and solemn, turned to her sister. "Eunice… it was Thomas Clark. He set the fire, seeking revenge for what he believed we stole from him—his inheritance."

Eunice's face paled with shock. "Thomas Clark? How did you know?"

"Because John saw him do it," Hannah said quietly, her voice laced with grief.

Sarah's arm around Hannah fell as she spun to face the women, her expression twisted in confusion and panic. "My John?" she asked, her voice trembling. "Where is he?"

Hannah covered her own face with her palms as she tried to hold back another wave of tears, and Abigail took over, her tone calm but filled with sadness. "John led us down to the docks. He pointed out Clark and helped us board my sloop. I ordered him to row away to safety, but—he disobeyed."

Sarah clutched her mother's arm, fear growing in her eyes as she harkened. Abigail's voice grew fainter, each word carrying a weight that threatened to crush her. "Clark… he fired his musket, aiming to kill me. But John…" She paused, the memory sharp and bitter. "John stepped in the way… shoved me aside, really." Abigail's voice wavered on her words, as though it slipped through a crack in a door she had been holding shut, "He… he saved me… with his… life."

A thick silence settled over the room, broken only by quiet sobs. The sorrow that filled the air seemed almost too heavy to bear, encompassing not only John's sacrifice but the turmoil that had tainted what should have been a joyous night.

Later that evening, as Sarah lay curled up in her bed, her mind a haze of disbelief and sorrow, Hannah crept in and sat beside her. She placed a gentle hand on her sister's shoulder, her own eyes red from crying.

"Before he…" she paused, holding her breath for several seconds before exhaling. "Before we lost him," Hannah whispered, "the last thing from his lips… he asked Mother for your hand."

Sarah's body stiffened, her tears coming faster, and she clutched the blanket to her chest. "What… did she say?" Her voice broke, but Hannah interrupted her gently.

"He said he loved you," Hannah continued, her voice cracking. "And Mother… gave her blessing before he…" She choked on her words, unable to finish.

They lay together in silence, each lost in their own grief. No more words were spoken; only the sound of quiet sobbing filled the room as they mourned the love that had been lost and the life that had been taken too soon.

CHAPTER 41

Black Sam Bellamy, May, 1716

IN THE LATE AFTERNOON before graduation, everyone was arriving at The Willow, and the school was aglow with anticipation. The last of the spring sun slanted through the tall windows of the open classroom, tinting the air with warm gold as it drifted toward evening. Inside, the space—once so disciplined and orderly—had been transformed into a genteel reception hall. Tables that had supported quills, slates, and Latin primers were now draped in fine linen and set with tarts, sugared fruits, pies, and porcelain cups of steaming tea and coffee.

Hope paused beside the doorway, letting her gaze sweep over the room. It seemed impossible that, only five months earlier, this same hall had flickered with the violent orange of flame, the air choking with smoke and frantic shouts. Though the fire had been contained to the kitchen and adjoining storeroom—both now rebuilt—the memory lay quietly in the beams, like soot refusing to surrender. Even with the windows thrown open and April's rains coaxing May's flowers to perfume the breeze, she could still detect the faintest ghost of smoke clinging to the wainscoting. MacCreedy's men had labored tirelessly to mend the damage, yet every soft groan of the timbers reminded her how near the school had come to ruin.

The girls moved about the room in delicate gowns, their steps measured but bright with confidence born of a year hard-won. Some stood with their escorts and parent chaperones near the garden door, speaking animatedly about the archery matches held in the backyard. Others lingered near the library alcove, reminiscing about the hours they had spent parsing French translations or reciting moral essays. A few gathered around the musicians' corner, laughing as they recalled their first hesitant attempts at singing under Mr. Warbleworth's stern ear.

Parents and guardians—dressed in elegant, modest attire befitting the occasion—exchanged polite greetings, offering congratulations with the warm pride of those who had watched their daughters transform. Their voices mingled into a gentle hum, punctuated by bursts of laughter and the clink of porcelain.

Garlands of greenery and early blossoms wreathed the walls, giving the room a sweet, festive air. The black slate board, decorated in flowing chalk script, announced:

"The Willow — Graduation Class of 1716." Beneath it, the girls' names were written in careful order, each one earned through diligence and quiet perseverance.

Yet woven through the merriment was a tender thread of wistfulness. The girls' smiles lingered a moment too long, their glances softened by the knowledge that this chapter—this year of unexpected friendships, challenges, triumphs, and secrets shared in confidence—was drawing to a close. Mothers brushed stray curls from their daughters' brows, resting proud hands on young shoulders, clasping hands a little tighter than usual.

The reception carried on in a perfect balance of pride and gentle melancholy—not an ending, but the moment just before it, suspended like a held breath. Tomorrow would bring ceremony, farewells, and the turning of a page. But for this afternoon, The Willow shimmered with all the quiet magic of a place that had transformed them—and would be remembered for shaping their futures.

An hour into the event, when the sun had set, and the gentle roar of convivial guests was high, Hope excused herself to inform the kitchen staff that the table of hor d'oeuvres needed attention. As she stepped out of the ballroom, she was surprised to see someone at the front door asking a member of the staff, "Where is Abigail?"

Without hesitating for an answer, the man began moving purposefully toward the ballroom and walked through the doorway.

Hope's stomach tightened with concern, and she moved quickly to catch up with him. "I beg your pardon?" she demanded. "Apologies, but you are?"

After scanning the other guests in the room, he said, "She told me to meet her here as a matter of importance. I am the captain of her yacht, James Holloway."

Seeing the commotion, Hannah came to their side to inquire into the matter. "Captain, you are aware of my mother's whereabouts?"

"Only that she was to meet me here, Ms. Hannah."

"Captain?" Hope repeated her request for an explanation, but Hannah only placed a gentle hand on the Headmistress's arm and said she would handle the situation. Hope nodded gratefully and turned away to resume her hosting duties.

Hannah pondered for a moment. "Then perhaps she went to the docks, thinking you might be there? Could there have been a mix-up in the timing?"

The old sea captain, his face weathered from years at sea, grumbled, "Not bloody likely. But I suppose I should have a look."

"I shall accompany you?" she suggested eagerly.

As Hannah and Captain Holloway hurried down the cobbled streets towards the docks, the cold air was filled with the distant sound of ships creaking and the occasional call of a nightbird. Dusk was turning to dark, lending an ethereal quality to their urgent journey.

Hannah, her mind racing with questions, finally broke the silence. "Captain, what's going on?"

Holloway, his eyes fixed on the path ahead, sighed deeply. "It's a bit of a mess, I'm afraid, and it's of my own making. I suggested to your Mother that we invite Hirana to The Willow after her Mother's death, Goody Hallett — 'Witch of Wellfleet.'"

Hannah frowned, puzzled. "But why would that be a problem?"

The captain glanced at her, his expression grave. "Because Hirana is the bastard child of the pirate Black Sam Bellamy, the Robin Hood of the Seas."

Hannah's steps faltered for a moment, her eyes widening in shock. "One of my Mother's clients. How did I not know of this before now?" she gasped, the words slipping out before she could think. "I've seen him in our house, and he did not seem much older than I. Hirana is already in her teens. How was Bellamy old enough to have sired her?"

Holloway rubbed his whiskered chin, recollecting stories told. "Bellamy signed on as a ship's boy in the Royal Navy in Devonshire at the mischievous age of seven. By nine, he was a powder monkey and, as a teen, a midshipman. While in port at Cape Cod, he met Hirana's Mother, his first and only true love."

As Hannah and Holloway continued their brisk walk toward the docks, Holloway's revelations about Hirana's troubled past weighed heavily on Hannah's mind. She could understand how the stigma of being a bastard and the burden of a notoriously absent father might loom over Hirana as a black flag emblazoned with the skull and crossbones of pirates. The night was quiet, save for the distant breeze stirring the waves and the sound of their hurried footsteps.

Deep in thought, Hannah recalled the young girl's demeanor throughout the year. A vivid image of Hirana, looking small and out of place at The Willow, flashed in her mind. "No wonder she looked so lost in the crowd," she said softly, her voice tinged with newfound understanding and sympathy.

Holloway glanced at her, his face reflecting a similar sentiment. "Yes, it's been a hard life for her. The shadows of her father's past loom large over her. It's a lot for any child to bear."

Hannah's heart ached for Hirana. The thought of the young girl, already burdened with the stigma of her departed Mother's tainted reputation and now facing the resurgence of her infamous father, filled her with a protective fervor. "We must do everything we can to help her," she said determinedly. "She deserves a chance to be seen for who she is, not for the circumstances of her birth."

Holloway nodded in agreement, his expression resolute. "Absolutely. And that starts with handling this situation delicately."

As they descended upon the docks, a cold sea breeze greeted them, carrying with it the promise and challenges of the vast ocean. Hannah looked out over the water, her resolve strengthening. This was more than just a mission to find her Mother; it was a commitment to safeguard a young girl's future.

Hannah's mind raced as they continued their brisk walk. The revelation added a complex layer to the situation, and she wished she had her twin musket's comfort. Now, she wondered if she should return to her room for them. Her Mother's dealings with pirates were always a delicate balance, and the involvement of someone as notorious as Samuel Bellamy could jeopardize their family's business and the tangled web of relationships they had built over the years.

Hannah braced herself as the masts towered overhead, with the outlines of ships swaying gently in the water. Whatever was unfolding between her Mother and Hirana's father, she knew it would require all the cunning and diplomacy her family was known for.

Hannah's eyes caught a familiar silhouette near the end of the dock. "Mother—" she began, raising a hand, but Captain Holloway gently grabbed her wrist and gave a subtle shake of his head. "Easy lass," he whispered. The lantern light from the wharf threw long shadows across the water, enough to reveal Abigail's outline and the tall figure standing beside her. The man's coat, dark and heavy, shifted in the night breeze, and the faint glint of metal—a buckle, perhaps, or the hilt of a blade—flashed as he moved.

Holloway leaned close, his voice barely carrying over the sound of water lapping against the pilings. "Aye," he said quietly. "That's the girl's pirate father, Black Sam Bellamy."

As the pair grew closer, it was evident that Abigail was in full persuasive mode, trying to convince Bellamy not to go to The Willow. Her words were firm, her gestures emphatic.

Neither Abigail nor Bellamy seemed taken aback by the arrival of Hannah and Captain Holloway, so engrossed they'd been in their heated exchange.

As the four figures converged on the dock, the tension was arresting. The moonlight cast long shadows, making the scene feel like something from a nautical legend. Samuel Bellamy stood tall, his raven-black hair tied back in a similarly dark bow, matching his clothing and imposing. His crazed eyes glinted with a mix of defiance and bitterness.

Upon seeing Holloway, Bellamy's lips curled into a sneer. "Ah, the river rat, too afraid to face the open sea," he taunted.

Holloway, unflustered, met his gaze. "Perhaps, Bellamy. Aye, but it's better to live as a lowly, lean rat than a dead fat cat. You might consider treading more carefully yourself, lest you end up at the end of a short rope."

After the brief, gritty introduction, Bellamy launched into a tirade, his voice rising and falling with the rhythm of his fervent beliefs. "I am sorry," he began, his tone dripping with sarcasm, "that you can't have your way. But truly, I scorn to do anyone harm—when it doesn't benefit me. You, Holloway, are a sneaking puppy, as are all those who willingly bow to laws crafted by the rich for their own protection. They're cowards, lacking the courage to defend their ill-gotten gains without their laws. But damn you all, you're nothing but a pack of crafty rascals. And those who serve them? Hen-hearted numbskulls!"

He paced back and forth, his voice growing louder. "They vilify us seamen, those scoundrels, when the only difference is this: they rob the poor under the guise of legality, while we plunder the rich, bolstered by our own bravery. Wouldn't you rather join us than grovel before these villains for crumbs of employment?"

His words, a challenge and a condemnation all at once, painted a world divided starkly between the powerful and the powerless, the oppressors and the oppressed. Bellamy's eyes burned with a fervor that spoke of deep convictions and a life lived on the edge of society's norms.

Standing her ground with a steely resolve, Abigail faced Bellamy as he finished his impassioned speech. Her eyes were unflinching, her voice steady and firm, cutting through the unease like a sharp blade.

"Samuel," she began, her tone laced with a mix of sternness and a hint of pity. "You will not ruin your daughter's life with your association. This is precisely the cycle she is here to break free from. The burden of having you as her father is a heavy shadow over her heart, one that is dragging her down as a cut anchor to depths she does not deserve."

She stepped closer, her gaze never wavering. "Your presence, your notoriety, it's a weight upon her, turning her into something akin to a wench visiting a ship at port. Is that what you want for your daughter? To see her reduced to nothing more than an extension of your own infamy?"

"You are not her mother," he spat with crazed anger. "I am her father," he declared as if that was all the defense he needed.

Abigail's voice rose slightly, imbued with a passionate intensity. "If you truly care for her, if there is any love in your heart for the child you sired, you will not rob her of this chance. This opportunity at the Willow is her path to rise above the misfortune you've seeded in her life. Do not be the cannon that sinks her. Do not be so complacent as to destroy her only chance to emerge from the shadow you've cast."

Her words echoed in the stillness of the night, a plea not just for Hirana's future but also a challenge to Bellamy's own sense of responsibility and honor as a father. Her words weighed down the atmosphere.

Abigail's gaze remained locked on Bellamy, her expression unyielding. She took another step closer, her voice carrying a sharp edge of truth that sliced through the night, causing him to take a step back.

"And let's not delude ourselves with romantic notions, Samuel," she continued, her words deliberate and piercing. "You've styled yourself as some modern-day Robin Hood, robbing from the rich to give to the poor. Ha, if you can call a whore or barkeep poor. But let's be clear about what's happening here tonight. In seeking this reunion, in insisting on your presence in her life now, you're not giving—you're taking. You're robbing from your own daughter. You're stealing her chance at a life unburdened by your legacy, a life where she can be judged for her own merits, not yours."

Bellamy's rugged composure didn't break so much as shift. The hard lines of his face eased, his jaw loosening, and for the briefest heartbeat the lamplight caught in his eyes—two sudden glimmers that vanished almost as quickly as they appeared. He swallowed once, hard.

"I just… need to look at her," he murmured, voice roughened but steady. "To remember her as she is now. She was only a scrap of a thing the last time." He breathed out, the sound more fragile than he intended. "Each voyage, I tell myself it won't be the last… but this time, I can't shake the feeling."

But he shook his head, stubborn in his resolve. It was then that Hannah spoke up. "I can go and bring her to visit with you if that would satisfy?"

"No," Abigail interjected firmly. "That will only confuse the girl."

The pirate's expression firmed, the fleeting softness gone as quickly as it had surfaced. His jaw set, shoulders squared with the quiet authority of a man used to storms and steel.

"Then we're at an impasse," he said, voice low and edged like a whetted blade. "I see her here, as agreed… or I walk up to your genteel Willow and call for her myself." His gaze didn't waver. "Tell me which you prefer."

Before anyone could respond, Hannah turned and dashed back towards the Willow, her silhouette disappearing into the darkness.

In the quiet that followed, Holloway spoke to Bellamy, his voice earnest. "Abigail gave me a new life, one without the constant fear of hanging from a rope or drowning alone at sea. You have that chance, too, Sam. You can choose a different path for you and for Hirana."

Bellamy kept his stance rigid, but his face betrayed a ripple of turmoil. The darkness around them thickened with a charged stillness, the whole moment suspended in a fragile, breathless pause.

The docks were dimly lit, the moon casting a silvery glow over the wooden planks and the gently rocking boats. Abigail stood face to face with the pirate, her posture firm yet tinged with empathy.

"I can help you disappear, Samuel," Abigail said, her voice steady and convincing. "You can live a life far from the dangers of piracy, a life of a prince if you so choose. But you must make that choice now, for your sake and Hirana's."

Bellamy, a rugged man with the sea etched into his very being, looked torn, his eyes reflecting a storm of emotions. He paced off into the night with his hands folded behind his back as if thinking about what Abigail was offering. He walked the rickety planks back and forth, occasionally waving his hand in the air and talking to himself. After a while, he turned and fixed his eyes on Abigail's, but as he was about to respond, Hannah appeared wearing a shawl, guiding a younger girl behind her. The girl's face was hidden from view, shielded by Hannah's protective stance.

Bellamy's eyes widened as they stepped into the moonlight, hope and fear evident across his features. The girl peered around Hannah, curious and apprehensive.

"Father?" her words tentative, a question suspended in the cool night air.

Abigail stepped forward as if to shield the girl from harm, but Captain Holloway reached out and steadied her stance with his own concerned frown. Bellamy hesitated, his tough exterior momentarily faltering. His eyes, usually so full of resolve and defiance, now shimmered with unspoken emotions. He took a step forward, his voice barely a whisper. "Hirana? My, have you grown."

The girl took a small, uncertain step towards him. Her eyes searched his face, looking for the man she'd heard of but did not know.

Standing steadily beside the girl, Hannah gently touched her shoulder, offering silent support. She understood the allure of this reunion, gambling that the weight of years and distant choices swaying between the pirate and his daughter had dulled their senses.

For a moment, time seemed to stand still on the docks, the only sound the gentle lapping of the water against the creaking boats. Then, slowly, tentatively, the girl moved closer to Bellamy, her voice a mere whisper. "I... I've wanted to see you for so long."

Overcome with emotion, Bellamy bent to be at eye level with her. "And I, you, my dear," he said, his voice heavy with passion. "I'm sorry... for everything."

The reunion, poised on the edge of a tender moment, took an abrupt and startling turn. Samuel Bellamy's eyes suddenly hardened, and he grasped her arm with a determination that brooked no argument. "You're coming with me," he announced, his voice leaving no room for discussion.

Abigail's stomach clenched in alarm, her eyes darting from the girl to Hannah and then back to Bellamy. "Whatever for? What of the code?" she demanded. The pirate code, an unwritten law of the high seas, strictly forbade women and children aboard a pirate vessel. Their presence confused the crew, leading to desires and heightening frustrated spirits.

"You would jeopardize your daughter's future for your own selfish reasons?" Abigail continued, her voice laced with incredulity and anger.

Then, the girl spoke up with a voice far more resolute than her years. "No, Father, I do not wish to follow your wicked ways, just as I once feared my Mother's bewitching ways. I want to stand on my own two feet."

Visibly stunned by his daughter's firm stance, Bellamy slowly released her arm. He looked at her with pride and sorrow in his eyes. Then, with a long sigh and a nod of acceptance, he stood up straight to face his now-grown daughter. "Well, at least I had the chance to see you," he murmured. "I do not know when I will see you again—if ever. But I know now you are in good hands." He nodded respectfully towards Abigail and tipped his hat to Holloway, pausing slightly, looking as if he wanted more before walking slowly towards the awaiting jollyboat. Over his shoulder, his voice breaking with fatherly sorrow, he vowed, "One last voyage, and we will be together."

As he moved into the moonlit shadows cast between the moored ships, his figure gradually faded, blending with the ocean breeze like a passing wave. Once he was out of sight, Abigail exhaled with relief, then turned to the young girl masquerading as the pirate's daughter, Hirana, with a scolding tone. "Sarah! What were you thinking? What if he had taken you onto his ship?"

Hannah stepped forward, her twin muskets now visible in her hands, both barrels peeking out from under her shawl. "Not bloody likely," she said with a steely edge to her voice, uncocking the weapons. Her eyes were fierce and protective, a clear indication that she would have gone to any length to ensure her sister's safety.

"But mother, Hannah told me that YOU wanted me to play the role of Hirana."

"Not bloody likely," Abigail growled before breaking her stern stance with a smile of appreciation for everything going well.

The night bristled with the residue of suspense and relief. The docks, once a stage for a potentially tragic unfolding, now bore witness to the strength and resolve of a family united in protecting one of their own. The moon continued its silent vigil overhead, casting a serene glow over a scene that had narrowly escaped descending into chaos.

CHAPTER 42

Graduation Night

ABIGAIL STOOD AT THE BACK DOOR, looking out at the young women assembled in the classroom. Roughly over half of the original class stood prepared to complete this journey and step into the next chapter of their lives. She felt a heavy tug of disappointment that the entire inaugural class of the Willow was not here for this momentous day, but she pushed past it; she would allow herself to dwell on that later. Right now, each of these faces present tells a story of growth, resilience, and transformation, even if other stories end abruptly or take unexpected turns.

Parents stood proudly behind their daughters, eyes filled with gratitude and admiration. The girls, adorned in their simple yet elegant graduation gowns, reflected pride and anticipation for their future. Outside the windows, the garden in full bloom and the pond waiting to be topped off by summer's rains served as a memorable backdrop for this momentous occasion.

Hope Terwilliger stood at the podium, on which sat a small stack of papers. Next to the podium was the clamshell-arrow demerit display, and on the ground near her feet was a tall bucket with wispy leaves hanging over the side. As Hope scanned the crowd, her heart swelled with emotion to see the young women who had blossomed under her guidance. She lifted her hand and gave a gentle, commanding wave. "Everyone, please—find your seats," her voice carrying the calm authority that always seemed to settle a room.

Chairs shuffled; conversations softened; a ripple of movement passed through the gathering as the guests and students settled themselves.

Only once the room stilled did Hope step forward, her posture poised, her expression bright with pride.

She began her speech with a warm smile.

"My, have our children grown in the past year," she said with a loving gaze at the students, some now as close to her as her own child. "I regret that some could not attend, but—" The Headmistress's eyes met Abigail's and knew she should not finish the thought. Instead, she held out her hand to direct everyone's eyes to the girls sitting proudly before her. "Today, we celebrate these fine young women's academic achievements and the remarkable individuals they have all become. Each of you has faced challenges and overcome them with grace and determination. You have learned the importance of resilience, empathy, and courage, not to mention a few new languages."

The Kidd yelled, "Oui, Oui!" causing everyone in the room to laugh and the Headmistress to click her comical castanets at her before continuing. "And I do not doubt you will carry these lessons with you as you enter the world."

The parents nodded, some wiping away tears, clearly moved by Hope's words. The students exchanged glances, their expressions a mix of excitement and trepidation.

"To our graduates," Hope continued. "You embody the values we hold dear at The Willow and in each of the new land colonies of America. You have shown that through hard work and perseverance, anything is possible. As you leave these grounds, remember that you carry a piece of The Willow with you. You are part of a strong, intelligent, compassionate women's legacy."

The girls sat a little taller, their eyes bright with the promise of the future.

"And so let us begin. Hirana Bellamy, would you step forward?"

As Hirana walked to the podium to receive her diploma, the Headmistress reviewed her accomplishments. "Her classmates voted Hirana as the most likely of them to become an innkeeper with a brewery and a cleaning service on the side." Amidst the cheers of her fellow students, she said, "Okay, I added the brewery and cleaning service on the side myself," which prompted more laughter.

Eunice said to her sister, "Innkeeper? Maybe your next endeavor will be setting her up in business?"

Abigail shrugged with a thoughtful nod of her head, adding, "It'll have to be far away from any pirating enclaves."

"Because of her father, Black Sam Bellamy?"

"Because of her adventuresome spirit."

Along with the sheaf of paper that was her diploma, Hope handed Hirana a willow branch from the tree in the backyard. "This branch," Hope said as Hirana waved the Willow in front of her face, "symbolizes your flexible growth and your connection to the school."

Hirana returned to her seat with a broad smile, amid cheering and laughter. Hannah and Sarah gave her a hug of accomplishment, trying to serve as surrogate substitutes for the lack of parents or guardians in attendance.

"Thank you, Hirana, for being such a good student. The next graduate is Dorothy Goodyear Whiting, voted most likely to become a preacher's wife."

She stood to the clapping of hands and hoots from the Kidd. Before moving to the front, she grasped her parents' hands as her mother said to her husband, the Preacher, with fondness, "What's so bad about that?"

The Headmistress continued, "Dorothy has grown by leaps and bounds, adding each of the girls here at The Willow to her list of lifelong friends. And I have no doubt she will continue to add to this expanding list of friends throughout the rest of her days."

As Dorothy returned to her parents, she stood before her mother and handed her the willow twig. Her mother showed it to her husband and said to her daughter, "You know, in ancient times, this was an olive branch."

Dorothy smiled and said with confidence, "I know!"

Hope waited patiently for Dorothy to settle back into her seat before continuing. Then, rearranging her notes, she announced, "Mary Dongan Nugent, most likely to become a politician."

Mary's Aunt laughed as she said, "In today's world, that means mother."

Everyone in the room laughed politely, not wanting to dispute the guest's words outright, as Mary stepped forward and took her certificate and willow branch.

"Mary," Hope said, "is always quick to offer another opinion that bridges the gaps between the other students—"

The Kidd yelled out, "Hannah and Gulielma Maria!" which set off a wave of laughter until the Headmistress clicked her clamshell in the air, and everyone became quiet.

"Yes, Gulielma Maria has received enough credits—"

"Clamshells," Kidd corrected, earning another sharp clack of the Headmistress's castanet.

"What? I'm her roommate. I have the right to, ah… kid her," she added, prompting the girls to stifle a giggle behind their hands as others clapped.

But when Kidd rose and bowed to the applause, Hope calmly lifted a clamshell and slid it down over the arrow labeled SB. A collective gasp rippled through the students. Kidd froze, mouth open—then slowly broke into a crooked grin.

"I always wondered," she said, "how many of those shells you'd stack on my arrow before you'd have to write my mother."

Hope raised her brows and, without a word, placed another clamshell, then another, each one clicking down the shaft until the arrow bristled with them. One more would surely spell academic doom.

"How many is that?" Hope asked, holding another shell above the tip as if genuinely considering it.

Kidd squinted. "Twelve…?"

"Mm. And how fortuitous," Hope replied, lowering the clamshell back into the bag with a dramatic clang, "that unlucky number thirteen remains unclaimed. Good to know for next time."

The room let out the breath it had been holding as the ceremony resumed.

Headmistress Hope cleared her throat—more to reassemble the moment than to scold—her eyes sparkling with a humor she didn't quite allow to bloom into a smile. Kidd's antics, though entirely inappropriate, had brought a welcome burst of levity to the joyous occasion.

With composed grace, she straightened her notes.

"Eliza Marble," Hope continued, her tone bright and steady as she shot Kidd a playful warning look, "voted most likely to become a Constable. Eliza is well known for her insightful questions and eagerness to resolve any problem, whether singing or midwifery; she is always ready to participate. Her impeccable view of the world has refreshed us all—daily," she added with a low, dry tone, eliciting laughs and giggles. "But, honestly, every community should have a strong woman like our bright and insightful Eliza."

Eliza made her way to the front of the class and took possession of her certificate and twig. Then, with a mischievous grin, she reached into the bag of clams and tried to place one over the Kidd's arrow, but was stopped at the last moment by the Headmistress. The Headmistress instead redirected it over Eliza's arrow, raising her eyebrows in silent inquiry as if to ask if Eliza wanted a few more before the ceremony was over. Eliza laughed, waving the willow twig in the air in celebration, saying, "Technically, I've already graduated."

Hope quickly added, "Technically, you're just a name on a piece of parchment."

Eliza walked back to her seat with her mouth agape, causing Kidd to pinch her arm as she passed. The sound of shell castanets clacked loudly when she shouted, 'Ouch.'

"Patience Carr voted most likely to become a homemaker. Her easygoing temperament and all-inclusiveness made her everyone's best friend."

"Aw," rang out around the room as the once shy and intimidated Patience bounced out of her seat and gave Hope a massive hug of appreciation. Then she took her diploma and twig and raced back to share it with her parents.

"Thank you," Waite Carr mouthed to the Headmistress, and she nodded quietly back, "You're welcome."

"The next two graduates come as a pair. You may not have known this, but they were integral to the Willow's building and planning from the beginning."

Each girl looked around, fixing their smiles on Hannah and Sarah, who stood in the back with their mother and Aunt.

"Truly, they were among my most steadfast pupils," she said with a thoughtful nod toward Abigail at the back of the room. "Their dedication made my work lighter, and their absence—like each of yours in your own way—will certainly be felt in the years ahead."

All eyes shifted to the sisters still left to graduate when Hope announced, "Sarah and Hannah." She deliberately omitted their surname, just as Abigail had requested. As the sisters and made their way toward the front, Hope added with genuine warmth, "I only wish that Hannah and Sarah had agreed to return next year as my assistants."

Before she could say more, Kidd shot up from her seat, cupping her hands around her mouth, hollering, "To teach swords and pistols!"

"And archery!" Patience chimed in boldly from across the room.

All the graduating students jumped to their feet with excitement and laughter as the two stood and walked to the front to receive their certificates and willow twig.

"The twig was Sarah's idea," Hope added.

Sarah laughed, extending her hand to accept the willow branch and swishing it in the air over her head, saying, "I got the idea when trimming the tree out back. The Kidd and I got into a little sword fight with the limbs, and well—"

Kidd popped to her feet before anyone else could react. With theatric flair, she reached beneath her chair and produced a small wooden sword, clearly smuggled in as part of a planned mischief. She tapped the practice blade to her forehead in mock solemnity, then extended it toward the two graduates at the front—issuing a grand, dramatic challenge as though the ceremony had suddenly descended into a field of honor.

A ripple of delighted laughter moved through the room.

One by one, the other girls rose to join her. Willow twigs were lifted to foreheads in unison, a playful salute, before each young lady shifted into her best approximation of a fencing stance. A soft chorus of swish-swish filled the air as they flicked their twigs toward the two standing at the front—an affectionate show of respect disguised as mock combat.

The room glowed with joy, pride, and mischief all at once.

The sisters held up their twigs, and Hannah announced, "Two against six. Sounds like good odds to me. What do you think, sister?"

The girls standing with the Kidd exchanged glances—first at the sisters, then at one another—and in a perfectly timed wave of self-preservation, each dipped into an exaggerated bow of surrender before scrambling back into her seat with astonishing speed. A ripple of shocked gasps rose from the parents around the room.

Within seconds, the once-unified phalanx of willow-wielding maidens had vanished, leaving the Kidd standing alone—sword raised, stance set, and expression frozen somewhere between triumph and betrayal.

Realizing she was now the lone warrior on a very empty battlefield, she darted her eyes left… right… Then down at her dull weapon.

"Well… traitors, the lot of you," she muttered, before dropping into her chair with the graceless plop of someone trying very hard to pretend that had been the plan all along.

Another sound of surprise fluttered through the parents and chaperones, some covering smiles behind gloved hands, while several students failed to contain their laughter. The Headmistress stood with her arms braced on the podium to thank everyone for coming to the first graduation ceremony of the finishing school, The Willow, when Patience said loudly, "Is that all? Haven't you forgotten someone?"

Shock and despair appeared on the Headmistress's face, forcing her to say, "Good heavens. How could I have forgotten my own daughter, Ursula?" She waved her hand to her daughter, standing in the back next to the kitchen door, to come forward. "My daughter Ursula. I couldn't have done any of this without her. She has worked tirelessly behind the scenes to run my original school, the church orphanage. I hereby bestow upon Ursula the honorary graduation certificate from The Willow. Thank you, my precious."

Everyone clapped politely, and when she returned to the audience, Hope asked, "Now, is everyone ready for refreshments?"

No one moved. The Kidd sat as quiet as a church mouse, her face beginning to glow a soft red, and her eyes began to water.

"What? Am I missing something?" The Headmistress asked, looking around for something amiss. "Sarah? Do you know what I missed?" But when Abigail's daughter began to speak up, the Headmistress shushed her with her clicking clam shells for her to be quiet. She then asked again, "Sarah? Did I miss someone?" She shook her head and, through slitted eyes, looked at the bewildered Sarah, standing next to her mother, to keep her silent. Then, with the room hushed with confusion, she shouted, "Sarah?!"

Slowly standing, with tears streaming down her face, Sarah 'The Kidd' Bradley faced the Headmaster, tears of joy wetting every eye in the room, including Abigail's.

Straightening her back and clearing her throat loudly, the Headmistress fought back her own tears, announcing loudly, "Ms. Sarah Bradley is all grown up and no longer a kid lost in the world of regret and sorrow. Voted most likely to be the ship's Captain—be that an innkeeper, ship owner, business entrepreneur, or simply a wife and mother. No matter the task, she will fight her way to the top, asking for no quarter and taking no prisoners. ARRGHH!"

"ARRGHH!" shouted everyone in the audience, students and parents alike.

Abigail and the Kidd's mother watched with pride as she stepped up, her face glowing with accomplishment. She grasped her certificate and held the branch up high, shouting at the top of her lungs, "ARRGHH!" and receiving another "ARRGHH!" from the audience. She then turned and hugged the Headmistress as the room chatter accelerated, and everyone stood to say good-bye and to say they would never forget their time at The Willow.

As the ceremony drew to a close, the graduates gathered around Hope, their faces full of admiration and gratitude. The Kidd's mother, Sarah, stepped forward to represent the group.

"Headmistress Terwilliger, we cannot thank you enough for your impact on our daughters' lives. You have shaped their minds and spirits, preparing them for the world beyond these walls. Your dedication and love have not gone unnoticed, and we are forever grateful."

Hope smiled, her eyes misty. "It has been my honor and privilege to be part of your daughters' lives. They are ready to face whatever comes next, whether it be a family or the French Army, and I am confident they will make us all proud."

The Kidd shouted in French, "Ces méchants chiens!" and the Headmistress, this time, picked up a clam shell from behind her podium and waved it at her.

"What," the Kidd exclaimed. "I'm just talking about those French frogs!"

The Headmistress shrugged her shoulders, muttering, "Nasty dogs, indeed," and replaced the clam behind her podium.

The graduates and their parents erupted in laughter and applause, the sound echoing through the classroom and spilling into the garden beyond. It was a moment of pure joy and shared accomplishment—a fitting end to a journey that had shaped them all in ways they had scarcely imagined.

One by one, families stepped forward with their daughters to offer the Headmistress their thanks and tokens of gratitude. Soon, the podium and the famed arrow-and-clamshell demerit display were adorned with charming, thoughtful gifts: a bound book of poems tied with silk ribbon, a bolt of fine fabric, a drawstring pocket purse, a posy cup overflowing with fresh flowers, a small box of rare imported tea, and a lace collar stitched by a proud mother's hand. Each offering was placed with ceremony, transforming the front of the room into an arras of appreciation and affection.

s the girls and their families mingled—embracing, laughing, and wiping away tears—their unbreakable bonds were on full display, forged, tested, and cherished. The air shimmered with promise, a sense that their lives, newly broadened and brightened, were stretching toward futures rich with possibility.

As the last congratulations drifted into soft chatter, Hope stepped forward to inspect the gifts now adorning the podium. Her hand paused over a small, humble drawstring pocket—plain linen, hand-stitched with careful, uneven seams. A tiny slip of paper was tied to the cord, marked only with the initials. "HB."

Hope's breath caught.

No lavish ribbon, no expensive lace, no parental hands guiding its making. Just Hirana's quiet effort—the only girl who had stood alone today, without mother, father, aunt, or family friend to beam with pride beside her.

Hope lifted the little pouch with both hands, as though it were more fragile than porcelain. She traced the crooked stitching with her thumb, tenderly, reverently. Then she pressed it to her chest, closing her eyes as her composure faltered.

A tremor passed through her. Her shoulders shook.

She raised the pouch to her lips—just a soft, trembling kiss upon the cloth—and whispered, voice cracking,

"I will cherish this... forever."

A hush fell around her.

From across the room, Hirana watched with wide, uncertain eyes, her posture half-defensive, half-hopeful. When Hope finally looked up, tears shining, their gazes met.

For the first time all evening, Hirana smiled—not the polite, guarded smile she wore for strangers, but something softer… something opening.

Hope returned it with all the warmth she held in her heart for all her girls.

And in that quiet, wordless exchange, a bond formed as surely as any forged by blood—two lives, stitched together by a simple linen pocket and the ache of belonging.

When the guests and students at last drifted either home or to the dockside inn to await the morning tide, the twilight deepened to a cool, velvety blue. Captain Holloway took charge of Hirana's departure as he had her arrival, escorting her to the inn and seeing her settled for the night; the quiet guardian of both comings and goings.

Abigail, Eunice, Hope, and Hannah settled together around the long table—now cleared of pastries and plates, yet still glowing with the warmth of shared celebration. Their shoulders relaxed; their voices softened.

"What a day it was," Abigail murmured, letting her hand rest over her heart. "I don't think I expected to feel this proud. Or this tired."

Eunice laughed lightly. "I expected both. What I did not expect were all the gifts— it's as though Hope were running for public office."

"That," Hope said with a fond sigh, "and every girl glowing like the sun. I swear, I felt like the one graduating."

Hannah leaned back, exhausted but luminous. "Everything went so smoothly. Better than any of us dared hope."

A pause fell—warm, reflective.

Then Abigail exhaled, gaze drifting toward the staircase where the dormitories lay silent. "It was wonderful," she said. "Truly. But… we all saw the empty spaces too, didn't we?"

Eunice nodded slowly. "Aye. Poor Hirana—no parent standing beside her."

Hope's eyes softened. "She was the bravest of all. She came anyway and stood tall. Today was all about her, too."

Hannah folded her hands together. "Next year," she whispered, "we'll make sure none of them feel alone."

And the women sat quietly for a moment, letting the promise settle among them like the soft glow of the last candle on the table—steady, warm, unspoken, but utterly sure.

After a moment, Abigail spoke again. "To be honest, the empty spaces of our missing girls bothered me more than I would have expected. It was disappointing not have them here to finish our journey together."

Hannah straightened up and looked at her mother. "But that was not the goal. This is everyone's journey. Every girl must forge her own path, and each girl has. Nothing is disappointing about that."

Eunice nodded emphatically. "Look at Maria Allamby—veered off course, quite literally. Her husband, that pirate Stede Bonnet, whisked her off to parts unknown."

"Well, I don't know if that is Maria charting her own course exactly," Abigail added. "What was it you wrote, Hannah? That the 'mystery of Maria's fate lingers over the day like an unwelcome shadow'? Quite poetic, my dear."

"Mother! You spied on me?" Hannah exclaimed, scandalized.

Eunice sniffed with dry amusement. "My dear, your mother spies on all of us. She probably keeps a journal labeled for each of us."

Abigail raised her brows. "Who's to say I don't?"

Hope continued before Hannah could sputter further. "And Gulielma Maria—despite earning the right to graduate—is heading to England due to her grandfather's impending death in London… I don't know that the girl who arrived here last autumn would have been selfless enough to do that."

"I liked her," Hannah said softly.

"Yes," Hope agreed. "She transformed the most of any girl this year. No longer arrogant or sharp-tongued… she became wise, responsible."

Sarah added, "And an excellent marksman and swordsman."

"I understand, second only to Hannah?" Abigail said teasingly.

Sarah drew herself up. "Now hold one moment. The Kidd and I were better than she was."

"Oh?" Abigail replied innocently. "That's not what I heard."

"Heard? Heard from who?" Sarah demanded, but Hope's silence displayed conspicuous agreement.

Hope, choosing mercy, smoothed the moment with a warm tone. "Her absence today was felt deeply. A mark of the remarkable young woman she grew into."

Eunice chimed in, eyes twinkling, "And then there was Lena van Hoorn—our fairy-tale ending. I suspect this is exactly the journey she longed for. Her suitor from the ball inherits a tidy fortune, sweeps her off her feet, and they elope to Hartford. A perfect love story. Quite nauseating, really. But good for morale."

They all laughed gently, the sound soft in the warm, candlelit room.

Abigail's eyes welled with tears as she thought of the many journeys that had begun at The Willow. Despite the absences, this day was a celebration of the strength and perseverance of each young woman who had passed through its halls.

The Willow stood empty after the inaugural class had moved out, yet its walls still hummed with the promise of future generations. The staff busied themselves, stripping down beds, cleaning the hearth, scrubbing floors and chamber pots, and preparing for the next class to arrive. In the meantime, Abigail, her sister Eunice, and her daughters Sarah and Hannah stayed down at the local inn after all the guests vacated the premises. Abigail spent her days visiting wealthy landowners, recruiting potential tutors, and meticulously straightening out the following year's school budget, shifting old and new staff members with a wave of amusement in her eyes.

One morning, Sarah and Hannah appeared for breakfast dressed in trousers, shirts, and large, flowing scarves. Abigail and Eunice stopped with their tea cups to their lips, observing their energetic behavior.

"And where are you two off on this fine day?" Abigail asked.

Hannah laughed, and Sarah nodded with conviction, "Fishing."

"Fishing?" Eunice said with disgust.

"Yes," Hannah reassured. "We felt that our education here at The Willow was lacking since King Hendrick didn't show up with his brave Iroquoian warriors to teach us how to hunt and play lacrosse."

"Yes, mother," Sarah added. "Why can't women also catch the fish before frying it up in the pan?"

"But where… who?" Abigail asked, almost spilling her tea.

"Constable Hullabee offered, and we accepted," Hannah imparted.

Sarah said, "Mother, my John loved to fish. We thought it fitting to learn to fish in his honor. If he loved it so much, then I want to feel that same love."

Eunice added, "Just remember, when you are fishing, men don't care much for polite conversations. Though they do frequently use this excuse for not catching any fish."

"Yes," Abigail smiled at her sister as she reached for a slice of butter. "Well, if you're going fishing, you'd better catch one big enough to brag about at church!"

Eunice shook her head as the girls walked toward the entrance of the inn. "Of all things, fishing? Next thing you know, they'll be off joining a pirate crew."

CHAPTER 43

Next Class of 1717, August, 1716

AS THE NEW STUDENTS ARRIVED at The Willow, nervous glances and wary expressions were exchanged between daughters and their parents. The scene buzzed with the usual hustle and bustle of arrival day: carriages rolled up, daughters stepped out clutching their bags, and belongings were sorted into room assignments by dutiful servants. Parents lingered nearby, reluctant to let go but knowing the time had come to part ways.

Headmistress Terwilliger stood poised on the grand staircase, her presence both commanding and reassuring. She watched with a practiced eye, gauging the new arrivals and their families. Her past students, Hannah and Sarah, stood nearby with Abigail and Eunice, observing the proceedings with a mix of curiosity and nostalgia.

As each family proceeded into the classroom, Abigail handed over all the letters from the parents to the Headmistress. "Just repeat what you did for my daughters, and everything will be as smooth as butter," she said with a confident smile.

Hope took the stack of parchments and, with an admiring glance at Hannah and Sarah, said, "If only I had an entire classroom of, ah, Huntingtons to teach."

"I do have another nine-year-old daughter named Abigail. But alas, she will not be ready for a few more years." The flicker in Abigail's eye showed that her involvement should remain concealed, ensuring that no one would be the wiser about where all the money it took to build the school's impressive establishment came from. "I've adjusted the tuition to support the budget my daughters tabulated from their class activities," she added.

Hope frowned slightly, "Really? I had no idea you were spying on my spending."

Hannah answered with a confessional smile, "Headmistress, why would you ever be surprised? You did teach us sound business practices, did you not?"

Hope chuckled, shaking her head. "I suppose I did. And it seems you learned those lessons well."

Sarah smirked, "I'm just glad coffee didn't blow the budget."

"On the contrary," Hope laughed. "I think it single-handedly forged a bond with the community. To this very day, people are stopping by to have a cup."

The sails on the sloop popped open as they set off from New Haven on their journey to their large stone house overlooking the Hudson River in Manhattan. After a summer spent helping Hope get the Willow ready for the new autumn cohort of girls, the four women were finally heading home. Abigail looked at her sister, Eunice, then at her daughters, and sighed. "Your younger brothers and sisters eagerly await our arrival."

Hannah smiled. "Funny thing, I think I've missed them. They have all grown up more as well. Maybe they will be a touch more tolerable."

Abigail nodded. "You and Sarah could teach them how to use a sword."

Hannah quickly added, "And pistols?"

Abigail remained silent for a moment, not wanting to provoke that argument.

"Uncle Willie taught me when I was just their age—" Hannah started.

Abigail considered it, then gave a noncommittal nod, neither fully accepting nor outright rejecting the idea. "We'll see," she said finally, leaving the possibility open but undefined.

"Mother, what news of the Collegiate School moving to New Haven?" Sarah asked.

"Why, Sarah?" her sister jested. "Do you want another formal ball?"

Sarah's steely green eyes peered at her through slits before saying, "What of it?"

"Oh?" Hannah gasped. "I should like that as well. What says you, Mother? You think we could be invited back for their social get-togethers?"

Abigail only gave them another noncommittal shrug as she looked out over the water with a feeling of accomplishment.

As the ship gently swayed on the waters of Long Island Sound, Abigail, Eunice, Hannah, and Sarah stood on deck, enjoying the crisp sea breeze. The sun was beginning to peak, casting a golden glow across the sky and the water below. The new class at The Willow had left them all in high spirits, but the young sister's curiosity had taken a different turn.

"What boys will be coming from the new Collegiate School?"

Hannah asked.

"Yes, mother," Sarah added, her eyes alight with curiosity. "How did you manage to convince the Connecticut legislature and the Board of Trustees to move the Collegiate School from Old Saybrook to New Haven?"

Abigail smiled, pride and accomplishment playing across her features. She walked over to the ship's shrouds, leaning against them as she gathered her thoughts, the ship's gentle sway providing a soothing backdrop to her recollections.

"Well, girls," Abigail started, her voice carrying a tone of reflection. "It wasn't a simple task. It required careful planning, strategic alliances, and, of course, a bit of cunning…."

"And lots of pirate money," Eunice added.

Hannah and Sarah, sensing the gravity of the story unfolding, moved closer, their attention entirely on their mother.

"You see," Abigail continued. "The first step was to understand the key players in the legislature and what motivated them. The promise of economic growth drove some…."

"And pirate money drove others," Eunice said.

Abigail's face puckered with a deep breath as she brushed her finger under her chin. She asked, "Need I say more? Each time a higher bid came into the trustees to nominate a different town, New Haven's pot would ripen just that much more. What else could I do with Henry Avery's pirated money?" she mused. "While still in Old Saybrook, I saw the few remaining students and tutors occasionally continued to study and teach, believing that better days were on the horizon. And as the pieces began to fall into place, the promise of a new beginning in New Haven grew ever closer in their hearts. At that point, all that was needed was someone to provide a small stipend for each person to relocate while the schoolhouse was being completed."

Abigail looked at her sister and daughters, her voice filled with resolve. "We played our part in securing New Haven as the new location. Upon hearing of our substantial pledge and the clear necessity for expansion, the legislature quickly allocated additional funding to the trustees for a new building. Shortly after our book drop in Old Saybrook's overwhelmed community, the trustees of the Collegiate School, recognizing the potential for a brighter future, voted to move the school to New Haven. As we speak, the building is being planned and built at this very moment."

Their journey continued, the sloop cutting through the water with ease.

Hannah and Sarah stood at the bow, looking out over the expanse of the Long Island Sound, each lost in their thoughts about what awaited them at home. The anticipation of seeing their siblings, the comfort of their familiar surroundings, and the memories of their time at The Willow blended into a mix of excitement and nostalgia.

After a quick stop in Flushing to drop off Aunt Eunice and pledging to see her whenever possible, they waved farewells.

Eunice cast them a parting goodbye, "The only thing sustaining me is the knowledge of your return—my life feels like a never-ending Sunday meeting without you."

Approaching Manhattan, the skyline came into view, and the bustling activity of the port could be seen and smelled even from a distance. Abigail took a deep breath, feeling the weight of her family's responsibilities and the joy of reuniting her children. Then, her thoughts fell to her oldest son. "I wonder what Jacob is doing right now?" she said to Hannah and Sarah, standing next to her, as she tried to recognize distant landmarks of the rapidly expanding metropolis.

Sarah looked at her mother with a blank expression. "Is he with Father in Albany?" she asked.

"Or maybe he's still with Andreas," Hannah said, a look of regret etched upon her brow.

Then Sarah dared to ask. "Does he know about Father's other family in Albany? And does he know he has a son waiting for him at home?"

"Ha, our brother the pirate," Hannah laughed. "A child in every port."

"I'm ready to be home," Abigail said, looking at her daughters with a frown. By ignoring the question, she was signalling that she did not want to discuss their father's second family again, but Hannah persisted.

"I wonder what father's other family is like," she said.

Her mother grunted to clear her throat. "Must not be too happy. The last I heard, your brother joined the Rangers and is tracking renegade Iroquois and Algonquin warriors out of French Canada in the Green Mountains of Vermont."

"Jacob is a Ranger? Whatever for?" Sarah asked, concerned.

Abigail snorted with satisfaction. "Probably to get away from his new stepmother," she said. "Now, who's ready to be home?"

"Ready as ever," Sarah replied with the expression of some regret. "Although

I'm going to miss New Haven."

"Let's hope the little ones have been practicing their manners. I can't wait to see them all, but especially Jacob's little Andreas, ah, I meant Jan. There's just something special about him that I love," Hannah laughed, expressing her hopes. "I'm so glad you went to Jasper and Maggie to bring him home to us."

"I just hope Jacob doesn't have them scattered all over God's creation," Abigail expressed her fears while letting her daughter call the boy what she will.

"But if he does, we know you'll find them and bring them home," Sarah laughed, and Hannah nodded in agreement.

"I just hope some of my own children realize I'm their mother," the family's matriarch murmured.

"Oh, mother," Sarah said, hugging her. "We know you are our mother."

Hannah, standing in the mix with a knowing smile, added, "Though I daresay you've spent so much time with us lately, the others must think we're your favorites." She laughed awkwardly, but each of them knew her words held a playful edge of truth.

Abigail gave her a side glance—sharp, but not unkind. She didn't deny it. Instead, she moved closer to her daughters, first brushing a stray curl from Sarah's face, then squeezing Hannah's hand, and resting her chin momentarily on her elder girl's shoulder with a warm hug.

"I love you each differently," she said softly. "But wholly. Even Jan."

"Jan? Are we to call Jacob's son Andreas 'Jan' now?" Sarah asked.

"Ha," Hannah chided. "I think she doesn't want to hear the name of my Andreas all day long."

"No," Abigail said with a defensive frown. Then her eyes softened, and she said, "Maybe. I like the name Jan. It reminds me of our Barbary pirate grandfather, Jan Janszoon van Salee."

"Because you want him to grow up to be a pirate?" Sarah laughed.

The moment passed in warm silence, filled not with protest, but the quiet understanding that Hannah wasn't entirely wrong—and that perhaps, being the favorite came with a bit more responsibility than privilege.

"Speaking of pirates. I hope Mr. McDermot will be happy to see me. Has he found another warm bed to sleep in, is a real question," Hannah moaned.

Abigail's expression softened with a touch of regret. "About your cat..." she began gently.

The girls turned to her, each wearing the same look—eyebrows raised, eyes narrowing in silent question.

Abigail cleared her throat delicately. "Mr. McDermot has, well... crossed the bar," she said, using the old sailor's phrase with the kind of reverence a pirate might reserve for a fallen mate.

Hannah blinked. "You mean he's dead? Oh, mother, why didn't you tell me this before?"

"And spoil all your fun? He was almost twenty. That's very old for a cat. He passed in his sleep under the empty birdcage in my office," Abigail confirmed. "Jan and your siblings helped Lawton bury him proper, right beneath the wisteria. Fitting, I thought, considering he caught his lion's share of rats under those very vines and around the cannon."

The girls fell silent, a blend of sadness and faint amusement flickering across their faces as they remembered Captain Kidd's cat's antics and his guarded ruby earring.

"He died a legend," Abigail added, managing a small smile. "As any proper ship's cat should." Then with a perk, she said, "But not to worry, Jan, well, it was actually Lawton, found another kitten, ah, probably one of his grandchildren—he was always on the prowl. They named it just—"

Hannah impetuously asked, "What?"

"McDermot."

Hannah let out a sigh of pent-up anxiety as Abigail smiled, knowing that no matter the challenges ahead, they were stronger and more united than ever before. The year's journey had shaped them all, and now, as they returned to Manhattan, they were ready to face whatever the future held.

CHAPTER 44

Yale College, August, 1718

OVER FIVE YEARS HAD PASSED since Abigail first read the request of her pirate client, Henry Avery, to build a school for girls. Now she stood before the newly finished Yale College hall, its stark timbers looming against a low gray sky. The students, all males in their late teens to early twenties, crossing the yard seemed small beneath it, and Abigail felt an unease stir within her, as though Avery's long shadow had reached all the way to New Haven and settled in the mortar. Now, she finally felt her obligations were doubly fulfilled. She had traveled back and forth from Manhattan to New Haven so many times that the Connecticut colony felt like her second home. Both of her daughters had turned into women here, and Eunice practically lived here year-round so she could visit with Constable Zachariah Hullabee.

The new building for the Collegiate School at New Haven was now completed and ready to welcome the students who had been studying in nearby homes for the last two academic years. The Board of Trustees, who had overseen the project, took great pride in the successful establishment of the new premises. Constructed with meticulous care and attention to detail by Mr. MacCreedy's business associate, Henry Caner, the building stood as a symbol of progress and a steadfast commitment to higher education.

Eunice stood back, surveying the building with a discerning eye. "A fine structure indeed," she quipped with a wry smile to her nieces, Hannah and Sarah. "It's a pity all this craftsmanship has to be squandered on a schoolhouse for boys. Imagine the progress we might see if such efforts were put into educating young ladies."

Abigail stood inside the impressive structure, her heart swelling with pride and accomplishment. The school's relocation from Old Saybrook to New Haven had been irregular, fraught with challenges and uncertainties. Yet, the new school stood here, a beacon of knowledge and opportunity for future generations.

She couldn't help but think of her daughters by her side as she walked through the halls. Both had spent part of their formative years in New Haven, and it had shaped them in ways she could not have imagined. One would soon be leaving a piece of her heart here, forever entwined with the spirit of the place.

"Yes, I wonder what Headmistress Terwilliger could do with a building like this?" Sarah marveled as they looked into each class and bedroom with satisfaction.

"What do you mean?" Hannah huffed. "Would you want to go to school with this many girls? Not me. We had enough."

"Well, only six by the end," Abigail corrected, alluding, as she still often did, to the class members who left before graduation.

"Mother, it's not their fault," Hannah chided. "Not every girl—or boy, for that matter—is suited to a full year of schooling. Most families still think that if a girl takes that much time away from home, she'll come back a year older, none the wiser, and halfway to being an old maid."

"That brings me to the subject of Eliza Marble," Abigail dropped into the conversation.

Sarah spun on her heel to face her mother. "Ah? Mother? What of our sweet Eliza?"

Abigail sighed and glanced at her daughters, her tone somber but laced with purpose. "I thought you should know, your old classmate, Eliza. She, like Marie Allamby, was already married before she came to The Willow. I didn't know this until after graduation. Her mother hid it, thinking we would not have let her into the school otherwise. She had lost a child just a month before we met her."

"Oh, no," Hannah cried.

Nodding with sadness, Abigail continued, "Her mother placed her at The Willow to get her away from her husband, a no-good scoundrel named Edward Low. But immediately upon graduation, she went straight back to him in Boston."

Eunice raised an eyebrow and quipped, "Well, I suppose distance really does make the heart grow fonder... or at least gives poor judgment a little breathing room."

"Do you feel like an old maid?" Abigail asked, looking first at Hannah and then at Sarah.

"Sometimes yes," Hannah said, "but other times I feel like I'm destined for greater things."

Sarah nodded in agreement.

Abigail frowned slightly, studying them both. "These greater things do not supplant having a family… do they?"

Hannah quickly shook her head. "No, Mother. We want families of our own—and to carry on what you've begun. We only wish to do it in our own way—and time." She looked at her sister for confirmation, but only received a look of melancholy.

Hannah touched Abigail's arm, echoing what she saw in her sister's tired eyes. "Truly, Mother. Tradition still matters to us."

Abigail exhaled, a quiet relief softening her features, saying, "Not to worry, my darlings. I dare say all those business classes Hope provided will come in handy when you two take over a few companies I have acquired through our pirate-backed Albany Investment Group. Ah, in your own time, of course."

"What do you have in mind?" Hannah asked with piqued curiosity. Despite what she'd just said, she was still eager to hone her newfound business acumen.

"Oh, let's see. There is a developing opportunity for whaling off the newly formed territory of Nova Scotia."

"Whaling?" she said with interest. "As in whale oil for lamps?"

"And other things like soap, candles, and tanning leather. Believe me, it is much better for tanning hides than dog droppings."

"It's got to be," Hannah said, causing everyone to laugh at the atrocious smell that usually emanates from a tannery.

"And then there is a shipyard in the James River area of Virginia."

"Shipyard?"

"That's right. The Golden Age of Piracy is coming to an end. With Blackbeard Edward Teach, Calico Jack Rackham, Black Sam Bellamy, and our beloved Black Caesar either dead or on the run, piracy is being crushed. Royal pardons issued to sailors offering amnesty have caused many to abandon the profession. I am afraid our traditional family business is also destined to dwindle to death as well," Abigail lamented.

Eunice sighed, "Every journey has its destination, as every tale must find its close. What would our great-grandfather Jan Janszoon van Salee do if not for pirating? Fishing, perhaps?"

"But what of our cousin Frances?" Hannah was not hiding the fear in her voice.

"Frances Farthington Spriggs?" Abigail sighed. "He is still at large, I suppose; I haven't heard hide nor hair of his activities. He deals his loot with his father in Hempsted, not me. Hah, he must have given up on you, my dear." She sighed again. "In this new light, it is most advantageous to our shareholders and us to divest our holdings into legitimate ventures in export shipping and import trade, business properties, and land holdings."

"So... what are you really saying?" Hannah asked hesitantly. "Is this truly the final chapter in a general history of the pirates?" She shifted her gaze, stealing a quick look to the side before lowering her voice. "And maybe... now... Can you tell me Henry Avery's real story?"

Inherently, Abigail knew her daughter could now begin to put the final touches on her clandestine book about pirates, most of whom had once been quiet clients of the family. And as long as no references to their own business dealings or the pirate bank were mentioned within its revealing pages, she would allow the work to continue. She also knew it was meant to remain her daughter's private venture, a secret stitched together in stolen hours. So she held her tongue, offering only a nod, neither encouragement nor criticism, and let the silence stand between them like a pact unspoken.

"Mother," Sarah said with a hint of anguish. "I do not think I am ready for such business obligations. Maybe when I'm older, right now, I'd like to live at home, sorting through my thoughts about John until I can find in my heart to love again."

Everyone remained silent, realizing that poor Sarah was still vanquished in thought by her loss at such a young age. Hannah's sisterly spirit chimed in, trying to elevate her temperament. "Okay, but when I rule the world like the Amazonian, one-breasted Queen Calafia of California, you must be one of my underlings."

Sarah's lower lip tightened, then began to quiver. Hannah thought she was on the verge of bursting into tears, but to her surprise—and to the visible relief of Abigail and Eunice—Sarah forced a resolute grin.

"I'm just saying, John set a high bar for the next one on my list, that's all."

"For me as well," Abigail agreed. "I thought the part of your heart that was broken was your pirating part."

"Not bloody likely," Sarah growled, and before any of them could protest, Abigail gathered her daughters into an unexpectedly tight embrace. Eunice stepped closer, slipping her arms around them as well, her hands resting gently on their shoulders, steadying and holding the moment together.

They lingered there longer than any of them intended, breathing in one another's warmth, letting old defenses melt.

When at last they eased apart, Sarah's voice was hushed. "We should do that more often. It felt… wonderful."

"I agree," Hannah whispered, her gaze meeting her mother's shimmering eyes with new tenderness.

"Me too," Abigail managed, drawing a handkerchief from her sleeve to blot the tears on her cheeks—tears she no longer cared to hide.

"Hey, what else do you have up your sleeve?" Hannah laughed. "I thought you said you would give me that alehouse and brewery on Wall Street?"

"I can, now that I know you won't drink all the profits." Then she smiled deviously and recanted, "Well, the heck with profits, eh? Arrgh, pirates do like their drinks."

Regaining their attention to the building's architecture and detailed woodwork, Eunice commented with a nod of satisfaction. "From what I see today, every aspect of this building meets the highest standards. Classrooms are equipped, and the library is stocked with an impressive array of books and manuscripts—"

"Including one—from Sir Isaac Newton," Abigail added.

Hannah immediately protested, "Oh, Mother, I thought that was for The Willow. How can the Headmistress deliver her inaugural lesson on gravity without it?"

"Didn't you learn anything while in school?" Eunice rebuked. "Gravity is everywhere. Not just at the Willow."

"So are nefarious people who would like to have Newton's work in their private library," Hannah said with a sardonic laugh that didn't belie the seriousness she clearly felt on the subject.

Eunice said, "That must be why Hope insisted on having the book under lock and key. Treasure not guarded is treasure soon parted."

"Good point, Auntie," Sarah laughed, touching the largest slate board she'd ever seen. "Pirate booty can be surprisingly good if used for the right purpose."

"I say we are lucky to have any books in this library at all," Abigail added.

Both daughters frowned.

"You see," she began. "When the books first arrived in Old Saybrook, we had to store them in local homes while decisions were made about the fate of the college. In those years, the people became fiercely protective of the books stored in their homes. They felt a strong sense of ownership and believed the volumes rightfully belonged to their town. There was considerable resistance when the decision was made to move the books to New Haven."

Hannah and Sarah listened intently as Abigail continued. "The constables had to go door to door, confiscating the volumes. Many people were reluctant to give them up, and despite their efforts, many volumes remain in Old Saybrook to this day. The townsfolk went to extraordinary lengths to prevent the books from leaving. They broke the wheels of the carts and even disabled one of the bridges leading out of town."

Sarah's eyes widened in surprise. "Did they really go that far?" she asked.

Abigail nodded. "Yes, they did. Eventually, only about half of the nearly 2,000 books made it to the new library here in New Haven. It was a disorderly process, but those who believed in the future of this school were determined to see it through."

As they walked through the room filled with shelves of books, Abigail added, "Each of these books represents not just knowledge but the perseverance and dedication of those who fought to build this institution. It's a reminder of the lengths people will go to for what they believe in."

As they left the library, Abigail's bedeviling emerald green eyes were ablaze. "Yes, I dare say, if Henry Avery were here today, he'd be proud of what his stolen money has accomplished," she mused.

"Maybe they should call the place Avery College?" Hannah suggested.

"Yes, that has a certain ring to it—an all-encompassing welcoming tone," Sarah agreed.

"Sorry, but the naming was not up to me. One figure stood out prominently among the people involved: Our old friend, Cotton Mather."

"Good God!" Eunice gasped. "Praise be they didn't name it after that canting crow—Boston's pulpit peacock, preening like a pint-sized evangelical pope."

Sarah laughed. "I'm sorry, but I can't help myself—every time his name is mentioned, I start to giggle. Why is it that the more religious a man claims to be, the more he seems to wrestle with demons of his own making?"

"I know what you mean, my dear," Eunice quipped. "Half the reverends I've met look like they're losing the bout."

"Mather particularly appreciated Elihu Yale's generous donation of books, supplies, and the portrait of King George to the school's cause," Abigail said.

"Ha, if he only knew his letter went nowhere and that portrait used to adorn our washroom," Hannah laughed.

"Oh no. His letter did end up somewhere. In my Manhattan desk drawer, right next to the original Henry Avery correspondence." She looked up at the portrait affixed to the library's wall and took in a deep breath of satisfaction. "Mather felt that since he personally had written to Yale, asking for his support, and Yale had responded with overwhelming generosity, he felt obligated to name it 'Yale College.' This gesture was met with unanimous approval from the board, and I believe the signage is already being designed."

Abigail continued speaking amongst shifting eyes and looks of dissatisfaction. "I didn't mind the naming of the school Yale College because I don't think I ever told you—Headmistress Hope Terwilliger's real name?"

Both daughters stood with bated breath, waiting to hear her following words to what they assumed was a long-held secret.

"It is Hopestill—Merryweather—"

"Merryweather Yale?" Sarah laughed.

"Of course, I remember that," Hannah added.

"Yes indeed, Yale," Abigail finished, looking at her smiling daughters with satisfaction.

"I almost had forgotten myself," Eunice admitted. "Her father and the interloper Elihu were brothers. She told us that fact at her father's home."

"So, in reality," Abigail concluded, "in my mind, the school is named after the Headmistress, Hope Yale."

Each of them, standing in the hall of future learning, reflected on the journey that had brought everything to this point. The vision of a thriving educational institution had once seemed like a distant dream, but it had become a reality through determination and unwavering support. The Collegiate School, now Yale College, was poised to make a significant impact, not just in New Haven but in the broader landscape of education, not to mention a few happier girls back at The Willow.

For Abigail, the moving of the Collegiate School was more than a professional achievement; it was a personal milestone. It represented the culmination of years of hard work, sacrifice, and faith in a vision that had finally come to fruition. Looking around, she felt a profound sense of fulfillment, knowing she had played a part in creating something enduring and meaningful.

Abigail, Eunice, and her daughters decided to visit The Willow one last time before heading home.

"I can't believe this is the beginning of The Willow's third year. Pretty soon, it will all feel ancient," Sarah said, shaking her head in amusement.

As they entered through the front door, their shared wave of nostalgia was almost immediately disrupted by a concussive 'BOOM' blasting through the interior from the outside garden. They could see through the windows a group of young women gathered in the backyard, handling muskets, and Hannah exclaimed, "That is what we did, down to the exact details."

"Wouldn't it be strange if every year you had to repeat the same thing over again?" Sarah asked her sister.

"Indeed, it has always puzzled me, who would want to do something like that?"

"Oh, come now. People do it all the time," Eunice said. "It'd be nothing more than listening to the same sermon every year from the same preacher, over and over again, without variation; such too is the life of a teacher."

While they were exiting the back door, one of the young students raised her hand and, when acknowledged by Hope, gestured to her musket and asked the question, "Headmistress, what is the cost of such a weapon, the musket hand cannon?"

Each of the women cocked their heads, simultaneously noticing something familiar about the young girl. Sarah's eyes lit up, "Isn't that Dolly? The baker's daughter?"

"She is part of the Charitable Endowment set up to enroll local students," Abigail whispered.

The Headmistress looked thoughtfully at the muskets before answering. "The cost, Dolly, depends on where it was made and if it was bejeweled with any adornments. But in general, it ranges from ten shillings for a second-hand item to over three pounds for a higher-quality piece made by a fine craftsman, such as what is found in France or the Netherlands. Why do you ask?"

Dolly hesitated to answer, but when she finally did, it showed the depth of knowledge she had already acquired from working in the community bread shop, knowledge that would benefit all those aristocratic daughters privileged to attend the Willow. "I was just wondering how many loaves of bread I'd have to bake to pay for such a boomstick; that's all."

"Ha," Eunice laughed. "Dolly's the perfect case of 'Ox sense over Opera sense' that this school needs to teach its students a rounded curriculum."

"Whose idea was this endowment?" Hannah asked.

"Hope," Abigail answered with admiration. "A stroke of genius if you ask me. We left the choice up to Reverend Morton to pick amongst the qualified candidates."

"The Reverend? But why?" Sarah asked.

"Twofold, really. By having him choose, people who wish their daughters to go to the school by free subscription feel obliged to go to his church and, by association, donate to the orphanage."

"And secondly," Eunice added. "Mothers of the daughters, such as the Baker's wife, Hattie, are a non-stop advertisement to everyone with a hankering for gossip, which is everyone in this town, of course, including me."

As they emerged into the yard, Hope only looked surprised for a moment before seamlessly integrating their presence into the ongoing activities. "Sarah," she called out warmly, "please make sure we have a few musket balls laid out."

Sarah frowned, and then, without hesitation, she put her head down and proceeded to walk toward the table laden with firearm paraphernalia.

Before Sarah had taken more than a couple of steps, a voice called back, "Yes, Headmistress." Sarah stopped abruptly, realizing a person was standing beside the weapons table, with her back to them, under the weeping willow branches.

Sarah's mouth went agape as Hannah, directly behind her, recognized the girl and called out, "Kidd?"

The Kidd turned, standing with a hand in the shot bag, rolling a few onto the table. "Hey," she said with a bright, mischievous smile. "I thought I missed you two. My carriage was late. Had to subdue a few bandits along the way with my sword."

Both Spragg girls puckered their faces and flattened their smiles, unsure, before Hannah asked, "No one told me you wanted to be a teacher?"

"You mean a teacher like my father was for you two?"

Eunice whispered to her sister, "Wouldn't it be amusing if the famed privateer, Captain William Kidd, went down in the history books as a teacher of girls?"

Abigail gritted her teeth and flattened her lips to growl from deep in her throat, "Not bloody likely."

Dolly could not contain herself—she leapt up darted forward, throwing her arms around both Sarah and Hannah in a fierce, breathless hug, nearly knocking them off balance before laughing and retreating.

"Ladies," the Headmistress announced to the class, clapping her hands together to introduce, pointing to smiling Hannah. "Hannah was the best marksman from the Willow's inaugural class."

The Kidd didn't hesitate to agree, bowing deeply, relinquishing her position at the shooting table.

Feigning indignation, Sarah, with a playful tone, said, "I can shoot one of those little things as well."

With a clicking of her clamshell castanets, Hope addressed her, "We only have time for one more 'live' demonstration before midday dinner. Hannah, would you mind?"

Hannah's eyes lit up at the sight of the weapons prominently displayed on the table, her gaze as sharp and focused as a hawk. A wave of yearning washed over her, recalling vivid memories. She remembered shooting the would-be pirate in the back of the head as he tried to rob her mother's sloop in Flushing Bay. Killing the arsonist merchant pirate Thomas Clark after the worthless filibuster shot at her mother, only to kill Sarah's husband, John. Then she remembered having her twin pistols ready to defend when her sister Sarah was masquerading as Black Sam Bellamy's daughter, Hirana. Muskets had become a part of her soul, imparting an addictive, fearless spirit of confidence that she not only loved but craved in this uncertain world of pirates, Indians, the French, and ordinary predators.

The Kidd said with wide open eyes and hissing laughter to the captivated students:

"You're not going to believe your eyes—or ears,
For she'll silence your doubts and conquer your fears.
Everything she does with precision shows.
Because my father taught her all that she knows."

Hannah nodded to the Kidd as she approached the muskets. She stood solemnly with her feet planted firmly in the lush garden grass, surveying the accouterments. She reached out to deftly feel the wadding between her fingers, then brought it to her nose to smell its oily residue, before biting bits of it into her teeth. She brushed her free hand across the sleek powderhorn while dropping her other hand from her mouth to finger the musket balls seductively, grasping two in her hand. Then, with a deep sigh, a wild, crazed look came over her face as she gritted her teeth and picked up the well-balanced hand cannon by the barrel to slowly slide the ramrod out into the hand holding the balls.

She glanced over her shoulder, no longer the mild woman who had strolled onto the lawn mere minutes earlier. The wide-eyed students watched, frozen, as a spark lit up Hannah's pirating face. Her emerald eyes flashed—steady, sharp, and daring. And with a wicked grin over her shoulder, she offered a rogue's warning to the class, the kind whispered before a plunge into danger.

"Ready?"

WHO'S WHO IN *THE WILLOW*

MARIE ALLAMBY

At 21, Marie Allamby believed she had married into stability when she wed Stede Bonnet in 1709. Daughter of the seasoned sea captain–turned–Barbadian planter William Allamby, she entered the marriage with hope, grief already etched into her young life after the loss of more than one child in infancy. Her husband inherited a plantation three miles east of Bridgetown, yet the comforts of land and status did little to steady the turbulence within their household. Whispers of failing finances, Stede's brooding temper, and his restless yearning for something beyond the cane fields haunted their marriage.

Marie sensed the final unraveling when Stede secretly purchased a sloop, christened it the *Revenge*, armed it with ten guns, and hired a seventy-man crew. Without explanation or farewell, he slipped away from their plantation and abandoned his gentleman's life to become a pirate. Marie learned later that he sailed under aliases—Captain Edwards and Captain Thomas—while fleeing the reach of the Admiralty.

News drifted back to her in tatters: Stede linking forces with Edward Teach, the infamous Blackbeard; the hijacking of ships throughout the West Indies; Stede's own incompetence at sea; his near death after battle; Blackbeard's manipulation in stripping him of command. Finally came the report from Charleston: captured on November 8, 1718, tried, and condemned to hang.

Marie bore this final blow with the same quiet endurance she had shown in burying her children. After his execution, she retreated into the only life left to her—the plantation, the silence, and the determined effort to shield herself and the Allamby name from the ruin her husband had chosen.

ANDREAS ANDREAS, AKA ANDREAS GRUBER

Andreas is the semi-fictitious uncle of Hans Gruber; both escaped their Rhineland village before the French army invaded, fearing conscription into the German military [*Newlander* Series]. Andreas is the twin brother of Hans' father, Dr. Christian Gruber, and was once trained as an assassin in the army during his youth. He is now a wanted man. While in Manhattan, Andreas met and fell in love with Hannah, but Abigail drove him away, sending her oldest son, Jacob, with him to Albany to live with his unfaithful father, Edward Spragg.

SAMUEL BELLAMY

Samuel "Black Sam" Bellamy was an infamous English pirate born in 1689 in the parish of Hittisleigh on Dartmoor in Devon, Kingdom of England. He became a sailor at a young age and, in his late teens, he joined the Royal Navy, where he fought in several battles. Although there has been speculation that he may have had a wife and child, there is no definite historical proof either way. Turning to piracy, he eventually captained the ship "Whydah Gally," which he famously captured from the slave trade. Known for his democratic pirate code and relatively humane treatment of his crew, Bellamy earned the nickname "Robin Hood of the Seas." His career was cut short when the Whydah Gally sank in a storm off the coast of Cape Cod in 1717. He had been coming home to see his daughter Hirana, and the storm led to the death of Bellamy and most of his crew. Despite his brief career, Black Sam Bellamy remains one of the most romanticized and well-known figures in pirate lore.

HIRANA BELLAMY

The daughter of the pirate Samuel Bellamy and Goody Hallett, the "Witch of Wellfleet."

SARAH "THE KIDD" BRADLEY

Born in 1696 in New York, **Sarah** was the stepdaughter of Captain William Kidd and Sarah Bradley. In 1731, she married Joseph Latham in Alstonfield, Staffordshire, England. They had at least two sons, John and William. Sarah passed away on August 26, 1743, at the age of 47.

BLACK CAESAR

Black Caesar was a West African pirate who operated during the Golden Age of Piracy. Once a tribal chieftain, he was captured and enslaved but escaped captivity and turned to piracy in the Caribbean. Known for his strength and cunning, Caesar became a trusted lieutenant of Blackbeard aboard the *Queen Anne's Revenge*. Following Blackbeard's death in 1718, Caesar was captured during a raid on Ocracoke, North Carolina. Accounts suggest he was tried and hanged for piracy in Williamsburg, Virginia. His story remains a symbol of resilience, rising from enslavement to infamy on the high seas.

WILLIAM BRADFORD

William Bradford was born in 1663 in Leicestershire, England, and later became one of colonial America's most influential early printers. After immigrating to the New World, he established himself in Manhattan, where his press became a bustling center of intellectual exchange. Beyond newspapers, Bradford produced almanacs, charts, pamphlets, legal documents, plays, and books that shaped the cultural and literary life of the colonies. His reputation for skill and discretion eventually led him to manage Abigail Spragg's publishing enterprise, *Metropolis*, where he oversaw the careful production of select manuscripts and guarded its more sensitive ventures.

Bradford also played a formative role in American printing history when he famously printed Governor Robert Hunter's play, *Androboros,* and redirected a young Benjamin Franklin to the Philadelphia shop of his son, Andrew. This act helped set Franklin on his legendary path.

He continued working until the end of his long life, dying in 1752 in New York City, leaving a legacy foundational to American journalism and the colonial exchange of ideas.

CAPTAIN WILLIAM KIDD

Captain William Kidd, born around 1645 in Dundee, Scotland, became one of history's most noted pirates, though he started his maritime career as a respectable privateer. Moving to New York City, he married the widow Sarah Bradley Cox Oort, who already had two daughters, Elizabeth and Sarah. He was commissioned by the English government in 1695 to hunt pirates and French vessels, commanding the ship *Adventure Galley*. Kidd's mission turned to infamy in 1698 when he captured the Quedagh Merchant, a ship carrying valuable cargo under a false French registry and flag. This act led to his branding as a pirate. Upon returning to Boston in 1699, Kidd was arrested and sent to England for trial. Despite his defense that he was acting under his privateer commission, he was used as a scapegoat, found guilty of piracy, and hanged until he was severely dead at Execution Dock, London.

PATIENCE CARR

Patience, born in Jamestown, Rhode Island, on February 14, 1701, was one of eleven children of Edward Carr and Hannah Stanton (whose name is changed in the book to her aunt Waite, so as not to be confused with Hannah Spragg).

Most notably, she was the granddaughter of Governors Caleb Carr and Nicholas Easton, men whose names still carried weight across Rhode Island and the New Haven Colony long after their deaths. Though they both died before she was born, their presence lingered in family lore—stories retold by aunts, uncles, and old neighbors who spoke of them with equal parts admiration and amusement.

She learned that they both had been deeply woven into the colony's civic and political life: a commissioner for Newport, an officer involved in militia affairs, and steady figures people turned to when disputes rattled the wharves or tempers flared in the taverns. Around the Carr household, tales often resurfaced of their service on the General Court of Trials, where they were said to judge firmly but with a knowing pragmatism. Patience heard more than once that they understood the lifeblood of a coastal town did not always arrive by proper channels—and that when sure sea-worn captains came bearing "unexpected prosperity," eyes had a remarkable ability to drift politely elsewhere.

MRS. HANNAH GIBBARD CLARK (THE WIDOW CLARK)

Mrs. Clark was married to Senior Thomas Clark, born in 1637 in Boston, Suffolk County, Massachusetts Bay Colony, the son of Deacon George Clark and Sarah Bowtell. As the son of early settlers, he came of age during a period of rapid growth and transformation in New England. On May 20, 1663, Thomas married Hannah in Milford, Connecticut, New Haven Colony. Together, they raised at least six sons and three daughters, helping to strengthen and populate their developing community. Both Thomas and Hannah were active participants in local affairs, and their son Thomas likely continued the family's tradition of civic—and possibly religious—service.

THOMAS CLARK

Son of Thomas Clark and Hannah Gibbard (the widow, Mrs. Clark).

BUNTY DOUGHARTY

Fictitious baker's wife who had a daughter, Dolly.

JEREMIAH DUMMER SR.

Jeremiah Dummer Sr. was a prominent early American silversmith and civic leader in colonial New England. Born in Newbury, Massachusetts, in 1645, he became one of America's first and most respected silversmiths, celebrated for his fine craftsmanship and intricate designs. His work is considered among the finest of the period, with many surviving pieces now held in museums and private collections.

Beyond his artistry, Dummer was active in public life, serving as a Boston selectman and a militia captain. Throughout his long career, he played a significant role in the colony's economic and social development. His legacy endures not only through his remarkable silverwork but also through his influence on future generations—most notably his son, Jeremiah Dummer Jr., who rose to prominence as a colonial diplomat and intellectual.

As an interesting footnote to his influence, Dummer died in 1718, decades before Paul Revere's birth; however, the celebrated patriot Revere entered the craft of silversmithing through a lineage that traced back to Dummer. Through the workshop relationships linking Dummer to John Coney—and Coney to Revere—many of the standards and techniques pioneered by Dummer ultimately shaped Revere's own celebrated work.

JEREMIAH DUMMER, JR.

A notable colonial agent and diplomat, Jeremiah Dummer, Jr., was born in Boston in 1681. The son of Jeremiah Dummer, Sr., he made significant contributions to American history, particularly through his work, 'A Defense of the New England Charters,' and his pivotal role in the founding of Yale College. He died in Boston in 1739.

HENRY AVERY, AKA "LONG BEN"

Born around 1659 in Devon, England, Avery began his maritime career as a child in the Royal Navy before turning to piracy. His most infamous act occurred in 1695 when he led a mutiny aboard the warship *Charles II*, renaming it the *Fancy* and capturing the *Ganj-i-Sawai*, a Mughal ship laden with immense riches, off the coast of India. This raid netted him and his crew one of the largest pirate hauls in history, making him one of the wealthiest and most hunted pirates of his time. His fate remains mysterious; some reports suggest he retired comfortably with his loot, while others imply he lived out his days in poverty. Only Abigail Spragg really knew.

EUNICE FOWLER

Abigail Spragg's sister Eunice Southard was born in 1670 in Hempstead, Queens, New York Colony, to Thomas Southard Sr., then 55, and Annica Antonise Van Salee, age 35. On 7 October 1690, Eunice married George Fowler in her hometown of Hempstead. Together, they became the parents of at least four sons.

JOSHUA GEE

Gee was born in Boston in 1667. His early life was very adventurous, but it took a dramatic turn when Algerian pirates captured him during one of his voyages. He was enslaved and forced to work for his captors, an ordeal that exposed him to the harsh realities of piracy and maritime warfare as well as various techniques in building and repairing ships. This experience, though grueling, enriched his knowledge and skills and, after securing his freedom—possibly through ransom or escape (see Phillip van Salee)—Gee returned to Boston with newfound expertise and determination. He established his shipyard on the banks of Boston's Charles River, where he built and repaired ships essential for trade, fishing, and transportation. His expertise in shipbuilding made him a respected craftsman and a necessary contributor to the region's economic growth. Gee's shipyard was known for producing durable, well-crafted vessels that were highly sought after for their quality and reliability. He died in his hometown in 1730.

GREEN DRAGON TAVERN (BOSTON)

The tavern was a famed colonial public house in Boston's North End and one of the most important meeting places of the American Revolution. Established on Green Dragon Lane (later Union Street) as early as 1654, it was a long-standing gathering place for sailors, merchants, and civic leaders. Tradition holds that Paul Revere was dispatched from the tavern on his famous Midnight Ride in April 1775.

The original building was dismantled in the early 19th century. Today, a tavern bearing the Green Dragon name operates near the historic site at 11 Marshall Street along Boston's Freedom Trail, commemorating the tavern's Revolutionary legacy.

CAPTAIN JAMES HOLLOWAY

Born around 1650, Holloway's piratical career was marked by boldness and strategic insight. Unlike some of his more notorious contemporaries, Holloway was reputed to be cunning and resourceful, often outmaneuvering both his prey and the naval forces sent to capture him. Despite his success, Holloway's career was fraught with peril. He was eventually brought to trial and, like many pirates of his era, sentenced to death. He is thought to have been executed by hanging, a common fate for those who chose the perilous life of piracy—or did Abigail's mother, Annica, save his life by sending another man to the gallows in his place? That is yet another tale from the Spragg family's secretive dealings with pirates that escaped Hannah's journal.

ZACHARIAH HULLABEE

Fictitious constable of New Haven, Connecticut.

BARNABAS JENKINS

Fictitious constable of New Haven, Connecticut.

DR. JONES

Dr. Evan Jones was born on January 25, 1689, the son of Dr. Edward Jones and Mary Wynne of Wales. His Quaker grandfather, Dr. Thomas Wynne, came to Pennsylvania with William Penn in 1682 and served as speaker for the first two Pennsylvania Assemblies of the Province in Philadelphia in 1687-88.

CLARA

A fictitious young, poor Palatine German girl left behind in Manhattan after the Germans were herded up the Hudson to process pitch and tar from pine trees for Her Majesty Queen Anne's Navy.

LAWTON

Abigail's faithful but fictitious butler. His African name was 'Tuo,' but because of his size, sailors started calling him 'Long Toe' on the slave ship. Andreas Gruber's sidekick, Rufus *(Newlander Series)*, later suggested he be called something more regal, like Lawton, and it stuck.

ELIZA MARBLE

Eliza Marble was a woman whose life intersected dramatically with the notorious pirate Edward "Ned" Low during the waning years of the Golden Age of Piracy. Born into a respectable family, Eliza's life took a fateful turn when she married Ned Low on August 12, 1714, at the First Church in Boston, Massachusetts. Their union produced a child, but tragedy struck when their infant son died. In the winter of 1719, Eliza gave birth to their daughter, Elizabeth. However, this period of new beginnings was marred by sorrow as Eliza died shortly after giving birth. Her untimely death left Ned Low grief-stricken and struggling to maintain stability. Unable to cope, Low lost his job and ultimately left Boston to become one of history's most vicious pirates.

COTTON MATHER

A prominent New England Puritan minister and influential figure in the early American colonies. Born on February 12, 1663, in Boston, Massachusetts Bay Colony, he was the son of Increase Mather and grandson of Richard Mather, both significant Puritan ministers. Mather was educated at Harvard College, where he earned his degree at the young age of 15. He followed in his father's footsteps, becoming a minister at Boston's Old North Church (Second Church) and dedicating his life to religious and intellectual pursuits. Mather was a prolific writer, producing over 450 books and pamphlets on various topics, including theology, science, and history. His most famous works include "Magnalia Christi Americana," a comprehensive history of New England, and "The Wonders of the Invisible World," a defense of his involvement in the Salem witch trials.

JOHN MACCREEDY

A fictitious general contractor and associate of the real Henry Caner, the builder of the first Yale College House in New Haven, Connecticut.

MR. MCDERMOT

The ship cat aboard the notorious pirate Captain William Kidd's vessel, the *Adventure Galley,* during the late 17th century. Known for his keen instincts and loyalty, Mr. McDermot was more than just a crew member; he played a crucial role in maintaining the ship's morale and controlling the rodent population, vital for preserving food supplies on long voyages. Though not much is recorded about the fate of Mr. McDermot, his association with Captain Kidd and his adventures at sea make him a unique and memorable figure in the lore of piracy. The cat was immortalized in the 1956 publication by Robert Lawson titled *Capt Kidd's Cat: The True Chronicle of Wm KIDD, Gent and Merchant of New York as narrated by His Ship's Cat McDermot, Who ought to know.*

MR. JAMES PECK

He was a prominent tavern keeper in colonial New Haven, Connecticut, best known as the proprietor of Peck's Tavern. Located along the docks, the tavern served as a crucial hub for sailors, merchants, and townspeople, providing food, drink, and lodging at the edge of the harbor. Peck's Tavern stood where the town loosened its collar and leaned toward the water—close enough to smell tar and salt, yet far enough inland to stay dry at high tide.

By the early 18th century, a busy port like New Haven could see dozens of vessels each year, and Peck's Tavern benefited directly from that traffic—often housing crews overnight, hosting negotiations, and circulating news from abroad. More than a place to eat or sleep, Peck's Tavern functioned as a clearinghouse of maritime life, quietly supporting the town's trade-driven economy and daily rhythms tied to wind and tide. When Long Wharf was constructed in 1723, it shifted New Haven's maritime gravity southward into the harbor where *Shell & Bones Oyster Bar and Grill, Fair Haven Oyster Company, Tavern on State* and *Gryphon's Pub* now stand away from earlier landing points.

REVEREND MORTON

Reverend Morton was a key figure in early 1700s New Haven, serving as a clergyman at the New Haven Church and Orphanage. He played a vital role in the community's spiritual life and was deeply committed to caring for orphans and needy people. Under his leadership, the church and orphanage became central to the colony's moral and social fabric, reflecting Puritan values of charity and community. Reverend Morton's legacy lies in his contributions to the growth and well-being of New Haven's early settlers.

MARY DONGAN NUGENT

A notable figure in colonial New York, Mary Dongan Nugent was known for her prominent family connections and influence on the colony's social and political life. As a member of the Dongan family, she was related to Thomas Dongan, the 2nd Earl of Limerick, who served as the Governor of New York from 1683 to 1688. Mary Dongan Nugent's family legacy and role in shaping early New York politics and society have made her a figure of historical interest, particularly in the context of colonial aristocracy and governance.

GULIELMA MARIA PENN

Gulielma Marie, born in 1699, was the granddaughter of William Penn, the founder of Pennsylvania, and the daughter of William Penn Jr. Named after her grandmother, Gulielma Marie carried the legacy of one of colonial America's most influential families. Although not as publicly active as her forebears, Gulielma Marie maintained the Penn family's Quaker traditions and connections, helping sustain their influence in both England and the American colonies. She remained a significant figure in the Penn lineage until she died in 1754.

CAPTAIN JOHN CORNELIUS PROUT

When Captain John Prout was born on 4 February 1648 in Boston, Suffolk, Massachusetts, his father, Timothy Prout, was 27, and his mother, Margaret, was 26. John married Mary Rotherford on 23 August 1681, in New Haven, Connecticut. They were the parents of at least one son, John, and four daughters. The Captain died on 20 September 1719, in New Haven, Connecticut, at the age of 71, and was buried in Center Church on the Green, New Haven, Connecticut.

THADDEUS PUDDING

A fictitious constable from Flushing, New York Colony.

REVEREND SAMUEL RUSSELL

The Reverend was an influential Puritan minister in colonial Connecticut and a key figure in the early history of American education. He was born in 1660 in New Haven, Connecticut, and graduated from Harvard College in 1681. Russell is best known for hosting the 1701 meeting of colonial ministers at his home in Branford, Connecticut, which led to the founding of Connecticut Collegiate College. This gathering was instrumental in later establishing Yale as a center for training future clergy and leaders for the colony. Throughout his life, Reverend Samuel Russell remained a respected religious leader, contributing to the spiritual and educational development of the early American colonies.

SAMUEL SEWALL

Samuel Sewall, a prominent judge, businessman, and printer in the Province of Massachusetts Bay, lived from 1652 to 1730. He is best known for his role in the Salem witch trials, an involvement for which he later publicly apologized in a 1697 statement of repentance. Sewall was also an early critic of slavery, publishing *The Selling of Joseph* (1700), one of the first anti-slavery tracts in New England. Serving as chief justice of the Massachusetts Superior Court of Judicature for many years, he left a complex legacy of moral introspection and reform. Sewall's later writings, including *Talitha Cumi* (1725), reflected his advocacy for the rights of women, orphans, and marginalized members of society, showcasing his evolution as a thoughtful and justice-seeking leader.

ABIGAIL SPRAGG, AKA MRS. HUNTINGTON

The great-granddaughter of the infamous and fabulously wealthy Dutch Barbary pirate Jan Janszoon van Salee, Abigail Spragg was born around 1669 in Hempstead

Swamp, Long Island, in the Province of New York Colony. She belonged to a prominent early American family with diverse Dutch and Moroccan roots. Her grandfather, Anthony Janszoon's eldest son, was among the earliest settlers of New Amsterdam (Manhattan) and a wealthy landowner, including ownership of Coney Island, then known as Conyne Island, leaving a lasting legacy in the region.

Although details of Abigail's life are limited, she embodies the rich cultural heritage and pioneering spirit of the van Salee family, which played a significant role in the early development of the American colonies. That heritage endured long after Abigail died in 1726; through her son Jacob's daughter Mary, she was the great-great-grandmother of Cornelius Vanderbilt, linking her lineage to some of the most historically significant Americans.

HANNAH SPRAGG

Hannah was one of Abigail Spragg's real-life daughters, living from 1690 to 1726. In this book, she is presented as the proposed author of *A General History of the Pyrates*, initially published in 1724 under the pseudonym "Captain Charles Johnson." This seminal work became one of the most famous historical accounts of piracy, offering detailed narratives of the lives and exploits of many notorious pirates.

The true identity of "Captain Charles Johnson" has long been debated. Some scholars believe it to be a pseudonym for Daniel Defoe—who is, in the *Newlander* series, Hannah's unscrupulous London editor—while others suggest it was a female author's clever revenge against another pompous writer named Charles Johnson, who had once scoffed that a woman could never become a serious author. Though intriguing, none of these theories has been disproven to date.

JACOB SPRAGG

Born in 1694 in Hempstead, Nassau County, New York, British Colonial America, Jacob was officially recorded as the son of Edward Spragg III, age 29, and Abigail van Salee Southard, age 30, though this fact can be debated. Over time, he transformed from a Manhattan city dweller into a rugged outdoorsman; Jacob Spragg served as a New York Colonial Ranger and fought in the long frontier struggles against the French and their allied tribes from the approaches to Montréal to the rocky shores of Maine. He married Dorothy Sarah Stodder on 18 February 1735 in Hingham, Suffolk, Massachusetts Bay Colony, and together they had at least one son and six daughters. Their third child, Mary, later married Jacobus Vanderbilt on 27 October 1746 in Monmouth, New Jersey, making Jacob Spragg the grandfather of their son, Cornelius Vanderbilt. Jacob died in 1745 in New Jersey, British Colonial America, at the age of 51.

SARAH SPRAGG

Sarah Spragg, who lived from 1691 to 1745, was one of the real-life daughters of Abigail Spragg, born into a prominent New York colonial family during a period of social constraint and quiet upheaval. Living in the shadow of her formidable mother, Sarah's life unfolded within the domestic, educational, and moral expectations placed upon women of her station in the early 18th century.

HANNAH SWARTON (NÉE JOANA HIBBARD, *C.* 1660 –)

Hannah was a New England colonial pioneer whose life was irrevocably shaped by frontier warfare. In May 1690, during the defeat of Fort Loyal at Casco Bay (present-day Maine), Hannah and her children—Samuel, Mary, John, and Jasper—were taken captive when a combined force of Abenaki warriors, Penobscots under Madockawando, and French-led troops attacked the settlement. Despite promises of safe passage upon surrender, most of the English men, including her husband John Swarton, were killed; only a handful of the more than two hundred inhabitants survived into captivity.

Hannah was held prisoner for over five years, first living among the Abenaki and later in the household of a French family in Quebec, enduring cultural displacement and hardship uncommon even by frontier standards. After her eventual release and return to New England, she recounted her ordeal to Cotton Mather, who preserved her experience as part of the broader Puritan record of captivity and providence.

Her death date is unknown, but her life stands as a stark testament to the violence of imperial conflict in late-17th-century New England and the resilience of women who survived it.

LENA VAN HOORN

During the colonial period, the van Hoorn family was among the prominent Dutch families in New York and New Jersey. The van Hoorns were involved in trade, agriculture, and local governance, contributing to the region's economic and social development.

JAN JANSZOON VAN SALEE

Also known as Murat Reis the Younger, Jan Janszoon van Salee was a notorious Dutch pirate and privateer who converted to Islam and became a significant figure in the Barbary Coast corsairs. Born around 1575 in the Netherlands, Janszoon became a privateer under the Dutch flag before turning to piracy. He eventually became a leader among the Barbary corsairs, operating out of Salé, Morocco, where he earned the title of "Reis" (a captain or leader in Arabic) and was appointed the Governor of Salé by King Al Walid Ben Zidan.

Janszoon, who died in 1641, left a legacy for his role as a pirate and his impact on European-North African relations during the 17th century. He is also remembered as the patriarch of a family that would later settle in the New World, with his descendants, including his sons Abraham and Anthony Janszoon van Salee, becoming early settlers in what is now New York City. Jan Janszoon van Salee's life encapsulates the complex interactions between Europe, North Africa, and the emerging American colonies during the early modern period.

PHILLIP VAN SALEE

Born in 1604, Phillip is the second of four sons of Jan Janszoon van Salee.

BASIL TINKLETUNE

A fictitious harpsichordist.

CORNELIUS WARBLEWORTH

A fictitious voice instructor.

DOROTHY GOODYEAR WHITING

Dorothy was born in 1700 in Southampton, New York, to Reverend Joseph Whiting and Waite Bishop, the daughter of Reverend John Bishop of Stamford, Connecticut, and granddaughter of Samuel Goodyear, Deputy Governor of Connecticut.

Reverend Whiting married Dorothy's mother after the passing of first wife, Sarah Danforth, who was the eldest daughter of Hon. Thomas Danforth, Deputy Governor of Massachusetts.

DAVID YALE

David Yale, who lived from 1660 to 1697, was a prominent settler and lifelong bachelor in colonial New Haven, Connecticut. He possessed a deep interest in alchemy—the early pursuit of transforming matter and uncovering the philosopher's stone. His fascination with the art reflected the intellectual spirit of the 17th century, a time when science and mysticism often intertwined. Yale's involvement in alchemical study underscores his engagement with the era's emerging ideas, blending rational inquiry with the search for hidden knowledge.

ELIHU YALE

Born in 1649 in Boston, Massachusetts, Elihu Yale spent his earliest years in New Haven, Connecticut, before his family returned to England in the early 1660s. He lived in London throughout his youth and early adulthood, and it was from England that he embarked on the career that would define him. Yale rose to prominence after traveling to India in the late 1670s, eventually becoming Governor of Fort St. George in Madras (now Chennai), where he served into the 1690s and amassed the considerable fortune that made his name known on both sides of the world. Returning to England, he lived out his final decades as a wealthy, if controversial, gentleman until he died in 1721.

Though often regarded as one of the most overrated philanthropists of his time—having never visited Yale College nor personally knowing the men who sought his support—his name endures as that of the institution's benefactor. Elihu Yale's life traces the complicated intersections of 17th- and early-18th-century colonialism, global trade, and philanthropy, stretching from Boston to New Haven, from London to Madras, and back again.

HOPESTILL MERRIWEATHER YALE

Headmistress Hope Terwilliger was the daughter of David Yale, Elihu's brother.

URSULA YALE

The daughter of Hopestill Merriweather Yale.

ABOUT THE AUTHOR

Mark Kraver, DDS, is a retired craniofacial-pain dentist and proud graduate of the University of Oklahoma, who traded drills and scalpels for pen and page to build an eclectic, ever-expanding literary world. He launched his literary career in science fiction with God of God, then turned his historian's eye to early America in sweeping series like Newlander, with spin-offs like Janszoon and The Willow.

Never content to stay in one lane, he also crafts sharp mystery and murder thrillers in The Alex Archer Chronicles, writes whimsical children's tales such as Spenser the Babbit, and explores the lyrical and the metaphysical in poetry collections including In the Realm of Dancing Syzygy, Credo, and Looking for a Friend.

A lifelong storyteller, Kraver now composes original music as The Mark Kraver Project, blending his poetry with modern soundscapes. Across genres, his work is bound by one thread: a drive to illuminate the past, imagine the future, and celebrate the wild, human stories in between.

www.ingramcontent.com/pod-product-compliance
Lightning Source LLC
Chambersburg PA
CBHW070858260626
47162CB00007B/2493

* 9 7 8 0 9 9 0 5 8 6 3 4 0 *